Black Wall Street New Dream Publishing Presents...

MY CALL II

MR. BONES' REVENGE

MY CALL II

MR. BONES' REVENGE

Ronald Gray

BLACK WALL STREET NEW DREAM PUBLISHING
Owned by
MY PROVIDER PRODUCTIONS LLC
www.myproviderproductions.com
blackwallstreetnewdream@yahoo.com

RONALD GRAY

My Provider Productions LLC
My Call II, Mr. Bone's Revenge
Copyright © 2014 by Ronald H. Gray
Revised Edition: 7/21/2017

Library of Congress Control Number: 2014906366
ISBN-10: 0692230475
ISBN-13: 978-0-692-23047-3
Author: Ronald H. Gray
Cover Design/Graphics: Ronald H. Gray
Printed in the United States of America

This is a work of fiction. Any references or similarities to actual events, real people, living or dead, or to real locales are intended to give the novel a sense of reality. Any similarity in other names, characters, places, and incidents is entirely coincidental.

Distributed by Black Wall Street New Dream Publishing
Submit Wholesale Orders to:
My Provider Productions LLC
Attention: Order Processing
233 Federalsburg South
Laurel, MD 20724
www.myproviderproductions.com
blackwallstreetnewdream@yahoo.com

RONALD GRAY

Dedication

Once again, this book is dedicated to family and friends who have witnessed my hard work and dedication and continue to believe in me. Their words, attitude and support toward me have not changed. "Never give up!"

RONALD GRAY

ACKNOWLEDGEMENTS

Again, I thank God in the name of King Jesus, for giving me this gift and opportunity to share another story. I continue to thank my family and friends for their encouragement and assistance along the way. I'm acknowledging and embracing all my ups and downs, pain and love. All these things have made me who I'm today. My journey continues and so do the stories. Is this just another story or is it a part of your life? Will you acknowledge if this is fantasy or your truth? This is it.

Another raw untold story until... now!

RONALD GRAY

Never Give Up
On Your
Dreams!

CHAPTER ONE

Mr. Bones

Early in the morning, a dark cloud of smoke appeared over Ron and Diana's house along with a very foul smell in the air. A group of vultures appeared and were flying into one another, dropping out the sky eating and feeding off one another on the ground. In the darkness, Mr. Bones appeared in the front yard. He was dressed in a dusty black coat holding a black cane in one hand and a small bag of bones in the other. He began stomping his feet, mumbling some words, and pointing his cane at the house.

"I told you boy, I was coming to get you. You made me wait too long but now it's my time and I'm going to get you and your entire stinking praying family. Look what I what I did to your wife because she became weak and married you too soon boy, pleasing you, instead of God. I put a strong lust spirit in her and now she is getting her freak on while you are out planning to do my dirty work," he started laughing. "I love disobedience to the word of God. Love it, love it, love it. It is helping me daily to take as many people to hell as I possibly can. I'm going there but I will not be alone." He started laughing and stomping his feet. "I'm the bones, I cannot be defeated."

He tapped his cane on the ground twice, mumbled some words and slowly transformed into a wolf. The wolf started viciously snarling and foaming at the mouth. It quickly takes off running around Ron's house thirteen times and stop at the front and changed back into Mr. Bones. He raised his arms.

"I'm the beast and the evil of this world, no man can defeat me. I killed your sorry daddy, put your sister Sandra in a coma, now it's destruction time for everybody else boy. It's my time for revenge." He tapped his cane twice on the ground and blood appeared, spreading across the ground like a spider's web until it reached Ron's house. Mr. Bones looked down, shook his head and spat on the ground. "I speak the curse of death on this property and this family. My blood will give you what you want and my blood will oppress then possess you all to do my will." He laid flat on the ground spreading his arms and legs out wide and slowly his body began to absorb into the ground until he was gone. The blood that was on the ground begun to travel back to where Mr. Bones laid and seeped down into the ground. Immediately the ground started vibrating and there was a loud cracking sound, and then silence.

RONALD GRAY   (2)

CHAPTER TWO
Ron's House

Stacy and Diana are in the shower together washing each other after having sex in one of the rooms upstairs. They stepped out, dried each other off, put lotion on each other and rushed to get dressed. They put their sweat suits back on so Ron and Keith would not suspect anything. Diana has a look of confusion on her face. She heard a low voice telling her, II Peter 2-9, *"The Lord knows how to deliver the godly out of temptations"*. She looked over her shoulder, put her hands over her face, and lowered her head in shame. She and Stacy walked down stairs to the kitchen so they could cook breakfast. Diana's guilt over what she has done was beyond words. She cried so hard while she and Stacy were in the shower, Diana thought she would pass out from being so emotionally upset but Stacy held and comforted her with words and gentle caresses. She loves Ron so much but something about Stacy's touch, affects her deeply but she can't understand why. She was thinking, *How, can I get a prayer through now? How can I look Ron in the face and feel the same?* She started crying.

Stacy felt bad now about what she did to Diana but not too bad. She knew Diana was hurting and feeling spiritually drained and guilty. She walked over and hugged her.

"It's going to be alright Diana and if you hate me, I understand. What we shared will stay between us and it will never happen again."

Diana looked at her with tears falling from her eyes.

"I don't hate you Stacy. It's me that I'm so angry with and I don't understand why I did it. Yes, I was curious but it was more so you." She stared at her. "Stacy, you are so beautiful and I wanted you but this can never happen again, ever." She looked up. "God help me." Diana lowered her head with tears still coming down her face.

Stacy held Diana and started rubbing her back while whispering words in her ear that even Stacy didn't understand where it came from. She lifted Diana's face up using both hands and stared at her and slowly moved forward until their lips touched, and they kissed very gently.

Diana knew this was wrong but for some reason, she couldn't stop herself. She kissed Stacy back sliding her tongue in her mouth kissing her with passion and they are caressing each other until Diana can feel herself getting wet, she leaned away from Stacy.

"I don't want to but we need to stop. I'm getting wet and I want you again."

Stacy quickly slid her hand inside her pants and rubbed her fingers across her wetness then rubbed them on Diana's lips.

"You did this to me, Diana, you made me wet as well. I love Keith so much but you deeply affect me emotionally."

Diana leaned forward and they kissed for what seems like hours and then she stared in Stacy's eyes.

"I want to please you like you did me. Bury my face between your legs and taste you so badly Stacy and lick and suck you until you climax." She lowered her head and then looked at Stacy. "I feel like I'm losing my mind. Can we be lovers? I know I just got married but I get so lonely when Ron is away. Now that he and Keith are business partners they will be spending a lot of time together. We could, comfort each other." She looked at Stacy.

Stacy smiled and kissed her and was thinking, *this could not have turned out better if I planned it.*

"I understand Diana and I will always be here for you but you can never tell Ron. This is just between us, not Keith or Ron, just us!"

Diana slid her hands down the back of Stacy's pants and grabbed her butt.

"I want this sexy ass of yours all for myself. Besides my husband, no one will ever touch me but you. I would appreciate the same thing from you Stacy." She kissed her and caressed Stacy's butt.

Stacy slowly pulled away from her.

"I'm all yours Diana but you are making me wet, so we need to stop unless you are going to finish what you started." She smiled at her and smacked Diana on the butt.

"Let's finish cooking so Ron and Keith can have some food waiting for them once they get back." She smacked Stacy on the butt and stepped away from her.

Stacy and Diana started cooking. They cooked pancakes, grits, scrambled eggs, bacon, and sausages. Diana set the table with the five-thousand-dollar Porcelain dinette set Ron got for her. After setting the table she grabbed Stacy's hand and they walked back into the living room to wait on the men. Diana plopped her body down on the plush white leather couch pulling Stacy down with her. They began to kiss passionately until they heard a beeping sound.

RONALD GRAY   (5)

Stacy jumped up.

"What is that?" She turned to look at Diana.

"Perfect timing. That was the alarm letting us know the gate was being opened, which means they are back. Good, because I miss my baby so much." Diana walked toward the kitchen but Stacy gently grabbed her arm.

"Diana, I hope you don't ever turn your back on me. The only person who has never left me is Keith." She lowered her head and tears come to her eyes.

Diana lifts Stacy's head up.

"I won't turn my back on you Stacy because all I have is my grandma and Ron." She hugged and kissed Stacy but Stacy pulled away from her but Diana pulled her back. "Don't do that." She grabbed her butt and kissed Stacy very passionately. "It's us, remember."

You can hear the rumble of Keith's Lamborghini as it drove up in front of the house. He and Ron removed their guns and put them under the seat. Ron looked at Keith.

"My brother, this is some car you bought and very fast."

"It is fast. How did you feel when I was on that long straightaway and hit two hundred miles an hour?"

"That one experience was enough for me my friend."

"Well, there is no turning back now partner because this is as real as it gets."

"Yeah I know but I'm good. Business is business. Besides, *A.M.O.A* remember."

"Always Money Over Ass! You damn right." They dap up.

"I wonder what Diana and Stacy have been doing because I'm hungry." Ron said.

RONALD GRAY   (6)

"They have been talking and telling lies like women do but I'm hungry too. I have one question before we go in. Was it worth the wait? Was she good partner?" Keith said grinning at him.

"Yes, Diana was worth the wait and a virgin just like I was. The girl was all that! Damn, she was good."

"About time, all that damn money you spent getting that ass, she better be good. I was beginning to wonder about you but I understand love. Now let's go inside so you can get back to your wife and I can hold my baby."

Ron hits Keith on the arm.

"When are you going to marry Stacy?"

"I don't know but it will be soon because she treats me too well to let her get away."

They got out the car and walked in the house. Keith walked over to Stacy.

Diana runs over to Ron, hugged and kissed him like she has not seen him in years.

"Hi, I missed you too." He kissed her again and grabbed her hips caressing them and then stop. "I know, don't grab your body in front of them."

Diana placed his hands on her butt.

"You are my husband now and I'm not ashamed of what we share, so do you."

"I like that." He caressed her hips and tongue kissed her like they are the only ones in the room. He can feel himself getting hard.

Diana whispered in his ear.

"I feel you baby and I want it. When they leave, bury your face between my legs again and make me climax, then fuck me from the back, doggy-style Ron." She started kissing him.

Stacy and Keith are still hugging and kissing. Keith stopped and stared at Stacy.

"I smell food."

Ron smacked Diana lightly on her butt.

"I smell food too,"

Diana kissed Ron on the lips.

"And you should, Stacy and I cooked, so come to the kitchen." She walked over to Stacy and winked at her.

Diana and Stacy walked toward the kitchen purposely shaking their butts extra knowing Ron and Keith would stare at them. They both looked back at them and smiled. Keith and Ron looked at each other and then at the girls and shook their head.

They are sitting down at the dining room table eating.

"Damn this food is delicious baby." Ron yelled out!

"It wasn't me this time. This was all Stacy's doing." Diana said with a smile on her face.

Keith looked up at Stacy and smiled.

"I better hurry up and make this official before someone tries to steal you away from me, in case there are some crazy people in the world that would try and cross me. You know what I'm saying Ron?" They dap up.

"I know that's right. I don't know what I would do if someone tried to touch Diana." He shook his head.

"I can't picture it myself, Ron." Stacy said.

"We know we have the best ladies on the planet." Ron said. Diana and Stacy started laughing.

"What's so funny? Don't you think you have the best man on the planet Diana? I know you're not clowning me after I married

RONALD GRAY   (8)

you, moved you into this mansion, took you shopping to lace this crib out, and then laid you down and gave you all this thick long goodness."

Stacy squints her eyes at Ron with lust. Keith pushed his plate of food away and stood up.

"Come here, Stacy. Let me slap that ass because you put your foot in that damn food. I can't wait to get you home to tap that ass."

Stacy winked her eyes at Keith.

"I know that's right. I can't wait until I can say, you married me and we moved into a million-dollar house."

Keith looked over at Ron.

"Look what you started man. Here she goes again." Keith looked at Stacy. "I know baby, real soon."

CHAPTER THREE

The Dream Continues

Ron picked the Marriott Resort and Stellaris Casino hotel in Aruba, located in the Palm Beach area. It's one of the most expensive hotels on the island. It is within walking distance to restaurants and various shops. They have a large suite with an ocean view and from the time they arrived in Aruba, Ron and Diana have been pampered night and day. Private escorts on all their tours, chauffeured driven car and boat, taking them anywhere they desire to go, facials and full body massages at their request. Ron is spending so much money in the shops, they all agreed to open any time just for him and Diana. Anything at their disposal all they had to do is ask and it is done. First thing in the morning and at night Ron and Diana have been making love, exploring every inch of each other's body. The love and passion between these two are beyond words.

On the fourth day of their honeymoon after walking on the beach, they walk to one of the local restaurants along the shores. The place is well decorated and not too crowded.

Ron is wearing sandals, sweat pants, and a short-sleeved shirt. Stacy is wearing sandals a one-piece bathing suit with a plunging neck line showing her beautifully shaped breasts with a sarong wrapped around her waist which does very little to hide her full hips and ample butt.

The moment they walked in, all eyes were on them especially Diana because she is very attractive and has a very sexy walk. Ron noticed four guys who look like trouble makers sitting at the

RONALD GRAY   (10)

bar staring at Diana when she walked by. They were staring at her butt pointing to it and making lewd comments. Ron chose to dismiss it because she is very pretty, with a great body and he needs to get used to her attracting attention, wherever she goes.

They sat down at one of the tables sitting across from one another waiting for the waitress. Ron reached for the menus that were laying against the metal napkin holder at the end of the table. He hands Diana one of the menus and they review it and decide on their choice of food and drink. A waitress comes over with two glasses of water and their silverware and she proceeds to take their order. Ron orders hot wings with blue cheese dressing and a large root beer soda. Diana orders the chicken salad with Thousand Island dressing and a large lemonade. The waitress said thank you and left. Ron and Diana tune everyone and everything else out and enjoy each other's company. Holding hands, leaning across the table kissing and laughing, while Ron is rubbing her leg under the table. The waitress brings their food and drinks and Ron says the grace. They kiss and start feeding each other.

After enjoying the meal and talking among themselves, Diana stood up to use the bathroom. She was so shapely her hips and butt can't help from shaking every step she takes. Ron was smiling, watching her walk away. He noticed the four guys at the bar staring at her and one of them said something to her as she walked by but he couldn't hear what was said. Diana ignored him and kept walking.

Ron becomes irritated looking at the guys act stupid and he's mean mugging them when Diana walked out the bathroom. The same guy who said something to her, smacked her on the butt.

Diana quickly smacked him and backed up. Immediately Ron jumped out of his seat, knocking his chair over moving fast to get to Diana. He hit the guy twice, knocking him down but his friends pulled out knives, one of them put the blade against Ron's throat.

Diana stepped closer to Ron.

"Stop", she yelled, "Leave him alone! You have made your point." She was staring at the guy holding the blade.

The guy Ron knocked down was getting up. As he stepped closer to him he put his knee in his groin then pulled out a blade. Two muscular male employees moved quickly from behind the bar to assist them. They ordered the guys to leave the restaurant and then threatened to call the police. The four guys looked at Ron and Diana, they put their knives away and walked out. The one who smacked Diana on her butt turned around and pointed his finger at Ron.

"We'll meet up again and prayer or nobody will be there to help you. Get out of Aruba." He pointed at Diana and smiled. "Pretty girl, you can stay and let me and my homies get some of that fat ass." He laughed and walked away.

Ron took a step toward him but Diana grabbed his arm.

"Ron let him go. He is not worth it, please baby."

He is furious but realized she was right. He could not take all four of them anyway. He turned to face Diana.

"You are right but my time will come. Let's get out of here and go back to the room." He kissed her and they left.

As they were walking back to their room, Diana could feel Ron's anger but she was talking and kissing on him to calm him down. She was also angry because it bothered her a lot when the

RONALD GRAY   (12)

guy smacked her on the butt. They reached their room and Ron hugged Diana and decided to take a shower to relax. Diana used that time to call Stacy, wanting to hear her voice. She told Stacy what happened and Stacy was angry and when she got off the phone with Diana, she called Keith. Keith was furious but wondered why Ron didn't call him. He hung up the phone and made a call then called Stacy back and told her to pack their bags, they were going to Aruba.

For some reason, Diana felt better after talking to Stacy. She joined Ron in the shower and they washed one another and Diana can feel Ron becoming more relaxed as she caters to him. They get out and dried each other off and walked straight to the bed and began making love. When Ron slid inside Diana she could not help but cry, not from pain but from her emotional state and the love she has for her husband.

"Oh Ron, baby you feel so good in me. Don't stop loving me baby, don't ever stop."

Ron was looking at Diana while thrusting inside her, kissing and sucking on her lips.

"Diana, I will never stop loving you." He pushed her legs back sliding inside her slow and deep, kissing her soft lips as well. They were kissing, sucking and licking each other until all was too much. They climaxed at the same time.

"Oh, Ron."

"Ahhhhhhhhh Diana."

He pushed deeper into Diana feeling all their love for each other hoping this desire will never change for them.

RONALD GRAY   (13)

CHAPTER FOUR

Introduction of the

Keith and Stacy are walking off a private jet in Aruba first thing in the morning on the fifth day of June. Ron and Diana are still on their honeymoon. Keith was wearing an Armani suit. Stacy was wearing nude color heels with a cream-color dress that comes just below her knees. It fits her body well showing her curves. Keith and Stacy are wearing Marc Jacob sun shades. Keith didn't tell Ron or Diana he was coming to Aruba. He made reservations at the same hotel they were in.

Walking off the jet behind them were ten young black men. All are athletically built wearing suits and shades. Keith handpicked and recruited these young guys some time ago for situations such as this. All the men are highly-skilled in martial arts and are expert shooters with hand guns and sniper rifles. Keith made them a legitimate security company named, *"Young Wolves Inc."* These men are on Keith's payroll. He employed thirty unique young men for his security company. However, these ten do whatever he asks and are sworn to secrecy. Their pay is much more because they're part of his special unit. Even their expenses are taken care of.

Keith hired an attorney to take care of the paperwork that would allow him and his men to carry guns domestically and internationally. It cost him six-hundred thousand dollars, that's twenty thousand per man but it was well worth it. Keith had two limos waiting to escort them all to the hotel. When they stepped out the limo people were staring at them, wondering who they were. Keith and Stacy felt like celebrities.

They checked into their rooms, five rooms for the, *Young Wolves* with two men sharing each room. Stacy and Keith had their own suite.

Ron woke up feeling great after he and Diana made love so wonderfully last night. He was determined not to show weakness after yesterday's fiasco, so he and Diana went back to the same restaurant where they ate last night. Diana didn't want to go because she knew Ron would do something horrible if those guys came back. But she also wanted to support her man. Ron and Diana are dressed the same except different colors.

There were twenty other people in the restaurant, eating and drinking, enjoying their day. Ron and Diana were sitting at a table laughing and having fun when the same four guys from last night walked in and over to a table. The guy who Ron knocked down pointed at him.

"Boy, what did I tell you? You Americans never learn. You think you own the world. We, run this entire beach area," he pointed at his friends. "Pay me and I might let you leave, boy." He laughed then he and his friends pulled their knives out.

The manager runs over to them.

"You four better leave. I'm tired of you coming in here, harassing my customers and shaking me down. Now leave before I call the police." Ron quickly stood up facing them and they pointed their knives at him and Diana stood up next to Ron.

The guy who smacked Diana on the butt stepped closer to Ron.

"Boy, you got a fine-looking bitch." He pointed his knife at Ron. "But I believe you want to die." He yelled!

Keith and Stacy walked in with the *Young Wolves* behind them and all are dressed in suits and wearing shades. Stacy was wearing a revealing top and skirt.

All the customers stop eating because of the commotion and some people got up from their table and left because of fear.

Keith walked up to the guy that stood close to Ron.

"Is there a problem?" All eyes are on Keith. "I said, is there a problem." The shades Keith has on hide the anger in his eyes, but he is ready to shoot up the place not caring about those four guys or the people watching.

The dude looked at Keith.

"Who are you supposed to be stupid fool?"

Keith, Stacy and the *Young Wolves* pulled guns out and aimed them at the four guys.

"Your worst damn nightmare! Now put the knives down or die," Keith says, removing his shades and putting his gun against the guy's head. He wants to shoot this guy so badly he must fight his own inner demons not to pull the trigger.

"Keith, Stacy." Diana said and smiled but quickly regrouped to play her position.

Ron was shocked to see Keith and Stacy but he will show his emotions later. The four guys dropped their knives and Ron stepped to the guy who called Diana a bitch.

"You smacked my lady on the butt and called her a bitch." Ron smacked him so hard he busted his lip. The guy just stood there looking at Ron, wiping the blood from his lip.

Diana walked over to Stacy and held her hand out. "Let me see it."

Stacy knew exactly what Diana was talking about. She pulled her sharp razor out and hands it to her. One of the *Young Wolves* walked over to Ron and hands him a gun. Diana walked back to the guy who smacked her on the butt looking at him with hate in her eyes.

"Hold your arm out." Diana said staring at him with anger.

"Hold your arm out fool unless you want a bullet to the head," Ron said pointing his gun to his head.

He held his arm out. Diana grabbed his arm forcefully and began to slice deeply into the center, straight down to his hand. He's screaming loudly because of the pain. She continued to grip his arm with force, blood was pouring out onto the floor and her hand was covered in blood. Diana wiped the razor off on the guy's shirt and gave it back to Stacy. The dude fell to his knees holding his right arm, moaning and crying. He looked weak in the face because he's losing a lot of blood. The other three started begging not to be hurt. The manager called the police and they arrived and took the four guys away. People in the restaurant started clapping their hands because they were glad the trouble makers are gone.

Ron, Keith, Diana and Stacy all hug each other while the *Young Wolves* are observing everyone and everything around them. Keith stood in front of Ron.

"I'm as real as they come. You have two days left on your honeymoon. When you leave, we leave." They dap up.

Five of the *Young Wolves* walked in front with their guns by their side. Keith, Stacy, Diana, and Ron walked behind them and

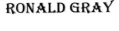

the other five followed behind them. They all left together in private limos Keith rented at the hotel. When the limos drove up in front of the hotel, a doorman was standing there waiting to open the door. Diana has her hand wrapped in a cloth that she found in the limo on the bar. She didn't want anyone to notice the blood stains on her hand. She told Stacy to get out the limo first, her and Keith and Ron will follow. The *Young Wolves* were the last to get out. Keith told them to order room service if they got hungry. Keith, Ron, Diana, and Stacy all walked into the lobby of the hotel. The hotel is breath-taking it is decorated so nicely. There are two giant waterfalls in between the two glass elevator doors where you can look straight through, seeing people and the beach in the back ground. They all are in the elevators on the way to their rooms. Stacy and Keith walked in Ron's and Diana's suite and sat down.

"Keith, I can't believe you and Stacy are here but your timing could not have been better. I won't ask how you knew about the trouble makers." Ron looked at Diana.

"Diana called Stacy and told her about what was happening and Stacy told me, but you should have told me. We are more than just partners, we are best friends. This is what real friends do, watch each other's back."

"True that." He gives Keith a serious look and he respects and appreciates him even more.

"Keith, I have never been so glad to see you in my life. I thank you and Stacy," Diana said smiling at them.

Stacy winked at Diana and smiled.

"Who were the guys in the suits Keith?" Ron asked.

"They are part of our security company which we will talk about later but know they will be around at times. The world is full of hater's partner." He stood up. "Ron, let me talk with you about something, out in the hall."

"No problem." He stood up and they walked out.

When they walked out Diana and Stacy walked over to each other and hugged.

"I was shocked to see you and Keith but thank you so much."

"Like Keith said this is what real friends do, watch each other's back," she smacked Diana on her butt, "and you got a lot of back to watch." Stacy started laughing.

Diana laughed and stared at Stacy.

"I have missed you so much."

"Show me."

"Stacy, you know I can't. Ron and Keith could walk in the door any second and this is my honeymoon." She looked at Stacy and hugged her and then they passionately kissed.

Stacy pulled away from her.

"I have missed you but we need to stop before I take you right here."

"When I get back we can spend some time together." She kissed her and they both sat down.

Ron and Keith walked back in.

"Come on baby, let's leave these two honeymooners alone because they need all the time they can get, to get their freak on." He stepped to Ron and pats him on the shoulder. "Handle your business partner." He takes Stacy's hand and they walked out with Stacy waving at Diana.

Ron walked over to Diana and she stood up.

"I'm proud of you for being brave and I love you."

"Likewise, but all that excitement has made me very horny for some reason. Enough talk, handle your business, my husband." Diana said and smiled at him.

He picked Diana up and carried her to the bed and laid her down. He removed her sarong and pulled her bathing suit to one side to bury his face between her legs. He glides his tongue slowly all over her wetness, and then pushed his tongue inside of her, flicking it from side to side.

Diana looked down at him and gripped the sheets.

"Oh Ron, that feels so damn good, don't stop baby."

CHAPTER FIVE

Hustler's Park

Keith and Ron are in the park sitting in Ron's Benz. They are wearing dress shoes, expensive pants, and dress shirts.

"Thanks again for having my back in Aruba Keith. But now, Diana is very unhappy with me because we just got back from our honeymoon and the next day, I leave for business."

"I understand but what we do is the nature of the beast in this business partner. Just remember what I told you about what a real woman wants and needs. Much respect, to be treated like a queen, spend money on her and keep some hard dick in her and your face buried between her legs and ass. On a regular basis."

Ron laughed.

"You are one nasty guy but your words might be true."

"Ain't no might be true, my words are "very true! Bobby Womack did a song about it called, "*A Woman's Gotta Have It.*"

Ron looked at him.

"Yeah, I know that old school song, very nice. Okay, your point is made but you are still a nasty dude. Anyway, I hope this thing with Stephanie works out and she needs to hurry up because I have other things to do besides waiting in some park. I could be home with my baby."

"Damn man, she whipped you that fast? You pussy whipped already. Oh, I forgot. You never had any so it wouldn't take much for you anyway." He hits Ron on the arm and started laughing. Ron looked at him.

Stephanie drove up behind Ron's car in her Bentley. She stepped out wearing heels and a tight dress, holding a gun, Ron and Keith got out with their guns in their hands by their side.

"Miss Walker, you are late," Ron said with attitude.

Keith looked at his watch.

"You need to be on time but you do look good as always. I will take your gun. You know the drill, pat down time," Keith said looking at Stephanie.

"You two are something else and all this patting me down stuff is beginning to get on my damn nerves. But I'm going to let you have your way this last time." She held her arms out. "Do your thing, Keith."

Keith put his gun away and Stephanie's and he began caressing Stephanie's body. Her breasts, stomach, back, legs and butt and then slid his hand under her dress to feel between her legs, never taking his eyes off hers.

"Very nice. You should let a young wolf like me take care of this body for you and stop faking."

Stephanie waved her hand in his face.

"Maybe later baby but right now let's get down to business." She looked at Ron. "Ron, how was your honeymoon?"

"None of your business and this is not a social call so let's talk business."

"You should be in a much better mood since you got some pussy unless that young pretty wife of yours is no good in bed. Be nice to me and I will show you how a real woman put it down." Smiling at him.

"No thank you." He looked at Stephanie like she was dirt.

"Whatever! So, have you two thought about my offer?"

"Yes, we have and the price is fifty million or we walk," Ron said.

A large Rottweiler dog was running in the park and began to slowly follow them closely. Stephanie knows if she does this they are going to make three times what she was asking for but she was pressed for time and wants to destroy Victor as soon as possible, so she agrees.

"Fine, fifty million it is." She pointed her finger at Ron and Keith, "but you two better deliver."

"We will do our part, you just do yours."

The dog stepped closer to them and Keith turned around looking at it.

"Where did this dog come from and why is it following us?" The dog was standing only a few feet behind them looking directly at Keith.

"Look at this crazy dog just standing there looking at me. I should shoot it."

Ron tapped Keith on his arm.

"Something tells me you better leave that dog alone Keith."

Keith stepped toward the dog and yelled.

"Get out of here! Stupid dog."

The dog does not move and then it stepped closer toward Keith. Stephanie looked at the dog.

"Leave the damn dog alone and get back to business."

Keith pulled his gun out and aimed it at the dog.

"Forget this, time to die, stupid dog."

More Rottweiler's suddenly appeared in the park and slowly began to surround them. Stephanie looked around at all the dogs.

"What in the hell is this? Keith, give me back my gun, now."

Ron looked at all the dogs.

"Keith, whatever you do, don't shoot that dog and don't move. I can feel this is the work of the devil."

Stephanie started to panic.

"Victor, this is his doing, he deals in witchcraft and voodoo."

Keith shook his head and laughed.

"Get the hell out of here with this voodoo garbage. These are a pack of wild alley dogs." He looked over at Ron. "S&D, when I shoot this one, you start shooting the rest."

The dogs that were surrounding them quickly run away, except for the one standing in front of Keith. It began to metamorphosis into Mr. Bones. He is dressed in all black with a black cane and a small black pouch in his hand. Stephanie screamed. Ron and Keith immediately began shooting at Mr. Bones and he fell to the ground.

"So much for the Voodoo but damn, I have never seen anything like that."

Seconds later, Mr. Bones stood straight up with his cane and pouch in his hand.

"No!" Stephanie screamed, quickly stepped out of her shoes and run toward her car, yelling. "Victor, I'm sorry, I'm sorry, forgive me." She got in her car and drove away spinning tires.

Mr. Bones pointed his cane at Ron.

"I have been waiting for you boy, chosen one. Stupid boy, you had it all. You had more power than me but you turned your back on God and now your soul is mine, Emmanuel. No holy spirit, no power," he pointed his cane at Keith. "Judas, you are trying to play both sides but now you are coming home with me. No more humping Stacy's fat ass for you, sinner."

Keith looked at Ron.

"The hell with this, let's go."

Ron and Keith took off running toward Keith's Lamborghini and they quickly drove away.

Mr. Bones raised his arms.

"You can't run from me boy. I'm the bones the prince and power of the air and I can go anywhere, attack anyone. You cannot beat the bones," He mumbled some words and tapped his cane twice on the ground and twelve Rottweiler dogs come running into the park surrounding Mr. Bones and laid down. He mumbled more words and began to metamorphosis back into a Rottweiler. All the dogs stood up and Mr. Bones runs away and the dogs followed him.

CHAPTER SIX

Keith's Condo

Ron and Keith are sitting on the sofa in Keith's condo and Stacy was in the bedroom.

"I can't believe what happened. I saw it and still don't believe it. A dog transformed into a man, we shoot him with a nine millimeter and a .357, with armor piercing bullets. The man hit the ground, seconds later, he stood straight up. How in the world is that possible?" Keith shook his head and waved his hands in the air out of frustration.

"I have seen the power of God but what we saw was the power of Satan himself and no flesh or worldly weapons can beat it. If Victor has that working for him then we are doomed and so is he, in the end."

"So, what are you saying? We should just stop and forget everything."

"No, I'm not saying that but you saw what happened and we can't beat the devil with guns and it seems Victor has the devil on his side, for now. Which means, we can't beat him and he probably knows our plans?"

Keith looked at Ron with an expression of irritation on his face.

"I don't give a damn! Nobody is going to keep me from making my money. That includes Mr. Augular, the voodoo man, and Satan himself. I got to get me and the devil can kiss my ass!"

Stacy walked into the living room wearing heels, tight fitting shorts and a top that comes just above her navel. She pointed at Ron and Keith.

"Are you two going to talk all night or are we going out. I didn't get dressed for nothing." She pointed to Ron. "You should be home with your wife who has been calling me looking for you. You are in trouble. And answer your damn phone."

"Hello to you too Stacy. You look good and call me S&D."

"S&D? Boy, don't make me laugh. Ron, you really need to choose and make sure you know what you are doing. Anyway, Diana is on the way over here. Keith, get dressed so we can go because I feel like dancing." She started moving and shaking her body.

Keith knew what was about to take place because he knows Stacy and how spoiled and persistent she can be. Not tonight, the timing was bad. He was not in the mood after what he and Ron have been through.

"Baby, you would not believe what happened to us today and I don't feel like going anywhere. This has been a nightmare of a day."

Stacy walked toward Keith and pointed her finger at him.

"Look, I know this business is crazy but if you don't get your black ass up and take me out you will be humping your hand for a week, and if you even think about cheating on me. I will put crushed glass in your food and watch you slowly bleed to death. You can believe that."

Keith quickly jumped to his feet and pointed his finger in her face.

"I told you I had a bad day and you're going to stop threatening me every time you don't get your damn way. Now back up off me."

Stacy slapped his hand away from her face making a gesture with her hands.

"Or what tough guy. Slap me, beat me, knock me down. Yeah, it would hurt and I would cry and then clean myself up, then I would do me. Seduce you, and while I'm fucking your brains out and you are screaming, oh baby it feels so good because I'm riding you like a pony. I would take my razor and cut your throat and watch you bleed, believe that."

Ron has never seen anyone like Stacy. She is very beautiful, erotic looking, and seriously sexy. And she was also smart, classy, strong, confident and full of courage. Deep down inside he admired her but he would never tell her or Keith that.

"Stacy, you are crazy. I hope my wife does not pick up any of your crazy ways and you need to be delivered"

Keith looked at Ron and back at Stacy.

"He is right, you are crazy and you do need to be delivered."

She looked at Ron and rolled her eyes thinking, You, need to be spending more time with your wife before I turn her hot ass all the way out.

"Whatever. Are we going out or not and don't play me?" She said frowning at him.

Keith shook his head.

"What choice do I have? My hand only goes around my guns and it is either crushed glass or a cut throat. Damn, what a life," he looked over at Ron, "S&D, where I go, you go."

"Wise choice." Stacy hugged and kissed Keith. "Baby, I'm going to make you feel so good tonight, put my freak moves on you." She rubs her fingers between her legs and rubs her fingers across Keith's lips. "Juicy drive you crazy, don't it baby?" She kissed Keith, winked at him, and walked into the bedroom.

"Keith, I don't care how fine she is. Stacy is crazy and you need to leave her."

"I know but I can't. She is a hundred percent real and down for me. A true ride or die, my brother. If you got a ride or die then you treat her like a queen. Anything less than that, you treat her like the piece of ass she is. Put that meat to her, bust a nut, pay her, and keep it moving," he smiled. "Stacy is a keeper. The girl makes my eyes roll back in my head and she got it going on. I can't leave her. I got to have her." He began laughing.

"Yeah, okay. Samson had to have Delilah and look what happened to him. David saw Bathsheba, a married woman but he had to have her. God cursed their son and he died but I know you can't help yourself. It's a lust demon."

"You know, sometimes I wonder about you. One day a preacher man the next day a drug dealer. You're funny man. Just keep sexing Diana my brother, good." He looked at Ron and laughed.

There was a knock at the door and Stacy walked out of the bedroom looking at Keith and Ron rolling her eyes at them.

"You two really are something." She answered the door.

Diana was standing there wearing a long dress holding a suit bag and a gym bag.

"Hi, Stacy!" She frowned at her.

Stacy looked at her up and down with a disgusted look on her face.

"You are kidding me. I know you are not wearing that going out with me."

Diana waved her hand at Stacy and walked past her into the living room, dropped the bags down, and looked at Ron with disgust. She stared at him with a serious attitude.

"Ron, you look real comfortable over there. Oh, and your phone must be broken, husband. I brought you a change of clothes. Ron, we need to talk, now."

Keith pointed to the other bedroom.

"Diana, don't beat him up. Cover up Ron, duck." He hit Ron on the chest and started laughing.

Ron picked the bags up and walked to the other bedroom with Diana behind him. She slammed the door. Ron dropped the bags and started undressing. He was standing in front of Diana wearing boxer briefs. He hugged her and started sucking on her neck. Normally this would turn Diana on quickly but she is very upset with him now, it was not working. She pushed him away.

"Is this how it's going to be Ron? You constantly leaving me and when I do call, you don't even answer your phone? I like our house a lot but I do not like being in that big house by myself. I'm getting sick of this. Our marriage was not supposed to be like this, Ron."

Ron knows he has been neglecting Diana since they got back from Aruba but the business stuff really excites him. He wants to make a lot of money so he does not have to work all his life.

"Diana, I apologize for not spending more time with you and this will change." He grabbed her waist pulling her into him and kissed her.

She pushed him away again.

"When Ron? When will it change?"

"I can't give you an exact date but it will be soon."

Diana was disgusted with him right now and her spirit becomes defiant.

"Fine Ron. You want to go out and stay in the streets, fine." She walked toward the door.

"Where are you going, Diana?"

She turned around looking at him with anger in her eyes.

"I'm going to talk to Stacy. You need to shower and get dressed, husband!" She walked out.

Keith and Stacy are sitting on the sofa kissing.

"Stacy, Ron will be ready soon and we can go."

Stacy stood up and looked at Diana and then at Keith.

"Keith, you need to shower and change clothes too but hold up. Diana, you can't go with me looking like you just stepped back in the sixties with that old lady dress on."

Keith started laughing and Diana pointed her finger at him.

"Stop laughing at me Keith and this is all your fault."

"Don't take your marriage problems out on me." He leaned back on the sofa laughing and pointing his finger at her.

Stacy walked over to Diana and grabbed her hand.

"Diana come with me. I have something that you can wear that will make Ron drool." She looked over at Keith. "Baby, will you go in the other room with Ron to shower and change? You have plenty of clothes in that closet to change into." She walked away holding Diana's hand.

Keith got up and walked in the other bedroom. Ron was getting dressed when he walked in.

"Partner your wife is highly upset with you. So, I suggest you give her a lot of attention tonight and do not get on her bad side. It's time for you to do what married people do, a lot of sucking up."

"Yeah, I guess you are right. Tonight, it is all about her. Now go shower and get dressed so we both can have some fun."

Keith got some clothes out of the closet and laid them on the bed then walked in the bathroom. He showered and got dressed. He is wearing custom made ostrich skin shoes, tailored dress pants with an ostrich skin belt and a short-sleeved dress shirt. A Rolex watch, platinum chain around his neck and diamond ring on his pinky finger to even out the look. Ron was wearing Gators, tailored dress pants, a gator belt and a tailored short-sleeve shirt. He has on a Rolex watch and a platinum chain on his neck. They walked out the bedroom but stopped in their tracks when they saw Diana and Stacy.

Stacy was wearing black heels, tight grey short shorts and a burgundy low-cut top exposing her breasts and it comes just above her navel. Diana was wearing grey heels, tight black short shorts and a white low-cut top exposing her breasts and it comes just above her navel as well. Looking at them would cause any man or woman to sin. Two gorgeous ladies with hips and ass for days.

"Diana, you are kidding me, right? Tell me this is a joke. You are not going out looking like that." Ron said and stared at her getting angrier by the second.

Keith sees Stacy looking hot on a regular basis but she looked great to him tonight. Seeing Diana like this was making him have thoughts about his best friend's wife he knows he should not have.

"Damn Diana you are trying to get somebody killed tonight." Keith was looking at her up and down with pure lust in his heart.

Diana smiled and put her hand on her hip.

"I think I look very sexy and classy." She smiled and looked at Ron.

"You do look sexy but classy Diana," she pointed at Keith and Ron. "You two need to get a grip and come on." Stacy said.

Diana can see the anger building in Ron's eyes but she has a plan for him tonight that will calm him down for good. He wants a sexy freaky wife, well he was about to get one. She walked over to Ron and kissed him.

"Baby let's not fuss, please. I want to look good for you and I want us to have some fun together, okay." She stared into his eyes while slowly rubbing his crotch.

He knows what she was doing and it's working.

"Yeah okay," he said frowning at her then turned to look at Keith. "Let's go have some fun partner." He and Diana walked toward the front door and he has his hand on Diana's butt caressing her cheeks.

Keith grabbed Stacy's hand.

"You heard the man, let's go, baby." He kissed her and they walked out.

RONALD GRAY   (33)

CHAPTER SEVEN
Eyes to See But Blind

Ron was driving his Bentley. He drove up in front of Victor's club but Victor and his bodyguards are not there. Three large bouncers are standing out front and there was a long line of people waiting to get in. They got out and Ron hands one of the bouncers a hundred-dollar bill and his keys to park the car, they walked in. It's Friday night and the place is full. The DJ is doing his thing making people bump and grind on the dance floor.

Diana grabbed Ron's hand.

"Come on baby, let's dance."

Ron pulled his hand out of hers. "I'm not in the mood to dance right now." He looked at her with anger. She stared at him.

"Why not? I didn't get dressed up to sit on a club sofa."

Stacy walked over to Diana and grabbed her hand.

"Come on Diana, I will dance with you." She kissed Keith then she and Diana walked to the dance floor.

Keith tapped Ron on the arm. "Don't sweat it, partner. Let's go to the bar and chill." They walked to the bar and ordered orange juice with ice and Keith sends his *Young Wolves* a text message because his instincts told him there was going to be trouble tonight. All eyes were on Diana and Stacy as they walked to the dance floor. The DJ switched to an old school fast song and started playing, *"Shake it Fast" by Mystikal*, just in time for Stacy and Diana to show off. Stacy tapped Diana on the arm. "I know you can do it so follow me and do what I do and we can blow these girls off this dance floor."

Stacy said smiling at her.

Not sure but she was determined to keep up with Stacy.

"Okay, I will try."

Stacy started moving her body slowly to the beat of the song and winding her back, then bouncing and shaking her butt slow while Diana did the same. Their bodies moved to the beat of the music like they have been dancing together for years. Winding and grinding side by side and popping their butt low and fast at the same time. Step for step, move for move people were staring at them. Men and ladies wanted to get with them but they shut everybody down.

A very attractive lady with a great looking body has been watching Stacy and Diana since they walked on the floor but it was Stacy that she was feeling. She walked on the floor in front of Stacy and started winding her back in such a way it looked like she was moving in slow motion. Any way Stacy moved, she moved and they danced together.

A very handsome clean-cut guy started dancing in front of Diana. Normally she would have ignored him but he was very good looking so she let him do his thing and danced with him.

Ten of the *Young Wolves* walked in the club wearing suits and dark shades spreading themselves out to observe. Keith and Ron noticed them coming in and nodded their heads at them. People knew of the *Young Wolves* and they were not to be messed with, on any level. People gave them much space.

Ron had calmed down after talking with Keith and he was in the mood to dance with Diana so they headed to the dance floor. What Ron saw made his temper rise instantly and his anger was in killer mode. Keith looked and he couldn't believe it. Diana was grinding her butt on some guy and Stacy was being herself, showing off her dance moves with some girl. Keith looked at Ron and saw extreme anger in his eyes that he has never seen before as he was staring at Diana. He knew Ron's thoughts as he would be the same if he saw Stacy dancing like that on some guy.

The *Young Wolves* saw all this and they unbuttoned their suit jackets ready to pull their guns and do whatever. Ron quickly walked over to Diana. Stacy saw Ron and Keith coming and she saw the rage in Ron's eyes. Diana never saw him coming because she was too busy grinding her butt on the guy. Ron snatched her arm and roughly pulled her towards him.

"What do you think you are doing?" He yelled at her.

The guy pushed Ron.

"Back up fool, she is with me." He lifted his shirt revealing a gun and mean mugging Ron as he looked at him.

Three of the guy's friends walked quickly next to him and raised their shirts revealing guns as well.

Ron lifted his shirt showing his gun and Keith quickly stepped next to Ron with his gun in his hand. The *Young Wolves* walked quickly on the dance floor and lined up next to Ron and Keith. They opened their jackets revealing two guns that each man had in their waist.

The music stopped, everybody stopped dancing, and a spot light was put on the scene. Twelve of Victor's bodyguards quickly walked to the area along with ten more standing by. The bodyguards knew of Keith and Ron and what the *Young Wolves* were about but they had strict orders from Victor to shut down any disturbance that happened in the club. And no one wanted to go against Victor. One of the guards stepped to Keith and Ron.

"We know who you are but it doesn't matter. Shut it down or get laid down." The bodyguards stared at them then looked at the *Young Wolves* and the other guys.

RONALD GRAY   (36)

Stacy was not new to this and she knows her man does not like to back down from anyone, regardless of the odds. She stepped closer to Keith and touched his arm.

"Baby lets go. We've had enough dancing."

Diana walked over and looked at Ron like he was wrong.

"I was having fun dancing, Ron."

Stacy, Keith, and Ron looked at her like she was crazy. Stacy grabbed Diana's hand.

"Come on let's go to the bathroom." She walked off holding Diana's hand.

The guy Diana was dancing with and his friends walked away and Victor's bodyguards left the floor but are still observing Keith, Ron, and the *Young Wolves*. The spot light was turned off and the music started playing and everyone began dancing. Keith and Ron were watching Stacy and Diana walk away seeing how they attract so much attention because of how beautiful they are and how they are dressed. With every step they took, you saw hips and butt shaking especially with the tight shorts they are wearing revealing butt cheeks when they were dancing. Ron and Keith saw the guy Diana was dancing with, he walked towards the same bathroom area Stacy and Diana walked to. Keith looked into Ron's eyes and saw rage. Ron walked towards the bathroom while Keith and the *Young Wolves* followed him. The bathroom was in a corner of the club and when Ron and Keith got close to it they saw the guy leaning against the wall waiting for Stacy and Diana to come out. Keith knew Ron was on fire from the look in his eyes.

"Just chill partner and see how the girls handle it. Just be cool." He said while looking at Ron.

RONALD GRAY   (37)

"Yeah, okay." Ron stared at the guy with his anger building by the minute.

Diana and Stacy walked out and the guy stepped to them. He extends his hand to Diana.

"Hi, my name is Devon. You dance very well and I would like to get to know you better."

"Look, I don't know you and we were just dancing." She held her hand up to his face. "You see this ring on my finger? I'm married and the only person I want or need to know is my husband, so no thank you." She and Stacy walked away.

The guy grabbed the back of Diana's shorts and pulled her back towards him.

"Look baby. You and your friend are fine and got hips and ass for days, let me take you both out and we can see what happens." He was staring at Diana and Stacy licking his lips.

Ron saw enough and he snapped. He quickly walked over to the guy with Keith and the *Young Wolves* behind him. He took his gun out and hit the guy hard in the mouth with his gun. Three of his front teeth flew out of his mouth with blood pouring out and then he hit him on the top of his head and the guy fell to the floor. Ron put the gun to his mouth and wanted to shoot the guy so badly he was grinding his teeth.

"Ron, please don't shoot him, baby, please." Diana said shaking her hand at him.

"Don't shoot him partner not in here." Keith said knowing Victor would kill him, Ron, and his entire family.

"Ron, he is not worth it so please don't, shoot him." Stacy said, seeing the rage in his eyes.

The *Young Wolves* were standing close by with their hands on their guns looking around waiting to pull and start blasting. They heard a lot of footsteps running behind them so they quickly turned around and pulled their guns out.

Twenty of Victor's bodyguards were standing behind them pointing Mac-10 machine guns at everyone. One of the guards stepped closer to them waving his gun.

"All of you get the hell out of here or die." He said with his eyes revealing no fear.

Two of the bodyguards dragged the guy that Ron hit out of the club and the *Young Wolves* put their guns away knowing they would be going up against Victor, which would be suicide.

Ron walked over to Diana and grabbed her hand and walked away. Keith and Stacy followed them out and the *Young Wolves* were behind them. When they got outside, Ron's Bentley was waiting. He, Keith, Stacy, and Diana got in and he drove away. The *Young Wolves* separate into pairs grabbing one of the five black 2012 Cadillac Escalade EXT trucks that were parked behind Ron's Bentley. They quickly drove away following him. Ron was looking over at Diana while driving and his temper was boiling because, in his mind, she caused all this. She looked at him and rolled her eyes. He slowed down and pulled over in an empty parking lot and stopped. The *Young Wolves* stopped as well.

"Get out." Ron yelled looking at Diana.

She looked at Ron like he was crazy.

"What? I'm not doing anything." She stared at him and rolled her eyes.

Ron balled his fist up and quickly hit the windshield so hard that it cracked.

"I said get out." He yelled again looking at Diana with so much anger, his eyes were red.

Diana looked at Ron and for the first time, she feared him because she has never seen him this angry. She quickly got out the car and leaned on the side of it.

Stacy got out and stood close to her. Keith has never seen Ron like this but he knew how he felt. He tapped him on the shoulder.

"Partner, I know you are heated and I would be too but don't say or do anything you will regret later. She is your wife and you wanted her a certain way, well you got it. We all know she was wrong for disrespecting you like that, grinding on that guy. But just be cool." He tapped his shoulder again.

"Yeah, she must think I'm soft." He got out and walked over to Diana.

Keith got out and walked close to Diana and Stacy. The *Young Wolves* got out as well and looked around and unbuttoned their suit jackets ready to pull their guns if they must.
Ron pointed his finger in Diana's face and yelled.

"Are you crazy? I saw you grinding your ass all on that fool. How are you going to be in a club with me and dance with another man disrespecting me like that? You must be crazy. Are you smoking dope." He yelled?

Diana knew she was very wrong but she was not about to back down from Ron now.

"Ron, get your finger out of my face and stop yelling at me. All I wanted to do was dance. You didn't feel like it so I danced with Stacy. I didn't plan on some guy dancing up on me like that. You are so busy with your business you are neglecting your wife. You have eyes to see but you are blind to what is really going on." She said staring at him trying to be brave.

"You think I'm stupid?" He stepped closer standing within inches from her face. "I saw you smiling and laughing while you were grinding your ass on that fool. Your ass cheeks were showing but I guess you wanted to really, show your ass."

Stacy stepped closer to Ron.

"Ron, she was just dancing and she made a mistake. Let it go, please."

He quickly turned his head in Stacy's direction and his facial expression and eyes revealed his anger.

"Does it look like I'm talking to you? Mind your business." Stacy knew Diana was wrong but she does not allow anyone to talk to her like this.

"Look, I know you are upset but don't take it out on me because I'm not the one. Don't get it twisted." Stacy looked at him with no fear.

Keith knew where this could lead to so he stepped closer to Ron.

"Ron, relax. Don't take this someplace we don't need." He tapped him on the shoulder. "Let it go, partner."

Ron looked at Keith, Stacy, and Diana and nods his head at Keith and got in the car. They all got in and Ron drove away but no one talked the entire way home. The *Young Wolves* reached Ron's house then they drove off. They all walked in the house and Ron looked at Keith and Stacy.

"You two make yourself at home, spend the night, do whatever. I'm going to bed."

He looked over at Diana with eyes still full of anger.

"Are you coming?" He said with attitude.

Diana was surprised Ron was even talking to her.

"Yes, I'm coming." She hugged Stacy and Keith and walked in front of Ron going to their bedroom.

Ron was staring at Diana's butt shaking.

"Yeah, I got something for that ass." He mumbled and looked at Stacy and Keith and walked away.

"Ron, you better not hurt her." Stacy said.

He looked back at Stacy and frowned.

Keith put his arm around Stacy's waist and they walked upstairs to the bedroom.

"We need to talk Stacy."

"Keith not tonight, please. I know you have a lot on your mind but can we just enjoy each other tonight and talk tomorrow?"

They reached the room and Stacy walked in first and Keith's eyes are locked on her body. He walked behind Stacy, hugged her and pressed his body against hers. He started sucking on her neck while his erection was pressed into her butt. Stacy missed him so much and wants him badly. She pushed her butt into Keith grinding on him and then turned around to face him.

"I have missed us spending quality time together Keith," she kissed him softly on his lips. "Baby, hold me and make love to me tonight. I want to feel your heart and your body."

"You are my heart, Stacy." He put his hands on her hips, pulling her into him and kissed Stacy with such warmth and passion, tears come to her eyes.

They removed their clothes, got on the bed, and began making love slowly and with great emotions. They made love in various positions until Stacy had three orgasms and Keith couldn't hold it and erupted inside Stacy, gripping her body with much love. They shower and fell asleep wrapped in each other's arms.

As Keith and Stacy were pleasing each other, Ron was on his mission. Diana was standing in the middle of the room with her back to Ron when he walked in. He closed the door, stepped out of his shoes, and walked over to Diana. He gently and slowly wrapped his arms around her waist and picked her up. Diana was surprised at this and didn't know what Ron was going to do since she knows how angry he is at her.

"Ron don't you hurt me." She said with real fear and concern in her voice.

He carried Diana close to the wall and put her down gently, pushed her against the wall facing it. He ripped her shirt and bra off and started caressing her breasts then slid his hands inside her shorts feeling her wetness.

Diana felt his erection pressing into her butt and all of this was turning her on greatly because of his attitude and roughness.

"Ron, stop. You can't just take me whenever you want to." But she didn't mean a word of what she just said.

Ron knew exactly what she wanted and he's in the mood to give it to her.

"Be quiet." He was rock hard and wants Diana badly. He quickly pulled her shorts and underwear off at the same time, kneel behind her and started licking her from the back.

Diana becomes wet in seconds with just a few long deep licks of Ron's tongue. He unbuttoned his pants pulling them and his underwear off and slid inside of Diana. Her being wet, he slid inside easy but she is tight. He gripped her hips and started pulling her into him back and forth.

The moment Diana felt Ron slide inside her she had a small orgasm but wanted so much more.

"Oh Ron, yes baby give it to me. Fuck me, Ron." She began pushing her body back into him.

Ron smacked Diana on the butt and started thrusting inside her faster and harder gripping her hips tighter. His dick was moving like pistons in a car inside Diana, faster and faster. She loved this so much, she placed the palms of her hands against the wall to brace herself and give her body more leverage to push back into her husband.

"Yes Ron, fuck me, hard baby. I have missed you so much, give it to me. I need this."

Ron pulled out of Diana and carried her to the bed putting her on her back. He pushed her legs back and slid his dick inside her, thrusting faster. Diana gripped the sheets and her body started shaking and bucking.

"Fuck me, Ron, I'm cuming baby, ahhhhhhhhh," she screamed so loudly she knew Keith and Stacy heard her but she could care less. "Ohhhhh Ron, fuck meeeeee!" She was pushing her body into him giving Ron all of her until she finally, deeply exhaled and relaxed.

RONALD GRAY   (44)

Ron was still hard so he pulled out of Diana and started licking and sucking her inner thighs then buried his face between her legs, licking and sucking all her juices, desiring to make her climax again. He gently rubbed both sides of his face against her wetness, back and forth wanting to feel and taste all of her.

Diana's first orgasm was intense but Ron was taking her to a deeper place, so she started grinding her pelvis into his face wanting more of his hot mouth. This was driving her emotions to another level and it felt so good. She tried to back up on the bed to get away from him but he gripped her legs tighter and pulled her back towards him.

"Come back here. Where are you going?" He sucked her clit and firmly held her legs so she could not get away from him.

Diana was twisting and turning her body because the pleasure was so intense. She tried pulling away from him again but Ron kept pulling her back. It was too much and she couldn't hold it any longer. Her orgasm felt like an inner explosion.

"Ahhhhhhhh Ron, I'm cummming so damn hard, ohhhhhhh baby."

Ron never wanted Diana to forget this moment. He was still rock hard so he stopped sucking on her and moved his body up and slid back inside of her. He pushed her legs further back and started pumping into her slow but deep and strong.

Diana thought she would pass out from the second orgasm but his lovemaking was so strong, it was making her entire body shake like she was having convulsions.

"Ohhhhhh Ron, you are trying to make me pass out. I'm sorry, I'm going to be good baby, I'm going to be good, ohhhhhhh Ron your dick is so hard baby. I can't take any more."

RONALD GRAY   (45)

"Yes, you can, take this dick, take it." He pulled her to the edge of the bed, never pulling out, and lifted her legs straight up in the air and started sliding his dick in her real slow. He would pull himself almost all the way out then slammed it back in. Doing this over and over until he felt ready to explode.

"Say it, say you want this dick." He continued pumping into her.

Diana knew she cannot get away from Ron and she feels like she is going to pass out because all of this is too much for her. Ron was taking his frustrations out on her which she liked but would never tell him that. She couldn't take this type of lovemaking daily. Another orgasm hits her like a shock wave, making her feel it in her brain and down to her toes.

"Ahhhhhhh Ron." She screamed even louder than before.

Diana's orgasm triggers his and he can't hold it but he wants to keep the pressure on her so for the next thirty seconds Ron thrusts inside Diana fast, like machine gun fire. His body motions and dick look like a blur. Diana's whole body was trembling and shaking. She leaned her head back.

"Nooo." She screamed so loudly and hard the muscles in her neck jumped.

"Ohhhhhh Diana, you are making me cum baby, ahhhhhh damn you got some good pussy." Still ramming into her like pistons.

Ron finally slowed down when he hears Diana crying. He slowly pulled out and held her. When he kissed Diana softly on the lips, tears are coming down her face and she kissed Ron back with more passion than they have ever shared.

RONALD GRAY   (46)

"I'm sorry Ron. I love you so much, baby. It will never happen again. I'm so sorry." She was crying and having mini orgasms at the same time holding on to Ron tightly. Diana has so much emotional pressure from climaxing so hard with back to back orgasms and the love for her husband. She can't hold it. "Ronnnn!" She yelled at the top of her lungs, crying then pressed her lips against Ron hard. Kissing and sucking on his lips while her body was still shaking.

Ron held her until they fell asleep. Two hours later they woke up, took a shower and went back to bed holding on to each other with a love that words can't express. Then they fell asleep.

Early in the morning, Diana heard a light tap on her bedroom door. She looked at Ron who was asleep. She slowly got out of bed so she does not wake him. Diana was wearing one of Ron's T-shirts and walked to the door slowly, on wobbly legs. She opened the door and Stacy was standing there wearing a big T-shirt as well. Stacy wiggled her finger for Diana to come out. They walked to the kitchen and sat down after getting some Gatorade to drink.

"I didn't want to disturb you Diana but Keith and I kept hearing you scream last night. Are you okay? Did he hurt you?" Diana stared at Stacy and can't help but start crying shaking her head because she was dealing with such deep emotions.

"No, he didn't hurt me Stacy but that man put something on me last night. I love him so much." She lowered her head then looked at Stacy. "It was beyond good but I'm still so horny and I don't know why. I just want more but not like last night. I want a soft touch and…"

RONALD GRAY   (47)

Stacy reached over and put her fingers over Diana's lips before she could finish her sentence. She grabbed her hand and they walked to the basement. Diana laid on the sofa pulling her T-shirt up. Stacy began to softly caress Diana's body with her hands, lips, and tongue. A delicate warm touch. Then she buried her face between Diana's legs licking and sucking her with expert skills until Diana explodes.

"Ohhhhhh Stacy." Diana climaxed hard, grinding on Stacy's mouth.

They hug and kiss for the next five minutes then washed up in the bathroom and they went back upstairs. Stacy laid next to Keith, kissed him on the cheek and drifts off to sleep. Diana laid down next to Ron holding him as tears come down her face. She whispered.

"Lord, please forgive me. I need help." She prayed until she fell asleep.

CHAPTER EIGHT

Sheila's House

Ever since Diana left home this morning in her Bentley she has been driving around for two hours going nowhere in particular. In most people's eyes, she had it all, a dream house with all the lavish furnishings, a very expensive wardrobe that she can change at will, expensive cars, lots of money, and a husband who loves her deeply. She loves him back just as much. Yet, Diana was not happy. Why? Her walk with God was not the same, not even close.

As much as she loves Ron she has to admit to herself, they should not have gotten married, at least not when they did. She was more motivated by her love for Ron instead of waiting on God. She got married too soon! Her walk with the Lord was very tight and she was very obedient to his word until she married Ron. The Bible reads, *"Be not unequally yoked together with unbelievers."* If you believe something then you will live according to what you believe. Ron's walk with Christ was tight but he changed after Sandra went into a coma and he blamed himself for this. Diana knew in her heart that Ron was not living for God when she married him and that makes them unequally yoked together. It does not matter how much Bible you know if you are not living it.

Diana was very upset with herself and she has no real peace anymore. She has cheated on her husband with Stacy and her guilt was beyond overwhelming for all her transgressions. Having sex with another female was a sin according to the word of God, and for her, that's all that matters because it was God who she was trying to please, not man. *What does it profit a man to gain the whole world but lose his soul or what shall a man give in exchange for his soul?* Diana needs help, she needs deliverance by God from her ungodly spirits and she knew who could help her. She does not want to face them but she must. They will understand because they both love her dearly. Her Grandma and Sheila are sold out to the Lord and prayer warriors.

Diana cried and prayed herself to sleep last night. She made love to her husband before she left, cooked him breakfast and said bye to Keith and Stacy before she left the house. As she drove up to Sheila's house, she was feeling so defeated but also felt like she was about to get her life in order. She stepped out the car wearing heels and a dress that she likes. The dress does not come up to her neck or down to her ankles nor is it skin tight but it fits her and she feels good about that. As she was about to knock on the door, it opened and Sheila was standing there with her arms opened wide.

"Come in Diana, we have missed you so much."
Diana stepped in and hugged Sheila very tightly and then walked over to Grandma Harris who has her arms opened.

"Come here, baby." She hugged Diana hard.
Diana couldn't keep it in any longer and emotionally broke down crying very hard in her grandma's arms. She dropped to her knees, crying out to God for forgiveness, deliverance, and to be healed. Grandma Harris and Sheila already knew what has been going on with Diana and Ron because of prayer and God revealing things to them. They prayed over Diana but it was the power of God that moved in her spirit to do everything that

Diana needs to be done. She stood up knowing God has bestowed mercy and restored her. She sat on the sofa, Sheila and Grandma Harris sat on the other.

"Baby, I'm so glad you came. We have missed you so much and thank God for his mercy and love for you." Grandma Harris said.

"Diana, I love you and I have since day one and I know you truly love my son but your salvation comes first."

"Thank you, Mrs. O'Neil. I made a big mistake. Yes, I love Ron very much and I still want to spend the rest of my life with him but we married too soon. I went to him instead of allowing him to first come to God, healed and delivered."

"Baby, you made a mistake like we all do. Okay, it happened but don't allow the devil to beat you up or hold you in condemnation. God has delivered you and now you have to stay delivered." Grandma Harris said smiling at her.

"I know grandma and as much as I want to be with Ron now, I know I can't until he gets fully delivered. I can't stay at the house anymore and that alone is going to break my heart. Not because of a luxury house but because I will miss being with my husband." She lowered her head and tears fall from her eyes.

"Diana, you can stay here. Grandma Harris is here most of the time anyway so it will be good for you and I know eventually Ron will come here for you." Sheila said.

"Amen to that." Grandma Harris said shaking her head.
Diana hasn't felt the peace she feels now for a while and she can't afford to lose it ever again, not for Ron or anything.

"Thank you both so much and yes, I would like to stay here until I can go home to my husband for keeps." She smiled from the inside out.

"First my son has to stop running from God and come back to him. Then he will come to you, Diana."

"Amen to that Sheila, Amen!"

Diana stood up and walked around the living room and looked at them both.

"I can't believe in such a short time of being married, I'm going to be separated from my husband." She stared into space looking around and then looked at them again. "This is very hard to ask but I really need to know and grandma, don't be mean." She looked down and exhaled hard and then looked at them. "While I'm separated from my husband, do we have sex?"

Grandma Harris looked at Sheila and laughed.

"Oh baby, I'm not laughing at you but I went through the same thing years ago with my husband, poor baby had a heart attack and died right after we had sex," she sighs. "Anyway, that choice baby will have to be yours and if you pray, God will guide you."

"Yes Diana, God will guide you and he will if you ask him but I know you will miss Ron dearly.

Grandma Harris started laughing again.

"I know she will because I know that young boy put something on her and she wants some more of all that good hot loving." Grandma Harris slapped her leg and started laughing.

"Grandma really, you are truly something else." Diana shook her head and rolled her eyes at her.

Sheila turned to look at Grandma Harris.

RONALD GRAY   (52)

"Grandma Harris, I can't believe you would say something like that in front of me about my son, shame on you woman."

"Oh, Sheila relax. You and I both know that boy is going to want his wife home and Diana wants to give him some more of her booty. They are newlyweds and they are in heat. You know how it is Sheila, young folk want to hump all the time." She looked at Diana and then Sheila and started laughing so hard she slowly slides down to the floor, still laughing.

CHAPTER NINE
James' Office

Rick Matthew was sitting in James Reed's office and James was sitting at his desk.

"Mr. Reed with each passing day I'm more determined to see Victor Augular in prison for life or dead. His destruction has become my life's mission and I feel compelled to see this case to the end, no matter what. Then I may retire."

"I can fully understand your persistence to see Mr. Augular behind bars where he belongs. I know he was indirectly responsible for David O'Neil's death and so many others including your partner. But we must be very careful in the handling of this case so when he does fall he will not get off on some legal loop hole."

"You are right but the man is so evil and I want him dead so bad," he stared at James, "you know I have dreams about killing him over and over. Then I wake up sweating and breathing heavy."

"Wow, this case has really affected you and you have taken it very personally which is why when this case is over, you should take some time off to relax and go have some fun."

"Yeah, maybe I need to go have wild passionate sex with a nasty girl," he laughed, "no offense counselor. But first, we must catch Victor. The slippery bastard, every time we get close to nailing him, he somehow slips through our hands and after what I have seen with the voodoo man and black magic. I see how he

RONALD GRAY   (54)

can sneak away so often. But the devil has no love for anyone, Victor will fall."

"He has been named the untouchable Victor Augular but he will fall regardless of using voodoo or whatever to protect himself. The devil is a master deceiver and the father of lies and he truly loves no one and as soon as the devil is finished using him. To hell, he will go along with Satan and all his followers." James said.

Rick laughed.

"Hell would be a perfect place for Victor and his murdering body guards and I want the satisfaction of bringing him down."

"So, do I but first we must prove he is responsible for the crimes we know he has committed. And that has not been an easy task."

"That's the main reason why I'm here. Victor has been watched very carefully and we have learned a few things."

"So, what happens now? Do you have any information that can be used to put him away?"

Rick nods his head.

"Yes, we do but every time we get close to him people start dying but the wrong people. He must have Satan himself working for him. You can't kill what you can't see."

"That's why it is so important in a situation like this to have God on your side."

Rick stood up and walked around then looked at James. "Tell me something counselor. Is God on our side because it seems like to me, the bad guys keep winning."

"It does appear that way but God is always in control and he will only allow the devil to do but so much, for so long. God will always have people who will stand for righteousness and help bring down the wicked. You and I have been drafted."

"I don't mind being drafted as long as I know who my enemy is and I want to win the war."

"Amen to that. For the record, you are on the winning side."

"From your mouth to God's ears. Now for the good news. We are about to serve federal subpoenas on Victor and his bodyguards and he will have to appear in court and even he doesn't know about this and he can't beat it. We are finally going to get that slippery bastard."

James stood up.

"Detective Matthew you have made my day and this is one court date that I will make. Now, what can I do to help?"

"I'm glad you asked counselor," he sat down, "sit down and I will tell you all about it."

CHAPTER TEN

Mr. Bones

Mr. Bones was standing in a graveyard. On the ground in front of him was a circle of bones and inside the circle are pictures of James and Rick. Mr. Bones was wearing all black with his cane in one hand and some bones in the other.

"Yes, I love it. It was the beginning of another wonderful morning for me to start doing what I do the best steal, kill, and destroy any and everything that I can. Stupid foolish people, I have them so blind because of their selfishness. They want what they want so bad, they put their trust in me. Dumb, very dumb! Don't they read the Bible? I'm the father of lies. How can you trust a liar? I can give you what you want but I can't give you what you need." He started laughing. "Even though I was kicked out of heaven because in my heart I wanted to exalt myself above the stars of God, but I still have the power because I'm the one and only, Mr. Bones." He looked down and stared at the pictures.

"Mr. Reed and Mr. Matthew your plan will not work and you will be destroyed by the prince and power of the air, me." He pats himself on the chest and mumbled some words then tapped his cane on the ground. The pictures float up in the air and Mr. Bones throws his bones at the pictures. The pictures and the bones burn up. "Now Victor, it's time I pay you a visit." He tapped his cane and smoke comes from underneath his feet and surrounds him, and he disappeared.

CHAPTER ELEVEN

Victor and Mr. Bones

Victor was not your typical drug lord who spends his money on expensive lavish homes. He sees this as a waste of money for him because he desires to travel a lot and not spend a lot of time in any one place. He chooses to spend his money on very lavish hotel suites, staying there until he becomes bored and then move on to another one. This also makes it harder to track his every move. Right now, he was staying in the Penthouse Suite at the Ritz Carlton in Washington, DC. With his money and clout, Victor refuses to accept there was something he cannot have. His concept was, he can buy it or take it, by any means necessary.

Victor was lying on a twenty-five-thousand-dollar king-sized custom-made bed, put in the room just for him. The hotel manager makes sure the room is available to him at any time. He is asleep lying on his stomach in his silk boxers along with three of the finest women any man could want. A Latina, Black, and a Caucasian. They are wearing tight boy shorts and nothing else. All three have flawless tight bodies with enough curves between them to make a man dizzy. The women were flown in on his private jet at his request. His heart was still heavy and hurt from Stephanie killing Sherry whom he missed very much so he uses other women for sex as a distraction.

When each lady was contacted, Victor's personal instructions for each was to sexually do whatever he asks. They were being paid fifteen thousand dollars a night. He woke up and pulled the covers back looking at all three women, shaking his head at how

RONALD GRAY   (58)

beautiful they are. He smacked each one on the butt to wake them up.

"Good morning ladies. I'm horny and want a foursome. I desire you three to be with each other first while I watch, then I will join in."

Two of the ladies said no because they are not into women. Victor walked over to his dresser and removed a stack of money and tossed it on the bed. It was an extra ten thousand dollars apiece. He stared at the women.

"Now get busy licking and caressing and stop talking." He looked at them like they mean nothing to him except for his pleasure.

They looked at each other, smiled, and started kissing and caressing one another and having sex doing all kinds of freaky sexual things while Victor sat on one of the chairs watching. He joined them an hour later doing everything sexually you can imagine. When it was over, they all got up and took showers. Victor had maid service come in to change the sheets. The women laid naked next to Victor but he has on silk boxers. The ladies fell asleep fast because they were all exhausted.

The room was dark because the curtains are closed but a cloud of smoke appeared at the foot of the bed. Mr. Bones appeared dressed in all black holding his cane and pouch. He tapped his cane on the bed. Victor opened his eyes but slowly slid his hand under his pillow and pulled out his .357 magnum and quickly turned over and pointed it at Mr. Bones.

"Damn, it's you. I told you not to ever creep up on me. What the hell do you want?" He lowered his gun.

RONALD GRAY   (59)

"My, are we emotional in the morning. Three sluts in bed with you and you still woke up grouchy." He laughed then stopped and pointed his cane at Victor. "Have you forgotten so fast Victor that I go wherever I want? You know who I'm." He stared at the women lying in bed and started licking his lips, "three women, damn you are a big freak." He hit the bed hard with his cane to wake the ladies up.

They all woke up and looked at Mr. Bones and screamed. He pointed his cane at them.

"Shut up that damn screaming you filthy, dirty, nasty women. Did you get enough dick and pussy last night? Sodom and Gomorrah was destroyed because of women like you."

All three ladies quickly try to cover up their naked bodies while getting off the bed and walked across the floor, quickly retrieving their clothes. As they were getting dressed Mr. Bones walked over and smacked one of them on the butt.

"Damn, all of you got fat asses. Yum, yum give me some." He licked his lips and laughed.

They looked at Mr. Bones but said nothing. The women quickly got dressed and run out the room with their cash in their hands.

Victor got out of bed holding his gun in his hand. He walked over to Mr. Bones and pointed his gun at his head.

"Don't ever creep up on me again or I will blow your brains out. The last time I shot you in the body and somehow you survived but this time it's in the head. You kill the head, you kill the body."

"You can't fight spiritual with the physical. Don't you know your word, Victor? For you wrestle not against flesh and blood but against the rulers of darkness of this world, against spiritual wickedness in high places. I'm that spiritual wickedness in high places. You can't beat the bones," he mumbled some words and tapped his cane on the floor.

Victor's gun turned into a rattle snake and he dropped it, quickly backing up. He looked down at the snake and then at Mr. Bones.

"How in the hell did you do that?"

"Once again you have already answered your own question. I'm the bones, now pick up your gun."

Victor looked at the snake and it turned back into his gun.

"Hell no! I'm not touching it. Now what the hell do you want and why are you disturbing my sleep? I was going to get some more ass from the ladies."

"Forget those sluts. I'm going to enjoy killing them later. I'm here to warn you. Your world is about to crumble. Attorney Reed and Detective Matthew are about to put you away for life. They have federal subpoenas for you and your bodyguards. I suggest you wrap up your business here and leave the country."

"I know of Attorney Reed. He has come a long way and is climbing the political ladder very well. I should have killed detective Matthew years ago. No problem I need to take care of some business in Bogotá Columbia anyway and the club business is boring me so I will sell it. Is there anything else?"

"Yes, move quickly and quietly through Maryland. Now I have to leave but remember time is very short." He mumbled some words, tapped his cane on the floor and disappeared in a thick mist.

RONALD GRAY   (61)

The mist lingers and moved toward the hotel door, it opened and the mist goes out the door and the door closed.

Victor stared at the door wiped his head with his hand and looked at his gun on the floor. He slowly bent down and picked it up and sat on his bed.

"What in the world have I done? No matter, because at the right time, I will find a way to destroy Mr. Bones and keep my empire. I want all the damn money I can get and as much as I can get, by any means necessary. Damn everybody else."

CHAPTER TWELVE
Torn in Love

Diana drove up to her house in her Bentley after staying at Sheila's for three days. She and Ron have been talking daily but all the conversations have been the same. He wants her home and never understood why she left in the first place. She missed him more than he could possibly know and believes she is doing the right thing. Diana stepped out of the car wearing heels and a form fitting dress just for him. Ron was in the basement sitting on the sofa wearing a T-shirt and sweat pants. He was watching a movie on his 90-inch, Sharp TV when he hears Diana coming down the steps. Diana was so happy to see him she could cry. She walked over to him.

"Hi Ron."

He was very happy to see her but refused to show it because he was still upset with her. He looked up at her and frowned.

"Oh, you finally decided to come home or are you just coming by to see me and get a change of clothes and roll out again? You really are something. A serious piece of work you know that?" He is staring at her.

"Ron, I do not want to argue with you so please don't do this. You know how much I miss you and how difficult this is for me to be away from you."

He stood up.

"None of this makes any sense to me. Damn, we just got married and you leave me because I'm not doing what you think I should. I deal with temptations every day just like you but I never stray. I love you greatly and no matter who I see out on these streets, all I want is you, my wife. Diana, I treat you like a queen, provide for you and give you much respect but none of that is enough for you."

His words penetrated her heart deeply and made a lot of sense. Women all over the world would love to have him.

"Ron, we have not seen each other in three days. Can you at least hug and kiss me."

"That's your fault, Diana. I'm not the one who left. All this hugging and kissing you want to do, are you giving up the ass?"

She stepped closer to him.

"Don't talk to me like that," she yelled at him. "I'm your wife, not some prostitute." She said with anger but trying to control it.

"Well, prostitutes give up the ass." He looked at her hips and butt and smiled.

It took silent prayer for her not to slap Ron when he said that but she promised herself those days were gone and all hitting is wrong.

"As your wife, is that all I am to you Ron, just flesh at your disposal?" She looked at him with hurt in her eyes.

Ron loves Diana so much and he never wants to hurt her and this situation is ridiculous to him but it was not his desire to make matters worse. He put his hands on her waist and pulled Diana into him and kissed her. He does not rub her butt because he didn't want her to think that's all he wants from her, although he desires her greatly.

The moment Ron's hands touched her body she felt weak, but when their lips touched it melted her heart and she started kissing him back with great love and desire. She placed his hands on her butt knowing how much he likes caressing it and how much she loves his hands all over her.

They hug and kiss each other like it has been years since they last touched. Diana felt his growing erection and she wants him just as much but she slowly pulled away.

"Ron, I want us together badly and this situation is breaking my heart," she lowered her head and tears fell from her eyes and then she looked at him, "but you lied to me, Ron. You are not finished with this devil lifestyle."

"Look Diana. Yes, I omitted a few details but that's the past. Come home and be a wife to me like I'm a husband to you. For better or for worse! The wedding vows, remember those. Your actions don't match the vows. The first little thing that happens in our marriage you don't like, you run off. That's why so many marriages are weak. People don't want to endure anything but talk about how much they love each other, it's all lies. I would never leave you, Diana." Ron stared in her eyes.

Looking at Ron and hearing his words ripped her heart in two because she knows he was right. What is she to do, stick around and maybe get caught up in one of his evil business dealings and go to prison or worse? Or, leave until he changed his life? She was so torn but right now, she wants her husband. She began undressing and stood in front of Ron naked.

"Please Ron. I know I've have hurt you by leaving but don't turn me down now."

Ron stared at his beautiful wife and all his anger disappeared. He removed his clothes and embraced Diana and they began making love as if for the first time. Slow with immeasurable

RONALD GRAY   (65)

passion. They end up on the sofa hugging and kissing with two hearts beating as one. The love between them was far beyond words. Two hours later and they are still in the throes of passion until they are satisfied emotionally and physically. They went upstairs to their bedroom, shower and got in bed and fall asleep. Ron woke up and looked at Diana getting dressed.

"Diana, where are you going? I know you are not leaving, after all, we talked about and just shared." He quickly threw the covers off him and got out of bed and walked over to her wearing silk boxers. Standing at arms distance from her, he yelled, "Diana, stop getting dressed."

Ron yelling and his words made her jump. She stared at him.

"Don't yell at me Ron. I need to go and you know why. If you only knew how hard this was for me."

"This is crazy. Are you bipolar?" He laughed but quickly changed his demeanor. "Diana, if it is so hard for you, then why are you leaving me?"

She finished dressing and stepped closer to Ron.

"Look at me, Ron. Do you really believe I want to leave my husband? The man that I love deeply and desire to spend the rest of my life with. No, I don't. Ron look me in my eyes and tell me you are not still directly or indirectly involved in drugs?"

He stared at her then turned his head, he could not say it.

"That's what I thought." She softly caressed his face with her hand then stared at her ring, "Ron, this ring on my finger means so much to me and I value it daily. Your walk with Jesus is not the same and we know it. I could work with that but this drug thing is just too much for me. Yes, I know you and Keith have several legal businesses that are making a lot of money but I'm

RONALD GRAY   (66)

not stupid and I do pay attention. In less than six months you have spent over ten million dollars like its water so don't insult me." She kissed him and stared in his eyes which caused tears to fall from hers because she loves this man so much.

Ron hugged her and started kissing the tears on her face knowing she was right but his heart was hurting.

"Diana, please stay. We can work this out I promise you."

She looked at Ron then walked toward the bedroom door, stopped and turned to look at him.

"Ron, tell me right now and I will believe and trust you. Tell me from this very moment that you are finished with any illegal activity and I will never leave again unless my husband is with me, hand in hand." She was looking at him with love and hope.

All Ron could do was look at her and feeling his heart breaking in pieces.

Diana's tears continue to fall from her eyes.

"You are crushing and breaking my heart Ronald Emmanuel O'Neil." She walked out of the room and out of the house and got in her car where she emotionally broke down and cried like a baby. Her heart felt like it's being ripped from her chest. She looked up and yelled.

"Lord, help me. I don't want to lose my husband." She leaned her head on the steering wheel crying so hard her body was shaking.

CHAPTER THIRTEEN
New Owners

Victor was sitting on the sofa in his office at the club drinking a glass of wine that costs twenty thousand dollars a bottle. He was wearing a $25,000 blue pinstripe Brioni Vanquish II suit. Three of his bodyguards are with him. The music theme for the club tonight is old school mixed with R&B. There are two DJs tonight, one playing R&B and the other playing old school.

Victor knew he was leaving so he wanted to have some fun before he left. You had to come dressed to impress tonight and security were turning people away at the door if they felt like they were not dressed appropriately. All drinks were free tonight no matter what you wanted to have. If the club had it in stock, you got it, and there was no charge except to get in, which was fifty dollars at the door per person, no exceptions. There was a long line of people standing outside the club waiting to get in. The club bouncers and two of Victor's bodyguards are standing by the club entrance. Mr. Greg Johnson drove up in front of the club in a Cadillac Escalade. Keith drove up in his Benz and Ron was with him. A limo drove up and Stephanie stepped out wearing a short tight dress. Greg, Ron, and Keith are wearing Armani suits. All four walked toward the club's front entrance. As they are walking towards the door one of the men standing in line stepped in front of Keith and Ron with his arm out toward them.

"Where do you people think you are going?" He pointed to the back of the line. "The line is back there, so start walking."

Keith and Ron quickly pulled out their guns and put them to the man's stomach. Greg pulled his gun out and aimed it at the man's head.

"The graveyard is full of people who don't know how to mind their own business." Keith said with calmness but anger.

Victor's bodyguards pulled their guns out and walked toward Keith.

"Is there a problem gentleman?"

Greg looked at the bodyguards.

"No problem at all."

Keith, Ron, and Greg put their guns away.

"Very good. Miss Walker, Mr. Augular is expecting you. If all of you will follow me we can go to his office." One of the bodyguards said.

The bodyguard, Keith, Ron, Greg, and Stephanie walked in the club which was packed and everyone was dressed to impress. Once again just like at Ron's proposal party, the ladies are going all out to be seen. Pretty faces, hips, and ass for days. Ron was thinking this was déjà vu for him seeing all the fine women in this place shaking their hips and ass like they are trying to get paid. His heart was sad because Diana was not with him but he must remain focused no matter what. The dance floor was full. The bodyguard standing outside the club reached into his pocket and pulled out his cell phone to call Victor.

"Mr. Augular, your guests have arrived...yes sir." He put his phone away.

Victor stood up and looked at his bodyguards. "Gentlemen, we are about to have company." His three bodyguards turn towards the door.

RONALD GRAY   (69)

One of Victor's bodyguards opened his office door with Keith, Ron, Greg, and Stephanie behind him as they walked in.

Victor waved his hand at them.

"Please come in." He walked toward Stephanie. "Miss Walker, you look very lovely as always." He hugged and kissed her.

The bodyguard who walked in with them walked out of the office.

Stephanie has never been so scared and nervous in her life.

"Victor, it is very nice to see you again but I'm curious. You mentioned you have a surprise for me. What is it?"

"Patience my dear. I need to talk with you but first, these gentlemen and I need to discuss some business. So, if you will give me a few minutes and entertain yourself in the club, we will talk when I'm finished with them."

"As you wish but remember it is not good to keep a lady waiting too long. We can become emotional."

"Well, I have seen you emotional and I wouldn't want that to happen again. I will be as brief as possible."

"You are smart as well as handsome," she kissed Victor and walked toward the door then turned around, "Victor, don't forget what I said. An emotional lady does interesting things." She walked out.

Greg watched Stephanie leave and looked at Victor.

"That's a very interesting lady you are dealing with, Mr. Augular."

"Yes, she is but a very temporary one." He sat down at his desk. "Please, gentlemen have a seat. It's time to get down to business."

RONALD GRAY   (70)

Keith, Ron, and Greg sat down in front of Victor's desk. One of his bodyguards stood by the door and the other two stood behind Keith, Ron, and Greg. Keith looked at Victor's bodyguards and then at Victor.

"Mr. Augular it is good to see you again but what is this meeting all about?"

"Mr. Keith Washington a man who is always about business. A very good quality to possess and you have a very special friend as your partner. Mr. Ron O'Neil, it is good to see you again sir. A chosen one by God but he left the Lord and joined the devil. Life is very interesting Mr. O'Neil. How does it feel to be dancing with the devil?"

"Mr. Augular I prefer to be called S& D and some choices are necessary to make in life to get what one desires."

"Very true and spoken with wisdom and strength. What does S&D stand for?"

Ron smiled.

"I'm glad you asked. It stands for Samson and Delilah, named after my two friends."

"And who might they be?"

"Allow me to introduce you to them." He stood up and pulled out his nine millimeter and a .357 magnum holding them up in the air. "Meet Samson and Delilah."

Immediately Victor's bodyguards pulled out their guns and aimed them at Ron. Greg quickly stood up and pulled his gun out aiming it at Ron. Keith quickly stood up and pulled his gun out and aimed it at Greg.

Victor waved his hand.

RONALD GRAY   (71)

"Gentlemen relax. Mr. Washington, Mr. O'Neil, I strongly suggest you put your guns away and sit back down. I don't want any blood on my office floor."

Keith, Ron, and Greg put their guns away and all three sat down and the bodyguards put their guns away as well.

"Mr. O'Neil, oh excuse me S&D, it would be better for you to control your spontaneous actions, your very life depends on it."

"Good advice Mr. Augular and you are probably right."

Victor stared at Ron.

"I know I am. Now, to the business at hand. I'm moving on to bigger and better things. Mr. Washington, my club is for sale. Would you and your partner like to buy it?"

Keith leaned forward in his seat and looked at Ron with astonishment.

"Are you kidding me? This place is the best club in all of Maryland. No doubt I desire it but how much and when?"

"For you and your chosen partner ten million dollars, fifty percent up front and this is a right now one-time deal. What's your answer?"

Ron looked at Keith.

"Take the deal, Keith, we can handle it."

Keith was looking at Victor thinking, Finally, I get to run things my way. This place is going to set it off for Ron and me.

"We will take it. How soon can we move in?"

"My attorneys will take care of the legal work and I will have them deliver the papers to you and the club will be yours after that. Concerning our other business, Mr. Greg Johnson will handle all your needs. I will be out of town for a while so the business is yours but a word of caution. No matter where I am, I can reach out and touch you so don't ever get too ambitious or mess up my product and all will be fine."

Keith looked directly at Victor.

"It will not be a problem Mr. Augular."

Ron looked at Keith and smiled.

"No problem at all."

"Very good gentlemen and that's it for now. We will take care of the paperwork later. Now, if you two will entertain yourselves in your new club I need to speak to Miss Walker." He stood up.

Keith, Ron, and Greg stood as well. Victor walked over to Keith and shook his hand.

"Mr. Washington, now it's time for me to see just how smart you really are. Take care of my business."

"No problem Mr. Augular. Small thing to a giant and I'm standing on top of the world."

"Enjoy it while you can sir." He extends his hand to Ron and they shake hands. "Mr. S&D, you are a very interesting individual. Even prison couldn't hold you. Twenty-five year to life sentence and you walk out in five years, as it was spoken. Truly amazing but now you are doing the devils work. Very interesting." He leaned forward and whispered in Ron's ear, "God is going to get you."

Ron stared at Victor.

"Things change Mr. Augular but I am who I am."

He whispered in Ron's ear again.

"God is still going to get you." he stepped back, "yes sir, you are who you are. If you gentlemen will excuse me, enjoy your club."

Ron and Keith walked out the office and Victor sat down at his desk. Once outside the office Ron and Keith looked at each other and give each other dap.

"Damn S&D, I knew things were going to move for us but not this fast. Partner, we are about to rock the world," he looked around the club, "first you get the money, then the power and the women will pursue you. You never have to pursue them." Keith looked at Ron. "Yeah, it does work that way. No offense partner but look at Diana. She is a prime example because she came to you when your pockets got really swollen."

"I have to admit money and sex rule this earth but Diana came to me because she loves me not the money. Now I'm paying the price for my deception. She left me." He stared out into space trying to control his emotions.

"Yeah, I know. I can't believe she left you. Damn, that's fucked up. Whatever happened to, for better or worse? I guess that's something people say in their wedding vows to make it sound good but the first sign of trouble, they get missing. To hell with that partner. A real warrior, a ride or die, will stand." Keith stared at Ron and shook his head.

Keith's words hit Ron's heart hard because he knows he was right.

"Yeah, I know. Let's walk around and check out our new club." They dap up again and walked away.

When Ron and Keith were walking through the club they see Stephanie walking toward them. Keith stopped walking and turned toward Ron and poked him in his chest.

"Ron, you need to slow down. You almost got us killed. This ain't no back alley. These people are highly trained killers and will bury us. Damn, I almost had a heart attack back in the office."

Ron put his hand on Keith's shoulder.

"Relax Keith, everything will be fine but it was interesting. Victor's bodyguards and Mr. Johnson pulled their guns on me super-fast but it didn't move me at all."

Stephanie walked up to Ron and Keith.

"That was quick. Is everything alright? Did he mention that devil man in the park?"

"Everything is fine. Mr. Augular is leaving town and he sold us his club. He is waiting to speak to you." Keith said.

Ron does not like Stephanie and has no problem showing his dislike for her.

"You look a little worried. Relax Miss Walker. You are far too beautiful to have wrinkles in your face. It would make you look, ugly." He smiled.

"Well, congratulations on your new club. And I'm not worried." She stepped towards Ron and whispered in his ear. "I'm glad you got married and got you some pussy, you needed some really bad. But it's too bad I don't have the time to teach you how to fuck that young pretty wife of yours." She smiled at him.

Ron looked at her thinking how fine she is but he despises her attitude and spirit.

RONALD GRAY   (75)

"No thanks. I want a fresh horse, not one that has been ridden for miles and worn out." He looked at her with serious dislike.

Stephanie laughed and blows Ron a kiss.

"Let me go see what Victor has for me."

Keith stepped closer to Stephanie.

"I don't know what he has for you but I know what I have for you. I'm young, strong, rich and nasty." He grabbed his crotch.

Stephanie caresses Keith's cheek.

"You are cute Keith and moving up in this business very fast but I'm not a twenty-minute woman and I would break your back." She leaned forward and whispered in his ear. "The problem with young people is you move too fast and don't take your time to please a woman. Your oral skills are lousy and you don't know how to nasty fuck." She grabbed Keith's butt and walked away toward Victor's office.

Keith and Ron stare at her.

"And you call me crazy. You are trying to get yourself killed. If Stacy ever found out you would be a dead man and quick."

"Yeah I know but I could handle Stacy and Stephanie."

Greg was standing in front of Victor's desk and one of the bodyguards was standing by his office door while the other two are standing away from his desk.

Greg looked at Victor.

"What do you want to do with Stephanie Victor?"

"Mr. Johnson do you have your friend with you?"

"Always Mr. Augular, always."

Stephanie walked up to Victor's office door and knocked on it. His bodyguard opened it and she walked in and stood beside Greg.

"Mr. Augular I understand you want to see me. I knew you were smart because you saved the best for last, me!"

Greg stepped back and stood behind Stephanie. Two of the bodyguards walked toward the sofa and stand and the other guard standing by the door locked it.

Victor walked over to Stephanie and stood in front of her.

"Miss Stephanie, a man would be a fool to overlook someone as beautiful and aggressive as you. You and that dress you are wearing have my full attention." He stepped closer and put his hands on her waist kissing her then caressed her butt.

Stephanie looked around the room and was thinking, *Victor is freaky but I know he is not about to ask me to participate in some group sex.*

"I know where your mind is Victor but please not in front of the men."

"Relax Miss Walker, I want to see what you are really made of." He looked at Greg. "Mr. Johnson, express yourself."

Greg stepped closer to Stephanie and put his hands on her hips caressing them. "Very nice hips, full and tight." He rubbed her butt and pressed into her so she could feel his erection."

Stephanie was getting very nervous but she was thinking, *If I don't let this happen Victor is so crazy, he and his men might rape me. The hell with that, I'd rather give it up.*

"Victor Augular, I had no idea you were so freaky but whatever turns you on lover. I can handle anything that you all bring my way, so let's do this."

Victor stepped closer to her.

"There is a first time for everything." He kissed her then stepped back.

RONALD GRAY   (77)

Greg kissed her on the neck then pulled her dress up revealing her thong panties and slides his finger inside her. He whispered in Stephanie's ear.

"Tell me how you want it."

Stephanie was so scared she could feel her heart rate increasing but she will do whatever she must to walk out this room alive and well.

"I want it slow and easy then hard and fast so stop all this talking."

"My pleasure." He put his arms around Stephanie's neck and broke it. He was still holding her body up. "I have never liked her anyway but she had a lot of heart." He let her body fall.

"You are right. She had a lot of heart. Too much, which made her dangerous but she truly was fantastic in the sheets. The Jezebels always are. As we are flying over the swamp in Columbia, we will dump her body out."

"What a beautiful waste. She was fine." Greg said looking at her body.

Victor looked down at Stephanie's body.

"Truly a waste, good piece of ass but I have never forgiven her for killing Miss Sherry Wilson." He looked at his bodyguards. "Gentlemen wrap her body and put it on the plane when we leave." He walked out of his office, closed the door, and stood there looking out over the club and the crowd of people. He sees Keith and Ron on the dance floor.

"Enjoy it while you can gentlemen. This was just a temporary setback. Maryland is mine and I will be back. Mr. Bones and I can never be stopped."

RONALD GRAY   (78)

CHAPTER FOURTEEN

Christine's Bondage

Christine lives in Bowie Maryland in a very nice three-bedroom town house with a garage. She has been hiding two secrets from her family. One, she lost her job as a legal assistant at a very prestigious law firm in Washington DC because of being late for work too often. She told her sister about her watching porn movies but she didn't tell her that she was addicted to it and she has a serious masturbation problem. It was her porn and masturbation problem that caused her to lose her job.

Christine's problem became worse after she spent time at her friend Tonya's house. This was also the turning point in Christine's life, for the worse. One night she received a call from Tonya asking her to come over because she didn't want to be home by herself and she would appreciate Christine's company. Tonya is twenty-six years old very attractive with an athletic body. This was really a set up on Tonya's part to try and corrupt Christine. They were sitting on the sofa eating popcorn when Tonya suggested they watch a movie, so she put a DVD in and they started watching it but Christine didn't know that Tonya had put in a porn movie.

When the movie came on Christine found it repulsive and started to leave but Tonya begged her to stay because she was very lonely and was tired of being home alone. The truth was, Tonya was attracted to men and women and she has been trying to get next to Christine for years. Physically she is very drawn to

RONALD GRAY   (79)

Christine but her dedication to the Lord made it impossible to really get close to her.

Tonya noticed Christine not going to church like she used to, not reading her Bible, or praying like she always did. Her conversation was more about guys and sex. She knew Christine was a virgin. As they continued to watch the movie that night Christine kept saying how repulsive the movie was but Tonya kept teasing and laughing at her.

"Just relax Christine you might learn something." Giving Christine a fake smile because inwardly she was just setting her up. Tonya purposely picked this movie because it had a lot of girl on girl scenes in it.

As the movie continued Tonya would look over at Christine watching her reaction to everything she saw in the movie. Christine would cover her face with her hands at certain scenes and Tonya would playfully hit her and wrestle with her to get her hands down, using this opportunity to touch and caress Christine's body. They both had on dresses. While wrestling at times on the sofa Christine's dress would come up and Tonya would playfully smack her on the butt repeatedly but Tonya would make sure her hand lingered there a little longer than necessary.

They finished watching the movie and fell asleep on the sofa with a blanket over them. Christine went to sleep feeling guilty but very horny with images of what she saw in the movie burned in her head but she didn't want to talk about this with Tonya. It was three thirty in the morning when Tonya woke up and Christine was still asleep, lying close to her. She carefully got off the sofa trying not to wake her up and put another porn movie in.

RONALD GRAY   (80)

Tonya started watching the movie and getting really horny and would look over at Christine to see if she was still sleeping. The longer she watched the movie the hornier she became until she started rubbing between her legs feeling her wetness. She carefully moved the blanket off Christine and her dress was above her knees. Tonya moved it up a little more to see Christine's underwear. Watching the movie and looking at Christine back and forth was turning her on more so she took her panties off leaving her dress on. She started masturbating, sliding her finger inside herself while looking at the movie and Christine. Tonya was trying to be quiet but was moaning a little because it was feeling good. She put the blanket back over Christine in case she woke up.

It was Tonya's moans that woke Christine up and when she opened her eyes what she saw shocked her and didn't know what to do. Here her friend was watching another porn movie and masturbating. Christine was embarrassed so she decided the best thing she could do was fake as if she was still sleeping. Tonya knew Christine woke up and was faking like she was sleep so she decided to use this against her. Tonya started to really get into masturbating and took her dress off caressing her legs, butt, and hips moaning at the same time.

All of this was very uncomfortable for Christine but she became horny and since the blanket would cover her actions, she slid her hand between her legs rubbing herself. From time to time she would look at the movie and Tonya, masturbating.

Tonya knew she was so close to climax and her moans were getting a little louder which was causing Christine to become even more excited and sexually turned on. Tonya was fingering herself and pinching her breasts at the same time making herself feel so good. She looked over at Christine and their eyes met.

Christine was truly embarrassed but didn't want to stop what she was doing and didn't want Tonya to stop either. Tonya moved the blanket off Christine because she wanted to see her flesh. She took a risk that she would stop but used one hand and moved Christine's dress all the way up. The very sight of seeing Christine's hand inside her panties turned her on so much she almost climaxed but wanted to hold it.

Christine could not understand what was compelling her to keep going but she was becoming less and less embarrassed so she pulled her panties off. Both girls were now facing each other watching each other masturbate and moved closer on the sofa and started fingering each other. Tonya had been waiting for this moment for years and was not sure if it would ever happen again, so she decided to go for it and really try and turn Christine out. She knew Christine was close to orgasm, so while she had her finger inside of her, rubbing her clit as well with her thumb, she slowly slid a finger in Christine ass moving it slowly in and out.

Christine felt like she was losing her mind because when she felt Tonya slide her finger in her ass it was a little uncomfortable at first but when she relaxed and Tonya continued sliding it slowly in and out, it felt so good to her. She started seeing the images in the porn movie and wanted more and did the same thing to Tonya, fingering her ass as well.

Tonya was surprised at Christine doing this to her but it felt very good and she could not hold it any longer and screamed.

"Ahhhhhhh don't stop, I'm cummming, finger me just like that, yes, yes ahhhhhh it feels so good, ahhhhhh." Tonya had not cum like that in so long, if ever and she wanted Christine to experience this as well and more, so when she calmed down and relaxed she got in a better position over Christine.

She pushed her all the way down on the sofa, pushing her legs back and apart. Tonya was looking directly into Christine's eyes as if she was trying to hypnotize her and inserted two fingers in her pussy and one in her ass. Back and forth, in and out, she was making Christine feel so good and she knew it.

Christine was so blown away by everything, she wanted to stop but it was feeling just too good to her flesh. Tonya leaned forward and kissed Christine, pushing her tongue against her lips and Christine allowed Tonya's tongue in her mouth and it felt natural, so she started sucking on it.

Tonya was having her dream come true as she moved her fingers faster inside Christine's pussy and ass.

Christine has never known such intense physical pleasure and she could not take this anymore. She started sucking Tonya's tongue harder and grabbed her hand, moving her fingers inside her faster and harder until she exploded with an orgasm like she has never known in her life. Christine started saying words and cussing like she heard in the movies but she has never talked like this before.

"Ohhhhhh damn, you are making me cum, don't stop, don't stop. Finger this ass and pussy, yes, make me cum baby, make me cum, ahhhhhh, finger fuck meeee." She was climaxing so hard her juices shot out like never before and Christine was shaking and trembling but still ramming Tonya's fingers inside her fast and hard. Christine even reached up and grabbed Tonya's neck and started sucking on it while she was climaxing,

RONALD GRAY   (83)

holding on to her for dear life. She felt like she would never stop climaxing but she finally calmed down. Tonya slid her fingers out of her, wiping them on a towel she had hidden under the sofa. She went to the bathroom, wet a wash cloth with warm water cleaning herself and then took it back to Christine cleaning her as well.

Tonya put her dress back on and pulled Christine's dress down. She was standing next to her by the sofa. She knew Christine felt lower than low now because she remembers how she felt her first time.

Christine finally looked up at Tonya.

"How could you have done this to me? I thought you were my friend. Do you have any idea what you have done to me?" She lowered her head and began crying very hard.

Tonya knew how to comfort her so she sat closer leaned over and hugged her.

"It's okay. I promise you it will all be okay." She hugged Christine lightly kissing the tears on her cheek and lifting her face up by her chin until their lips met and they slowly kissed. Christine was still crying and whimpering but for some strange reason, having Tonya close like this gave her some comfort. Without realizing it, Christine spread her legs apart and started fingering herself while Tonya was still kissing her tears.

Tonya knew how to affect Christine, what to say and do. She had her mouth inches away from Christine's.

"Yes baby, that's it, go ahead and please yourself. I know it's good, yes just like that." She licked and sucked Christine's lips as Christine fingered herself into another quick orgasm while Tonya was telling her it is going to be okay.

RONALD GRAY   (84)

"Yes, ohhhhh yes, this is good, so gooood ahhhhhhh yessssss."

"That's it, let it go, make yourself cum baby this is your body, all yours." She whispered in her ear. "I know you want some dick baby and I'm going to help you get some. Look at me. Say it. Tell me you want some dick?"

Christine felt so ashamed but her inner desires were overwhelming.

"Yes, yes I want some dick in me so bad." She lowered her head but kept fingering herself.

Tonya continued to hold Christine after she climaxed until they fell asleep again.

It was never okay for Christine after that and she was never the same. She struggled with serving God and her constant sexual thoughts and desires daily. She never revealed this to her family or anyone. Tonya would call or text her constantly but she knew she had to stay away from her but the damage had already been done. If she wasn't looking at porn she was masturbating at home, at work, even in her car sometimes while driving. Christine wondered if she would ever be the same again or would she have to live with this deep, dark secret for the rest of her life. Her daily prayer was, "Lord Jesus, help me."

CHAPTER FIFTEEN
The Hospital

Dr. Hardy was standing close to the front desk of the visitor's entrance of the hospital when he sees Sheila, Grandma Harris and Diana walking down the hallway. He walked toward them.

"Mrs. O'Neil, Miss Harris and Diana it is good to see you again."

"Dr. Hardy good afternoon and I thank you for being here because I know you have a busy schedule. How is my daughter?" Sheila said.

"Hi Dr. Hardy."

"Diana, you are growing into a beautiful young lady. I hope God blesses you with a wonderful husband someday."

"Dr. Hardy, stop flirting with my baby and she has a husband. Look at that beautiful ring on her finger."

Diana started smiling and held her hand up so he can see her ring.

"Wow, that's some ring on your finger. More than I could afford. This must be your miracle man Mr. Ronald that finally came to his senses and married you so no one else could have you. Smart man."

Diana had a big smile on her face while looking at the ring and then looked at Dr. Hardy.

"Yes, that's my baby and he does treat me like a queen."

Sheila put her hand on Diana's shoulder.

"And he should. I raised him well."

Grandma Harris nods her head.

"Amen to that Sheila. Anyway, Dr. Hardy as good looking as you are how come you are not married? You like women, don't you? You ain't doing that down low thing, are you?" The devil is a liar."

Dr. Hardy started laughing.

"Miss Harris, I like you and yes I like women and there is a lady in my life who I wake up and see every day."

"You are not married. I know your type, why buy the cow when you can get the milk for free. Lord deliver him. Diana baby, you save all your milk for that fine young husband of yours."

Diana looked at Grandma Harris and rolled her eyes.

"Grandma I'm not a cow and I only want my husband to ever touch me and I'm not a baby either."

Grandma Harris stared at Diana and shook her head then looked up.

"Lord, please keep me from sinning. As soon as they think they are grown they start talking back, but you are in the right place for when I swell your lips up, good. I might get that eye too." She stared at Diana.

"Grandma Harris don't embarrass her like that." Sheila said looking at Diana then at Grandma Harris.

"Miss Harris, you truly are something else." He looked at Diana's hand again. "Congratulations on your marriage. You two deserve the best. By the way, how is that young man?" He looked at Diana.

"He is being deceived and he is breaking my heart." She lowered her head.

Sheila stepped closer and hugged Diana because she understood.

"Just hold on baby it is not over and you made the right decision."

"Did I?" Diana looked at Sheila.

"Continue to pray baby and follow the voice of God." Grandma Harris said.

"Amen for that. Now, if you lovely ladies will follow me, we can go see Sandra. By the way, Sheila where is Christine?"

"Well, the devil is really attacking my family. Christine is feeling very guilty and responsible for Sandra being hurt so she stays away but she has not been her usual self for a while. I have been feeling her distance but I know God will deliver my entire family soon."

"Amen to that and I know one day Ron will say, Lord, it's *My Call* and come back home to him." Grandma Harris said.

Doctor Hardy shook his head and looked at them.

"I started something. It doesn't take much to get you three started. Let's go see Sandra before you all start shouting in the hallway."

They walk to the elevator and rode to the floor where Sandra was, got off and walked into her room and stood next to her bed. Sheila was staring at Sandra lying in bed and was trying not to become emotional but she couldn't hold back the tears.

"Dr. Hardy do you know how long she will be in a coma?"

"That's just it, we have run several tests and there are absolutely no medical reasons she should even be in a coma. Sandra's condition has no medical basis to it at all. It's weird, very mysterious."

Grandma Harris touched Sandra.

"Her condition is not a physical one but was caused by spiritual wickedness in high places and no medicine can bring her out of this coma or heal her body."

"Grandma, I know the forces of darkness caused this but the Holy Spirit of God will deliver Sandra. *This sickness is not until death but for the glory of God.* I know it." Diana said speaking with a voice of authority.

Sheila slowly grabbed Sandra's hand.

"I know my Lord in his time will deliver my baby."

"We will continue to run tests on her but you are right, no medicine can bring Sandra out of her coma or heal her. Only time and the hand of God can do that."

Sheila stepped closer to Dr. Hardy.

"Doctor Hardy, I thank you for everything and I know everyone is doing their best. Will you give us some time alone to pray with her please?"

"Of course, and take your time. There are many others praying for Sandra and your family." He walked out.

Sheila stepped closer to Sandra, leaned over and kissed her on the cheek then held her hand. Grandma Harris and Diana are on the other side of the bed.

"Mrs. O'Neil, I miss Ron beyond words and being away from my husband is heart breaking but I know God will have his way. He really should be here."

"And he will be Diana. It may not seem like it right now but I know Ron loves you deeply and the Lord but the devil has him blinded right now but God will deliver him."

Grandma Harris looked at Sheila.

RONALD GRAY   (89)

"The devil is messing in the Lord's blessing. That's why before the victory of Jesus, things always look like a defeat for a short while. When Jesus was in the grave the devil thought he had a victory but Jesus came out of his grave in three days just like he said he would, all power in his name."

Diana lightly stomps her foot.

"I feel the presence of the Lord in this room." Sheila started stomping her foot.

"Lord, have your way. Let us pray and praise his holy name. Oh Father, let thy will be done, protect my family. Deliver my son from the hands of darkness and heal my daughter. *We call those things which be not, as though they were.* Thank you, Lord."

Grandma Harris claps her hands.

"Yes Lord, *death and life are in the power of the tongue* and we pray and speak divine healing, deliverance, peace and protection, in Jesus' name."

"Grandma Harris and Diana, I thank God for you two. The devil has been working overtime on my family. First my husband David, then Sandra and now Ron. Lord knows I need help. And Christine, that child has been so distant and I don't know why."

"Sheila, I know this is a very difficult time for you and your family but you hold on to the Lord. He will keep his word above all else and you will see the mighty hand of God no matter what. The devil is a liar."

"Thank you, Grandma Harris. The Lord has never left me but I feel so overwhelmed. My baby is laying here in a coma, Christine blames herself and Ron. Lord, I don't even know where my son is." She started crying.

Diana walked over to Sheila and put her hand on her shoulder.

"Mrs. O'Neil, I will continue to pray and fast for you and your family and I know where Ron is."

Sheila looked at Diana and smiled.

"You are very sweet Diana but I don't want to put you through any more than you have already been through but see if you can talk to that hard-headed husband of yours."

"No problem. We saw each other about two weeks ago. He became very upset with me when I left again and I have not seen him since. I have some words for that husband of mine because I and the Lord are tired of his rebellious spirit."

Sheila smiled at Diana then lowered her head with great sadness in her eyes.

Grandma Harris wants to change the spirit of sadness in the room with laughter and she knew exactly how to do it. She placed her hand on Diana's shoulder.

"Diana, you said it's been two weeks since you and Ron have seen each other?"

"Yes, Grandma and I miss him so much."

She stared at Diana and shook her head.

"That's sad. I know what you really miss. You miss giving him some of your little booty. That kitty cat of yours is on fire and you want him to scratch it." She started laughing so hard she had to hold on to the bed railing to keep from falling.

Diana looked at her and shook her head.

"Grandma Harris, I think the older you get the nastier your mouth becomes. You really should be ashamed of yourself."

Sheila said while looking at her but holding back her own laughter.

Grandma Harris was looking at Sheila with tears of laughter coming from her eyes.

"Sheila, you know how much I love you and David was a great man. Please take this the right way. You need to pray and ask God to send you another good man. You are still young, pretty and have a tight body. Your butt has not started sagging like it does when you get old. So, you need to be blessed with a husband so you can get your kitty cat scratched too." She started laughing again.

Diana put her hand over her mouth but the laughter comes out anyway.

"Oh my God Grandma, I can't believe you said that. You are being so disrespectful right now." She stared at her.

Sheila looked at Grandma Harris with embarrassment and slight anger in her eyes.

"In the name of Jesus, I can't believe you sometimes Grandma Harris."

She is still laughing.

"Oh please, you two are too sensitive. I'm an old woman. My husband died years ago and I have not had a man since, but if I had a husband he could scratch my old kitty cat. Between Jesus, Viagra and my good cooking he would stay strong and ready." She started laughing again.

Sheila and Diana looked at each other and started laughing.

"Lord Jesus, help us all." Diana said.

CHAPTER SIXTEEN
New Beginnings

Diana drove up in front of the club in her Bentley and sees a big new sign on the front of the building that reads *New Beginnings*. She got out the car wearing heels and a dress that comes just above her knees. It was the afternoon so the club was not open but a few people are working throughout the club checking on things. Stacy was in the club working behind one of the bars doing inventory. She was wearing heels, low-cut top showing much cleavage and a mini skirt that hugged her body showing her hips and ample butt. Keith is sitting behind the desk and Ron is sitting on the sofa in their office. Both are wearing Armani suits. Music was playing in the club. Diana rung the bell on the door and Stacy answered it.

"Hi Diana, come on in, Ron said you would be coming by."

Diana closed the door and she walked in next to Stacy but she felt Stacy's attitude and coldness towards her. She stopped walking and touched Stacy on the arm. Stacy stopped walking and looked at Diana.

"Stacy, I have called you several times but you never returned any of my calls. Why?"

Stacy stared at Diana with attitude.

"You have to ask? You lied to me and you know it. You said you would never turn your back on me but you have, but what can I expect? You left and turned your back on your own husband, so I know I got nothing coming."

Diana knew this was coming which is why she kept calling Stacy so they could talk.

"Stacy, I'm still your friend and I have not turned my back on you or my husband. We are going through some rough times right now."

"You know what, I'm so tired of hearing that from married people. As soon as something goes wrong in their marriage they separate. I expect that attitude from weak-ass people but I thought you were different with all that praying you do. Keith is not perfect and neither am I but we have been by each other's side since day one through some very tough times. Warrior to warrior! You talk so much about God and faith but as soon as difficult times come, you run." She put her hand in Diana's face. "Save all that conversation." She walked off.

Diana grabbed Stacy's arm and pulled her back. Stacy used this opportunity and grabbed Diana's waist pulling her closer and kissed her lips. Diana quickly pushed Stacy away.

"No, I'm not doing that any more Stacy. God has delivered me from all of that and I'm going to stay delivered. We can be friends but in a Godly way for me." Diana looked at her.

Stacy looked at her and waved her hand in front of her.

"Whatever Diana, you do you and I will do me but this is real talk. You are acting very stupid. You have no idea how many good-looking women approach Ron but he turns them all down because of his love for you. A man, regardless of how much he loves you, can only resist that much temptation for so long. These women out here today are scandalous. They are practically throwing pussy at Ron. He needs attention and affection. I don't get you. First, you wouldn't give it up because you two were not married, and then you get married and have a disagreement and you leave your husband. Ron is young, good looking, has a nice body and rich. You are leaving him to all these female wolves who would suck his dick with the quickness."

Diana knows everything Stacy just said was true and she has been torn in her choice.

"I've been praying so hard Stacy. I didn't want to come here but I need to talk to Ron. Prayerfully he will allow the Lord to touch his heart and repent of his ways and come back to God."

Stacy looked at Diana and was thinking, *Here we go again, miss goody talking about Jesus and repenting. Knowing all she should do is go back home and give that ass up.*

"Yeah, okay. Praying is great but when was the last time you did the smart womanly thing and gave Ron some pussy, sucked his dick or something? Damn, I don't get you." Stacy said that just to irritate her.

"That's none of your business Stacy." She said waving her hand in Stacy's face looking at her with anger.

Stacy started laughing then looked at Diana.

"Come over to the bar and I will get you something to drink."

They walked to the bar and Stacy goes behind it and pours Diana a glass of orange juice.

"I know orange juice. Diana, Ron's mind is made up and he and Keith work well together but he needs his wife at home so he can get some of that fat ass of yours that you shake so well." She hands Diana the glass and she takes a sip.

"Great sex does not make a relationship. There has to be trust and honesty and the word of God is the foundation."

Stacy looked at Diana and had enough of her pompous attitude.

"Damn, you should be a preacher. Look, girlfriend, I respect your walk with Jesus but a man wants more than scripture reading in bed. He wants you to be able to fully sexually please him from head to toe. Love-making is fine but a man wants a freak in the sheets licking, biting, sucking and some serious fucking. Of course, the church will not talk about that part." she pointed her finger at Diana. "You better get real girl and wake up before another woman has your man dick in her mouth."

Diana has a disgusted look on her face.

"Your mouth and spirit is foul. You Jezebels are alike. You think wearing revealing clothes and having sex can keep a man."

Stacy leaned closer to Diana.

"You got some nerve. Now I'm a Jezebel, again? You were not calling me a Jezebel when I had my head between your legs, making you scream my damn name. Not your husband's but mine. I'm through with you. Do you but you need to let Ron bend your ass over on a regular basis and slide up in that thing and bust that nut and he might come back to you." Stacy is looking at her and could not hold back from laughing.

"You truly are beyond disgusting and I didn't come here to argue with you. Where is Ron?"

"In the office with Keith. Walk with me and I will show you." They walk toward the office and Diana was walking next to Stacy and staring at her skirt.

"That skirt you are wearing is very short and tight. If you lean over even a little, your underwear will show."

Stacy looked at Diana and smiled.

RONALD GRAY   (96)

"My baby likes it and that's all that matters and I noticed Ron can't keep his eyes off my hips and ass and that ain't no mouse in his pants that keep moving while he is staring at me." She sticks her tongue out at Diana.

Diana rolled her eyes at Stacy and she stopped walking.

"Stacy, I love my husband deeply and I do not want to lose him regardless of what you might think. So please tell me, is Ron seeing anyone and don't lie to me."

She turned and looked at Diana.

"Would it matter to you if he was? Diana, be for real. I really don't understand ladies like you. You leave Ron, you don't want to fuck him and you don't want him to fuck anyone else but you think he should stick around and be faithful. You could at least slob that dick really good, damn."

"God your mouth is disgusting. Yes, it would matter to me and you know it. I'm tired of hearing so much about sex, sex, sex. Money can buy sex. What about focusing on things that money can't buy? Like your salvation."

"I respect that but you still need to go back home and give that ass up, daily." She laughed and smacked Diana on her butt.

She rolled her eyes at Stacy.

"You can't keep your hands off me, can you?"

"I can, but I don't want to." Stacy smiled at her.

They continue to walk to the office and Stacy knocked on the door and they walked in.

"Ron, get up and come hug your wife."

He stood up smiling.

"Diana, it is good to see you."

Keith stood up.

RONALD GRAY   (97)

"Diana, come into our new empire. Stacy and I will go elsewhere." He walked over to Stacy and put his arm around her waist and kissed her. "Very sweet, and S& D, you better come and hug Diana or I will." Keith started laughing

Diana looked at Keith and rolled her eyes at him.

"Later for you Keith." Diana said.

Stacy reached under her skirt and pulled out a switch blade and clicked the blade out in front of Keith's face.

"And when you hug her you may as well get that ass because it will be the last hug and body that you feel."

Keith reached behind his back and pulled out a gun and held it in front of Stacy's face.

"You are going to stop threatening me. I told you about that, so don't get shot wearing that tight mini skirt."

"That gun does not scare me and you love me wearing this tight mini skirt. Now kiss me and I will forgive you."

"You better be glad I love you." He kissed her.

Diana was shaking her head.

"You two were made for each other and you both need deliverance."

Stacy pointed her finger at Diana.

"You need to let your husband, put some dick in you."

Ron walked over to Diana and grabbed her hand.

"Diana, come over here and sit down. Keith, you and Stacy finish that slobbering on each other somewhere else, please."

He and Diana walk over to the sofa and sat down.

"My pleasure." Keith put his gun in his belt and put his arm around Stacy's waist and they walked towards the door with Stacy holding her knife down by her side. Keith put his hand on

Stacy's butt caressing it. He turned his head and looked back at Ron. "It looks good doesn't it partner. She got a hot ass." He smiled at Ron and he and Stacy walked out the office leaving the door open.

Ron was still holding Diana's hand while he was staring at Stacy's butt as she walked away. Diana looked at Ron and she quickly pulled her hand away from his.

"What's wrong with you? Why are you looking at her like that? You men are dogs in heat. I told you about disrespecting me. If you want to look at her butt, wait until I leave."

Ron walked over and closed the door and back to Diana, and stood in front of her.

"Do we have to always argue? I'm very glad to see you and I have missed you. Come here."

Diana looked in Ron's eyes as she heard his words. It melts her heart because she missed him so much. She knew the things she did with Stacy was very wrong and she would never want Ron to find out. If Ron was with another woman, it would crush her heart so she had to ask.

"Ron, I know you deal with a lot of temptation but I want to know, so please be honest with me." Staring in his eyes. "Have you been with someone else?"

"Diana, you really are something but the answer is no. I love you and I'm in love with you and I want only you, no matter what I see. You are my God-given wife whom I desire to spend the rest of my life with." He held his arms out to her.

Diana began to cry because Ron's words touched her heart deeply but they also made her feel guilty for all that she has done. Yes, she knows God has forgiven her but would Ron if he were to ever find out? She quickly stood up and hugged him tightly, holding him and kissing him with all her love.

Ron hugged Diana just as tight because he missed her tremendously. He lifted her dress up from the back and slid his hands inside her underwear on her butt caressing it, sliding his hands lower feeling between her legs until he felt her wetness. He was sucking her neck knowing it was one of her weak spots.

Diana desires him badly right now and his hands feel so good on her body but she really needs to talk to him.

"Baby, you know I miss you deeply but can we please talk?" Ron looked at her.

"Diana, not this hot and cold stuff again. We are married," he backed up "this is getting ridiculous. Do you want me to have sex with someone else? Damn, I treat you like a queen and I still can't get any pussy." He stared at her with anger in his eyes.

Diana quickly grips the side of her dress to keep from slapping the taste out of his mouth after talking to her like that.

"Yes, we are married but I'm getting sick of you constantly making derogatory comments to me about sex like that's all I'm good for. Is that why you married me, Ron, for sex?"

"No, and stop asking me stupid questions. If all I wanted was sex, I didn't have to get married for that. Get real Diana. We would not be having these types of conversations if you were treating me like I treat you. Look at me, Diana. Do I neglect you in any way?"

She looked at him.

"No Ron, you do not but you have neglected someone far more important than me, your first love, Jesus. You cannot have me and live for the devil. You cannot serve two masters. Let's sit down so we can talk."

He sat down and stared at Diana realizing how good she really does look but he can tell she was not the same, she looks better. He knows that great holy glow when he sees it and she has it. God has blessed her.

"Diana, have you seen Christine? How are mom and Sandra doing?"

"Guilt is keeping Christine away, Sandra is still the same, and your mom is very worried about you. You are breaking her heart and mine and you don't even care."

"You are very wrong I do care but my mind is made up and this is what I want."

"No! It is not," yelling at him. "The devil has you blind. Please come back to the Lord and let God use you, please."

"I tried that and look what happened. Sandra is in a coma because of me. Diana, this spiritual calling was not my choice and I don't want it. It's time for me to live and have fun."

Diana is so frustrated she grips Ron's hand very hard.

"Stop talking stupid Ron. Have you forgotten how God used you in prison, how God delivered you from prison in five years? Now, look at you. You are living for the devil. He is deceiving you. Don't you know if you die in this spiritual state you are going to hell? Ain't no once saved, always saved, I can live my life any way I want and still go to heaven. That's a lie from the devil. That lie is deceiving a lot of people."

He removed his hand from Diana's.

RONALD GRAY   (101)

"Nice grip. I appreciate what God did but that was then and this is now. I like my life. I'm making plenty of money and I have a new empire to run and control."

"Gain material things, break your family's heart and mine. Turn your back on God. Thus, losing your soul, fuel for hell and why did Keith refer to you as S&D? Is that some devil name?"

"No comment on S&D and I told you I love my family and you but I'm who I'm. I still want my wife home, that will never change." He slid closer and grabbed her hand and looked in her eyes, "Diana, please come with me. Nothing is the same without you by my side, nothing."

Once again, his words gripped her heart. She desires to be home next to her husband so badly. Even now she was giving God her thoughts. Lord, am I doing the right thing? What do I do?

"I can't Ron I just can't. Please understand."

"No, I don't understand. I would never leave you it's just that simple. Yes, sex is very important in marriage. Women throw themselves at me daily but my own wife, who said she loves me won't even give up the pussy or the throat."

Diana stood up and stared at him so hard her eyes hurt.

"Stop saying that P word," she yelled at him. "I'm getting out of here before I say and do something that I might regret." She walked away.

Ron quickly walked over and grabbed her waist.

"Diana wait, please stay for a while so we can spend some time together since you will not come home."

"No Ron. I'm tired of you insulting and disrespecting me and I will not stay in this lust house another minute."

RONALD GRAY   (102)

"Keith and I are owners of this lust house, as you call it."

"What? This devil's den? A place like this cost millions. Oh my God Ron, you are doing the devil's work and selling drugs," she pointed her finger at him, "Why Ron, why? After all that God has done for you. If you only knew how much I love you." She started crying, "You are breaking my heart."

He put his arms around her.

"Diana, I never wanted to hurt you but it's so hard for me. I feel spiritually oppressed."

She put her hands on his chest.

"Ron, I understand it is a spiritual warfare that you are dealing with. Only God can deliver you. Please come back to church and let God have his way with you, please."

Ron lowered his head then looked at her.

"Come home Diana where you belong. I'm not a monster." He pulled her closer into him and kissed her slowly and passionately on the lips while caressing her hips. "Diana, I want you so badly. Let's go back to the sofa baby so you can slob this dick down, get your mouth wet."

Diana slapped him so fast it surprised her and then put her finger in his face.

"How can you talk to me like that? I'm your wife Ron, not some slut you picked up in a club."

"Yeah well, wives suck dick. At least good ones do anyway."

Diana stepped closer and swung at Ron but he moved out of the way and quickly pulled her into him kissing her and grabbed her butt under her dress caressing it, then quickly backed up so she couldn't hit him.

Ron was staring at Diana and has a big smile on his face.

RONALD GRAY   (103)

"Diana, you got a round sexy ass and I would put my hands on your hips and lick that from the back."

Diana stared at Ron wondering how he can talk to her so ugly and disrespectful. She stepped closer to him but he backed up.

"You better not slap me anymore."

"I'm not going to slap you, Ron." She stepped closer to him and stared into his eyes as tears fall from hers. "Is that all I'm to you, a pretty face, hips, and butt? What about the real me, Ron? What about my heart, mind, and my soul? Do any of those things mean anything to you anymore?" She wiped tears from her face. "I love you, Ron Emmanuel O'Neil." She kissed him again and walked out of the office.

Ron stared at her leaving and felt horrible about how he talked to her.

Diana continued to walk through the club and sees Keith and Stacy standing by the bar hugging and kissing. Keith has his hand on Stacy's butt.

"Girl, I would slap the devil in his mouth to get some of this ass."

Diana stopped in front of them.

"Keith," she yelled and pointed her finger at him. "I blame you for Ron's continued spiritual decline. You are helping to corrupt him."

Stacy pointed her finger at Diana.

"Don't blame my man because you left your husband. I see your dress is a little wrinkled. Did you wise up and give your husband some loving?"

Diana is so sick of Stacy's smart mouth. She walked over and stood three feet from her. She looked at Keith and stared at

Stacy. Stacy was not sure what this girl was up to so she reached under her skirt and pulled her blade out clicking it and holding it by her side.

"Don't get cut. Don't try to take your sexual frustrations out on me because you ain't fucking your own husband."

Keith has never seen Diana like this and he is enjoying it.

"Stacy, I can't believe you would pull a knife on me but that blade does not scare me and what I do with my husband is none of your business." She looked at Keith. "Keith, you and Stacy operate in spirits that really disgust me." She stepped a little closer to Stacy. "I thought we were friends but you can kiss my ass."

Stacy smiled at Diana then moved closer and got in her face.

"You don't really want me to respond to that but if you wash it," she leaned forward only inches from Diana's lips, "I would turn your hot ass all the way out and you know it. So, don't fuck with me." She said staring into Diana's eyes with burning fire.

Keith was staring at Stacy and the very thought of Stacy's words about her kissing Diana's ass has him aroused.

Diana knew she went too far with Stacy but she was very angry right now.

"You two really disgust me. You make me spiritually sick." Diana walked out of the club and got in her car. She leaned her head on the steering wheel and then hit it with her hand.

"Lord, forgive me for my unholy actions and words. Forgive me and I thank you for coming to my rescue and giving me strength. Forgive me, Jesus." She drove away.

CHAPTER SEVENTEEN
Sheila's House

Diana, Grandma Harris, and Sheila are sitting in the living room at Sheila's house. Grandma Harris and Sheila are sitting on one sofa and Diana on the other.

"Diana, did you get a chance to see Ron today?" Sheila asks.

"Yes, I did and it is going to take the hand of God to deliver him. The devil has Ron very blind and deceived."

"Baby, where was he and what was he doing?"

"Grandma, I saw that husband of mine at the night club where he proposed to me. He said he and Keith now own it. Stacy was there being her usual self. There is no way those two could afford that club legally."

"He is my son but I'm not stupid. It sounds like Ron is involved in drugs a little.'

"Mrs. O'Neil, you would have to see this club. It would take more than just a little involvement in drugs. I'm no club expert but I know that place is worth millions and I know Ron has a mind of his own but that Keith is behind all of this."

Grandma Harris looked at Sheila.

"I have never told Ron this but I have always believed it was Keith who he was protecting and why he went to prison but I don't understand why he would do that."

"I have also thought Keith was behind my baby going to jail because he was always so protective of Keith. Anyway Diana, how did he look? Has he lost any weight? Just the thought of him running those streets breaks my heart. If I could just get my hands on that boy."

"Physically he looked very nice, strong, and solid but his spirit is foul. He needs much prayer. He also said and did something that I didn't like and I slapped him and I feel bad about that. He is very arrogant. I know I'm his wife but I'm not some hooker." She lowered her head.

Grandma Harris rubs her hands and smiled.

"Lord, I want to hear this. Baby, what did he say to you that caused you to slap him?"

"It is not something that I want to repeat especially in front of Mrs. O'Neil and it is embarrassing."

"Now I know I have to hear this. What did that son of mine say to you and don't leave out any details?"

"Go ahead child and tell us. We love the Lord but we have heard it all. What did he say to you?"

"Well, since you two must know. Mrs. O'Neil, your son was very persistent about having sex with me but I refused and he got angry with me. It was what he told me to do and how he told me to do it that was very hurtful and disrespectful. I can't repeat the rest, it's too embarrassing."

Sheila stomps her foot.

"Oh, just say it, child."

Diana looked at Sheila and decided the only way she can repeat what she said to Ron was to say it fast and get it over with.

"Fine, all Ron wanted was to hump me like some dog and he told me to suck his you know what. I refused and then he said all good wives suck you know what. I got angry and slapped him." She cannot face Sheila, so she looked away.

Sheila stared at Diana.

"I can't believe my son. Diana, I respect what you did." Grandma Harris is laughing.

"Lord have mercy. My husband would talk to me like that whenever I refused to have sex with him. Until I put these lips on him one day and dropped him to his knees. I think I did it the same day he had a heart attack and died on me, poor baby."

Sheila was thinking, *I cannot believe this woman.*

"Grandma Harris please, you should be ashamed of yourself for talking like that especially in front of Diana."

"Ashamed! The only thing I should be ashamed of is these big bloomers I'm wearing. I have to keep pulling them up. But why should I be ashamed for pleasing my husband? Please, Lord knows I may be old but an old rat still love cheese and I miss my husband's cheese."

Diana was laughing.

"Grandma you are too much. Any man would be blessed to be with you because you are still a hand full of energy."

Sheila was looking at Grandma Harris and shook her head and then looked at Diana.

"Diana, as a woman I do understand why those things Ron said would make you so angry."

"Diana, you knew before you went over there he wanted some of your kitty cat." Grandma Harris started laughing and clapped her hands then pointed her finger at Diana. "You did the woman thing and teased that man then you turned him down and that's why he told you to suck his thang." She was laughing even harder.

"Grandma, that's not funny. I'm not some whore." She rolled her eyes at Grandma Harris. "I can't believe you sometimes."

"Diana, I'm sorry that Ron said that to you and you should have slapped him, but you are his wife now and we all know men expect that." Sheila said.

"Shame on Ron for wanting you to do such a horrible thing but I know he wanted some of your kitty-cat badly," she laughed and then got serious. "Shame on him for grabbing your little butt." She looked at Diana and laughed.

Sheila looked at Grandma Harris.

"Grandma Harris, stop laughing and teasing her. No woman should be disrespected in any way, wife or not. I know Ron wanted some of her little butt." Sheila smiled at Grandma Harris.

Diana stood up and rolled her eyes at them then shook her head.

"This is not funny and you two should be ashamed of yourselves for laughing at me." She walked toward the kitchen then stopped and turned around looking at them. "Just for the record, my butt is not that little. My husband likes it." She walked into the kitchen purposely shaking her hips and butt.

Sheila stared at Diana never seeing this side of her.

"Diana Brown, did you go over there teasing my son? If you did, shame on you." Sheila said shaking her finger at Diana.

"Yes, she did. She went over there shaking her little tail in his face and got him all horny but when he wanted her to get on her knees and get busy, she got upset and slapped him." She pointed at Diana "They call women like that penis teasers. Diana, are you a penis teaser?" She started laughing hard.

"Grandma Harris stop. Now that's just too much and you are being too nasty." She looked over at Diana in the kitchen.

"Diana, is there anything else you can tell me about Ron?"

She turned to look at Sheila.

"No, that's all I know and even though he upset me I'm glad that I saw him but only prayer and Jesus can deliver him from the powers of darkness."

Grandma Harris looked up and folds her hands together.

"Yes Lord."

"Amen to that Diana. Amen to that." Sheila said.

"And Lord, please deliver my baby from being a penis teaser to her husband." She looked over at Diana and began laughing so hard tears come to her eyes.

CHAPTER EIGHTEEN

Ricks House

Detective Rick Matthew lives in a four-bedroom house in a quiet neighborhood in Bowie, Maryland. He was sitting on his custom ordered one-thousand-dollar lazy boy chair in his living room listening to jazz. He went to Victor's club for a few hours because he felt like listening to some music and doing some police work at the same time. He was watching Ron and Keith because they are under investigation but they do not know it. They never saw him in the club.

Rick kept a low profile by mingling and talking with a few ladies and dancing but stayed focused and observed the actions of the people at the club. The club was very busy as usual but he enjoyed being there seeing so many beautiful sexy women. Rick was flirting with a very attractive young lady with a body that would make any man dig into his pockets and pay. Her name was Cynthia. She told Rick she was twenty-seven and was a car salesperson at Euro Motors in Bethesda, Maryland. He thought about the last conversation he and James had concerning him going out and having a good time. He was sure the counselor never meant this place but oh well, you only live once. Anyway, he gave her his number and she moved on. He could tell she was a gold digger and his pockets are not that deep for this young girl. He watched as Cynthia approached Keith, flirting with him, but Stacy walked over and shut that down very quickly. She introduced Cynthia to Ron and they spent the rest of the night together, dancing and talking.

Rick smiled and leaned farther back in his chair thinking about that scene. He knew that girl was wasting her time with that young man. He is newly married and his wife is fine but I guess women don't care too much these days about a man being married if he spends money on them and he does not become too demanding. He exhaled, turned up the volume and just relaxed to the sound of the music. "Yeah, my time will come real soon. I can feel it, real soon." He smiled.

CHAPTER NINETEEN
The Last Deal

Keith has always been a visionary and a deep thinker. He desires to build a large business complex which would be the headquarters for his and Ron's company. He likes the name, *The Young Wolves,* so he decided to keep that and have every business they own to come under the umbrella of, *"Young Wolves Inc."* This complex would cost millions to build and run. He has some of the money but not enough for the long term, so he wants to do one last big deal.

He knows no one does crime for years and not eventually get caught so he has been thinking for a while what deal he and Ron could put together that would make them a great deal of money quickly and retire from crime forever. It finally came to him but it took him a while doing serious research to get all the information and put everything together. They are going to sell legal and illegal drugs at the same time. The legal drugs they are not supposed to sell of course, but business is business. The product is pills and marijuana. They want to purchase twenty tons of high-grade weed which is forty-thousand pounds. Their purchase price is five hundred dollars a pound, which comes to twenty million dollars. The street price is two thousand dollars a pound, which comes to eighty million dollars gross.

They want to steal ten million, 20mg Levitra pills and sell them on the streets at eight dollars a pill, which comes to eighty million dollars. The gross from both deals is one hundred sixty million dollars.

Keith and Ron went over this plan for two weeks covering every detail they could think of until they were satisfied it could work and how to work it. They realized it was always the distribution part that proves to be the complicated process, so they put together a thirty day, forty-state nationwide distribution plan. Sell one-thousand pounds of weed in forty states in thirty days. They recruited a temporary team of four-hundred men with ten men in each of the forty states, selling weed and pills at the same time. Five-hundred dollars a day per man for four-hundred men is two-hundred-thousand dollars a day for thirty days, which makes that six-million dollars.

Keith invested just about all he had saved to make this deal happen, twenty-million dollars to buy the weed. Ron invested ten-million dollars for the men and miscellaneous costs. After recruiting everyone and putting them in place, it was deal time.

Phase One: Keith, Ron and ten of the *Young Wolves* flew to Montego Bay, Jamaica on a large private jet. They all stayed at the luxury Half Moon Hotel which stretches over four-hundred acres, including two miles of beach. Their front for being there was doing research for a movie production. The *Young Wolves* always arrived at the assigned meeting place to purchase the weed three hours early to set up spots to hide. Snipers on their team were set up in a four-point position to cover every angle and every man had *Mac 10* machine guns. All the meetings went smoothly and the shipments were already in route to Maryland.

Phase Two: Stealing the ten-million *Levitra* pills which are manufactured by Bayer Corporation in Germany but distributed by GlaxoSmithKline. In comparison to getting the drugs, this was easy to accomplish. Keith paid to get the inside information on the drug shipments and when they shipped out. He had it arranged to have twenty pallets shipped on two trucks with each pallet having fifty boxes on it and five-thousand pills in each box, which comes to ten-million pills. Of course, he had the route of the trucks. The *Young Wolves* would highjack the trucks.

The deals were done in three days with the pills and weed acquired and put in place. Thirty days later, every pound of weed and every pill was sold. Every man and every debt was paid. Keith and Ron made a profit of one-hundred twenty-four million dollars from this deal which they split in half, sixty-two million dollars apiece. They also had several authors working for them writing books that sold extremely well in the urban market. Ron wrote one book that sold three-million copies at four-dollars a profit per book. That's twelve-million dollars in legit money, by himself. Now it was celebration and investment time.

CHAPTER TWENTY
EuroMotorcars Dealership

Ron and Keith wanted everything about their company, *Young Wolves Inc.* to be first-class in the way everyone dressed and what they drove. Each member of the *Young Wolves'* elite security team had new condos and new Cadillac Escalade EXTs. Now it was time to upgrade. Ron appreciated the service he received when he purchased his car from EuroMotorcars, which sells Rolls Royce, Mercedes-Benz, and Bentley automobiles. This is where they would purchase the upgrades.

Ron and Keith drove to the dealership in Ron's Bentley. Behind them were ten *Young Wolves driving* their Escalades. All were dressed in Armani suits and wore sunshades. When they walked into the lobby of the dealership every head in the place turned in their direction to look at these well-dressed, well-built handsome young men. Ron called earlier to speak with the same salesperson who sold him his car but he no longer worked there.

Cynthia was sitting at her desk when they drove up. She stared at them from the time they drove up until they all walked into the lobby. She recognized Keith and Ron immediately. The sales manager came out and introduced himself to Keith and Ron. He knew money and a good deal when he saw it but he didn't know how good this day was going to be. Ron mentioned to the sales manager he wanted Cynthia as their sales rep. After informing the manager they wanted to trade ten 2011 Escalades for ten new S600 Benzes with no financing, straight cash deal, the manager almost choked as he hurried and walked over to

Cynthia's desk with Ron and Keith behind him. The *Young Wolves* were walking around the lobby looking at other cars.

Cynthia was wearing a low-cut dress showing just enough cleavage to get attention. The dress fit her curvaceous body well hugging it like a glove, and high heels that made her legs look great. Cynthia is extremely attractive by anyone's description. She's five-feet-seven, one-hundred-forty pounds of traffic stopping beauty, beautiful face small waist, hips and ass for days.

The manager introduced Keith and Ron to Cynthia. She informed the manager they had already met and she would be taking very good care of them. The manager nodded his head and walked away but kept his eyes on them to make sure everything went smoothly. He was not about to lose this deal for anything.

When the manager left, Cynthia put her plan into effect. She wanted Keith but she knew Stacy would kill her for even trying to push up on him. So, she set her sights on Ron, especially after Stacy told her Ron was having problems with his marriage and he was separated from his Christian wife. She was very nice looking and had a great body but she was not fucking him right. When she saw Ron in the club and how fine and well-built he was, she didn't give a damn that he was married.

Cynthia hugged Keith and Ron.

"It's good to see you two again and you look great."

They stared at Cynthia from head to toe with lust.

"Cynthia, you look very nice and your body is fitting that dress very well." Keith said smiling at her.

"Thank you, Keith." She said knowing he was a flirt but off limits because Stacy was around.

"Cynthia, you do look absolutely gorgeous and it is good to see you again." Ron said.

"Likewise, now let's go to the other lobby so we can talk because the seating area is more comfortable." She retrieved an ink pen and pad from her desk and started walking.

"No problem, lead the way." Ron said.

Cynthia wanted to sit in the other lobby because it had a comfortable sofa to sit on and she didn't want to sit at her desk because she would not be able to flirt using her body like she wanted to, hiding behind a desk. She made sure to walk slow and sexy for Ron and Keith, knowing they were staring at her hips and butt like all men do whenever she walked.

Keith knew she was putting on a show but he didn't give a damn what she thought about him. He was young, handsome, rich, and bold and could say whatever.

"Damn Cynthia, you need to stop making your hips and ass shake like that when you walk. You make a man go in his pocket and pull out some money when he sees all that." He laughed.

Cynthia turned her head slightly to the side while walking.

"Keith, you are something but make sure you pull out, enough money baby." She smiled and kept walking.

They reached the lobby and sat down and Cynthia sat across from them making sure they got a peek of her underwear as she sat down and crossed her legs.

Ron was looking at her legs then looked at her face.

"How much?"

"How much for what Ron?" She said with a frown on her face thinking he was trying to treat her like some low life slut.

"You said the man had to pull out enough money, how much is, enough money?"

"Well, are we talking personal or business?"

"It's always business with me so how much for ten S600s?"

"Yeah, right you want ten S600s today. This is not April fool's Day and my time is priceless." She said with an attitude.

"So is ours so don't play yourself. All ten cars today, how much?" Keith said.

Cynthia was looking at both guys and then licked her lips, knowing they were testing her to see if she was going to say something smart or reveal her true gold digging ways.

"Personally, I make my own money baby and if a man can meet me halfway, I'm good. Business wise you say you want ten S600s that cost one hundred and seventy-five thousand a piece equaling one million, seven hundred fifty-thousand dollars. If you are serious I can give you two thousand off each car which would come to one-million-seven-hundred-forty-thousand dollars," she said, slowly uncrossing her legs revealing her underwear and smiled at them. "Your move."

Keith and Ron looked at each other and then Ron reached into his pocket and pulled out the company American Express, Black card. He leaned forward slightly touching her leg with his fingers and stared into Cynthia's eyes. He gave her the card.

"Put it on the card please and write your personal phone number down for me."

Cynthia's mouth dropped open while looking at the card.

Keith and Ron stood up.

"We will be in the lobby waiting. I would greatly appreciate if you would get someone to help you with all of the paperwork for the ten cars, so it will not take long."

She looked at them trying to be cool but she knew these young brothers are for real. She stood up and looked at them.

"So, it's like that?"

Ron stepped closer to her and whispered in her ear.

"Is that ass of yours, like that?" He stepped back and stared at her with a serious look on his face.

Cynthia was not about to be played. She looked around the room then looked back at Ron.

"You damn right this ass of mine is like that." She got out one of her business cards and gave it to Ron. "Call me and maybe you can find out about this ass of mine and more," she said while smiling at him. "I will have all of your paperwork and the keys to your cars very soon gentleman."

They looked at her and walked away.

Two hours later Cynthia and the sales manager walked over to them carrying a brown envelope. The manager gave each man the keys to the cars that were parked out front. No one has ever seen anything like this and it created some inquiries about who these young black men were who could come in and purchase ten S600s at one time. The manager shook all their hands and he walked away, smiling. Cynthia was calculating in her head how much of a commission she would receive on this deal and what she would do with the money. She made sure to give Ron a nice hug before he left. She had plans for him. Everyone in the dealership watched Ron, Keith, and the *Young Wolves* drive away.

CHAPTER TWENTY ONE

Divine Intervention

Ron purchased a two-bedroom condo in Keith's building before he got married but spent very little time there, until recently. Diana does not know about the condo. He hired an interior decorator to decorate his place at a cost of eighty-thousand-dollars for her fee and the furniture. He was sitting on the sofa wearing silk pajama pants and a silk tank top T-shirt and slippers. Music was playing on the stereo and Cynthia was sitting next to him wearing heels, a low-cut top, and a mini skirt.

"Ron, I have to admit the people on my job are still talking about the entrance you, Keith, and your ten business associates made but the ongoing conversation is your purchase of the ten S600s. It has never been done before and to watch young good looking black men do it, was something to see."

"Thank you but we are just doing our thing. Don't let this go to your head but you are most definitely a *full seven* Cynthia."

"I have been called many things but what is a *full seven*?"

"A *full seven* is a woman who is beautiful in the face, small in the waist, got hips, full lips, pretty painted finger tips, big butt, and a pretty smile."

She smiled and rubs Ron's leg.

"Wow, okay I receive all of that and I thank you. I must remember that phrase, *full seven*. I like that but it never goes to my head because looks come and go."

"Very true and love is far more important."

"Yes, it is. I enjoyed dancing with you at the club tonight. You move well on the dance floor but I want to find out what other skills you have."

Cynthia is looking at him trying to feel if he is serious about this love stuff or speaking lies to get in her panties. She feels he is the real thing. He is too good-looking and rich to have to lie to women to get sex.

"I feel you baby but in the world that we live in, it is hard to find real love. So, we settle for what we can get and hope for the best."

"Not me. I'm determined to have both."

"I understand that but let me ask you this. Stacy told me a little about you. I know you are newly married to a very nice-looking Christian girl with a good-looking body. So why am I here? I'm far from judging you but I want and need to know what I might be getting into."

"Good questions that deserve honest answers. The short story, I love my wife deeply but we don't agree with my lifestyle. I left the old life behind but I enjoy the fruits of my labor and go some places that my wife does not like and I don't agree with my wife and some others that I have this great calling in my life to save the world."

"I appreciate your directness and your story is all too familiar. So where do I fit in? And please be direct because I detest liars."

"Direct it is. I'm not sure at this point where you fit in. It's too early to tell but I need a woman that can ride with me, watch my back and I watch hers. It's just that simple, and satisfy me in bed, that's a must."

RONALD GRAY   (122)

Cynthia was looking at him and thinking, *Damn I may have hit the jackpot. As soon as I put all this body and good nasty loving on this brother, he will be hooked on me and what I do. Then he can leave his boring wife and get with a trooper in the bedroom and out.*

"Well, I don't brag or boast on what I do. I allow my production to be my best resume as it should be. Let's take it one day at a time and see what happens with us."

"Works for me and at this point, that's what I had in mind. Speaking of moving, you and that mini skirt you're wearing, move a lot of men in your direction. You look good baby."

"I'm glad you noticed. I have heard some interesting things about you, very interesting."

"Positive things I hope."

"I heard that you and Keith do business with Mr. Victor Augular, you two are the new owners of the club, and you just gave me the icing on the cake," She pointed her finger at him. "You, need a real woman in your life."

"I see Stacy told you a lot. What are you looking for?"

"I could lie but I won't. I make my own money as I said but I wouldn't turn down a man with a lot of money who was willing to spend some of it on me. I'm all class but a freak in the bedroom. Hopefully, we can become great friends and maybe more, only time will tell."

"Not bad. I expected you to lie like so many others do. Just be real, it saves a lot of time." He leaned forward and kissed her. "Nice, your lips are very soft." He kissed her again slowly and passionately. "Very nice indeed."

"Don't start something you can't finish. You move well on the dance floor but I want to see how well you move in bed."

"Absolutely." He stood up and extends his hand to her, which she takes and they walk to his bedroom holding hands. He turned the stereo on in the room and sat on the bed. "Take that mini-skirt off and let me see what you are working with."

Cynthia knew as soon as he got a look at her body, which was all that, he'll be all in. Thanks to good genes and spending many hours at the gym. She was standing in front of him.

"Absolutely," she smiled and slid her mini-skirt down to the floor and is now standing there staring at Ron in her heels, thong panties and matching bra. She put her hands on her hips, "do you see anything that you like?"

Ron was staring at her thinking, *Wow I thought Diana had a nice body but this girl is all that, damn.*

"Yes, I do. Damn you are fine."

In Keith's condo, he and Stacy are sitting on the sofa wearing sweat pants and T-shirts listening to music. Stacy has been feeling guilty because of the way she has been treating Diana and how she talked to her the last time they saw each other at the club.

Keith hugged and kissed her but she didn't respond to him.

"Baby, what's wrong? You have been quiet all day."

She kissed him and rubs his chest.

"I know baby. I have been treating Diana badly and it has been bothering me. The fact is, she has not done anything to me but be nice to me and be my friend. I need to talk to her and Ron."

RONALD GRAY   (124)

"That's why I love you so much. You do have a kind heart underneath all your toughness," he kissed her softly on the lips rubbing her leg, "but tonight can you focus on us? Besides, Ron is busy tonight getting ready to get his freak on with Cynthia."

Stacy leaned away from him with a frown on her face.

"What! What is that supposed to mean Keith? Did you do something?"

He held his hands up.

"Relax, I didn't do anything. Ron is a grown man and he is living his life as he pleases. Cynthia was flirting with him at the car dealership and they connected and she is with him tonight at his condo. He probably has her legs in the air right now." He started laughing.

Stacy quickly stood up.

"No Keith," she yelled at him, "he can't do this, it would break Diana's, heart. Damn you men can't control your dick." She walked toward the door.

Keith stood up looking at her.

"What are you doing? I know you are not going to that grown man's condo."

She turned around and looked at him.

"Yes, I am and since this is partly your fault, you are coming with me. And Keith now is not the time to argue with me and please don't stop me. I need to do this."

Keith stared at her and was thinking. *What am I about to get myself into.* He and Ron are best friends so he would get past this but Stacy would never understand.

"I hope you understand what you are getting me into Stacy. Let's go."

RONALD GRAY   (125)

They walked out and go to Ron's condo. Stacy knocked on his door very hard. There was no answer so she bangs on the door repeatedly.

Ron and Cynthia are sitting on his bed kissing when they hear the loud banging on his door.

"Damn, who is that banging on my door like they are crazy," he kissed her again, "relax I will be right back." He grabbed his gun out of his dresser drawer and walked to his door and looked through the peep hole seeing Keith and Stacy. He shook his head and quickly opened the door.

"What? Are you two crazy banging on my door like you don't have good sense. Go home."

Stacy put her hand up and walked right past him and stood in the living room and Keith looked at Ron and shook his head.

"Not me partner. I don't block."

Stacy looked at Keith and rolled her eyes then looked at Ron putting her hands on her hips.

"Well, I do. Where is she? Where is Cynthia?"

Cynthia walked out in the living room in her heels, bra and thong panties.

"Is the building on fire? Hi Stacy, hi Keith." She looked at Keith and smiled.

Keith was staring at her lusting in his heart a hundred miles an hour. This girl got body.

"Damn Cynthia." Keith said as he stared at her.

Stacy looked at Keith with instant anger in her eyes but even she had to admit, Cynthia was beautiful and has an incredible body.

"Keith, there are enough people in the grave yard," looking at him then Cynthia. "Hi Cynthia. We need to talk." She walked over to Cynthia grabbed her arm and they walked back to the bedroom.

Ron looked at Keith.

"This better be good partner. What's up? Do you know how close I was to taste and putting my dick in her, damn?"

"I mentioned to Stacy that you and Cynthia connected and she was with you tonight. She snapped and dragged me up here."

"You talk too much."

Stacy and Cynthia are talking and she waved her hand at Cynthia.

"Get dressed. You are not fucking Ron tonight or any other night. And don't argue with me because I'm not in the mood." She is looking at Cynthia with malice in her heart.

Cynthia looked at her like she was crazy. She knows Stacy well so she started getting dressed.

"I can't believe this."

Stacy was watching her dress and had to hold herself back because she was instantly drawn to her. She stepped closer and smacked Cynthia on the butt.

"Hurry up and get your hot ass dressed, no dick for you tonight, at least not from Ron."

Cynthia got dressed then looked at Stacy because she was past irritated with her.

"Damn Stacy, you are going to tell me about this later. Are you fucking Ron and Keith?"

Stacy wants to smack her so badly and get in her panties.

"You got a smart mouth. I love Keith and Ron is not my type, money or not. Let's go. Get some dick somewhere else."

They walked out. Ron and Keith are on the sofa talking.

"Say goodbye to Cynthia Ron, she is leaving."

They stand up and Ron walked over to her.

"Business calls but I will make it up to you."

She pointed her finger at him.

"You better." She stepped closer hugged and kissed him.

Ron put his hands on her butt rubbing it.

Stacy does not like seeing Ron doing this to her and hurting Diana. She grabbed Cynthia's arm.

"Enough of that, let's go. I told you, ain't no fucking."

She and Cynthia walked out and Keith and Ron looked at them and shook their heads. They dap up.

"Later partner talk to you tomorrow."

"Yea after all of this we definitely need to talk."

Keith walked out and Ron locked his door and walked back to his bedroom. On his bed are Cynthia's thong panties. He picked them up and looked at them.

"Damn, I got to get that hot ass."

CHAPTER TWENTY TWO
Rick and Cynthia

When Cynthia left Stacy, she began thinking about what she could do and who she could call to make her kitty pure. She thought about the nice-looking older guy who was flirting with her at the club. She has been around the block and she knows the streets and can read people well. She knew Rick was a cop but her mindset was you never know when you may need one and it's always good to have one on your side instead of against you. The way she was feeling she was not looking for love, romance, or a long conversation. She wanted some good satisfying sex and a little money to line her pockets with. Cynthia knew she could get both from Rick as hard as he was macking her. While they were talking she felt between his legs and knew he was working with something. Just like carrying rubbers, she learned long ago young or older, she always carried Viagra, Cialis, and Levitra. Guaranteed to get the job done, one way or another.

Besides she likes older men, no games, more mature and freaks in the bedroom. They have no problem getting nasty doing whatever to please you just the way any real woman wants it. When she got home and showered she called Rick and arranged for them to meet at the Embassy Suite hotel in Virginia across the street from the King Street subway station. She was not in the mood to drive and deal with traffic tonight. They talked on the phone for an hour. She was surprised when he told her how old he was. She figured he was about thirty-eight but he told her he was forty-eight. The man looked good, clean cut with a tight body. They had a clear understanding, tonight it would be all about her and if it worked out then it would be about pleasing him later. She told Rick she wanted him to take his time and please her entire body, front to back top to bottom. She wanted it all. He made her one promise.

To do anything to her that she wanted him to do and to lick, kiss, caress, suck, bite, touch her entire body. When Cynthia heard that it was good enough for her, besides she already read him and knew he was a freak in bed. She decided to keep it simple in her dress since she was going to spend the night. She had heels on and soft pink greisen goddess, very low cut draped dress, that's very easy to get out of. Her favorite matching bra and thong panties and carrying her overnight bag of essentials.

Rick was already there and he chose a very nice suite in the hotel. The first thing he did before he forgot was to set the stereo to a nice jazz station. He was surprised when Cynthia called him but she has been on his mind as she would be on any man's mind. You just don't forget someone as fine as her. He laughed to himself because he figured the young man could not get the job done. He never did abuse his body like so many cops did. No drinking, smoking or drugs and he worked out four times a week. He knew she figured him for a cop. Her type always could, street smart and wise to the game. He could care less. He also had his own thoughts concerning her. Sex her good tonight and keep her on speed dial when he wanted some fun. No harm, no pain. He was far from rich but he had invested well and saved his money over the years. Truth be told, he could put his hands on three-hundred-thousand easy. Not bad for a detective.

Rick showered when he got to the hotel. After brushing his teeth and tongue he looked in the mirror while putting lotion on his body. He liked what he saw. Handsome face, toned body, small waist and a decent six-pack. Not bad. He knew he could put many young guys to shame. He put his silk boxers and a tank top on when he heard a knock at the door. He went to the door and saw through the peep hole that it was Cynthia. He opened the door and smiled.

"Hi, come on in, you look good."

"Hello yourself and thank you." She walked in carrying her small bag. She was very satisfied with how Rick looked up close and in the light. She could also tell he was fresh out the shower, he smelled good. She looked around the room and really liked how lavish it was. Cynthia dropped her bag by the bed.

Rick stood in the middle of the room looking at her.

"It is good to see you again."

"Likewise, I was looking forward to coming over here. Especially after all the things you said you were going to do to me over the phone. You did mean every word right, it wasn't some game to get me over here."

"Sweetie, I don't play games." He walked over to her and slowly pulled her into him lightly brushing his lips against hers and slowly kissed her feeling how soft her lips are.

Cynthia liked him already. Nice move, nice soft kiss. She didn't come here for romance but you never know. She wanted more so she slightly opened her mouth to allow his tongue in.

Rick liked the way she felt in his arms and when she opened her mouth it was what he was waiting for. He slid his tongue in and their tongues connected well like they have known each

RONALD GRAY   (131)

other for years. He placed his hands on her butt and pulled her tighter into him. He found out she had more ass than he remembered. He continued slowly kissing her.

Cynthia was enjoying this already because she loved it when a man took charge. It showed he was sure of himself and confident but not cocky. She could feel his erection growing and it made her smile and wet which is a big improvement from early tonight.

"You know how to make me want more of you," she kissed him, "baby let's not waste time talking."

"You spoke my thoughts." He kissed her with more passion and removed her dress, bra, and panties and stood back admiring her stunningly beautiful body.

"Can you handle all of this baby?" She said licking her lips.

"You damn right I can. You are one fine woman and your body is incredible." He was thinking. *This young girl has no idea what she was in for.*

He bent down putting his hands between her legs underneath her and on her butt and picked Cynthia up putting one of her legs on his shoulder and her other leg on his other shoulder with her crotch very close to his face.

"Rick what are you doing? Don't you drop me, put me down?" She is a little nervous but anxious to see what he was going to do to her.

"I will put you down when I'm finished." He carried her to the other side of the room and put her back up against the wall with his hands holding her up while her legs are resting on his shoulders. He buried his face between her legs, licking and sucking on her with such passion until her entire body started shaking from her first orgasm.

"Oh Rick, I'm cumming baby, don't stop, oh my God, I'm cumming baby, ohhhhhh Rick, I'm cumming."

Cynthia climaxed so hard and so quick it surprised her and she was still shaking and thinking. *Damn this man is good.*

Rick knew what he was doing and how he wanted to affect her so he carried Cynthia to the bed and gently laid her down on her stomach. Not wanting her to recover he started kissing, licking, biting and sucking on her body. Her neck, arms, back, butt, legs, and feet. He moved up to her butt again and started licking, kissing and sucking on it.

Cynthia was feeling so good from this man's touch and want him badly inside her. All his sucking and licking was driving her crazy and she wanted more of him. As she was adjusting to this great feeling, he does something that she has heard so many other ladies talk about but never had it done to her.

Rick gently spreads her butt cheeks apart and began licking between it, sliding his tongue back and forth up and down her ass then makes his tongue stiff and pushed it into her butt as far as it will go, knowing it was driving her crazy. He stopped and quickly grabbed two pillows putting them underneath her so her butt will be high in the air giving him more access and continues to lick her butt deep and slow.

"Ohhhhhh Rick, damn your tongue feels so good in my ass baby, lick it, stick your tongue deep in my ass Rick. I know you want to fuck this ass. Damn you are trying to turn me out I know you are, ohhhhhh lick this ass baby."

RONALD GRAY   (133)

Rick continued to explore her sexy butt until she climaxed again. Play time was over. He turned her over on her back grabbed her ankles, pushing them back and slid his dick inside.

"Ohhh Rick, damn you baby. That's it, just ram it in me, give me what I need, ohhhhh I need this good dick down."

Rick slows down and slowly pulled almost all the way out of her and slams back in deep, doing this over and over. Picking up his pace until he was drilling her and can feel her passions building and knew she was on the brink of another orgasm.

"Take this dick, take it, damn you are so tight and wet, ohh you feel good Cynthia, take this dick."

This man was giving it to her so good it was blowing her mind. She couldn't hold it any longer because his thrusts are like a machine.

"That's it, fuck me, Ohhhh I'm cummming Rick, I'm cummming baby, fuck me good, don't stop, ohhhhhhh please don't stop, fuck this pussy, ohhhhhh Rick, I'm cumming."

Rick could no longer hold it because Cynthia was so wet, hot and tight. She was pushing her body into him.

"Cynthia, I can't hold it, baby, I'm cuming, your pussy is so good, ohhhhhh I'm cumming baby, damnnnn Cynthia." He kept fucking her until every drop of his seed was inside her. He slides out and laid next to her.

Cynthia was laying there totally blown away by this man and all that he did to her body and how good it felt. She was thinking, *Most definitely I will spend time with this man. If she was not careful she could fall for him, hard.*

Rick rolled over toward her softly kissing her lips.

"Will you join me in the shower?"

RONALD GRAY   (134)

Cynthia was so relaxed and she does not want to move at all right now but she can't let him think he put it on her like that, although he did.

"If you will help me up, yes I will join you in the shower."

Rick gently helped her get up and they walked to the shower. They washed each other slowly, kissing each other along the way. As Cynthia was about to step out Rick gently grabbed her by the waist, turned her around and pushed her against the shower wall with her back to him. He put her hands against the wall, pulled her butt towards him and kneeled placing his hands on her hips. He started licking and sucking her pussy from the back and slid his tongue inside her.

"Oh Rick, not again baby, oh you are going to be my man. That's it baby, in and out, stick that tongue in me, it feels so good. Yes, baby you can have me, fuck me any way you want, just keep sucking my pussy baby, ohhhh damn you are going to make me cum again, damn you, ahhhhhhh."

Rick continued licking her then stood up and started sucking on her neck, caressing her breast and lightly pinching her nipples. He was rock hard again so he slowly slid inside her and she was so wet. He grabbed her hips and started fucking her from the back.

"Oh Rick, you can't keep doing this to me, oh you feel good," she looked back at him sliding his dick inside her. "You are not going to just push dick in me, I'm fucking you back." she started throwing her butt into him, "yes baby, just like that, fuck me good. Ohhhhhh, you are my man, you are my man baby, fuck this young tight pussy. I'm cummming Rick it is so gooood, ohhhhhhh get this damn pussy, ahhhhhhh baby." She climaxed

RONALD GRAY　　　　(135)

so hard again it made her dizzy. Cynthia was leaning against the shower wall trembling and trying to hold herself up while this man is fucking her so well.

Rick knew his sex game was tight and was driving Cynthia wild but between her tight, hot pussy, her body shaking and trembling like it was and talking dirty to him claiming his dick. He couldn't hold his nut any longer so he gripped her hips tighter and increased his thrusting, exploding inside Cynthia hard.

"Damn baby your pussy is soooo good, ahhhhh, yes." He finished unloading in her and they washed each other again and stepped out the shower and started drying each other off. Rick can't help from staring at Cynthia because she was beautiful and her body was a ten. He wrapped a towel around his waist, leaving her naked but gently grabbed her hand and they walked out the bathroom. He laid her down on the bed and begun taking his time to lotion her entire body, nice and slow.

Cynthia was laying there thinking. Oh, my God, this man was something else. I have been with my share of men but he put it down like no other. I got to keep him. Now, if he has some money, I will shut all other bitches down trying to push up on him.

Rick was enjoying catering to Cynthia like this and he can read her thoughts. After a woman gets some great loving from a man, the next thing was, does he have some money. He already made up his mind to keep her around for a while and see how things go, so he was going to give her a few dollars. He stopped massaging her and walked over to his pants and pulled out a knot of money, peeling off ten hundred dollar bills putting the rest back in his pocket and walked back over to her. He leaned over kissing and lightly bites Cynthia on the neck. She turned over and sees the money in his hand, holding her smile in.

He kissed her lips.

"I'm not trying to insult you but this is for you. Can we spend some time together getting to know each other better? When you have time."

Cynthia was staring at him.

"When I have time. I may be young baby but I'm no fool. You damn right we can spend some time together. I don't know what you are taking to put it on me like you did but you need to keep taking it because I'm shutting all other hoes out." She raised up and took the money from his hand, putting it underneath the pillow. Then laid back down on the bed with her hand behind her head, fighting sleep. "Thanks, Rick but you didn't have to do that," she pats the bed with her hand, "now come over here and lay down with me. I'm tired, you tried to fuck my brains out baby but I got you next time, believe that." She smiled at him.

Rick smiled and removed his towel and laid next to her caressing her body. Cynthia rolled over on her stomach to finally get some sleep enjoying his delicate touch which is making her even sleepier. Rick was staring at her incredible body and her butt sticking up in the air. This very sight was making him desire her and he is hard again. He slides down her body gently spreading her legs apart seeing her wetness and started licking it.

Cynthia was almost asleep when she felt his warm tongue between her legs. She would have made him stop because she was very tired and wanted to sleep but his tongue was moving so

RONALD GRAY   (137)

slow on her wetness and it felt so good, she let him keep going, hoping he would stop soon.

Rick knew she was very tired but opportunities like this do not come along every day so he was going to take advantage of it. He stopped licking her and moved his body over hers and very slowly, very gently slid his hard dick inside her. He didn't put any of his body weight on her because he was holding himself up on his hands. Many years of doing push-ups were paying off. He was all the way in now and he didn't move because he wanted her to respond to him.

Cynthia was so wet again and so close to another climax when Rick stopped licking her but she was okay with that because she was so tired and thought he was going to sleep too. Then she felt his hard dick slowly slide inside her, it made her insides jump. She was thinking. *Does this man ever get enough? I know my pussy is good but damn.*

"Rick no. I'm too tired you wore me out baby, please let me sleep."

He ignored her words and pulled his dick almost all the way out and slid it back in with just a little more force seeing and feeling her butt shake. Rick began slowly sliding in and out of her. He leaned forward and whispered in her ear.

"Do you really want me to stop?" Slowly increasing his pace.

As tired as she was his dick was feeling too damn good.

"No baby, don't stop. Ohhhh please don't stop. You are my man baby, you are my man. Own this pussy."

CHAPTER TWENTY THREE
Keith's Condo

Keith was sitting on the sofa wearing a dress shirt, dress shoes, and dress pants. Stacy was sitting beside him wearing low-cut boots, a blouse and dress pants that hug her body.

"We need to talk. What's up with you blocking on my partner. When did you become Diana's keeper?"

"Keith, it was a conscious call and it just hit me. Diana is one of the good ones. Yes, she has a save the world attitude that gets on my nerves sometimes but she is a good person trying to do the right thing, in a messed-up world. Ron should be ashamed of himself. Diana is not that bad in bed that he has to go out and be with another woman."

Keith was staring at Stacy wondering what has caused her to have such a change of heart.

"Yeah okay. I'm feeling your heart but how do you know Diana is not bad in bed. Are you doing her?" He started laughing knowing what he said would irritate her.

Stacy looked at Keith and was thinking, *If you only knew and I pray to God that you never find out.*

"Stop being disgusting Keith. Women talk and she told me Ron was very pleased with her in bed and she was very satisfied with him."

Keith leaned back on the sofa and started laughing.

"They never had sex, anything would be good to those two. Cynthia, now she got it going on and with all that body. I know she would put something on a man."

RONALD GRAY   (139)

Stacy stood up and pointed her finger in his face.

"Oh, so you want to fuck her now. I told you about your mouth and disrespecting me. Don't get cut first thing in the morning."

Keith stood up and pointed his finger in her face.

"Look, I told you about threatening me."

The doorbell rang and Ron was standing at the door wearing a tailored sweat suit.

"Get your finger out of my face and go answer the door, tough guy," she stepped closer and kissed him, "I'm as hot as fire and I drive you crazy, don't I baby."

He bent down and reached under the sofa pulling out a gun and stood back up looking at Stacy holding his gun by his side.

"One of these days you are going to make me blow your brains out," he walked over to the door and looked through the peep hole, "perfect timing," he opened the door, "Mr. S&D, come on in my brother." He put his gun behind his back in his belt.

"What's up Keith?" He walked in and sees Stacy and was thinking, *Damn, she is fine. Keith would be a fool to cheat on her*. He continued walking into the living room. "Hi Stacy, we need to talk." He removed his jacket and laid it on the sofa and he was wearing two shoulder holsters carrying his two guns. He sat down on the sofa and stared at Stacy.

Keith was sitting in a chair in the living room knowing where this was about to go.

Stacy was looking at Ron feeling his irritation.

"Don't stare at me. You should be ashamed of yourself and yes, I'm glad I interrupted you and Cynthia about to have sex.

How can you even think of cheating on your wife? Damn, marriage vows don't mean a thing to people anymore. Can't you control your dick? Okay yes, I think Diana is stupid for leaving you and not fucking you like she should but you are stupid for trying to fuck another chick because you can't say no to your dick." She stared him down not caring what he thought of her right now.

"Stacy, relax damn. Maybe you should be a marriage counselor." Keith said laughing.

"Keith, you think this is funny. Okay, if I don't give you some love in two weeks, are you going to cheat on me?" She walked over to him putting her finger in his face, "you do and I will slice your dick off in your sleep, believe that."

Keith had enough of her mouth and threats. He quickly picked her up and put her over his shoulder.

"Keith stop put me down, you better not hurt me," she looked at Ron, "Ron help me."

Ron was laughing and pointed his finger at her.

"Handle your business partner. I will be here when you finish, get that mouth."

"Amen, my brother. See you in a while." He carried Stacy into their bedroom and kicked the door shut.

He put Stacy on the bed and quickly started taking her clothes off until she was naked but she was still fighting him.

"Keith, are you crazy? You can't just take me anytime you want. Now stop." She started kicking her feet at him.

He quickly took his clothes off and his dick was sticking straight up. He grabbed Stacy's legs and pulled her to the edge of the bed and started licking and sucking on her wetness, making sure his tongue hits all her spots.

Stacy tried to slide up on the bed to get away from him although his mouth was sending her over the edge and close to climax very quickly. She was not about to give in to him now.

Keith pulled her back to him, making his tongue dance inside her and sucking her clit.

"Ohhhhh Keith, noooo baby, I'm cumming." Her body started twisting she is climaxing so hard.

He continued sucking Stacy holding on to her legs tightly because she was trying to get away from him even though she was climaxing so hard. He stopped and slid his hard dick inside her and for the next hour. He had Stacy on her back, her stomach, on the bed, on the floor, and up against the wall while biting and sucking on her neck. Before he exploded in her, Keith put Stacy on the bed on her stomach with two pillows underneath her and her butt was sticking up in the air as he was ramming inside her. In and out, back and forth making her butt shake every time his body connected with hers.

Stacy was loving this from Keith and although he put it down before, this was different. He felt extra hard and big inside her and it was blowing her mind which was why she could no longer hold back.

"Ahhhhhhh yes Keith, fuck me baby I will be good, ohhhhhhh baby I'm cummming Keith." She put her hands underneath her so she could push up into him, matching his powerful thrust that was sending her entire body into mini-orgasmic convulsions.

Keith slowly pulled out and smacked her butt repeatedly but not too hard, making her cry but not from pain. He slid back in and put that old school move on her. He gripped the sheets on both sides close to her waist and started dicking her down machine-gun style. Fast and deep.

Stacy was crying and screaming at the same time calling Keith many names but was still pushing up into him trying to get all this fantastic loving he was giving her.

As if they could read each other's mind and body, they both exploded at the same time.

"Ahhhhhhh Stacy."

"Ahhhhhhh Keith."

Keith continued to thrust inside her until he went soft, then pulled out and started kissing and gently biting Stacy all over her body, making her jump, twitch and shake trying to get away from him while crying telling Keith how much she loved him.

Keith held her for a while then he got up and helped Stacy up but when she took a step, she fell because her legs were wobbly and her body was weak. Keith laughed and carried her to the shower. They washed and dried off and he carried her back to bed. He put on sweat pants and a T-shirt to go check on Ron but first he kissed Stacy on the cheek.

"You better stop playing with me, Stacy. I run this. You remember that and play your position as my queen." Looking down at her, frowning.

Stacy looked up at him.

"Yes baby, whatever you say. Just let me sleep."

Keith kissed her cheek again and walked out the room.

She watched him walk away and tears fell from her eyes.

"If he asked me to marry him right now I would say yes. Damn, I love that man." She gripped her pillow and closed her eyes.

Ron heard them having sex and it made him miss Diana even more. He got up and went to the kitchen and fixed himself some breakfast. Scrambled eggs, bacon, grits, toast and orange juice. He was sitting at the kitchen table when Keith walked out and looked at him.

"Damn man, make yourself at home. All the money you make and you can't go to IHOP," he started laughing, "where is mine and it better be some food left."

Ron looked up at him still stuffing food in his mouth and he pointed to the stove.

"On the stove." He continued eating.

Keith got his food and started eating.

Ron looked at Keith.

"Is she alive? I heard you two."

"Yeah well, I got to hit it like that from time to time. The girl got a lot of mouth and attitude besides she loves it when I dick her down like that. She goes right to sleep and sleep half the day."

"Real men do real things partner do you." They dap up.

"Enough about my love life. You better go get your wife and put fire to her."

Ron stared at Keith knowing he was right and so was Stacy in all that she said.

"Yeah, I got to handle that because I miss her. Speaking about business. Our plans worked out like a dream come true and we made enough money to definitely retire from crime for good,

RONALD GRAY   (144)

but knowing the spirit of Victor, he will not let us go unless we make him a great deal of money as well."

"I have been thinking the same thing and you are right but the man is already a mega-billionaire. He is too damn greedy and I know he knows about our deal and he is going to want more money in his pockets, greedy damn man."

"I have a plan that will make him a lot of money and allow us to walk away from him for good. Business and pleasure moving a lot of weight at one time, at one place and have fun at the same time. By the way, where is Stephanie?"

"Now you are talking and I know it's a good plan because your last one was great but damn man you tried to take over the whole drug market. Stephanie is dead partner. They killed her. So, break the plan down to me."

"Stephanie is dead? Wow, that's sad but whatever, anyway my plan is we are going to have a very large and expensive fashion show. Top models from various states and a popular group to entertain everyone. I'm talking big show, five stars all the way."

"It sounds great and the pleasure I see but where is the business?"

"That's the best part. We also put the word out and invite major players that want some serious weight in drugs. A multi-million-dollar deal covered by the fashion show which is just a front with all that glitter and flesh to draw all that money."

Keith smiled.

"I knew you were smart and I like it. I like it a lot and we can do this," he stood up, "and I know just the person who can help us set this fashion show off."

RONALD GRAY   (145)

Ron stood up and faces Keith.

"Perfect and when we get the details of the show and find out who and how many are coming we call Greg Johnson and get plenty of weight to move."

"We put plenty of muscle and guns on the scene and drop anyone who gets out of hand. Big events like that, people do stupid things."

"What do you think? Are we in there?"

"Like thongs in a woman's butt. Partner, you are a genius. Now let me make a call," he walked over to the table in the living room and got the phone and sat down on the sofa. Ron put the dishes in the sink and walked over to Keith.

"Shantai, hi this is Keith...I have something that I want to talk to you about. Can you meet me at my club...no problem just call me back when you are finished...bye sweetheart." He put the phone back on the table.

Ron looked at Keith like he was crazy.

"Bye sweetheart. You live very dangerously considering Stacy is crazy. Keith, you really need to slow down and take Stacy very seriously. If you ever cheat on her and she finds out partner, you are a dead man. She will put you in the ground. I notice the way she talked to you and the look that I see in her eyes. She is one hundred percent serious. You need to think about that. I don't understand you anyway. You have a great lady who treats you like a king, she is super fine, sex your brains out. My own wife won't even give it to me when I want it, and we just got married. Any man would love to have Stacy but you still want more. That's why so many women call us dogs, because of guys like you. Anyway, what's the deal, are we in or not?"

RONALD GRAY   (146)

"Damn man, you are clocking my business and my baby like that but you are right. I do need to check myself. Stacy is all that and then some. You know, I really do think she would kill a brother if I cheated on her," he stared out into space for a few seconds then shook his head and stood up, "damn all that, let's work this plan so we can get away from Victor. It's in the mix partner."

"Good, then it's show time with fine women and plenty of money."

"Just the way I like it. Watching pretty faces, hips, and ass shaking and making money. What more can a man ask for." He smiled.

Ron looked at him and shook his head.

"His life! You cheat on Stacy and I will be attending your funeral brother. You remember that." He gave Keith some dap.

CHAPTER TWENTY FOUR
Mr. Bones and Doctor Eyes

Mr. Bones was standing in a grave yard dressed in black with his cane in one hand and his pouch in the other. He was looking down at eight large grey shiny headstones. On each one is engraved the names Sheila, Ron, Diana, Christine, Sandra, Grandma Harris, Keith, and Stacy. The light from the full moon makes the names stand out boldly. On the ground in front of each headstone was a small pile of bones and a dead black cat. Mr. Bones walked in front of each headstone, mumbled some words tapping his cane twice on each one. The bones start vibrating and slowly, float up in the air. The black cat floats up meeting the bones, which started circling around the cats. The cat catches on fire and explodes in the air, shooting cat flesh and bones everywhere. Mr. Bones tapped his cane twice, slides across the ground backward, in front of the headstones. He throws his cane and pouch high in the air and raised his arms, mumbling some words and he slowly began to levitate. The wind started blowing hard, lightning started flashing hitting the ground and thunder sounds so loud it could be heard from fifty miles away. Mr. Bones was hovering thirteen feet in the air holding his arms out when his cane and pouch float down and land in his hands.

"I'm the Bones, all power is in me. I call those things into existence that shall be. I speak it, so it shall come to pass. Death to Sheila! Death to Ron! Death to Diana! Death to Christine! Death to Sandra! Death to Grandma Harris! Death to Keith! Death to Stacy! I come to steal, kill and destroy the entire human race." His body turned around in the air, "I curse them all to hell." He mumbled words and he slowly floats down to the ground. The winds, lightning and thunder stopped. He tapped his cane twice on the ground and the ground started shaking.

"I command the spirit of Doctor Eyes to awake and do my will. He yelled. "Doctor Eyes, wake up, now." He tapped his cane hard on the ground and six feet underground a vibration started and travels to Beaufort, South Carolina underneath the home of Doctor Eyes making his house shake.

Doctor Eyes is a very powerful root worker who has a reputation to get anything done that you ask. People come to visit him from across the nation. He is dark skin complexion six feet six, two-hundred-eighty pounds with salt and pepper hair. He looks about a hundred years old but no one really knows how old he is. He's lying in bed asleep when his house started shaking. His eye lids opened but he has no eyes, all you see is an open hole. He sat up in bed.

"Who is calling me?"

Mr. Bones tapped his cane twice.

"Come to me, Doctor Eyes, now." He opened his pouch and pours bones in his hand and throws them in the air. They travel across the sky until they hit Doctor Eyes' house. Smoke appeared from underneath his bed covering his body and he disappeared. He appeared in a cloud of dark smoke standing in front of Mr. Bones.

"Who are you and what do you want? Do you know who I am?" He said with a very deep gravelly-toned voice.

Mr. Bones walked around him mumbling some words looking at Doctor Eyes.

RONALD GRAY   (149)

"I'm Mr. Bones and I know who you are. We serve the same master. I summoned you because I'm going to help you become even more powerful and in return," he pointed his cane at him, "you will help me one day."

"I'm Doctor Eyes, I need no help." He pointed at him.

"Shut up fool. You are blind but I'm going to help you see." A black cat runs in front of Mr. Bones but with lightning speed, he quickly snatched it off the ground and hit it in the back of its head with his hand and its eyes pop out and land in his hand. He throws the cat on the ground, it runs off. Mr. Bones grabbed Doctor Eyes by his neck.

"Open your eye lids, boy."

Doctor Eyes opened his eye lids and Mr. Bones placed the cat's eyes in his eye sockets. The eye balls are blood red with a yellow dot in the middle. The moment Doctor Eyes received his eyes he could not only see everything in the physical realm but he was able to see things in the spiritual world. He looked at Mr. Bones and stepped back.

"Nooo," He screamed very loudly, dropped to his knees and started shaking because he has never seen such powerful spirits in his life and he has seen many. He stood up shaking and looked at Mr. Bones. "You, you are the devil."

"Yes, I'm incarnated in the flesh. Now stop all that stuttering and shaking. I have increased your powers tenfold. You will be able to do so much to help me trick and deceive more people, taking them to hell. Stupid fools think they can dance with me and not pay. If you come to me I can give you everything that you want but only God can give you what you really need but who waits for God anymore these days." He started laughing.

RONALD GRAY   (150)

"What do you want from me now, Mr. Bones?" Looking at him, he is no longer shaking and he feels stronger than ever before in his life.

"For now, just keep deceiving people but in time I may need you and you will know when and you will be there." Staring at him with eyes that keep changing colors, from coal-black to blood red.

"No problem."

"I didn't think so. Now you can go back to living in your old raggedy house." He tapped his cane twice on the ground and black smoke comes under Doctor Eye's feet, surrounding his entire body. Mr. Bones tapped his cane once hard on the ground. "Be gone." He yelled and Doctor Eyes and the smoke disappear.

Doctor Eye's house started shaking and he appeared in a cloud of black smoke sitting on his bed. He laid down on the bed and opened his eye lids wide. His eye balls come out and float over to his dresser where a small box opened and the eye balls float down into the box and the lid closed.

"Damn, I feel powerful. Keep coming to me people, keep coming. Hell is enlarging." He started laughing.

Mr. Bones was standing in front of the headstones staring at them.

"I'm going to get all of you people. You fakers, backsliders, hypocrites and weak Christians. I'm killing you all and taking you to hell with me. You will burn forever."

CHAPTER TWENTY FIVE
Attorney Reed Office

James was in his law office standing in front of the desk that Diana was sitting behind. He was looking at Diana with sadness in his spirit not looking forward to telling her the news.

"Diana, I was praying the news I heard about your husband Ron was not true but unfortunately it is. He and Keith Washington are in way over their heads doing business with Mr. Victor Augular and I know they now own his night club."

"Yes, I know and it is breaking my heart being away from him but I did go see Ron during the day at that club to hopefully convince him to come back to the Lord and stop doing what he is but the devil has him spiritually bound. That club is beautiful but it's a trick of the devil."

"True indeed, all that glitters is not gold. I'm very good at what I do and would do anything for Sheila and her family but all eyes are on Mr. Augular and anyone associated with him. When Mr. Augular falls everyone falls with him and the system will have no mercy."

"I pray for my husband body and soul so much. I know God can't lie and his prophecy will be fulfilled but at what price, on Ron's behalf. Mr. Reed, I truly do love Ron and I do not want to lose him, ever. Not being at home and this separation from him is very hard for me." She began to cry.

"Diana, I know it is very hard but just hold on to your faith and don't stop praying. I don't mean to get too personal but I do care about you and you know that but please be careful when dealing with Ron. Even though you two are married now, being around him could cause you legal problems. You know how it goes, guilty by association."

"Mr. Reed, I know you are just showing concern for me and I greatly appreciate it and you are right I need to be very careful with Ron. I'm sorry, I don't mean to cry," she stood up, "I pray so hard for him and love him so much but he is truly hurting me," she cries harder, "I'm sorry, forgive me. I need to go to the bathroom." She walked away crying.

Rick Matthew walked into the office, smiling.

"Rick, come on in sir. I have been waiting for you."

"James, it is good to see you," he walked toward James and they shook hands, "I have some information for you concerning Mr. Augular."

"Perfect, let's go to my office," they walked to his office, James sat behind his desk and Rick sat in front of it. "So, tell me some good news about this seemingly untouchable man."

"News I have but bad news. We don't have him. He did it again," he shook his head. "That man always seems to be one step ahead of us. We couldn't serve the papers on him because he and his body guards are gone and he sold his night club. He beat us again."

James slams his hand on his desk!

"I know he sold his club. That man has earned his title well, Mr. Untouchable. Good God, this makes no sense. No one is above the law and he can't run forever. Even with Mr. Augular using voodoo, he will pay because the devil has no friends."

"You know I have never believed in voodoo or any supernatural stuff until Mr. Augular came on the scene. The man

RONALD GRAY   (153)

really is untouchable with crooked politicians, large money, and voodoo. I can't deal with all of that." Rick rubs his chin.

"In the natural, no one can. Those who are truly born again, they have the power to defeat the devil and all his evil spirits."

"You know I was raised in the church but it never took but after all, I have been through in these last years, life and death have been on my mind a lot lately, especially life and taking the time to enjoy it." He turned his head to the side and smiled. "Really enjoy it. Anyway, we do know that Mr. Augular and his killers flew to Bogota, Columbia but he could be anywhere by now."

"He can't be touched in Bogota anyway. Even in the states, his political connections run deep. He is very protected by so many people because he is making them so much money. I have a friend in the IRS office and this friend informed me that Victor is now worth over ten billion dollars. But he feels his wealth is probably twice that and more because the man hides his money very well in bank accounts all over the world that not even the federal government can touch. Despite his mass wealth, he will be brought down no matter what."

"Well, when he falls I'm going to retire and enjoy the fruits of my many years of hard labor. Yea, I got to enjoy it more."

Rick stared at James and smiled.

"Do you know something that I don't? That's the second time you made that comment about enjoying life and had that guilty smile on your face. Share the news."

"Let's just say ain't nothing wrong with appreciating life and what it has to offer. I took your advice," he smiled, "there are some fine things in this life to enjoy."

"Okay, I got it now. You met some nice lady and you two went out and had a good time together. Good for you. A nice settled lady is good to have."

Rick started laughing and leaned back in his chair.

"Well, I don't know how settled she is but she sure is nice, real nice. Talk about fine and a body to make any man pray for more energy."

"No, don't tell me you met some young thing and she put it on you and turned you out. How old is this woman?"

Rick looked at James and rubbed his chin and then smiled.

"You got it backward counselor. I turned her out, really turned her out. She is twenty-seven and all woman."

"What? You should be ashamed of yourself, a man your age dealing with a baby."

"There you go with that baby thing. You have been living a sheltered life too long my friend. She is no baby, she is smart, street wise, and very mature. This is no fantasy or romance novel. We both know what we want and are doing," Rick smiled, "don't hate on me, find your own," he leaned forward in his seat, "this girl is so good it should be illegal with the things that she can do."

James shook his head and pointed his finger at Rick.

"I will take your word for it and I hope you know what you are doing. Anyway, just be careful."

"I will and will stay in touch with you. Don't worry about Mr. Augular, he can't stay away forever. When he does come back, well let me just say, voodoo doesn't make him bullet proof and I will never forget what happened in Miami or to my partner Steve."

RONALD GRAY　　　　　(155)

"And I will never forget Sheila's husband David, but justice will prevail above all. Even for the Mr. Untouchable Victor Augular and his entire crooked organization."

"Amen counselor" he stood up, "time for me to leave and do some police work and have some more fun."

James stood up.

"I will walk you out." They walked toward his office door then James stopped walking and turned to face Rick, "be very careful my friend dealing with this case and in your personal life," he looked at Rick and takes one step toward the door, stopped and looked at him again, "one question," he put his hand on Rick's shoulder. "Is she really that fine and with a banging body?"

Rick looked at him and laughed.

"Counselor, she is beyond beautiful. She is what young people call a *Full seven*. Pretty in the face, slim in the waist, hips, lips, pretty painted finger tips, big butt, and a pretty smile." Rick makes a hand gesture. "Even in a dress, you can sit a cup on that ass."

"I didn't need that image in my head. You guys have all the fun." He laughed.

"You did ask. Take care of yourself counselor."

They walked out of his office and stopped in front of the desk where Diana was sitting.

"I will be in touch and don't worry Rick. Mr. Augular will fall." They shake hands and Rick walked out.

Diana looked up at James.

"Mr. Reed is everything all right."

"Diana, I have a feeling that very soon Mr. Augular and his empire are going to fall and anyone connected with him, including Ron and Keith," he looked at Diana, "I will not be able to protect them, Diana. Don't stop praying."

"I will never stop praying for Ron, his life, and soul. I thank you for everything that you have done and for giving me this job."

"You are more than welcome and you earned the job but God help Mr. Augular, wherever he is."

"Amen to that, Mr. Reed."

CHAPTER TWENTY SIX
Bogota Columbia

Victor is sitting outside under a large canopy in the back of his spacious private villa in Bogota Columbia. There is a large pool in the back and attractive ladies are walking around or lying down in lounge chairs around the pool in bathing suits. Two of his body guards are sitting at the table with him and the other three are walking around the pool observing their surroundings. All the bodyguards are wearing dress slacks and shirts carrying automatic weapons. Victor has on dress slacks and a dress shirt. One of his bodyguards approached his table.

"Mr. Augular, the grounds have been checked and all communications lines as well, everything is clear. Is there anything else?"

"No, that's fine for now but I'm expecting an important guest but I don't know when he will arrive or how but he will show up."

"That presents a security problem because no one could just walk in here. Security is far too tight and no one is that good unless you are talking about that devil Mr. Bones."

As the bodyguard was talking a very attractive lady wearing a revealing two-piece bathing suit walked up to the guard and purposely bumps into him. She looked at Victor, caressed her butt and walked closer to his table.

"Mr. Augular there is something that I desire to speak with you about, in private if you have the time."

Victor stood up.

"I'm interested in what you have to say but first I need to take care of some business. Afterwards, you will have my complete attention." He walked closer, kissed her on the cheek, and slid his hand inside her bikini bottom caressing her butt.

She looked at Victor with a very seductive smile.

"You have warm hands. I look forward to the rest of your direct attention. Call me when your business is complete." She caressed his cheek and walked away shaking her butt adding an extra bounce in her step.

Victor stared at her butt as she was walking.

"Very nice." He sat back down and looked at his bodyguards sitting next to him.

One of them turned to look at Victor.

"Mr. Augular what are you going to do about the hotel owner Frank Cantina? My source tells me he rejected your lucrative offer and he is going to move against you. Do we go to him or let him come to us?"

"Mr. Bones informed me that my two young entrepreneurs are about to put together a major drug deal through a big fashion show. Mr. Cantina does not know it yet but he will show up and so will we."

"Good and I hope he does something stupid because I'm bored and desire to kill a few people."

"And you are going to get your chance," he looked around at his body guards, "gentlemen play time is over. We will show up at this fashion show and Mr. Cantina will sign his hotel over to me. Then we kill him and take all the drug money. We will also kill Keith Washington and his chosen friend Ron O'Neil. After that we move our operation to Atlantic City, go completely legit and take over."

The guard rubs his automatic weapon.

"Very good sir, I like that. I never did like the two young punks anyway and I want to see just how God protected this Ron O'Neil really is."

Victor waved his hand at the guard.

"No, I have someone particular in mind for Ron, spiritual warfare. Good versus evil, the devil himself, Mr. Bones."

Suddenly a thick cloud of smoke appeared behind the bodyguard standing in front of Victor. The two guards sitting next to Victor quickly stood up and aimed their weapons at the smoke. The two guards walking by the pool aimed their weapons at the smoke. The guard standing in front of Victor quickly aimed his gun at the smoke and stepped away.

"What in the hell is that. Everybody inside," he yelled. We have you covered Mr. Augular."

All the ladies start screaming and run inside. When the smoke cleared Mr. Bones was standing there dressed in all black holding his cane and black pouch.

"Mr. Augular, you called. What can I do for you and tell your men to put their guns away because I'm already in a bad mood and want to kill somebody, really bad."

One of the guards stepped closer to Mr. Bones.

"How in the hell do you do that? It doesn't matter. Mr. Augular, say the word and we will cut him in two."

Mr. Bones pointed his cane at the guard.

"Boy, I told you I'm in a bad mood." he yelled, "Don't go to hell today and see your whore of a mother and your sorry drunk of a daddy. I gave him a heart attack and I gave your cheating mama aids. Sorry, dick sucking slut that she was."

The guard is so angry he is grinding his teeth while staring at Mr. Bones. He wants to pull the trigger so badly to cut his body in two after what he just said but he knows his time will come.

Victor stood up.

"Mr. Bones, you do make an entrance. Gentlemen relax, I need to speak with Mr. Bones privately, so excuse us, please."

The three bodyguards close to Victor lowered their guns and walked toward the other two guards at the end of the pool. All five are watching Victor.

"Mr. Bones, please sit down we need to talk."

He mumbled some words and tapped his cane on the ground, a chair slid over to him. He sat down and put his cane in his lap. And then opened his pouch and poured the bones in his hand.

"What can I do for you Mr. Augular?"

"Very interesting Mr. Bones. You need to teach me your tricks someday. Things have changed and I'm moving my operations to Atlantic City but there is some business that I need to take care of in Maryland before I leave."

"Say no more, the bones always know," he mumbled some words and threw his bones on the table and waved his hand over them. They begin to shake then stopped. "I have already informed you of the big fashion show in Maryland that Keith and Ron are arranging. It will go well. You want Mr. Cantina there and you want him dead."

"Good, I need protection for this deal but I also want Keith and Ron dead before I leave."

"So, shall it be. I have been waiting for Ron O'Neil to step out of the will of God so I can destroy him but he was still spiritually protected by God."

"So, what are you saying? You can't kill the boy. I thought you were the best. I guess Jesus does have all power."

Mr. Bones grabbed his bones and put them in his pouch and then stood up holding his cane and black pouch.

"Don't push it, Victor. I'm the best and can do anything. Consider Ron dead. I have to leave and I will see you back in Maryland." He walked away toward the pool.

A very attractive lady wearing a revealing one-piece bathing suit walked out of the villa and passed Mr. Bones. He turned around and looked at her.

"Girl, you sure have a fat ass on you. Shake what your momma gave you. All that junk in your trunk."

She turned around and looked at Mr. Bones with a look of total disgust on her face.

"Shut your mouth and you look ridiculous. I know you are hot wearing all that black. You look really stupid."

Mr. Bones leaned toward her staring so hard that his eyes looked like they would pop out.

"I was trying to be nice but now you made me mad. I know you. You have been whoring around a long time," he pointed his cane at her. "You are a nasty big butt freak. You take it up the butt and suck dicks like lollipops. Well, your lollipop dick sucking days are over and you can suck a dick good. Deep-throat type women. Suck a man's dick so good, you make him go cross-eyed. Now you and your fat ass are coming home with me." He quickly grabbed her hips and put his arm around her waist.

"Victor, help me, help me, Victor." She yelled.

"Shut up he can't help you," he smacked her on the butt. "Damn that thing jiggles." He mumbled some words and tapped his cane on the ground while staring at her. "Time to go to hell, you, stupid fat butt sinner."

She screamed and smoke appeared around them and when it cleared they are gone. The other bodyguards walked toward Victor and stood in front of his table and one of them touched him on the shoulder.

"Mr. Augular I don't know where you found him but he is unlike anything I have ever seen. He is the devil incarnate."

Victor stood up.

"Actually, I met him in the grave yard. He made me an offer that I could not refuse but I didn't know who he really was at that time. Now I'm sick of him and after our business in Maryland is over, I want him dead."

"Mr. Augular, we are the best at what we do but this guy is not human. The man or whatever he is has super-natural powers. How can we kill him?"

Victor walked around then stopped and stared at them.

"You will not. Mr. Case will. Mr. Bones is a powerful spirit, operating in a body. Mr. Case is an expert at destroying the body. Gentlemen, no one will defeat me and I mean no one. Not even the devil himself incarnate, Mr. Bones."

The same lady that was flirting with Victor earlier walked out of the villa toward his table. She stared at Victor then turned to look around the pool area and looked back at him.

RONALD GRAY   (163)

"Victor what in the hell was all that," she looked around again and back at Victor. "Never mind, I don't want to know. Are you finished with your business, Mr. Augular?"

He stepped toward her.

"As a matter of fact, I'm and you mentioned having a desire to speak with me. Well, I'm ready to listen."

She stepped closer to him.

"There are some things that one should not discuss in public. Will you come with me, please?"

He put his arm around her waist.

"It will be my pleasure," he whispered in her ear. "How is your head game? He kissed her on the cheek.

She smiled and looked at him.

"Why don't you let me show you? Production beats conversation any day. I do it all baby. I suck it, grip it, and hand slips it, and you can have all of me, front and in the back." She put her arm around his waist. They walked away with the guards following behind them and Victor's hand is inside her bikini bottom caressing her butt as they walk.

CHAPTER TWENTY SEVEN
Betrayal from a friend

It is Friday night. Christine and Tonya are sitting in a jail cell together. Both are dressed very nicely wearing heels and tight dresses. They were on their way to a club. Christine is thinking this entire scene over in her head. How did she end up in jail for the first time in her life? She regrets ever answering the phone. She had been ignoring Tonya's many phone calls and text messages for some time but on this one night, she was feeling very lonely and bored. She wanted to go out somewhere but didn't want to go by herself.

She remembers saying out loud sitting on her sofa at home. "I'm bored and want to go somewhere," somebody call me! She laughed and looked around to see who was watching and felt like she was losing it. Twenty minutes later, Tonya called her cell phone. She looked at the caller ID and was going to ignore her as usual, but the urge to answer it was overwhelming. So, she answered the phone, regretting that she didn't follow her instinct. Tonya talked her into going out and she was coming over to pick Christine up.

Christine knew this was a bad idea but she wanted to go out. She picked out something to wear, jumped in the shower and was dressed when Tonya arrived at her house. The moment she answered the door she knew it was a mistake. Tonya was standing there looking even better than the last time they saw each other. The night they watched porn movies ruined Christine's life.

RONALD GRAY   (165)

She didn't want to tell Tonya but she did miss her friendship and seeing her again brought back all kinds of thoughts and memories of them together which Christine was trying not to even think about. Tonya walked in and hugged Christine tightly, too tight for Christine's comfort. She invited Tonya in and when she did Tonya grabbed and smacked her on the butt and laughed. Christine ignored her. They shared some wine together, then left.

Christine was driving when Tonya decided to pull out some weed and started smoking. She told Tonya to put it away but she slid her hand up Christine's dress which made her jump and swerve the car a little. A police car was behind Christine and she was pulled over. Christine was arrested for driving while drunk and possession of marijuana. Her car was taken and she and Tonya was booked and put in jail on a fifty-thousand-dollar bond, apiece. She felt so ashamed and foolish. Once again her disobedience to God cost her pain, first her sister Sandra, now this. She finally broke down and called Sheila. Tonya was trying to play hard. Christine and Sheila talked, and then Sheila called James. Christine was waiting on James to come and get her out. She looked over at Tonya and could not stand the sight of her, sitting over there with that smug look on her face.

Tonya knew she had messed up badly and had no way of getting out of this situation except to depend on Christine. She knew right now Christine didn't want anything to do with her and was giving her a look of pure hate, so she had to play on her emotions and her spiritual beliefs.

"Christine, I know your mom's attorney friend is coming to get you out but please don't leave me here. I have no one to call and it's the weekend, all kinds of women will be coming in here. They might try to jump or rape me or something, please help me. Christine knew Tonya was running game on her but she still could not leave her in jail. If something happened to her while she was here, she would never be able to forgive herself, so she decided to help her if she could. She was not sure if James could or even would help her. She looked over at Tonya and spoke with much attitude.

"I don't know what I can do for you but I will try to help by talking to Mr. Reed and see what he can do if anything."

"Thank you, Christine. Is he married? Is he nice looking?" Christine could not believe this girl.

"Are you kidding me? You are in jail and all you can think about is sex. Unbelievable." She exhaled and shook her head at Tonya, "not that it matters but no he is not married and yes he is very nice looking, satisfied."

Tonya started scheming in her head already on how she could use this situation to her advantage.

"I was just asking. I wonder what is taking him so long, it is already one o'clock in the morning."

"I don't know but he is a man of his word. If he said he will be here, he will. Oh God, I hope he comes soon."

James has worked hard for years in his legal field taking on high profile cases reaping him large percentage pay outs. Now he is a multi-millionaire and he lives in Potomac, Maryland, the richest area in all of Maryland. He has an eight million dollar, four-car garage, seven-bedroom mansion sitting on three acres. He was relaxing at home in his sweats when he got the message from Sheila about Christine being arrested with a friend. Once again, he was shocked. Sheila was crying very hard on the phone practically begging him to go get her baby out of jail. He would never turn his back on Sheila and he told her he would do what he could to help.

Sheila and her family have been through so much and he knew she was depending on him. He would not let her down. He got up, got dressed in his usual business attire of an Armani suit, custom-made shoes, no less than two thousand dollars, dress shirt and expensive tie, Rolex watch and his nine-millimeter gun. In his business, you never know what will happen. He sprayed on some Clive Christian cologne at twenty- three hundred dollars a bottle. He walked to his garage and got in his white two-hundred ninety thousand dollar 2012 Bentley Mulsanne and put the gun in the glove compartment and drove to the jail.

James made some calls while he was driving to get the details about Christine and her friend's arrest. He already arranged for them to be released in his custody. It pays to have friends in the right places. Everyone knew James was a straight up guy and that his word was priceless. He arrived at the jail and signed them both out and waited for them to be brought out.

Christine and Tonya were escorted out to James by one of the correctional officers. The moment Christine saw him she ran and hugged him, holding on for dear life. She was so happy to see him she hugged him again and kissed his neck.

"Mr. Reed, thank you so much for coming to get me. God, I thank you. I don't know how I'm ever going to repay you."
James knew she would be happy to see him but didn't expect this and he noticed how tight her dress was. He had to suppress his thoughts of her for brief seconds when Christine pressed her

RONALD GRAY   (168)

body on him so tightly. She is very attractive and has a serious body on her. James felt bad for even having these thoughts about her. She was his dear friend Sheila's daughter. He brushed it aside and noticed Christine's friend staring at him like he was the last pork chop on the table. Now, this girl was fine but off limits to him as well.

"It is no problem Christine and don't worry about paying me back, we can talk later. Your mom and I have been friends for years. You know I will always look out for her and the family." Tonya was staring at James and thinking. *This man is fine, well-dressed and wearing a thirty thousand dollar Rolex watch. Yea, he is loaded. I know how I can pay him*, she laughed to herself. She walked over and introduced herself, extending her hand out to James.

"Mr. Reed, hi I'm Tonya and I truly thank you for all of your help. Now, can we get out of this place, please?"

"I second that, I'm so ready to leave this place." Christine grabbed his hand.

All three of them walked out of the building toward his car. The moment they got to his car Christine and Tonya say at the same time.

"Is this your car?"

James laughed because he is used to people responding like this when they find out what he drives and where he lives.

"Yes, the car is mine, get in." He opened the door for them and Christine got in the front and Tonya got in the back and he drove away. While he was driving James was thinking he should make a few things clear.

RONALD GRAY   (169)

"I was able to get you two released into my custody after I signed your fifty thousand dollar bonds, but the DA would only do that if I agreed to have you two on house arrest at my place. Tonya, I don't know you but because you are friends with Christine I agreed to help you but know this, I never play games with the legal system and if you decide to run. I know some professional skip-tracers who are very good at catching people no matter where they go and they will bring you back. If this happens, I will make sure you get the max. Is that clear?"

Tonya leaned forward in her seat putting her hand on James' shoulder and her face close to the back of his neck. Anything she can do to seduce him, she will.

"Mr. Reed, I would never run and I appreciate all that you have and will do for me. I will find some way to pay you back." She was thinking. *If he only knew how good my head game was.* She leaned back and enjoyed the ride in this exquisite car.

Christine knew exactly what Tonya meant when she said that. They reached the gate to the front entrance of his house. He pushed a button on the steering wheel, the gate opened, and then he drove through, stopping at his garage. He pushed a button on a remote and the garage doors opened revealing his Lamborghini, S600 Benz, and Cadillac Escalade.

"Oh my God, will you look at this house and your cars, I need to go to law school." Tonya said smiling and hitting James on his shoulder.

"Mr. Reed, I have known you for years and never knew you had it like this until now. Wow, my brother, you are truly balling."

James laughed.

RONALD GRAY   (170)

"Well, I thank you, Christine. Tonya as far as you going to law school, let's focus on getting you out of this trouble first."

After pulling into the garage they got out and go inside his house through a side door in the garage. They walk in and as everyone else, they are amazed at the size and the decorations in the house. He gives them the tour and showed them to their separate rooms upstairs. James gives them two of his new large T-shirts to wear for tonight, promising to do better tomorrow.

Tonya and Christine take a shower in their rooms and put on the T-shirts with nothing on underneath. Christine put her and Tonya's clothes in the washing machine in the basement. After getting out of the shower Tonya walked to Christine's room with her T-shirt tied on the side so it will fit tighter and show her figure. They talked for a while feeling much better now since they were out of that nasty jail cell. Tonya sat on Christine's bed as they were talking and she would lightly touch her as they talked trying to seduce her. Christine was feeling horny but refused Tonya's advances so Tonya finally left Christine's room.

James was coming out of the shower in his room when his cell phone rang. He quickly wrapped a towel around him and answered it, knowing it's Sheila from the caller ID.

"Hi Sheila...yes, I have your baby and her friend...I know you want to fuss at her but I do not think now is the best time, let me talk to her first...yes, I promise I will talk to her...yes you are more than welcome...I know you trust me to handle this situation and I will keep you posted...yes, I will call you tomorrow, I promise...goodnight Sheila."

As he put his phone away he heard someone calling his name. Having so much on his mind and not really thinking, he walked to his bedroom door with the towel still wrapped around his body. When he opened the door, Tonya was standing there looking very sexy with her T-shirt hugging her body. She made sure when she tied it in a knot that it fit just below her butt cheeks, hugging her ample butt. It was then that James realized he was still wearing the towel around his waist. He became immediately aroused by seeing Tonya like this, which revealed the outline of his erection under his towel.

Tonya could not be happier to catch James like this, seeing the embarrassment on his face and his erection that she was staring at. He had a nice body as well.

"Mr. Reed, I apologize for disturbing you but I wanted to say thank you again for getting me out of that nasty hell hole."

James was caught off guard by her appearance and he was trying to stay focused but he could not take his eyes off Tonya's body. Her nipples were protruding under her shirt and she has nice-sized breasts and he knew she didn't have on any underwear. His erection was growing by the minute, sticking straight up under his towel and he was rock hard. Trying to regain his composure, he focused on looking at her eyes.

"Tonya, hi. I apologize for how I'm dressed but I do live alone and didn't expect anyone to knock on my door. You are welcome for my help, just don't forget what I said and all will be well and I will do what I can to help you."

Tonya looked down at his erection and knew he was working with something.

"It looks like you could use some help now yourself." She smiled and looked down at his erection again then looked back up at him. She stepped closer to James, quickly reaching out

RONALD GRAY   (172)

putting her hand under his towel grabbing his erection feeling his size and the heat from it. Yea it was nice she thought. She leaned forward and kissed his lips stroking him at the same time.

Tonya's hand felt good on him but James was caught off-guard by her boldness. He quickly slapped her hand away and stepped back from her.

"Tonya, you got the wrong impression about me. Go to bed." He closed his door in her face and stood against the door rock hard thinking how badly he really wanted her. Talk about a moral struggle, the girl was all that.

Tonya walked away disappointed but thought to herself, *another time Mr. Reed, another time.* She walked back to her room and masturbated thinking about James making love to her then she fell asleep.

James laid down on his bed to relax and he dozed off. He slept about an hour before he got up because he was thirsty. He walked to his kitchen to get some ice for his drink, still wearing his towel. As he walked in the kitchen his refrigerator door was open and Christine was bending over looking in it. Her T-shirt was tied the same as Tonya's except now, her shirt was up on her lower back showing all her butt and crotch area. She has a small waist, hips and a nice, round big butt. James stopped walking and stared at her bending over and he was rock hard once again.

Christine felt someone behind her. Thinking it was Tonya and feeling horny, she decided to tease her a little just to irritate her knowing she was not going to do anything with her. Without even looking back, still bent over, she reached between her legs and started rubbing herself then slid one finger inside, sliding it in and out making herself very wet and very horny. She knew Tonya loved dirty talk so she decided to give this to her as well.

"I know you want some of this nice tight, wet pussy Tonya. I can feel you staring at my ass." She laughed and turn around to get the shock of her life when she saw James standing there staring at her with a towel wrapped around his waist, with a full erection and a tight body. She quickly covered her mouth with her hand in total embarrassment.

"Oh my God, Mr. Reed, oh my God, I'm so sorry. I didn't know it was you." She quickly untied her T-shirt, pulling it down which it fell below her knees. She was beyond embarrassed for her and Mr. Reed but she also wanted to know why he never said anything and stared at her the entire time and was rock-hard under his towel.

Twice in one night, James was caught off guard but this was so much worse. Seeing Sheila's daughter like this and her seeing him like he is now, is just too much. His decision! Say nothing. He quickly walked to the cabinet to get a glass then walked to the refrigerator. Ignoring Christine standing there, though his erection was still present, he opened the freezer but inadvertently brushed against her thigh as he got ice out. Then walked down to his fully furnished basement and started watching his big screen TV, drinking Cîroc.

Christine stayed in the kitchen for a while, thinking. She didn't know what to do but she felt like she had to say something to James. Twenty minutes later she walked down to the large basement. It was dark and the only light was coming from the TV. Christine was walking very quietly and saw James sitting on the sofa. She stopped about ten feet from him when she noticed he was watching a porn movie and was masturbating. She was already horny but seeing James like this, stroking his big dick, made her wet and increased her desire for him. She walked closer to the sofa. James was so frustrated he thought watching a good porn and relieving himself would release some stress, so he did and was close to release when he heard his name called again.

"Mr. Reed."

James quickly turned his head and the last person he wanted to see right now was Christine and she was standing close to the sofa. He quickly grabbed his towel to cover himself.

"Christine, what are doing down here? I can't believe this is happening to me." He said frowning.

Christine sat on the sofa next to him but James moved away from her. She was staring at his hard-on under the towel and looked up at him.

"Mr. Reed, please listen to me before you freak out. I'm not a little girl. I'm over twenty-one, you are not my daddy, and I'm not trying to set you up. I'm an adult, attracted to another adult. I have never been with a man and I want you to be my first. Please let me do something to pay you back for helping me, please." She said with a look of seduction and innocence at the same time.

James was looking at her like she was crazy.

"Christine, you can talk to me. Are you on drugs?"
"No, I'm not and don't do this. Don't treat me like I'm some child or that I'm playing a game."

"Fine! This never happened and you need to go to bed, goodnight." He said with attitude.

RONALD GRAY   (175)

Christine moved closer to him, rubbing his leg making sure he does not totally lose his erection. She quickly slid her hand under his towel and grabbed his dick. Feeling a real one for the first time is very exciting and stimulating for her, making her desire him even more. It is so hard and hot in her hand.

James stood up to get away from her but she quickly grabbed his towel pulling it off him. He is standing there with a full hard-on.

"Christine stop," he yelled, "this is all wrong. I'm going to bed and you should too and give me back my damn towel." He leaned forward and tried to grab the towel away from her.

Christine used his forward motion to grab his hand, pulling him on the sofa and he lands on his back. She is so horny she grabbed his erection which is sticking straight up in the air and lowered her mouth on it, quickly sucking it like she saw the women doing in the porn movies.

James can't believe this is happening to him and wanted to stop her but it felt good, her mouth is hot.

Christine continued sucking and licking his dick like she has been doing this for years and every image in those porn movies she saw was coming instantly back to her. She could tell he was close to erupting in her mouth, so she stopped.

"I want you to be my first, don't leave me like this, I'm so horny and wet, make love to me, please."

James can't believe he is even considering what Christine was asking but his body moved all on its own. He leaned forward and kissed her for the first time. Her lips are so soft and warm and she allowed his tongue to invade her mouth sucking on it. He lowered her body down on the sofa pulling her T-shirt up. James slowly licked and sucked on her breast making her nipples erect. He kissed and licked her neck, stomach, hips, and legs then moved back up slowly spreading Christine legs apart licking and sucking on her wetness.

Christine was trembling from his touch and ready to climax from his tongue action.

"James, I want you now, please put it inside me. I want to feel you but don't be rough."

He can't believe what he was about to do. She is a virgin, but again, his body betrayed him and he moved up spreading her legs further apart and back. He slowly started sliding himself inside her and she is tight but wet, which helps him. He pushed himself in more and more until he was all the way in.

Christine has been looking forward to this day for years and wanted him so badly, but this hurt. She had to bite down on her lip to keep from screaming. She didn't know it would hurt this much and he is not small but it was too late now to turn back. She was determined to continue this to the end. So, she slowly started moving and some of the pain was replaced with pleasure. She started moaning now because it was feeling good, so she grabbed James butt, pushing him into her even more.

"Oh, James please don't stop, make love to me, I want you." With each passing, second, he was feeling guilty but the calling of his own sexual desires to be satisfied was great along with his desire to please her. Feeling Christine relax and watching her being satisfied caused him to slowly increase his thrusting, making her wetter. He was feeling his own nut coming close so he started sliding inside her faster and deeper.

"Oh yes James, that's it, make love to me, you feel so good inside me," she pulled his neck down so she can kiss him and wrapped her arms around his neck kissing his lips with passion, staring into his eyes, "Oh this feels good. I will be your lady James, just give it to me," she bites his lips and wrapped her legs around his waist pulling him into her, "you want me to say it, baby. I want you to fuck me, fuck me, James. You can have me whenever and however you want. I will even let you have my ass. Just don't leave me like my daddy did. That's it, fuck your bitch. Ohhhh James, yes I'm your hot bitch, now fuck me James, I'm going to cum, ohhhh I'm cumming," she gripped him tighter with her legs, "you feel so good in me, don't leave me James, please don't leave me, ohhhh James I'm cummming on you!"

The moment Christine mentioned her dad, James wanted to vomit. He felt so guilty at what he was doing to her but couldn't stop because she was feeling too good and he was close as well.

"I won't leave you Christine, I can't hold it baby, and you are so tight, ahhhhh."

She knew this was what so many men like, a woman who is wet, tight, and freaky to make love to. She started throwing her body into him as hard as she could to make sure she fully pleased him.

They both finished and James was soft but still inside her. He slowly pulled out and was about to get up when Christine pulled him back down, grabbing his neck looking directly in his eyes.

"No! Where are you going? You said you would not leave me," she started crying, "don't leave me. Don't ever leave me James, please don't leave me. You can have me, just don't leave me," she was crying even harder holding on to him tighter and kissing him hard on the lips and staring in his eyes. "James, I promise to be whatever you want me to be. I will treat you so good and be nasty for you, suck your dick every day when you come home from work. I'm your lady, your hot bitch, and I will be as freaky as you want me to be. You want to watch me," she leaned back and slid her finger inside her moving it fast looked in his eyes, "Is this it baby? Is this what you want? Oh, it feels good and I like making myself cum." She increased her pace faster and faster.

James reached down and stopped her.

"Stop!" He pulled her into him holding her tight.

Christine started crying hard.

"Just don't leave me. My dad left me. Don't ever leave me. I will do anything that you want, just don't leave me, please."

He held her tight and was thinking. *What in the world have I done, Lord what have I done. Forgive me Lord, forgive me.* He continued to hold her.

James and Christine were so into what they were doing on the sofa, they never noticed Tonya standing at the foot of the stairs watching the entire scene. She slowly walked back up the stairs and into her room lying down on the bed. She was so turned on by all that she saw. She quickly took her T-shirt off and started caressing her entire body. Tonya is rolling all over on the bed, back and forth caressing her body. She was so horny. She had her finger in her pussy and ass, pleasing herself until she exploded. Her juices were all over the bed, but she still couldn't stop fingering herself. She wanted more. She continued until she was exhausted and fell asleep.

RONALD GRAY   (179)

James was finally able to get Christine to calm down. He carried her up the stairs and into her room, laying her down on the bed. He was walking away to leave when she grabbed him, begging him not to leave her. James didn't want to but he laid next to her, holding her until she fell asleep in his arms. James was thinking. *How could he ever look Sheila in the eyes again, how could he look at Christine the same*? He slowly slid away from her and got on his knees by the side of the bed to pray.

"Father, forgive me for what I have done and have mercy on my soul," tears begin to flow from his eyes and he laid face down on the floor muffling his crying. "Forgive me, Lord, Sheila trusted me, now look how I have sinned and betrayed Sheila. How could I have done this horrible thing? Forgive me oh Lord, please."

CHAPTER TWENTY EIGHT

James House

James is lying on his bed in his silk pajama pants and although his blinds are closed in his room, the sun is still peeking through which makes him think about the true power of God. How light will always overcome darkness and right now he feels so dark and guilty thinking about all that happened last night. He is determined to deal with this situation fast and direct. He was thinking who he could call in the DA's office for a favor which he does not like doing but this is an exceptional situation for him. He was going to help Christine at all cost no matter what. He made a few calls to some friends explaining the situation and they promised to check into it and call him back later. James was thinking so hard he drifted off to sleep.

Christine was lying in bed under the covers still wearing her T-shirt thinking about many things. What happened with her and Tonya sexually, getting in legal trouble, ending up in jail and having sex last night with James. She felt horrible about seducing him and her own shame was eating her up on the inside. Although it hurt for a while and it didn't help that James was not small, but after she relaxed it got better and it was so good. As bad and as guilty as she feels now, she wants more sex. Thinking about it was making her horny so she pulled her cover down, pulled her T-shirt up and started rubbing between her legs, making herself wet. Christine was so into what she was doing that she never noticed Tonya standing there in her door way.

Seeing Christine like this made Tonya instantly horny and to think, she was coming to apologize to her for everything and was going to promise to leave her alone sexually. Also, she was going to tell Christine she saw her and Mr. Reed last night having sex but was going to keep this to herself. Now she realized she could use that sexual encounter to her advantage.

Tonya quietly walked into her room and closed the door walking over to the bed staring at her.

"You look so sexy doing that."

Christine jumped and quickly pulled the cover up to cover herself.

"Tonya, what are you doing in my room? Get out of here, now."

"No! I want you so badly right now." She pulled the cover off Christine, laid down next to her, quickly kissing her.

Christine pushed Tonya off her.

"Stop, I want you out of here now! Are you crazy?"

Tonya quickly grabbed Christine's T-shirt, pulled it up and started rubbing her wetness then slid her finger inside her.

"Christine, I want you, please let me have you. I saw you and Mr. Reed last night in the basement having sex. I saw everything, Christine. How does it feel to finally get some dick and no longer being a virgin?" She started kissing and sucking her neck while fingering her.

Christine felt so low and ashamed not wanting anyone to know what she did, let alone Tonya of all people. She wanted Tonya to stop but it felt too good, she started crying.

"Tonya, please stop. Don't do this to me. I want to live right, ohhhh Tonya."

RONALD GRAY   (182)

Tonya knew she had Christine now so she passionately kissed her and Christine kissed her back with their tongues in each other's mouth.

"Do you want me to stop Christine, do you really want me to stop?" Fingering her faster and deeper.

"No, please don't stop, it feels so damn good baby, ohhhh Tonya, I'm cumming."

They continue to have sex until falling asleep in each other's arms.

It was eleven o'clock and James, cell phone was ringing. He answered it and listening to the person talking put a huge smile on his face. He hung up the phone and jumped off the bed dancing in place.

"Thank you, Jesus, thank you Lord!" He calmed down and sat on the bed. He was told all charges against Christine and Tonya were dropped, it never happened and the incident would never be spoken of. However, he had to lose the fifty-thousand-dollar bond money on Christine and Tonya to which he quickly agreed. A hundred grand is a small price for him to pay. He was so excited he put a T-shirt on walking to Christine's room to give her the good news. As he was approaching her room he saw Tonya coming out wearing her T-shirt. He stopped walking, wanting to keep his distance from her. She walked within arms distance to him, grinning.

"How does it feel to have sex with a virgin James? Shame on you. I saw you two having sex. I'm not Christine and I would have fucked you so damn good."

Christine walked out and sees Tonya standing close to James.

James quickly walked away from Tonya and over to Christine, smiling at her.

"Good morning Christine. I was just coming to your room to give you some great news. I called in some favors, you and Tonya's charges have been dropped. It never happened."

Christine heard him but was in shock and then the news hit her. She started jumping up and down, screaming running over to Tonya where they both started jumping up and down.

James was just looking at them, thanking God to himself that all of this happened so fast.

Christine walked over to James hugged and thanked him, then walked into her room closing the door but still jumping up and down, thanking God. Tonya walked over to James but he backed away, not trusting her at all.

She stepped closer to him.

"Thank you for everything, Mr. Reed. Is there anything I can do to show you my appreciation," she leaned forward? "You already got your pay from Christine?" Smiling at him.

James stared at her because she is very attractive but dangerous to deal with.

"No, I'm okay. You and Christine will be leaving today," he stared at her. "Try to stay out of trouble, if you can." He said with a smirk on his face.

She blows James a kiss and walked away shaking her butt hard.

James was looking at her butt and speaks just above a whisper.

"Damn she got a fat ass."

Tonya stopped walking and looked back at James.

RONALD GRAY   (184)

"I heard that. Baby, you don't have to just look at my ass, you can have it. My pussy and ass are so sweet." She pulled her T-shirt up and turned around showing all her butt to him, caressing it. She looked at him and walked to Christine's room door then stopped to look back at James. "Too bad you don't want all of this. Christine loves to bury her face between my legs." She winked at him and opened the door and walked in.

James was standing there thanking God for giving him the strength to do the right thing because he wanted to teach her a lesson she would never forget. She has a perfect round, heart-shaped butt begging for some serious attention. To have her and Christine would be most men fantasy, but the result would be spiritual death. He shook his head not wanting to figure it out. He quickly walked back to his room and called Sheila telling her the great news. She screamed so loudly in the phone it hurt his ear but he fully understood. He listened to her and then made an excuse to get off the phone, feeling guilty talking to her because of what he had done. He shook his head.

"Lord, forgive me."

CHAPTER TWENTY NINE
Separated but Close

Stacy has been feeling guilty lately about how she has been treating Diana and ignoring her, so she decided to call and invite her over so they could talk. Dressed to impress, Stacy was wearing tan Dolce Gabbana pumps, dark blue jeans tailor made by a designer from Milan to fit her curvaceous body, and a short sleeved, low-cut, cream colored blouse which perfectly reveals just enough of her breast. She shops in Bijan, the most expensive store in the world located in Beverly Hills, on Rodeo Drive and shopping is by appointment only.

Diana called Ron that morning telling him how much she was missing him. They agreed to meet later that day for lunch. She was going to visit Stacy first so they can talk and then go see Ron. She knew he would try to seduce her, so she wanted to look nice for him but not slutty.

Diana put on a Victoria Secret bra, thong underwear, Dolce Gabbana cream-colored heels, black tight jeans from Gucci and a grey blouse showing just a little cleavage. She checked herself in the full-length mirror at Sheila's where she is staying, she had to admit, she looked good. Naturally pretty face with flawless skin, long legs, small waist, hips and a nice, round butt. All of this for her husband. Grandma Harris and Sheila teased her before she left about how she was dressed knowing she was going to give up some booty to her husband. She smiled, hugged them both and got in her Bentley and drove off to see Stacy.

Diana was a little nervous about going to see Stacy because of their past but that's where it will stay, in the past. She parked her car in front of the building and walked in. She could feel the guard's eyes staring at her when she was walking away from his desk going to the elevator. It always made her uncomfortable when guys stared at her with pure lust in their eyes but she was trying to get used to it. She really missed Ron whenever this happened because she knew he would always protect her.

Diana got off the elevator walking to Stacy's condo when this guy opened his door to take his trash out and sees her.

"Damn lady, please tell me you just moved into this building. You are gorgeous and your body is lovely, damn you are fine."

Diana could not help but laugh at what he said. She turned to look at him, not bad looking she thought but nothing compared to my Ron. She kept walking. She knocked on Stacy's door.

Stacy opened the door and was surprised to see how Diana was dressed.

"Damn girl, you look good, come on in."

Diana walked in and they stood in the living room staring at each other.

"Stacy, you always look good and hi."

They hugged and Stacy grabbed her butt but Diana pushed her off.

"Stop, you know that's over between us and you know how I'm living."

"I know but I had to at least try you," smiling at her, "come and sit down so we can talk."

They sat down on the sofa.

"Diana, I don't apologize too often to anyone but I have been feeling bad about how I have been treating you. You are a good friend and Keith is my only real, true friend, so not having you around makes me miss your funny acting self." She looked at her. "Girl, you are looking really good and I know you didn't get dressed up like this just to come see me. If you did, I know I'm going to get me some Diana booty." She started laughing.

Diana playfully hits Stacy on her leg and laughed.

"You are something else and I miss you too, and no, I didn't dress like this to see you. I'm meeting Ron later and I wanted to look nice for him. I want him to see what he is missing."

Stacy claps her hands.

"Thank you, Jesus, you are using your brains. Diana, I know where you are coming from and I'm not trying to get in your marriage but living right or not, Ron is still your husband. No, I don't agree with you moving out, to me that's just crazy but it is your choice. Not having sex with your own husband is just stupid! He is faithful to you," she is thinking. *Thank God I walked in on him and Cynthia because she would have taken him away from you, the girl is a super freak, so she heard*, "and he loves the ground you walk on. Ain't no way, I would just give a man like him up to these gold digging, get on their knees, suck dick quick, freaks out here."

Diana shook her head.

"Stacy, you really are something and you have a way with words but you are right and you know how much I love my husband. I have been praying, asking God for wisdom but some things are just common sense. Ron is living foul but he is a good man to me and I do not want to lose him. I don't want to be used just for sex but I do miss my husband."

"And you should miss him. You two are a great match for each other. You are hot in the pants although you try to cover it up. I know you miss getting all that tongue and good dick. He is licking and sucking that sweetness and the dick is good, right?" She leaned back laughing.

"You are so disgusting Stacy and it is none of your business about how good my husband's loving is."

Stacy pointed her finger at Diana.

"See, that's your problem. I didn't say loving. I said dick, not penis or loving but dick. Say dick. Say yes Stacy, I miss my husband's good, hard dick." She said laughing.

Diana hit her on the leg.

"I'm not saying that at least not to you." Smiling at her. "Look, let's go have some fun and go shopping before you meet up with Ron, my treat."

"Girl, you read my mind," she reached into her jean pocket and pulled out a credit card, showing Stacy. "Ron got me a Visa black card, in case I needed anything."

Stacy reached into her jean pocket and pulled out a credit card.

"I have Keith's Visa black card, with his security code. It allows me to spend up to five hundred thousand dollars, without his permission. So, let's shop."

"Let's shop. How about Georgetown?"

"Paris, France would be better but Georgetown it is. Let's go." They get up to leave and Diana is walking in front. Stacy was looking at her hips.

RONALD GRAY   (189)

"Damn girl, Ron is going to be glad to see you with those tight jeans on, shaking butt and hips."

Diana turned around and looked at Stacy.

"I shake it very well for my baby." She winked at her and opened the door to leave.

Stacy walked up behind her and smacked her on the butt.

"I know how well you shake that ass."

Diana turned around and looked at her, smiled and kept walking. They walked out and got in Diana's Bentley and drove away.

They drove all over Georgetown, going from shop to shop, buying shoes and clothes. Stacy and Diana look like super stars walking down the street. Men and women stare, and people tried talking to them but they ignored all of them. They ended up at Market Street Diamond jewelry store, looking at some diamond bracelets. Two men and one lady were working in the store. Two young guys came in being loud and dressed like thugs. They wore nice new gear but thuggish. You could tell they had money but were not used to having it. They stared at Diana and Stacy hard. One of the guys stepped closer to them.

"Damn you two look like super stars waiting to be pampered." He pointed to his friend, "my homie and I are celebrating, so why don't you two roll with some real ballers like us and get treated like queens."

Stacy and Diana looked at them and laughed.

"Thanks, but no thanks, we don't step down, we step up. You two have a nice day." Stacy said looking at them.

The other guy walked closer to Diana, lightly touching her on the butt.

"No disrespect baby, I see that ring on your hand but some ladies wear rings as a front. You and those tight jeans hugging your hips and ass look damn good. Let me spoil you for the day and we will see what happens."

Diana backed up from him becoming instantly angry, pointing her finger in his face.

"One, I don't know you, and two, don't you ever touch me again, and three, get away from me!"

"Look, I was trying to be nice to you bitch, you are not all of that, so back down and keep it real." looking at Diana like she was dirt.

Stacy quickly got her cell phone out and sent Keith a text message with their emergency code then walked over to Diana pulling her razor out and stepped to the guy talking to Diana.

"Fool, are you crazy disrespecting her? Do you call your mother a bitch?" Staring at him with hostility in her demeanor.

The other guy sees the razor in Stacy's hand and he knows she is a real street girl. He pulled his gun from his pants and walked over to her holding his gun down by his side.

"I see that razor in your hand and you see this gun. Don't make me put a hole in you and your friend." Staring at her with contempt in his eyes.

Stacy and Diana look at his gun. One of the men working in the store walked over to them.

"Excuse me but this is not the streets. Whatever problems you all have, take it outside and don't come back. We don't tolerate this type of behavior in here."

The guys looked at the man and Stacy and Diana look at each other then walked toward the door. Both guys grabbed them on the butt when they were walking. Diana quickly turned around swinging at the guy who grabbed her butt but he backed up and pulled a gun on her, pointing it in her face. Stacy quickly turned around swinging her razor on the guy who grabbed her, but he also moved away and aimed his gun at her. The store owner pointed at them, yelling for them to all get out before he calls the police!

Ron was driving his Bentley and Keith was in his Benz. They quickly pulled up in front of the diamond store with five S600s Benz's right behind them with two *Young Wolves* in each car. Keith and Ron quickly got out of the car, walked to the store and the *Young Wolves* followed them. Keith, Ron and the *Young Wolves* wore black boots, black pants, grey shirt, and a grey jacket that said, *"Young Wolves Inc."* on the back, and all of them were carrying Mac-10's machine guns under their jackets. Stacy and Diana walked out of the store and ran over to Ron and Keith, and hugged them.

The two guys walked out but their guns were in their waist and they saw all the men. They knew of the *Young Wolves* and now realized they were in major trouble but they refused to back down.

Stacy and Diana pointed to the two guys saying they are the ones who grabbed them. Keith and Ron walked over to them revealing their Mac-10s. The *Young Wolves behind* them did the same.

"You two fools put your hands on these two ladies?" Ron pointed to Diana and Stacy.

The two guys looked at each other trying not to show any signs of weakness but they knew the odds are against them. One of them stepped closer to Ron.

"We didn't know they were with you, but damn man you can't blame a brother for trying. As fat as the hips and asses are on these bitches, you know the game." Smiling at Ron and Keith.

Ron hit the guy with an upper cut to the chin and one to the jaw, knocking him down then pulled his gun out aiming it at him. The other guy reached for his gun but Keith and the *Young Wolves* pulled their Mac-10s out aiming it at him. The very thought of someone else grabbing Stacy's butt was making Keith angrier. He hit the other guy in the jaw with his Mac-10. Blood and teeth fly out of his mouth as he hits the ground. The store owner and the other employees come out of the store waving at them to leave because he called the police. People driving and walking by are looking, wondering what is going on. You can hear the police sirens getting closer. Keith nods to his men. Four of them quickly grabbed the two guys on the ground and put them in the cars and drove off.

Diana walked up to Stacy looking at her with concern.

"What is going to happen to them?"

Stacy stared at her.

"You don't want to know."

"What does that mean? I do want to know. Okay, they grabbed our butts but they don't deserve to die just for that. This is crazy."

"Diana, you really need to get a grip. I'm the lady of a high-profile young, black, rich man. And you married one. Get real."

The other six *Young Wolves* are standing by looking around. Keith nods at them again and they drove off. Keith and Ron dap up and Keith grabbed Stacy's hand, got into his Benz and watched everybody else get into their rides. Everyone quickly drove off.

Three police cars pulled up in front of the jewelry store. Two police officers are in each car. They got out and begun asking people questions. The only thing consistent with everyone's story is, the guy's jackets said, *Young Wolves Inc.* The officers nod their heads at each other, knowing who they are.

Ron and Diana ride in silence back to the house. He pulled up to the house, got out and opened the car door for her, helping her get out.

Diana tapped Ron on the arm.

"Ron wait," she grabbed his hand and stared at him, "thank you for coming to help me, it means a lot to me."

"Diana, you say that as if I'm some stranger, or I don't care about you. Remember this, we are separated by your choice. Stupid choice but I'm still your husband who loves you deeply, so get real and stop playing these games, bring your butt home where you belong." Staring at her, he stepped closer and kissed her on the lips.

Diana can't help but kiss Ron back and looked at him feeling his words of truth and irritation in his voice. She does not like being treated like property but she knows this is not the time. She knew in her heart that he was right.

They walked into the house and to the bedroom. Ron stopped and stared at her, realizing just how beautiful and sexy she looked today. He grabbed her by the waist looking at her.

RONALD GRAY   (194)

"You do look great and you know it. Damn, you are wearing those jeans. You got a fat ass on you," smiling at her. "I don't blame those fools for trying to talk to you. If I saw you for the first time, as fine as you are, I would try to talk to you too. Pretty face, hips, and ass for days." He smacked her on the butt.

Diana smiled and pushed him away.

"Ron, you have a one-track mind, you know that. All you men lose your mind over a woman in a pair of tight jeans."

"No, we don't. It's not the jeans baby, it's who is wearing the jeans and what she looks like. Tight jeans on an ugly woman with a flat ass don't mean a thing. Now when you are as gorgeous as you, hips and ass like you got," he caressed her hips and grabbed her butt squeezing it, "men get distracted and try hard to get next to all that fine body." Smiling and laughing at her.

Diana playfully hit him in the chest.

"Some things never change. Ron, what is going to happen to those guys and please don't lie to me." She is looking at him.

"Beat up really bad and let go. I don't want to talk about that. I miss my wife." He hugged and kissed her. He takes his jacket off and his Mac-10, laying it on the floor, then stared at Diana. "I really do miss you Diana."

She can feel the care and love coming from his words which make it hard to hold back her tears. Diana removed her shoes, blouse, and jeans. Ron takes his shirt and pants off. He moved closer to her.

"Separated but close." He kissed her.

"I don't want to be separated any more Ron, please let this ungodly lifestyle go." She pulled him closer, kissing him from her very heart and soul. They walk to the bed and lay down and begin making love on a level that can only be described as *When two become one*! For the rest of the day they give themselves to each other in every way they can. Diana gives her body and heart to her husband repeatedly. She cooked for him and he feeds her. They make love, sleep and do it all over again. They finally end up in the living room on the floor where they made a bed with blankets and pillows.

"I love you Diana, come home."

"I love you Ron, you, come home." She kissed him and they hug and fall asleep.

CHAPTER THIRTY
Plan Interrupted

The two guys who grabbed Stacy and Diana are Chuck and Dwight. They are cousins who live in a three-level five bedroom three car garage house in Waldorf, Maryland. They live in a rural area. Their house sat on four acres and is about a half mile from another house. Chuck and Dwight's parents were very close and they spent a lot of time together, including going to church together making sure to take Chuck and Dwight. They were ten years old when all four of their parents were out one night coming from a club and they were robbed and shot. They all died.

Their aunts took them in and kept them in church, but soon the spirit of rebellion began to overcome them and they would no longer listen to their aunts. After turning fifteen they started selling weed and hanging out in the streets late at night. One night their aunts were preparing to go to Bible study, telling Chuck and Dwight to hurry up and get dressed. They told their aunts they were never going back to church again, cursed their aunts out and told them to go to hell. Their aunts cried and told them to get out. As they were packing their belongings to leave, their aunts told them to repent of their sins and come to God. They laughed at their aunts and told them, they don't need God, they got money. They walked out carrying suit cases and laughing but their aunts were on their knees crying and praying.

For the last eight years, Dwight and Chuck have been inseparable. Their objective in life, make a lot of fast money, by

RONALD GRAY   (197)

any means necessary. They went from selling more weed to pills, robbing jewelry stores and selling thousands of cartons of cigarettes. At one time, they each had a hundred and fifty thousand dollars. They invested that in cocaine and never looked back. Now, at twenty-three years old, they each have a million dollars and three vehicles. Two corvettes, two 750Li BMWs, and two custom-ordered Lincoln Navigators that cost ninety thousand dollars.

It has been two weeks since the *Young Wolves* beat them within an inch of their lives for grabbing Stacy and Diana and was told to leave town. The anger between them has not diminished and their objective was revenge, but the question is how? Chuck and Dwight know they do not have the fire power, man power, or connections to go up against Keith, Ron, and the *Young Wolves*. They do not care and want revenge against them badly. So, they decided to kidnap Stacy and Diana and sexually assault them, then kill Ron and Keith when they come to rescue them. They plan on killing the girls later.

Dwight and Chuck went to South Carolina and recruited ten young, hungry-for-money killers, to help them carry out their plan. First, they wanted to have a nice house party to celebrate, and then go to war with the *Young Wolves*.

Tonight, was party time and Dwight made a phone call to a night club that he and Chuck go to and requested ten of the finest girls the club has. At three-thousand dollars per women, plus tips, no girl said no, not even the ones who usually don't do private house parties. The girls came in one long stretch Benz limo and stepped out carrying small hand bags and wearing heels, mini skirts, short tight shorts, tight jeans, and dresses with long slits on the side showing lots of sexy legs. They were all very attractive, small waist, hips, and butt for days, just as Dwight and Chuck wanted. Guards were posted around the house while the party was going on. Cars were still driving up to the house with some of Dwight's and Chuck's friends and more girls. The theme of the party is, please all the men any way they want. You could hear the music and that loud bass from a distance. People were scattered throughout the house, in the basement, main floor and upstairs.

This party was Sodom and Gomorrah in every way. Drugs were flowing, weed, pills, and cocaine, as much as you wanted. Everything for tonight was free and every kind of alcoholic drink you could think of was present. Ladies were entertaining the men to the fullest. Bumping and grinding, lap dances, strip dancing, having sex in the basement, in all the rooms upstairs, and performing oral sex acts in any dark corner they could. The house was dark because the lights were out in the house, except red and blue lights.

Dwight and Chuck were in the same bedroom with four other girls. All six of them for the last three hours have been having a private freak party. Sex, drinking, smoking weed, popping pills, and snorting cocaine and trading partners engaging in every perverted sex act you could think of and in every position laughing and just being wild and free.

What they didn't know was this was the last day of their lives. Victor heard about what went down with Keith, Ron, Stacy, Diana and the *Young Wolves*. He knew about Dwight's and Chuck's plan of revenge and their recruitment of the ten guys from South Carolina. His information is compliments of

Mr. Bones of course. Victor will not allow anything to interrupt this big drug deal that Keith and Ron have been working on. For Victor, it's not so much the money involved in the deal but the many connections that the deal will bring for future business dealings. No love for Ron or Keith, just protecting them for business purposes only.

A large dark cloud appeared in the sky that covered the light coming from the moon and a black cloud of smoke appeared in the yard close to Chuck and Dwight's house. When the smoke cleared, Mr. Bones was standing there dressed in black with his cane and black pouch in his hand. Mr. Case is dressed in his ninja suit with his sword on his back. Mr. Bones looked at Mr. Case.

"Look at all these people doing what they want and what I want them to do. Sin! Time to kill and bring more people to hell with me," he pointed his cane at Mr. Case. "Start killing."

Mr. Case runs quickly across the yard but you can't even hear his feet hit the ground. He sees four guys walking around carrying automatic weapons. He reached inside his suit and pulled out four throwing knives. With years of experience and a deadly aim, Mr. Case throws his knives hitting each one in the chest, and then cuts their heads off.

Mr. Bones throws his bones at the house and it erupts in flames inside and out. People are yelling and screaming, running through the house, jumping out windows and running out of the house on fire. Mr. Case does not discriminate between men and women. He kills everyone as they come out, swinging his sword with lightning speed, cutting off arms, legs, heads, and cutting people in half. Blood, bodies, and body parts are everywhere.

RONALD GRAY   (200)

Finally, Dwight and Chuck jump out the window naked landing at Mr. Bone's feet. They both are badly burned but are still alive. He pointed his cane at them.

"Fools, you were on the right track but you left the church, cursed out your aunts and started living for me. Your aunts became your parents and you ungrateful fools disrespected them. The Bible says, *"Honor your mother and father, that your days maybe long upon thy land, which thy Lord, God give thee."* Now, look at you. In the house fornicating and doing freaky things," he laughed, "I love it." He tapped his cane on the ground twice and it sounds like cannon fire going off and shook the ground. "Come and get it." He yelled.

Seventeen large wolves appear in the yard in a cloud of black smoke. They spread out running across the yard and start eating the burning bodies. Ten wolves run over to Dwight and Chuck biting and eating them. Five were on Chuck and five were on Dwight biting their legs, arms, and head. They were yelling and screaming and begging for mercy but there is none when you are dealing with the devil.

These wolves were tearing through their flesh like seasoned meat pulling their arms and legs clean off and snapping their bones like twigs. The wolves' heads were so large it allowed them to open their jaws wide enough to grip the very skulls of Dwight and Chuck. Biting down hard sinking their powerful razor-like teeth in crunching their skulls like dog biscuits. More wolves run over, helping to eat their flesh, insides, and bones. All you can hear is snarling, growling and bones crunching and the wolves were eating them very quickly like this was their first meal in days. Blood was shooting in many directions as the

RONALD GRAY (201)

wolves were enjoying this meal. The wolves eat their flesh and bones until nothing is left. They lick their mouths, looking around for more bodies but nothing is left, so they run off. The house burns down with a few bodies still in it. Over thirty people are dead. Mr. Bones tapped his cane, he and Mr. Case disappear in a cloud of black smoke.

CHAPTER THIRTY ONE
The Hospital

Ron and Diana walked into the hospital holding hands. He was wearing an Armani suit and Diana has on heels and a dress.

"Ron, I know this is not easy for you but I'm glad you came. I'm also glad that you're taking care of all her medical bills."

"You think I'm heartless. I think about Sandra every single day and what happened to her. If I had never touched her, she may never be in a coma." He let go of her hand.

Diana stopped walking and looked at Ron.

"Baby, stop blaming yourself. This is not your fault." She kissed him and they continue to walk.

They reach Sandra's room door and Ron exhaled heavily then gently grabbed Diana's hand and they walked in. A nurse is in the room wiping Sandra's face with a towel. She smiled at them and walked out. Ron and Diana walk over to her bed. Ron just stared at her until tears began to fall from his eyes.

"I'm so sorry Sandra, please forgive me. Just wake up and get well no matter what." He gently rubbed her arms and face. He looked at Diana. "She looks so peaceful."

"Many prayers have gone out to the Lord on her behalf and I don't care what it looks like, it is never over until God says it is over. You know that Ron better than me. Look how God moved you out of an impossible situation and look how you pay God back. Look how you are living." She said with building anger.

"What is that's supposed to mean? Are you judging me, again?"

Diana knew she should not have said that, but thinking about what God has done for Ron and looking at how he is living now is making her angry. She does not want to push him away when she feels he is close to doing the right thing and they have been getting along so well recently. She has not fully come back home but she has been spending more time with Ron. Of course, the great sex they have been having has something to do with it.

"Let's not argue Ron especially in here. Doctors don't really know if someone who is in a coma can hear what is being said around them." She held his hand.

Ron removed his hand from hers and leaned over to kiss Sandra on the forehead. He wiped his eyes and walked out, standing in the hallway against the wall.

Diana turned her head looking at Ron walk out then kissed Sandra on the cheek and looked up.

"Lord, please forgive my husband and all his sins and deliver Sandra from her coma, oh Lord. Heal her body from head to toe and deliver her from all afflictions. Thank you, Lord." She leaned forward and kissed Sandra again, then walked out and sees Ron leaning against the wall.

Ron walked over to her.

"Are you ready to go?"

Diana looked at him, praying to herself for strength so she does not snap and tell him how she really feels.

"No, I'm not ready to go. We just got here. Ron, how can you be so distant and cold toward your own sister?"

"I'm not cold but I don't like seeing my sister just lying there in a coma and there is nothing that I can do about it. You make me sound heartless, I'm far from that. If that was the case I

RONALD GRAY   (204)

would not be here. Now I'm ready to go because I have business to take care of."

Diana has heard enough of his selfish attitude when others are suffering as well.

"That's it! I'm so sick of hearing you always talk about business. Business this, business that. What about God, Ron? What about us, our marriage? You talk more about business than you do God. The Bible said, *"Out of the abundance of the heart, the mouth speaks,"* remember that, my brother." Staring at him with anger in her eyes.

Keith walked down the hallway toward Sandra's room, followed by ten of the *Young Wolves*. All are wearing Armani suits and wearing shades and carrying Mac-10s inside their suits. Ron and Diana look up and see them coming and Ron smiled. Diana looked at Ron smiling and it took prayer to keep her from slapping that smile right off his face. Five *Young Wolves* wait on one side of the wall and five on the other. The look around. Keith kept walking.

"Ron, I apologize for this interruption but something has come up and we need to talk." He looked at Diana seeing the extreme anger in her eyes. "Hi Diana."
She stared at Keith, rolled her eyes at him, then looked at Ron.

"Ron, I know you are not leaving me again to take care of God knows what evil, dirty business. You really need to think about it before you walk away from me today, and I mean it. I'm sick of this."

Ron stepped closer to her, putting his hands on her waist.

"Diana, let's not do this now. Let me go do this and we can hook up tonight. Okay?"

RONALD GRAY   (205)

She stepped back from him and put her hands on her hips and looked at him with disgust and total frustration.

"Hook up! Hook up!" she yelled, "I'm not some girl you picked up at the club, had sex with and hope to get some more booty from later," she stepped closer putting her finger in his face. "You better not leave me tonight Ron." She said with tears building up in her eyes.

Ron knew if he left Diana tonight she may not come back home for a long time but he was willing to take that chance. He kissed her lips, looked deep in her eyes seeing her hurt and pain.

"Diana, I promise to be back later and I got you, okay."

"Ron, if you leave me tonight. I will not be home when you get there and I'm not sure when I will be back, if ever."

He hugged and kissed her.

"I love you." He stared at her then turned to Keith. "Let's go partner."

Diana stared at Keith so hard and with so much anger she can feel her heart thumping in her chest. Ron and Keith walked away and the *Young Wolves* followed them.

Diana looked at them walk away and tears fall from her eyes. She walked back to Sandra's room and fell to her knees, crying hard and praying.

"Lord, help me, I can't take this." She laid on the floor crying and calling on God so hard her body is trembling.

CHAPTER THIRTY TWO
Spiritual tug of War

Mr. Bones is in a room in the hospital close to Sandra's. He's dressed in a white doctor's uniform, holding his cane and black pouch. He's standing inside a circle of bones with a picture of Sandra on the floor with a circle of small bones around it.

"Foolish, stupid people, don't they know I'm the most relentless and persistent adversary in the world. I keep coming and I never give up. Look at that child in there laying on the floor doing all that crying and praying. It will do her no good. I'm the power. I put Sandra in a coma. I put lust spirits in Christine. I put the spirit of confusion in Diana and caused her to separate from her husband, who I'm destroying. The precious chosen one," he laughed, "now look at that boy, deceiving himself because he is doing my will, not the will of God. I deceive people and give them what they want, but I love no one and I hate the world. God kicked me out of heaven and my fate is doomed and hell is my home but I will not be alone. Only those born again can escape me." He mumbled some words and takes his hand off his cane and it stood up by itself. He opened his pouch and removed some bones and laid a bone on Sandra's picture then mumbled more words and his cane tapped itself on the floor twice and the picture catches on fire. He grabbed his cane and raised both arms.

"I'm the bones, no one can beat the bones, no one, not even you, Ron, chosen boy." He mumbled some words and he began to change into a snake and curls itself around the cane.

CHAPTER THIRTY THREE
Sheila's House

Grandma Harris, Diana, and Sheila are in the living room on their knees praising God. They stood up and walked around for a while then back on their knees, praying. The praise and praying that has been going on in this room were so strong and powerful you can feel the presence of the Lord. The Bible says, *"Call on me in the day of trouble and I will deliver you and you shall glorify me."* Sheila feels she is at her very end and can't take any more. Diana is very tired and feels she has done all she can for her marriage and Grandma Harris is a veteran in this walk with Christ but even she is tired.

Three hours later all three stand up and sat on the sofa. Grandma Harris and Sheila sat on one sofa and Diana sat on the other. They looked at each other, exhaling and smile.

"Wow, physically I feel tired but spiritually I feel rejuvenated and spiritually strong. I know the situation is still there but I just don't feel the weight of it anymore. The presence of the Lord is in this house greatly, I can feel it." Diana said while smiling.

"Amen, baby, that's how God works if you humble yourself to him. Lord knows after all that praising and praying, I feel good. Thank you, Lord."

"Amen Grandma Harris. I felt beyond tired and beat down going through so much back to back with my family. Now," she exhaled, "I feel brand new and ready for another day in the Lord. Diana, I know you have been dealing with a lot in your marriage but how are you doing and how is Ron?"

RONALD GRAY   (208)

Diana was staring into space thinking about if she should answer according to how she really feels or not answer at all. She is tired of holding her true feelings in.

"Well, I have been praying, seeking God for wisdom, wondering if I made the right decision to leave my home and husband. What happened to, for better or worse? What kind of woman and wife am I, if I run away as soon as something negative happens in my marriage? Ron has his faults but he would never leave me, this I know for a fact but I left him. He treats me like a queen although we do bump heads at times, and how do I show him my loyalty? I leave him when he disobeys God. Marriage is about enduring through problems, not running away. That's one of the reasons why the divorce rate is so high in marriages, in and out of the church."

Grandma Harris and Sheila looked at each other wondering who would speak first.

"Diana, how long have you been feeling this way because you said a lot and I can tell it came from deep within you."

"I have been feeling this way for a while, Miss O'Neil." Exhaling and lowering her head.

Grandma Harris is looking at Diana and she can feel how torn she is in her spirit and she knows how much she loves Ron.

"Baby, I know in marriage you have to make some very difficult choices and you separating yourself from Ron was very hard for you but look at it like this. Ask yourself exactly why you left. Was it about you, Ron, or your marriage? Not living for God is one thing but being involved in criminal behavior is something totally different. What about your overall safety?"

RONALD GRAY   (209)

"Diana, you made some very strong statements about marriage for which I agree with them all but as much as I love my son, if he is still involved in criminal activity, then you have to be concerned about your own safety.'

"All this is true but I need to be honest with myself. Did I leave for my safety or for disappointment," she lowered her head then looked at them both, "the truth is, I left Ron out of anger and hurt. He deceived and lied to me and I wanted to teach him a lesson but what lesson did I teach him, none. I showed him immaturity and selfishness, not honor and commitment to our wedding vows. This is the truth." She stared at them.

"You are young Diana so don't be too hard on yourself. Your call is one of judgment but I do compliment you on being honest with yourself. You will be able to be a blessing to others."

"Baby you are growing up fast and having to make hard choices that you should not have to make but as Sheila said, you can be a blessing to so many people who are going through the same thing. God is giving you and all of us strength to carry on and he gives us joy even in the time of much hardship. So just hold on baby, hold on. God has us all. I noticed you have been dressing really sexy lately going to see your husband." Winking at Sheila then smiling at Diana.

"Grandma Harris don't start teasing her. Leave her alone. She is young and she loves her husband and wants to please him like a real woman and wife should. Just like real men need to understand just because they pay bills and provide for the house, there is so much more that women want from them. Quality time spent together, romance, and courtship."

"Thank you, Miss O'Neil. Oh, romance and courtship." She stuck her tongue out at Grandma Harris and smiled.

"Don't be sticking your tongue out at me young lady. I know all about romance and courtship. My husband and I had our disagreements but we never stopped courting each other, unlike what people do today. Sex ain't romance and that's all you young people do nowadays. All that humping but there is no real closeness in the mind, heart, spirit, and soul."

"You are right about that Grandma Harris. Not really getting to know each other, no courtship or romance. Just humping each other like dogs. It's all sad." Sheila said nodding her head.

Grandma Harris started laughing knowing what she is about to say is going to irritate Diana.

"Diana, I know the way you have been dressing recently, Ron has been trying to hump you. Have you been humping your booty on that man baby? Or, are you still being a penis teaser." She started laughing.

"Oh my God, Grandma Harris! We just finished praying. You should be ashamed of yourself." Sheila said waving her hand at her.

Diana stood up and looked at Grandma Harris.

"I love you grandma but you are nasty and nosey since you've commented on it, yes, I have been humping my husband but not enough but I will be changing that as soon as God allows me to. Thank you." Looking at Grandma Harris she walked into the kitchen.

Sheila's mouth was open, staring at Diana because she was surprised at what she said and how she said it.

RONALD GRAY   (211)

"Diana, you are something and I think you inherited your Grandma's ways. Both of you are nasty."

"I'm not nasty, thank you very much. I'm just an old woman who knows it is nothing wrong with humping your husband and I'm still praying for you Sheila. Praying that God blesses you with a good husband, who loves the Lord. So, you can start doing some more humping." She started laughing again.

Sheila looked at Diana and Grandma Harris who are both laughing. She pointed her finger at them.

"Both of you should be ashamed of yourselves and you need to repent of that lust spirit that you speak on so much."

Grandma Harris waved her hand at Sheila.

"Child hush. What we are talking about is not lust. Sheila, you and I both know married people have sex, so you need to stop acting so stuck up and pray that God sends you somebody who you can marry. As the young people say today, get your freak on." She started laughing and pointed her finger at Diana. "Diana, you better go home so your husband can hump your little booty." She waved her hand at them because she is laughing so hard.

CHAPTER THIRTY FOUR

Anger Released

Mr. Bones is standing behind the night club dressed in all black with his cane and black pouch in his hands. He is angry and is tired of all the praying that has been going on, making his job hard. He decided to increase his attack on those who are already living foul and he will increase their disobedient spirits to destroy them faster. He mumbled some words, tapped his cane twice and throws his bones against the building.

"Death is in the power of the tongue." He pointed his cane at the club, "I speak death, violence, hatred, jealousy, betrayal, lust and demonic possessions to this building and everyone who is in it and those who will ever come inside this building from this day forward." He laughed and tapped his cane twice and disappeared in a cloud of smoke.

The *Young Wolves* are scattered throughout the club wearing grey three-piece suits with their Mac-10s under their jackets. Keith and Ron are in their office at the club both are wearing Ralph Lauren suits. Keith was sitting behind the desk and Ron was sitting on the sofa. Stacy was working at one of the bars in the club. She was wearing heels and a tight dress that leaves little to the imagination. The club was full and music was playing.

"I called Greg Johnson and briefly explained the situation to him. He should be here soon. I'm also waiting for Shantai. She and her mom's modeling connections will be perfect for this and the girl is fine. We hung out for a while, talk about the head game, damn," he shook his head and smiled, "I wouldn't mind reuniting with her pretty face, small waist, hips, and ass."

"Don't forget about Stacy, who I have to admit, she is physically all that. You know Keith, I'm surprised you have lived this long. Keep your mind on business. This deal is going to put us in the position to get away from Victor, so stay focused and keep your head where it belongs, on business."

"Relax partner, I laugh and joke, but with me, it is always A.M.O.A. Take my word for it, my mind is very focused but I do like to flirt at times. I know where home is and Stacy is my home. Speaking of business, are you any closer to convincing Diana to come back home?"

"I was but after you showed up at the hospital and I left, Diana snapped, and she has not been home since. I'm not going to lie. I miss her a lot but I just want to get this last deal with Victor over with so we can get away from him and his entire organization and run our own."

"You should miss your wife just like I miss Stacy when we don't spend enough time together, but for me, it's A.M.O.A, Always Money Over Ass! Remember that my friend."

"Every time you say that it sounds worse but I got it."

Greg Johnson walked in the club looking around seeing all the sexy ladies with their fine bodies but none of this distracts him at all. He is wearing a suit and walked over to the bar where Stacy and another bartender are working.

"Hi, you must be Stacy?"

"Mr. Greg Johnson, yes, I'm Stacy. Keith and Ron are expecting you. They are in their office."

"Thank you," he leaned forward looking at Stacy, "you look very nice. Is Keith taking very good care of you?"

Stacy frowns at him.

"Better than you ever could," she said with much attitude and coldness.

Greg smiled.

"Minor, where he would end I would begin." He walked away toward the office, knocked on the door and walked in.

Keith was sitting at the desk and Ron was sitting on the sofa.

"Gentlemen, I see you are enjoying your club. Time to do business." He walked over in front of the desk and sat in a chair.

"Mr. Johnson, perfect timing. As the sign on the building said, *New Beginnings*, and that's what this is about for my partner and I. Doing new things. I know you are busy so we will be brief. S&D came up with this idea and it's a winner."

"Panties and money all under one roof. We throw a big fashion show, call all the major drug players who sit on the side and watch the girls. They make purchases on the outfits, only they are actually telling us how many kilos they want, ten outfits, ten kilos and on and on." Ron said looking at Greg.

Keith looked at Ron then Greg.

"Easy money. No drugs on the premises and before the show is over we get the total and meet everyone in one place. Plenty of guns on the scene to cover everything. Pass the money, pass the drugs and everyone is happy easy money."

"Nothing is ever that easy in this business but I like the idea. Only, the buying is going to be much bigger than you thought. I will invite big players that Mr. Augular has been doing business with for years and no one will buy under a hundred kilos of cocaine and heroin. Gentlemen, everything that we move will be uncut."

"We need an army to control all that money and drugs but we have an elite team of security guards."

Greg looked at Ron.

"Yea, I know about your security company, *Young* Wolves Inc. I see you have learned some things from Mr. Augular. But you two do not have to be concerned about security. The two of you will put the show together and I will handle the drugs and security."

Keith stood up pointing at Ron.

"S&D and I came up with this. We don't need you trying to take over. We can handle the show, security, and the drugs, middle man." Mean mugging him.

Ron is aware that Keith has a temper so he quickly stood up and so does Greg, who waved his hand at them both.

"Relax gentlemen, I'm not here to insult your capabilities but the fact is you two lack the experience to handle a deal this size without help. It is my job to make sure everything flows smoothly. Mr. Augular is aware of the move that you two put together and made all that money selling drugs and pills. Not bad at all but you two will make more money on this deal, enough to retire. I just need to make sure everything goes smoothly."

"Things will flow smoothly anyway with or without your help. You are right, S&D and I are ready to move on to some legitimate businesses. We will do our thing and you do yours, easy money."

Greg despises these two but he must continue to hide it for now.

"Very good and now I have to go and discuss the details of this deal with Mr. Augular and put this in motion."

Ron shrugs his shoulders.

"It is already in motion," he pointed at Keith and himself. "We put it in motion."

Greg looked at Ron then Keith.

"Absolutely gentlemen. I will be in touch." He walked out of the office and closed the door behind him and stood there looking out over the club.

Keith walked over to Ron.

"I don't like that guy and never did."

"Neither do I."

"Good, when this is over, we kill him, dig a hole and dump his body in it."

Greg is standing outside of the office door.

"Stupid young punks. When this is over I'm going to kill them both." Walking away he reached the bar and sees Stacy looking at him. He licked his lips and smiled at her and walked out of the club.

Shantai walked in the club just when the DJ started playing the old school song; *A Freak Like Me* by Adina Howard. Shantai was beautiful. She is twenty-five years old, five feet five and a hundred thirty-eight pounds of sexuality. She was wearing Prada heels, a short top that shows off her breasts and flat stomach and a long tight Prada skirt hugging her hips and a perfectly round butt. Eyes follow her as she walked over to the bar where Stacy was.

"Hi, I'm looking for Keith Washington. My name is Shantai and Keith is expecting me."

RONALD GRAY   (217)

Stacy stared at her noticing how attractive she is. Beautiful face, tight body, flat stomach, and enough hips and ass that would make any man follow her. Her tight dress has her on display.

"Hi I'm Stacy, Keith's lady. He mentioned you would be coming by." She turned to the other bar-tender. "Take care of the bar until I get back."

He looked at Stacy.

"No problem Stacy."

Stacy walked around the bar toward Shantai and looked her up and down.

"Come with me. Keith is in his office with his partner Ron."

They walk through the club and Stacy can feel people watching them walk but she dislikes walking beside Shantai because this girl does have it going on, and she is used to shutting everything down, not this walking beauty.

Shantai was looking at Stacy while they are walking and sees she was very pretty and built just the way she likes her woman. Keith never knew the real reason why she stopped seeing him. She knew he could never fully deal with her being bisexual. She looked around the club while walking seeing how nice the place was.

"I always did like this club and now Keith owns it. He must be doing very well, making all the right moves, especially with Mr. Victor Augular."

Stacy looked at Shantai with disdain and plans to keep an eye on her and hopes she does not have to teach this bitch and Keith a lesson.

"You seem to know a lot about my man. How well do you know Keith?"

Looking at Stacy she can feel her jealousy.

"We spent some time together getting to know each other better, but all of that's history. You are sucking and riding him now." She turned her head and looked at Stacy and smiled, "well I hope."

Stacy stopped walking and touched Shantai to get her attention so she can stop walking. Stacy immediately thinks about how fast she can get to the razor underneath her skirt so she can cut this bitch for talking so disrespectful out of her mouth concerning her activities with Keith. She stepped closer to Shantai.

"I don't know what you are used to but if you don't want your throat slit, you need to be very careful what comes out of your mouth about Keith and I."

Shantai is looking at Stacy thinking how weak she is for falling right into her trap. She said what she did on purpose just to see how Stacy would react. She is even more attracted to Stacy now and thinking what Keith would do if she seduced Stacy and turned her out. Shantai stepped in Stacy's face and smiled.

"Relax Sweetie. Keith is the past but you could be the present." She gently caressed Stacy's face with the back of her hand then rubbed her butt and whispered in her ear. "Nice ass."

Stacy was surprised and not sure how to react to her. Part of her wants to slap the taste out of her mouth then cut her throat but another part of her is turned on. Diana is the only female she has been with but since Diana changed her ways, she misses that one-on-one woman's touch but has been suppressing those desires, until now. Shantai is the type of woman she could be

RONALD GRAY   (219)

with. She feels herself getting wet just thinking about them in bed and what they could do to each other, but she will not be played by her or any woman.

"You got me mixed up with somebody else. I don't go that way. And don't you ever put your hands on me again if you like breathing."

Shantai was going to leave Stacy alone but since she threatened her again, she was going to try Stacy and prove something to her at the same time.

She looked over at Stacy and grins.

"Okay, sure you don't, my mistake."

They continue to walk through the club then they pass this very dark corner close to a bathroom and no one is nearby. Shantai was thinking this was too good of an opportunity to pass up. She looked around to double check the area then quickly grabbed Stacy by her waist and pulled her into the corner where she pushed her up against the wall. Not giving her any time to react, she kissed Stacy on the lips while sliding her hand underneath her dress using her fingers to push her panties to one side and started rubbing between her legs feeling her wetness.

Stacy is shocked and is about to hit Shantai in the throat until she felt how soft her lips are. Then realizing how quickly Shantai got her wet and how good her fingers feel between her legs, she moans.

"Ohhhh damn."

Shantai has never been wrong; she can tell the true hidden desires of any woman. She slid her finger inside Stacy, in and out and rubbing her clit at the same time with her thumb making her even wetter. She slides her tongue across Stacy's lips.

RONALD GRAY   (220)

Stacy can't seem to control herself and allowed Shantai to have her way and opened her mouth to allow Shantai's tongue in.

Shantai slides her tongue in Stacy's mouth and they kiss with passion and she quickly pulled Stacy's dress up seeing the razor in its special small pocket. Shantai smiled and was thinking. *I like her more already, a true gangster bitch, razor and all.* She snatched her thong panties down putting them inside her bra and spreads Stacy's legs apart then grabbed her butt gently spreading her butt cheeks apart and softly biting Stacy on the lip.

"Do you want me to stop?"

Everything in Stacy is fighting these feelings she's experiencing and wants to say stop but she does not. She wrapped her arms around Shantai's neck kissing her even harder.

"No, don't stop, it feels so good and I'm so close to climaxing."

Shantai rubbed Stacy's butt with her own juices then dropped down to her knees spreading Stacy's legs even more. She started licking and sucking her wetness with expert precision until her juices start running into Shantai's mouth. She knows Stacy is about to cum and what would send her over the edge. While her mouth is buried between Stacy's legs she slowly slides her finger in her ass moving it slowly. Then she gently sucks Stacy's clit making her whole body shake.

Stacy was embarrassed for allowing this girl to take her like this but she loved the finger in her ass and Shantai's mouth locked on her clit, at the same time. She can no longer hold it in but she does not want anyone to hear her scream so she put her hand over her own mouth.

RONALD GRAY   (221)

"Ohh Shantai, I'm cummming don't stop, please don't stop, finger my ass baby, ohhhh you are making me cum, don't stop, don't stop, ahhhhh."

Shantai continues to suck Stacy's clit and finger her ass even faster sucking and licking all her juices as she explodes in her mouth.

Stacy's body was shaking because she was climaxing so hard. She grabbed the back of Shantai's head pressing it into her even more. Feeling and hearing Shantai suck and lick all her juices caused her to climax harder. She finally calmed down but her body is still slightly shaking. Shantai slides Stacy's dress back down fixing her clothes, then kissed Stacy passionately while palming her butt with both hands. Then they walked inside the bathroom in silence to clean up and walked out too a dark area of the club to talk in private.

Shantai fully understood the afterthought of women like Stacy after having sex with women because they think they are boss bitches. She understood Stacy is a control freak so she knows what to do and what to say to make her feel like she is still in charge. Shantai takes the softer woman's approach to make it better and easy for Stacy. Shantai looked directly in her eyes, showing fear to Stacy.

"Please don't hit me or cut me but I wanted you so badly the moment I saw you, I was drawn to you. If you want, this never happened and I will never tell a soul. I'm not a lesbian but I'm bisexual and you are so damn pretty and taste so good just like I knew you would. Are you going to hit me?"

Stacy does not know how to respond to Shantai. She can't deny the strong attraction that she has for her or how good

Shantai made her feel. She was thinking, *Shantai made her feel this good up against a wall in just a few minutes, she can only imagine what they could do in bed together with no time limits.* She loves Keith with all her heart, so how could she let this happen? She stared at Shantai.

"No, I'm not going to hit you but after you and Keith take care of this business deal. Stay the hell away from him. As far as what just happened between us," she lowered her head then looked in Shantai's eyes, "I don't have an immediate answer."

Shantai knew exactly what to do now to have future dealings with Stacy. She kissed Stacy slowly but passionately, knowing Stacy can smell and taste her own juices. Shantai grabbed Stacy's hand and they walked back inside the bathroom which is empty. Stacy was not believing what was happening but she had to leave so she quickly walked toward the bathroom door but Shantai grabbed her by her waist pulling Stacy in one of the bathroom stalls, closed and locked the door.

A lady walked into the bathroom very quietly and enters one of the stalls but neither Shantai nor Stacy heard her.

"Where do you think your hot ass is going," she started kissing Stacy and reached underneath her own dress sliding her finger inside herself feeling her own wetness then rubbed her finger across Stacy's lips.

Stacy knew she should back this girl off her because she can feel her own desires building up again, but she doesn't. Instead, she allows her to do this and even opened her mouth sucking on Shantai's fingers. The smell and taste of Shantai turned her on greatly and she kept sucking her fingers with passion.

RONALD GRAY   (223)

Shantai was thinking. *I got her. Now it is only a matter of time and place.* She leaned forward looking directly into Stacy's eyes.

"Do you want me? Do you want to have your face buried between my legs and ass? Do you want to be my friend and lover?"

Without any hesitation or thinking, Stacy started shaking her head.

"Yes, yes, I want you," she grabbed Shantai's butt with both hands and pulled her closer, "I want you to cum in my mouth then I want to fuck you with an eight-inch strap on until you scream my name while I'm fucking you so damn good and deep. No one will ever know about us, ever and I meant what I said about Keith."

"No problem, just you and I but I want you so badly right now, but another time, another place." Shantai gives Stacy back her thong panties and softly kissed her on the lips.

Stacy put her panties back on and fixed her clothes then quickly grabbed Shantai around her waist and turned her around so she is facing the stall wall. Stacy pressed her body against Shantai's ass and whispered in her ear.

"I will be tasting this pussy and fucking this fat ass of yours, believe that." She grabbed Shantai's butt firmly and gently bites her on the neck.

"Whenever you think you can handle all of this, you let me know." Shantai said.

They walked out the stall and washed their hands and adjust their clothes before walking out, going to the office.

What neither of them was aware of is they were being watched the entire time. Cynthia had been in the club for a while when she saw Shantai come in and was drawn to her as well. So, when she saw her and Stacy walking away she followed them but kept her distance then she saw Shantai grab Stacy pulling her into the corner. She hid in a dark corner not knowing she was about to have one of her fantasies come to pass. To see two women together.

When they went inside the bathroom it was Cynthia who later quietly walked inside and went to another bathroom stall just to listen to them, she heard it all. Cynthia became so turned on she started masturbating making herself climax but had to muffle her own moans so they would not hear her. Never in a million years would she think Stacy, her friend, was into women. She knew how Stacy felt about Keith and how protective she was of him and what they share. If she knew Stacy was into women she would have approached her long ago because she was always attracted to Stacy in a sexual way and wanted her badly but was too afraid to say or do anything to let her know. Now, she wanted Stacy and Shantai. She was thinking. *Time, only a matter of time.* She walked out of the bathroom stall towards the sink, washed her hands and adjusted her clothes. She looked at herself in the mirror, smiling and walked out of the bathroom.

Stacy and Shantai reached the office door and walked in. Keith was sitting at his desk and Ron was sitting on the sofa.

Shantai walked in first.

"Mr. Keith Washington, you have moved up in the world."

Keith smiled.

"Shantai," he walked toward her, "you look wonderful and sexy as ever," he hugged and kissed her on the cheek, "I'm sure you and Stacy have already talked."

Shantai turned to look at Stacy then looked back at Keith.

"Yes, we have and you have a very nice lady and she loves you, so be good to her before someone comes along and takes her away from you." She turned her head looking at Ron and looked at Stacy again smiling. "Who is this good-looking gentleman on the sofa? He must be your partner Ron, very nice."

Ron walked over to Shantai and shook her hand.

"Hi Shantai and you do look very lovely. Come over here and sit down so we can discuss some business." They walked toward the sofa with Ron behind her staring at her butt. "Shantai, no disrespect intended but you could hurt someone with all those curves you are working with."

Shantai decided to have some fun with Ron and flirt with him even though she knows he is married. You never know what the future held. She turned around and looked at him.

"You mean you were watching my ass while I was walking. I'm glad you noticed." They sat down.

Stacy does not like Ron trying to get next to Shantai and she knew why. Because she desires Shantai all for herself and she does not like him messing around on Diana so she must be careful about what she says.

"Shantai, don't waste your time with him, the package is pretty but he is married. Well, I have to get back to work." She looked at Keith. "Baby I will talk to you later."

"Absolutely," he hugged and kissed her, caressing her butt and whispered in her ear, "I want to taste you."

RONALD GRAY   (226)

Stacy smiled and lightly slapped him.

"You are so nasty." She walked toward the office door then turned and looked at Keith. "Keith, I love you." She walked out but her heart was now heavy and she was feeling very guilty for what she did with Shantai. Seeing the love in Keith's eyes that he has for her was making her feel horrible. Stacy made up her mind right then to never be with Shantai again no matter what and hopes that Keith never finds out.

Shantai looked at Keith.

"Keith, I can tell she really loves you, don't hurt her. Although she is little possessive of you."

Ron looked at Shantai.

"More like, fatal attraction."

"All is good, now let's get down to business," he grabbed a chair and sat in front of them, "Shantai, I thank you for coming. Ron and I want to put on a big fashion show with your help and the people who you and your mom know. The show will be the talk of the town for a long time."

"Your timing is perfect. My mom and I have been talking about doing something really nice and this could be it, how big and when?"

Ron touched Shantai's leg.

"We want a very big show with new models on the scene and well-known ones as well. Modeling dresses, slacks and swim wear. We want it all and we will have someone or a group to perform during the show, someone very popular."

"Help us put the show together and get all the ladies and the designers. Let us know the details and we will take care of

RONALD GRAY   (227)

everything else. All of the advertising paper-work, security and the entertainment, everything."

Ron was very attracted to Shantai but does not want to make a fool of himself, plus his heart was with Diana but this lady was doing something for him and he can feel himself getting hard just thinking about what he would like to do with her.

"What do you think? Are you interested?"

"Yes, very interested. Now what is my fee for all this work and since you two are living very large, do not insult me," she looked at Keith and pointed her finger at him. "Keith, you know better."

"You are smart and beautiful, a wonderful combination. For your help, we will pay you twenty-five thousand and throw in two, first class round trip airline tickets plus hotel fare for a week to anywhere you want to go in the world."

"My, my, you do know how to make a lady feel wanted. My mom will like that very much. Yes, I will do it and I want half my money up front and the balance plus the tickets at show time. You two know this is going to take a lot of work and it cannot be done overnight if you want it done correctly."

"Shantai, relax. We know it will take some time but I have confidence in your abilities to get this done or you would not be here. So how long do you think it will take before you will be ready for the show?" Keith said.

"What you two desire and how you want everything to be first class, keep in mind we are talking about a lot of work. Give me three maybe four weeks tops, to put everything together and I will give you my best."

Keith smiled and lightly touched Shantai's leg.

RONALD GRAY   (228)

"How good is your best?" He caressed her leg again.

Shantai moved his hand off her leg.

"I see some things have not changed," she turned her head to stare at Keith, "Keith you know my best so don't play and you do have a lady so don't mess that up."

"Shantai, we are here for business so overlook Keith. Anyway, your time frame is very reasonable, so go do your thing and let us know when you are ready."

"Thank you, Ron, I'm glad someone is remaining focused," she looked at Keith and rolled her eyes at him then smiled. "Well, unless there is something else, I will make my exit and get started."

"I'm looking forward to this. The best fashion show in all of Maryland, in the mix." Ron said.

Shantai stood up and held her hand out toward Keith.

"Keith, don't play. I need half the money to get started, please." Still holding her hand out to him.

"Not a problem," he reached into his pocket and pulled out a stack of money, counting it and hands Shantai twelve-thousand, five hundred dollars, "half of what we agreed to." He caressed her hand as he gave her the money.

"Thank you very much," she put the money inside her bra. "Well gentlemen, I have to go, there is a lot of work that has to be done for this show to be a success." She walked toward the office door then stopped and turned around. "Ron get my number from Keith and call me." She likes Ron already and can see the hunger in his eyes for her, married or not. She would like to find out how good he is in bed. She pointed at him. "Ron, will you come here please."

RONALD GRAY   (229)

He walked toward her.

"This is just a little something for you to remember me by," she hugged and slowly kissed him. "Call me, it will be worth your while, I promise you that."

"I would be a fool not to."

Shantai kissed Ron again, waved at Keith and walked out.

Keith walked toward Ron.

"Damn she is fine, my brother when you hit that make it last a long time and don't be no five-minute man."

Ron nods his head.

"She is very lovely but business is first and its show time. Since it is going to take a few weeks to put all of this together, I need to spend some quality time with Diana. Take her somewhere very nice."

"Smart move my brother, if she would go with you but whatever it takes to get her on your good side again, you need to do it."

"True that," Ron stared into space, "I just had an idea come to me. How about all four of us take off somewhere very nice. We can spoil Diana and Stacy for about two weeks before we have to get into this last big deal."

"Partner, you are always thinking and I like the idea a lot. Some place tropical, great weather and we can do what I know the girls will not turn down, spend money and do some serious shopping."

"Great and we all will have a good time, but where do we go?" He was quiet for a few seconds then snapped his finger. "I got it, we can island hop. Take the private jet to wherever we want to go. This way we can see different things and not get bored."

"Once again, you said it all and it's play time before business show time."

"I feel good like we can do whatever and that's a great feeling."

"Amen to that my brother." They hug and dap up.

Shantai is walking through the club and sees Stacy standing by herself leaning against a wall slowly moving her body to the beat of the music. She walked over and stood very close to her.

"Hi Stacy, I see it is hard for you to keep your body still. Are you okay?"

The moment she sees Shantai all her erotic passions come to the surface begging to be satisfied. She was fighting her own inner demons. She was torn between her love for Keith and her feelings for this girl whom she just met but shared something together that was so good. Deep down inside she wants it to happen again. But she knows she can't.

"I'm fine, I just like to dance. Look, what happened with us can never happen again."

Shantai expected this to happen. It always does with control freaks but she wants Stacy and is not about to be defeated.

"I understand how you feel but will you at least walk me to my vehicle?"

"Yeah I can do that, lead the way."

They walk through the club and outside to the parking lot turning men and women's heads. The night air is a little cool on Stacy's skin and she put her arms around herself. Shantai intends to take advantage of Stacy. They reach a black 2012 Mercedes-Benz airstream, interstate van. Stacy pointed at the van.

"This is yours, I mean it looks nice but who drives a big conversion van these days."

"Smart business people do. I spend a lot of time on the road and this is my office on wheels. It has everything that I need inside and when I'm parked doing my work, no one can see inside because of the dark tint that I have on the windows in the back. Would you like to look inside?"

Stacy knew this was the last place she needs to be right now, but she would like to see how it was laid out on the inside. It might give her some business ideas.

"Sure, why not. It might give me some business ideas."

They stepped into the van from the side doors and Shantai closed the door when they were in. Shantai sat in one of the chairs in the back and Stacy sat in another seat. Stacy was surprised to see just how much room this van has and she noticed the bed in the back and all the latest electronic equipment, computer, printer, flat screen TV and a nice stereo system.

"So, Stacy, what do you think? Do you like what you see?"

Stacy knew what she really meant by that statement and she should leave now.

"I'm surprised, this van is very nice inside. It is an office and home on wheels. Very nice indeed but I have to go." She got up from her seat reaching for the door.

Shantai moved toward Stacy and grabbed her by the hips and pulled her back but she trips over the seat and they both fell to the floor. They looked at each other and started laughing. They are lying side by side.

RONALD GRAY   (232)

"Stacy, are you okay. I'm sorry, I didn't mean to make you fall."

"Yeah, I'm okay but I really have to leave."

"Please don't leave, just stay for a while so we can talk."

"You know I can't and I should not be here." Stacy can feel the heat from Shantai's body and knew she had to get up.

Shantai leaned forward and kissed Stacy gently on the lips while sliding her hand up her dress.

Stacy leaned away from her.

"Stop, I can't do this again with you." Her mouth said no but her body was aching for Shantai's touch. She was already wet.

Shantai knew Stacy's desires and does not plan on letting her out this van until she has had her way with her. She started rubbing Stacy between her legs, feeling her wetness through her panties then quickly but gently pulled her panties off.

Stacy can't do this, she must leave, but it is too late she feels Shantai's finger inside her sliding in and out and it feels so good.

"Please stop, don't do this, ohhhh it feels good."

Shantai lifted Stacy's dress and buries her face between her legs licking her juices then stopped and kissed her on the lips sliding her tongue in her mouth. Shantai slides her finger inside her own wetness rubbing it until she can feel just how wet she is. Then rubs that finger across Stacy's lips and slides it in her mouth back and forth and slides her finger back inside Stacy, fingering her.

"Is this what you really want? Do you like my pussy juices in your mouth, *"Ahora mis espíritus son en usted, freak a freak"*, meaning, now my spirits are in you, freak to freak. Tell me you want me."

Stacy can't fight it anymore.

"Yes, I want you. Your juices taste so good, I got you in me, yes oh yes. You know I do, *"Freak me oh me encanta"*, meaning, freak me oh, freak me," Stacy can't believe she just spoke in Spanish and understood what she just said. No more fighting it. She is going to have Shantai here and now.

She quickly removed all her clothes and Shantai's as well. Stacy was staring at Shantai, seeing how sexy and good looking this girl's body really is. Damn, she is fine. She knows what she wants to do to her and waste no time showing her. She pushed Shantai on her back pushing her legs up in the air and started licking and sucking between her legs. She slides a finger inside her while she is licking her. Seeing how Shantai was responding is making her feel great.

"Ohhh Stacy, baby I like that, don't stop."

Stacy pushed her legs farther back so she can lick her ass and pussy back and forth knowing how good it feels.

"That's right baby, lick my ass, ohhhh it feels so damn good, ohhhh Stacy I want you to hit this pussy good."

Stacy knew exactly what she meant and is determined to please her completely.

"Where is it? Where is the strap-on?"

Shantai pointed to a cabinet close to the floor, arm's distance reach for Stacy.

"In there, oh baby hurry I want you to make me cum so hard."

Stacy opened the cabinet and sees it. She is grateful for all the porn movies she has watched or she would not know how to put it on and surprisingly she put it on fast.

RONALD GRAY   (234)

Shantai turned over on her stomach and looked back at Stacy with the eight-inch strap on wrapped tightly around her and sees the desire in Stacy's eyes, she knows she is going to enjoy this.

"I want you to slide it in me, I'm already so wet for you."

Stacy looked around and sees a small pillow and put it underneath Shantai so her butt can be higher in the air. She moved over Shantai's body and slowly slides the eight inches inside her feeling how tight her pussy is, slow at first inch-by-inch until she is all the way in.

Shantai knew it would be good but this is so much better than she even thought. She started raising her butt up and down, feeling the eight inches slide in and out of her. She is so wet.

"Ohhhhhh yes Stacy, that's it baby, give it all to me."

Stacy never thought she would be so turned on by fucking another woman but this is increasing her own desires. She started moving a little faster in and out of her going deeper with each stroke.

"Ohhhh that's it baby, fuck me, ohhhh fuck me, Stacy, it feels so good, this is your pussy baby, I'm yours, ohhhh, you are making me cum, ohhhh fuck me."

Stacy is pumping in and out of Shantai faster and faster then slows down. Nice deep slow strokes making her feel every sensation of her movements.

"That's it, ohhhh just like that, I'm cummming, fuck me Stacy, ohhhh fuck meeeee."

Stacy keeps humping until she knows Shantai is totally satisfied. Looking at her butt in the air like this is such a turn on for her. She slowly slides out taking the strap-on off and laid it to the side then turned Shantai on her side so she can lay facing her.

RONALD GRAY   (235)

They start kissing each other slowly while caressing each other's body.

"Stacy that was so, so good to me, please don't leave me. You know I want you to and..."

Before Shantai can finish her sentence, Stacy put her finger on her lips to stop her from talking. She leaned closer to her.

"I know, just relax okay."

They start kissing and Stacy lifts one of Shantai's legs up in the air, Shantai held her leg up while Stacy slowly slides her finger in her ass and started licking and sucking her wetness at the same time until Shantai climax again. They remain in the van and continue to please each other in every way. Spending time slowly caressing, licking, and sucking each other's entire body front to back, top to bottom, like they are the only two people in the world. They have made each other climax four times and lay there exhausted.

Shantai was looked in Stacy's eyes, lightly caressing her hips.

"Stacy, please believe me when I say that was absolutely wonderful. Are you going to break my heart and leave me like so many men do after they get what they want from you?" I would never do that to you."

Stacy knows how it feels to give your body and heart to someone and they dump you. As much as she loves Keith she just can't do Shantai like that. Diana left her. She looked in her eyes and put her hand on Shantai's butt.

"Don't lie to me. Is this mine? Are you going to be with someone else?"

Shantai was not expecting this from her but she was truly into Stacy and she would never intentionally hurt her.

"Yes baby, I'm yours for as long as you want me. I know you will never leave Keith, but I still want you and you can have me whenever you want. I will be so good to you and for you. I promise you that."

"Good, then I'm yours."

They slowly kissed, enjoying the feel of each other's lips and tongue.

"Shantai, I have to go. I don't want to but I have to."

"I know you do. Call me tomorrow okay," she kissed her so passionately.

They use towel wipes to clean themselves and then got dressed and hug. Stacy got out the van and looked around then looked up.

"Lord, what have I done to myself and Keith?" She walked back in the club.

Cynthia watched Stacy and Shantai walk out of the club and followed them outside and saw them get into the van. She was sitting in her car that happened to be parked close to the van the entire time they were in it. She could hear some of what they were saying and saw the movement of the van. As soon as Stacy left and walked back to the club, Cynthia got out of her car and walked over to the van and knocked on the side door. Shantai opened the van door thinking it was Stacy coming back. When she saw Cynthia, she was disappointed.

"Who are you and what do you want?" She said frowning and with attitude.

"My name is Cynthia and we need to talk."

RONALD GRAY   (237)

"I don't know you and we have nothing to talk about, so get away from my van." She tried to close the door.

Cynthia grabbed the door and stopped her.

"Yes, we do have something to talk about. You and Stacy and what you two were just doing in this van," she stared at Shantai. "You two were fucking. Now, do we talk or do I go and talk to Keith."

Shantai stared at Cynthia with hate in her eyes.

"Come on in."

Cynthia climbed into the van.

A cloud of smoke appeared and Mr. Bones was standing outside the van. He watched Stacy walk in the club and Cynthia got in the van. He laughed.

"More victims of my evil unholy desires and spirits. I love it. I just love it." He raised his arms, "no one can beat the bones. I come to deceive the entire world." He mumbled some words and he can now see and hear Shantai and Cynthia moaning, twisting, and shaking on the van floor. Shantai has Cynthia's legs up in the air and has her face between her legs.

"Oh Shantai, that feels so good, ohhhh you are going to make me cum."

Mr. Bones was still looking and quietly laughing. "Do it girls, do it." He walked away from the van laughing, "Stupid foolish people. Don't they know there is no loyalty doing my desires, I lie to everybody. I'm the devil. My spirits deceive, trick and destroy." He continued to laugh then walked away touching and cursing each car as he walked through the parking lot.

CHAPTER THIRTY FIVE
All for love

It is Friday afternoon. Ron and Keith are coming back from Gold's gym in Rockville, Maryland. They are in Keith's Lamborghini doing a hundred twenty miles an hour on the beltway going to Ron's house. Keith and Ron told Stacy and Diana they had a surprise for them and they would all meet up at the house after their work out. Keith drove up to the gate at Ron's house. It opened and he drove to the house. They stepped out wearing sweat suits.

"Keith, that's some car but you need to slow it down. I would like to have another birthday."

"Relax my brother. Sometimes, I need to open it up just a little, but yesterday I was doing a hundred and eighty miles an hour and she was purring like a kitten begging for more."
They lean against the car and continue to talk.

"Yeah okay, if you say so. I will stick with my Bentley. Anyway, we have discussed all the details about this trip so let's go inside and tell the girls. I know Stacy will be ready to go in a second but it is going to take some talking on my part to get Diana to go with me, which is stupid and she is trying my patience."

"Better you than me but remember this. You wanted her and now you got her. So, roll with it partner."
Stacy and Diana are sitting on the sofa in the living room watching TV wearing T-shirts and tight shorts.

"What do you think these two are up to now? I'm still upset with Ron and he knows it."

"I don't know Diana but on a real, you need to look at what you have in life and let all of that foolishness go. You are living a dream lifestyle and you have a husband, not a boyfriend, but a husband that treats you like a queen. Wake up before it's too late. Anyway, we are about to find out what is going on because they just drove up in front of the house. Please do me and everyone a big favor, no drama today with Ron, damn. After a while, enough is enough. Just be the wife who appreciates what you have. Feed the man, sex the man, suck the man and fuck the man." She looked at Diana. "You are sucking and fucking him right." She started laughing knowing that would irritate her.

"Some things never change with you and your filthy mind and mouth. You are beyond nasty, you know that."

"That may be true but my baby loves my nasty mind and mouth." She sticks her tongue out at Diana.

Diana looked at her and shook her head.

"I'm sure he does. You two belong together."

Ron and Keith walked into the house and see Diana and Stacy sitting in the living room. Stacy walked over to Keith, hugged and kissed him passionately on the lips. Keith put his hands on her butt pulling her into him.

Diana was looking at how happy they always seem to be and she can see Stacy's butt cheeks as Keith is pulling and grabbing her butt. For a few seconds, her mind wandered and she had flashbacks of her and Stacy together. It instantly turned her on and made her horny but she quickly prayed and blocked those thoughts from her mind.

RONALD GRAY   (240)

Ron was standing there looking at Keith and Stacy and he noticed her butt cheeks as well. He was thinking. *Damn this girl got a thick, fat ass.* Then he looked at Diana desiring her very much. He walked over to her.

"Hi baby, can I get a hug and a kiss?"

Diana was staring at Ron and everything that Stacy said ran through her mind and she instantly made up her mind to show him love, no matter what or whom. She stood up.

"Yes, baby and so much more." She hugged and kissed him with nothing but love and desire in her heart.

"That was nice and you look good. You squeezed all those hips and butt in those little shorts." He said laughing.

Diana playfully hits him on the arm.

"You need to stop but I have something for you," she grabbed his hand and walked past Keith and Stacy. "You two make yourself at home, we will see you a little later," she continued walking and go to their bedroom. Diana takes Ron's clothes off and she got undressed and they took a shower together, dry each other off and get on the bed. For the next two hours, they make passionate love to each other over and over.

When Diana and Ron left, Keith and Stacy looked at each other knowing what time it was. They went upstairs to one of the bedrooms and did the exact same thing. All you could hear throughout the house was moaning and screaming. Hours later they all met down stairs in the basement. Stacy and Keith are sitting on one sofa and Ron and Diana are sitting on the other. Ron and Keith are wearing silk pajama pants and a T-shirt and the girls are wearing shorts and a T-shirt.

"So now that we have taken care of some personal business." Keith said.

Stacy rubs Keith's leg.

"You sure did baby, you sure did." She looked at him smiling and kissed him.

"Don't be nasty Stacy. Leave all that in the bedroom where it belongs." Diana said looking at Stacy and Keith.

Ron kissed Diana.

"Sex is not just for the bedroom baby. Bedroom, bathroom, kitchen, the wall and anywhere you can get busy. It does not make a difference, just get you some." Ron said and started laughing.

"That's what I'm talking about partner, set it off." Keith was laughing knowing Diana didn't like what he or Ron just said.

Diana pointed her finger at Ron and Keith.

"You two are just very nasty. Anyway, enough of all that. What is the surprise?"

"Keith and I have decided to take you and Stacy on a two-week vacation by private jet. We are going to island hop to Tahiti, Bora Bora of course, Venezuela, and Monte Carlo. You can shop until you get tired and we can ship all the clothes and anything else back home so you don't have to be concerned about dealing with customs every time we fly to another destination. First class accommodations all the way of course."

"What do you think?" Keith said.

Stacy looked at Keith.

"Is this a joke, Keith? Are you setting us up for some bad news?"

"It's no joke baby and I would never do that to you. What do you think?"

Stacy looked at Diana and they just stared at each other. Then they both jumped up at the same time and start screaming and run and hug each other. They run back to Ron and Keith kissing them repeatedly. Ron gently grabbed Diana's hand.

"Come on baby lets go to our room, I will give you a back ride upstairs."

Diana stood up and hopped on Ron's back. Her shorts got pulled up tightly on her butt revealing a lot of her butt cheeks Diana was so happy she does not pay attention to this or even care, she was holding on to Ron as they were going up the stairs.

Stacy was kissing Keith but when Diana hopped on Ron's back, she watched her and saw it all. She became instantly horny and missed them being together. She noticed Keith was looking as well and noticed his erection but for the first time, it didn't bother her.

"Keith it's cool baby, some things you just can't help and Diana is pretty and has a nice ass. Ron needs to have dick and tongue between her legs on a regular," she kissed him, "but the only ass you need to concentrate on is mine."

"You are absolutely correct baby," He pulled Stacy's shorts and panties off and pushed her down on the sofa and started licking between her legs to make her wet and hornier. Stacy stopped him and pulled his pants and underwear off and pushed him back down on the sofa slowly sliding down on his dick facing him. She put her hands on his chest for leverage, bouncing her body up and down.

Keith put his hands on her butt helping her ride him.

RONALD GRAY   (243)

"Damn Stacy, I love you. Your pussy is so good."

"It's all yours baby. Ohhhhhh Keith." Shocked by her own thoughts, the image of Diana's butt as she was going up the stairs on Ron's back came to her. She was visualizing Diana on her hands and knees on the bed with her ass up and Keith fucking her from the back. This made her ride him even harder and she had an incredible orgasm but hated her thoughts and tears came to her eyes as she was still riding Keith.

CHAPTER THIRTY SIX

Money talks

Keith, Stacy, Ron, and Diana left two days later along with ten of the *Young Wolves*. Keith contacted a private elite escort service out of Atlanta to have ten ladies keep his security team happy. Ron contacted VIP Airliners and leased a private jet for two weeks to take them on their trip.

Four and half hours and two thousand eighty-four miles later, they landed in Caracas, Venezuela and checked into the luxurious Gran Melia Hotel. They reserved twelve rooms. Two large suites were for, Ron and Diana, and Keith and Stacy. Ten large rooms for the *Young Wolves and* their ten lady friends. Ron and Keith put a budget on this trip, no more than three million dollars.

Keith contacted his attorney before they left to make sure his security team could carry their weapons on this trip. The attorney's answer was, not possible because of international politics. Keith paid him five hundred thousand dollars more and it became very possible.

The ten ladies who were with the *Young Wolves* varied in nationalities but they all were very attractive and had tight sexy curvaceous bodies. Any man would like to have one of them wrapped around his arm. Everywhere they went people stared, wondering who these very nice-looking men and ladies were. Their clothes were expensive, their choice of travel, was nothing but the best, first-class, and they received VIP treatment always. They went on tours, ate at the best of restaurants and shopped at

RONALD GRAY   (245)

the best of stores. For everyone, it was eating, sleeping, shopping, and having sex was their itinerary, in Caracas for four days straight.

On the fifth day, ten and a half hours later they were in Monaco Monte Carlo. They checked into the five-star Le Meridien Beach Plaza hotel along with the best of luxuries, this hotel has its own private beach. They all had the same VIP accommodations and were treated to the best of everything, but all of them had one thing on their mind, the gambling casinos. So, after everyone checked into their rooms, sexed, showered, and changed clothes, they took limo rides to the Casino de Monte-Carlo.

All the men wore Armani suits and the ladies wore expensive, full-length evening gowns with long slits on the side. This place is no stranger to stars and celebrities. They come from all over the world but when these twenty-four-people walked in dressed to impress, all eyes were on them. The *Young Wolves* had the ladies by their side, but they remained aware of all their surroundings, all the time and carried their Mac-10s under their jackets. This was their job, and they did it very well. Even hotel security knew of them and was told by management, hands off, and to give them whatever they wanted.

Diana and Stacy were having the time of their life with Ron and Keith. They were treated like queens, catered to by the best the hotel and casino had to offer.

The ladies with the *Young Wolves* were being swept off their feet like never in their life. Yes, they were escorts but the men treated them with dignity and class, so they made sure not one man had anything to complain about in the bedroom and out.

Sexually whatever the men wanted they received and then some. Everyone was on cloud nine and having the best of time.

Keith and Ron figured they saved the best of relaxation time for Stacy and Diana, for last. After spending four days in Monte Carlo shopping and gambling, on the tenth day they were flying to Tahiti. Eight hours forty-three-minutes and four-thousand, seven hundred, twenty-three miles later they landed in Tahiti and had to take another short flight to Bora Bora. The scenery was brilliant and the waters are beautiful.

Ron and Keith selected Bora Bora for last because after all the excitement of the other two places and all the shopping and gambling. They knew everyone would be a little tired and wanted to relax and be pampered by who they were with. This was the place to do it. Bora Bora is a very laid back beautiful island. They stayed at the Four Seasons Resort and picked the Lagoon-View Over-Water Bungalow. Each room had a king-size bed and plenty of amenities. The south pacific temperature was a nice 82F and just perfect for walking on the beach and going for a swim in the beautiful waters.

This was everyone's private time to relax and be themselves but for Ron and Keith. It was a special time to reconnect with their ladies.

Diana wanted to look very sexy for Ron so she called Stacy and asked her to come over to her bungalow. Ron left to talk with Keith. They agreed to meet at a certain spot on the beach close to the bungalows. Keith and Ron had on sandals, short pants, and T-shirts. They arrived at the spot first and saw Diana and Stacy walking toward them dressed very seductively.

The girls had on sandals, a small top that barely covered their breast and a thong with a sarong wrapped around their waist. This was a private section of the beach, for them only but Ron got instantly angry at Diana seeing her dressed this way and he knew that Stacy talked her into it.

Keith looked at Ron and saw the anger but with all the fun they have been having he was not going to allow Ron to mess it up, so he stopped walking too quickly talk to him.

"Ron, I know you are angry at how Diana is dressed, but don't go their partner, not now. She is a grown woman, trying to please only you and if you can't see that then maybe you're the one with the problem, not her." He put his hand on Ron's shoulder. "Let her live homie or you will lose her. Men would kill to have a woman that fine by their side that they can trust. You have that, so appreciate it, before it's too late."

Ron looked at Keith and realized all that he said was true. He exhaled and smiled.

"You are a true friend and you are right. I have been squeezing her too hard and no one likes that."

Stacy and Diana also stopped walking to talk.

"Ron is going to have a fit when he sees how I'm dressed but I would only do this for him and out here. He better not go off on me or this is going to turn ugly real fast."

"Relax Diana, all will be well. Call it a woman's intuition. If he can't appreciate you wanting to please him, then you need to think real hard about being with that man," Stacy leaned back to look at Diana's butt, "damn you look good in that thong all in your ass. If Ron does not want you, I will take you." She started laughing.

"Stacy, you really are something, my body is for my baby only. Speaking of bodies, Keith is going to attack yours. You look gorgeous Stacy. Thanks for being my friend." She hugged Stacy and she takes advantage of the hug, to caress Diana's butt. Diana playfully pushed her way. "You never give up, do you?"

Stacy smiled at her. "Never."

Ron and Keith are walking and stop in front of them.

"Damn baby, you look stunning and I'm so glad we are on this private beach. Come here sexy," Keith hugged Stacy and started kissing and caressing her, all over her body.

Diana was looking at Ron, trying to read his attitude.

"Ron, before you say anything."

He was so glad to see Diana and how she was dressed was instantly turning him on, he hugged and tongue-kissed her very passionately while caressing her hips.

Diana was so happy. She also became instantly turned on by his touch and positive attitude and she felt his growing erection. It increased her deep burning sexual desire for him. She pressed her body tightly into him, wanting him inside her so badly. Not really thinking, but allowing her deep emotions and sexual hunger to come to the surface. She placed her hands on top of his, forcing his hands on her butt and moving them around.

"Oh Ron, I want you so bad, lick me from the back and fuck me baby," the moment those words came out of her mouth she realized what she said and was so embarrassed because she knew Stacy and Keith heard her.

Stacy and Keith stopped kissing and were looking at these two when Diana said those words. Both were surprised at what she said.

RONALD GRAY   (249)

"About time, do you, Diana," Stacy said. She grabbed Keith's hand and they walked away.

Ron kissed Diana and they walked away holding hands.

Stacy and Keith found a secluded spot near some rocks and did everything but sexual intercourse. Keith developed a bad cramp in his leg so he walked back to their bungalow to relax and put some heat on it. Stacy wanted to go with him to pamper him but he said he would be fine and for her to enjoy her walk on the beach and he would catch up with her later.

Stacy started walking and came to a spot close to some rocks and tall trees. She heard some noise and thought it was some type of animal at first and was about to run away when she heard a familiar sound. She heard Diana moaning. Curiosity got the best of her and she moved closer very quietly and was crouching down, peeking through the trees. What she saw instantly sexually stimulated her greatly.

Ron was lying down on a big boulder with his shorts off and Diana was totally naked sitting on top, riding him. Her head was thrown back and her eyes were closed and her hands were gripping his legs. She was so close to climax when she leaned her head forward and opened her eyes to see Stacy staring at them. She was shocked and so embarrassed but something in her would not allow her to stop. At this point, Diana didn't care. She locked eyes with Stacy and increased her tempo riding Ron's dick. With each passing second, Diana became more turned on by Stacy looking directly at her. She knew she was wrong but the deep erotic desires suppressed within her for so long were coming to the surface. Diana started caressing her breasts and nipples making them hard.

RONALD GRAY   (250)

"You feel so good, oh your dick is so hard. Fuck me Ron, this is your pussy, fuck me harder." Riding him faster and harder staring at Stacy the entire time and licking her lips.

Ron never knew Stacy was behind them watching and listening to everything. Diana's aggressive attitude affected him. He put his finger close to Diana's mouth.

"Suck on this finger baby, get it nice and wet."

At that time Diana would have done anything to please him. She grabbed his finger and started sucking on it like she was sucking on his dick but never taking her eyes off Stacy's. She was licking, sucking and slobbering all over it.

Seeing all of this had Stacy so hot between her legs she wanted to scream but she knew she could not start masturbating because she could never hold her orgasm in.

Ron moved his finger from Diana's mouth and was caressing her butt again until he slowly slid it inside her ass.

Diana was so incredibly turned on she loved the feeling.

"Oh Ron, that's it baby, slide that finger into my ass. Finger fuck this ass baby, it feels so good. I know you want this ass, Ron." When she said that she leaned forward a little and stared even harder at Stacy to let her know that she was really talking to her.

Diana could no longer hold it and she screamed her desires out, not caring who heard her.

"Ron, I'm cummming baby, oh Ron push that dick in me deep, fuck me. Ohhhhhhh Ron." She was shaking and trembling but never took her eyes off Stacy.

"Oh Diana, you are making me cum baby, pussy is so damn good, ahhhhh Diana."

RONALD GRAY   (251)

Diana pressed her breasts to his face for comfort and love. They both relaxed and Diana winked at Stacy.

Stacy walked away probably hornier than she has ever been and could not walk back to her bungalow fast enough to get her hands on Keith.

Ron and Diana stayed there for a while hugging and kissing then they walked back to their bungalow.

When Stacy reached her bungalow, Keith was sitting in a chair with a big smile on his face when he saw her. He just came out of the shower and had a towel wrapped around him.

Stacy quickly removed her clothes, snatched the towel from around Keith and started sucking his dick to get him hard. When he was rock hard she got on top of him and started riding his dick like a mad sex-crazed woman that she was at that time. They had sex all over that place but the entire time all Stacy could see was Diana's face.

The *Young Wolves* had so much fun with the ladies and every night it was whatever they wanted, however, they wanted. On the last night of their trip, you could hear very loud moans and screams of sexual ecstasy. Everyone was having sex on this night and loving it.

Early Sunday morning they were all on the long flight back home. Twenty-one hours later they arrived at BWI airport and another private jet was waiting for the girls to take them back to Atlanta. The girls were so tired of being on a plane that they talked the men into staying the night with them to rest then leave tomorrow. Keith Okayed it and the girls left with the *Young Wolves*. There were other men there from his security team to follow them home. Two limos were waiting for them.

Keith and Ron walked over to one of the limos putting luggage in the trunk. They gave each other dap and Stacy walked over to Diana and hugged her but she whispered in her ear.

"I love you Diana."

Diana looked at Stacy smiling.

"I love you back Stacy," she looked over at Ron and Keith to see if they were looking before she gave Stacy a quick kiss on the lips and walked toward Ron. They got in the limo and it drove away.

Keith walked to Stacy and kissed her.

"Did you have a nice time baby?"

"Keith, I had a great time and I will never forget this trip, thank you so much baby." They kissed and walked to the other limo and got in and it drove away.

CHAPTER THIRTY SEVEN
The fashion Show

It was Friday afternoon, a week after they arrived back from their trip. Diana has not returned any of Stacy's calls and Ron has been in and out of the house for a week spending very little time with her. The fashion show was taking place at the Convention Center in Washington, DC. The room was large with a seating capacity of two thousand people and it has been decorated beautifully. The MC was talking while the models are walking down the runway. Security guards are walking around the room wearing black dress shoes, black dress slacks, and long sleeve dress white shirts. Twenty of the *Young Wolves* are present dressed the same way as the security guards, except on the back of their shirts was written, *Young Wolves Inc.* Stacy and Ron are sitting next to each other close to the runway. Ron was wearing an Armani suit, and Stacy was wearing a seven-thousand-dollar dress from Italy that was cut low in the front revealing her cleavage and hugged her body just right showing all her curves. With three thousand dollar shoes to match.

There are thirty drug dealers sitting close to the runway looking at the models. The drug dealers are supposed to be large store owners, from across the globe, bidding on various clothing items. Each dealer held up a small card with a number written on it, so Ron and Stacy could see it. Stacy and Ron wrote the numbers on their iPad. Keith was standing by the entrance way to the room talking to Greg Johnson. He and Greg are also wearing Armani suits. Stacy was feeling uncomfortable, sitting so close to Ron and looking at so many attractive ladies. Since observing Diana and Ron having sex, those images are forever burned in her mind. Spending time with Shantai are other images she has been dealing with, causing her to have a lot of very nasty erotic thoughts and watching all these women was not helping. She must keep crossing and uncrossing her legs, hoping no one would notice how horny she was. She has even become sexually attracted to Ron, which was so bad on all levels.

Cynthia walked in wearing black Prada heels, a grey very expensive, low-cut, body hugging bodysuit. With her looks and body, she could put the models on stage to shame. The suit fits her like a second skin, and all eyes were on her, with every step she took, and she knew it. So many men and women were lusting over her gorgeous face, round sexy breasts, small waist, hips, and ass. That's why she adds a little extra in her step, making her hips sway and butt shake. She sees Stacy sitting next to Ron, and wants to approach her badly but realize this was not the time, she was determined to get in Stacy's panties, no matter what. Looking at Ron, sitting next to Stacy, irritates her because she had plans for him, such a waste. She thinks about Rick and the wonderful time they had together which makes her smile. She was looking forward to spending more time with him.

Greg looked around the room, then at Keith.

"Everything is going well. The right people are here, the place is full and security is very tight, as it should be. I gave specific orders to remove and physically punish all trouble makers."

"Things are flowing well and this event was sold out the day after it was advertised on the radio. The ladies here are so fine they could stop a pit bull in its tracks." Keith said grinning.

"Keep your mind on business. The ladies are just a tool for the money, other than that, they mean nothing."

Keith stared at Greg.

"You are one cold individual. Do you even like women?"

"Yes, but only for sex. Other than that, they are useless and they all talk too damn much about nothing. That's why when they start all that talking and won't shut up, you put dick in their mouth to give them something to do." He walked away.

Keith watched him walk away and shook his head.

"I thought I was rough on the ladies, this guy is just evil." Sheila, Grandma Harris, and Diana walked into the room where Keith was. All three are wearing long dresses and they walked up to him.

Sheila tapped Keith on the shoulder.

"Hello, Keith Washington."

He turned around and was very surprised at who was standing in front of him.

"Miss O'Neil, Grandma Harris, Diana what are you doing here? This is the last place I expected you three to be."

The very sight of Keith right now makes Diana angry because she knows he is very responsible for Ron's continued criminal lifestyle but the trip they all shared was wonderful. She is not naïve, a five-star trip like that was extremely expensive and she knew where the money came from.

"Well, we didn't come to see you. Where is Ron you lust demon?"

RONALD GRAY   (256)

Keith was looking at Diana like she was crazy. One minute she seems okay with everything and the next, she was all attitude. He pointed his finger at her.

"You know what Diana, I think sometimes you are bipolar because your attitude and behavior changes so much and so quick."

Grandma Harris was looking around the room then looked at Keith.

"Keith Washington, don't pick on my baby and I don't appreciate you, Stacy, and Ron sneaking her off for two weeks traveling the world. Only God knows what you all exposed my baby too. I will deal with that later. Come here and give me a hug, you, disobedient boy."

Keith hugged Grandma Harris and turned toward Sheila.

"Hi mom, can I have a hug?"

Sheila gave Keith a look that was ice cold

"Boy, don't make me sin and get your lips swollen in front of all these people. Where is my son? We need to talk and don't play with me. I'm not in the mood for foolishness."

"Yes mam," he pointed toward Ron, "He is sitting over there next to Stacy."

Diana rolled her eyes at Keith.

"That figures, she is probably trying to corrupt him like you are." She realized what she did was so wrong by allowing Stacy to see her and Ron having sex. She probably wants to be with him now.

Keith was thinking. If she only knew what I would like to do to her and that smart mouth.

"Diana, you and Stacy are supposed to be friends. What happened to that? Oh, that's right she does not go to church. You are one hot and cold judgmental mental person."

Shelia reached over and pinches Keith real hard.

"Shut up boy. I know what you two are doing. Living foul! Shacking up together but you will not marry her. Boy, if I had the time I would tell you a few things about how all women should handle men like you."

Keith looked at Sheila and smiled.

"Miss O'Neil, a man like me can't be handled, only appreciated." He looked over at Diana and winked at her.

All three of them walked past Keith, Diana purposely bumped into Keith as they walked toward Ron and stand behind him.

Sheila pat Ron on his shoulder.

"Ronald Emmanuel O'Neil."

He quickly turned around and his mouth dropped open.

"Mom, what are you doing here? Grandma Harris and Diana, I can't believe you are here." Stacy turned and looked at them.

Grandma Harris smacked Ron on the head.

"Stand up and come hug your mother boy before I knock your eyes out. You, young people, are something else. Lord forgive me but Ron O'Neil," she makes a fist and shook it at him, "I feel like busting your lips, good."

"Hello Miss O'Neil, Grandma Harris, Diana." She rolled her eyes at Diana.

"Hi Stacy. It is good to see you again." She was torn because she does love Stacy, but her spirit is so foul and she can feel her strong lust spirit.

"Hi Diana. I'm surprised to see you here but the trip we had was wonderful. I know you and Ron had a nice time." She said this to her knowing she was still embarrassed about being seen having sex with Ron. Diana turned her back on her again. She felt like slapping the taste out of her mouth at times for having such a holier than thou attitude. She wouldn't be so uptight if Ron was putting that dick and tongue to her like he should. She needs a serious dick down like every woman wants at times. Just like I gave Shantai in that van. She was smiling on the inside.

Grandma Harris smiled at Stacy.

"Hi baby. I'm upset with you but Jesus still loves you," she pointed her finger at Stacy, "but you need to be delivered."

When Grandma Harris said that Stacy was thinking. *If she only knew what Diana and I shared and what I'm dealing with now, she would really think I'm possessed.* She looked at Diana and shook her head because she felt betrayed by her again. She's being such a hypocrite and I would love to be drilling her from the back with that strap-on. Stacy shook her head. God help me.

Ron walked over and hugged Sheila and Grandma Harris.

"Hi Diana." He extends his arms toward Diana to hug her.

She hugged him and whispered in his ear.

"I'm not going to create a scene but I could slap the taste out of your mouth for tricking me. One moment you are all over me and then you are back out in the streets but I have something for you, husband." She looked at him with cold eyes.

Ron whispered back in her ear.

"I hope it's something hot, tight and wet." He smiled and kissed her lips.

Diana grabbed her own leg to keep from slapping Ron. She looked at Stacy feeling how angry she was towards her and she knows why. But she had to make a choice for her own salvation.

Two of the security guards walked over to Ron. One of them tapped him on the shoulder.

"Mr. S&D is there a problem sir?"

Ron turned around to look at him.

"No, there is no problem, this is my family."

Sheila lightly hit Ron to get his attention.

"Mr. S&D, boy what is that mess? Some foolish devil name he tricked you to embrace. You just don't know how bad I could beat all the black off you right now. God, hold me."

Diana hit Ron.

"Answer your mother. What does S&D stand for?"

Ron stared at Diana and spoke softly to her.

"I'm tired of you hitting me. You haven't been giving up that booty on a regular basis since we got back from our trip. Stop hitting me Diana, I mean it. The letters stand for, Samson and Delilah. Look it's great to see all of you, but this is bad timing. I have some serious business to take care of."

Frank Cantina and four of his bodyguards walked in. Keith and Greg turn around to face them. Three of the security guards walked over and stand next to Keith and Greg.

Greg extends his hand.

"Mr. Cantina, how are you doing sir? I was not aware that you would be here. What can I do for you?"

Frank ignores his hand.

"I need to speak to Mr. Augular. I went to his club but was told he sold it and he was no longer there. I heard about this big show and I figured he would be here."

Keith stepped closer to him.

"Mr. Augular sold his club to me he is not here but you are welcome to enjoy the show and talk to me if you need anything."

He looked at Keith like he was scum.

"Thank you for your assistance but I don't deal with errand boys."

Keith pulled his suit jacket back to show his gun.

"Who are you calling errand boy, old man? I don't give a damn who you are. If you disrespect me again I will body slam your old ass, right here, now try me." He looked at Frank, mean mugging him hard.

The *Young Wolves* are always watching Keith and Ron. Seeing Keith get angry put them on high alert. They all have two nine- millimeters strapped to their legs, and are ready to bust off against anyone, even Victor, and his bodyguards. Frank's bodyguards open their suit jackets to show their guns.

Victor and his five bodyguards walked in behind Frank and his bodyguards. Victor was wearing a two-toned, brown forty-three-thousand-dollar, tailored, completely hand-stitched Brioni Italian suit, and twenty-five-hundred-dollar Berluti shoes. He's holding his two, fifty-seven magnums in his hand, and all his men have on Armani suits that are already unbuttoned, revealing two Mini Uzis- sub-machine guns strapped to their shoulders.

Victor learned long ago, never tell all your business and at a big event like this, he expected trouble. He made one phone call to Mr. Case, asking him to send some of his best-trained men to this event, but for them to stay low key. He knew Keith's *Young Wolves* would be here and he quickly scanned the room when he walked in and he saw some of them. Mr. Case sent Victor thirty men, all highly-trained like him. They are scattered throughout the room, all wearing automatic weapons underneath their suits and are instructed to protect Victor, at all cost. When Victor walked into the room, their eyes were on him and Mr. Cantina, ready to attack at any second. Mr. Case's men are thirty walking-death dealers for hire, at five thousand dollars a day.

Victor walked into the room, very cocky and arrogant like he owns the entire world.

"Gentlemen, is there a problem?"

Frank and his men turn around.

"Mr. Augular."

Victor walked closer to him.

"Mr. Cantina, I suggest that everyone relax and sit down and enjoy the show before I become emotional. We will do business after the show is over."

"Mr. Augular, we need to talk." Frank said.

"We will, after the show," he stepped closer and stared at Frank, "is that a problem?

All of Victor's thirty men are watching him like a hawk and when Victor stepped closer to Mr. Cantina, his men pulled back their suit jackets ready to pull out and start blasting.

He looked around at Victor's bodyguards, then at Victor.

"No problem. Let's enjoy the show." He and his men walk off and sat down.

Victor looked at him walking away.

"Wise choice." He looked out over the crowd and nods his head knowing his men were on high alert.

Victor and his men put their guns away.

Greg shook Victor's hand.

"Mr. Augular it is good to see you."

"Mr. Augular, your timing is perfect. How are you sir?"

"Mr. Keith Washington this show of yours was a great idea, now if you will find me a good table I will sit down and enjoy it."

Greg turned to look at Keith.

"Keith, make sure your partner S&D is handling his end, and I will see to Mr. Augular."

Keith stepped closer to Greg.

"This is my show. I'm running this, not you, and don't you forget it. By the way," he pointed his finger at Greg, "you ain't bullet proof." He grits his teeth and walked toward Ron.

Victor stepped closer to Greg.

"Mr. Johnson, I know how you feel and when this deal is over, he is all yours. Now let's enjoy this show."

Greg walks with Victor and his bodyguards to a reserved table and they all sat down.

Shelia, Diana, Grandma Harris, and Ron are all sitting at a table when Keith approached them.

"Ron, we need to talk, now."

"Just a minute I need to talk to my mom."

Sheila looked at Keith with venom in her eyes, and then looked at Ron.

"Ron, listen to me. Christine is very depressed over all of this and still blames herself, and something else is bothering her, but

I don't know what it is. You need to go and talk with her and visit Sandra again. Just sit and talk with her. Come back to the Lord son. You can't run from God."

Diana touched Ron's hand.

"Ron, words can't express how much I miss you but you are destroying yourself and our marriage, lusting over all these women. I deeply love you, but right now, I could slap you blind."

"Diana, your threats are getting old. I haven't slept with anyone because I love you, so relax," he looked at Sheila, "mom I really don't mean to hurt you, but this is serious business and it's a lot of money. I will see my sisters later and besides, I don't need God anymore. I'm out of prison, making so much money now, I should have my own mint. I'm on top of the world and I can't be touched." He said smiling.

Sheila's mouth dropped open and she stared at Ron. She cannot believe what just came out of his mouth.

"Lord have mercy, my son is possessed. I can't believe you would say that." She started crying and Grandma Harris put her arm around Sheila.

Diana's mouth dropped open as well. Never did she ever expect to hear Ron of all people say those words. Which lets her know how deeply, spiritually bound he really is.

"Ron, are you crazy," she yelled, "I can't believe you just said that. Are you demonically possessed boy?"

Ron stared at Diana.

Grandma Harris pointed her finger at Ron.

"Ronald Emmanuel O'Neil, you are the chosen one, but God is about to bring you down to your knees. You remember that."

Keith stepped to Ron and tapped him on his chest.

"Ron, Mr. Augular is here and some other big players with his men. You need to get back to work, now."

He stood up.

"Damn, you should have said something sooner Keith," he looked at Sheila, "Mom, I have to go but I will talk with you after the show," he leaned toward Diana, "Diana, just for the record, I'm not demonically possessed and I miss you just as much. You are still the only woman for me which was why I married you." He kissed her on the lips and walked back to his seat next to Stacy.

"Ron wait." Diana yelled and waved her hand at him.

When Ron sat down next to Stacy she hit him on his arm.

"It is about time you came back. I'm tired of all this writing and sick of these men looking at me like I'm a pork chop."

"Relax Stacy, everything will be fine. Besides, pork chops are good." He looked at her, licked his lips and smiled.

Stacy hit him on the arm again.

Diana looked at Keith and had to quickly repent from the thoughts she was thinking about him right now. She pointed her finger in his face.

"Keith Washington, I blame you for adding to his sinful ways and I really dislike your foul spirit but I pray that you repent and give your life to the Lord."

Keith waved his hand in her face.

"Yea, yea, well pray for me," he laughed. "Pray that I keep making this money." He walked away and sat next to Stacy, "hi baby," he kissed her, "now we can sit back and enjoy the show."

Stacy looked at Keith and reached over to hold his hand. She missed the closeness they always share but he has been so busy

RONALD GRAY   (265)

lately. Now she feels very guilty about all that she has done. She knows deep down inside she has truly betrayed Keith and the tight bond they have. What she would give to turn the clock back and not have allowed herself to be touched by Shantai or Diana. She feels so violated and dirty. Yet, she can't stop thinking about Shantai and how good she made her feel. Today for some odd reason she has been having sick dirty thoughts about Shantai and her friend Cynthia repeatedly. She wants them both, at the same time. Oh God help me. She leaned her head on Keith's shoulder and whispered in his ear.

"I love you Keith and will do whatever I have to do to keep you." A tear escaped her eyes.

Keith looked at Stacy and wondered what was really bothering her, but he doesn't have the time now to think about it. He needs to stay focused on this deal which was life and death.

The fashion show continued with the MC calling the ladies and men out to the runway. The ladies are modeling dresses, slacks, and swim wear. The men are modeling suits, pajamas and swim wear. There was a break during the show and a group sings several songs and then the show continued until it was over.

Victor looked at his men.

"The show was great and the ladies were outstanding, very beautiful. Now it's time for the best part. Collecting my money," he looked at Greg, "Mr. Johnson is everything ready."

"Yes sir, the warehouse is set up and my men are in position, we could start a war with all the fire power in that place. We control everything."

"Very good sir. Get everything to the warehouse so we can end this and move on. We take care of the paperwork for the

RONALD GRAY   (266)

hotel and kill Mr. Cantina before we leave here. Stupid idiot, he should have taken my offer."

People are leaving the room. Cynthia has been watching Stacy the entire night, waiting for the right time to approach her, now is that time. She walked toward her when she sees Shantai. She can't believe Shantai is here. She didn't see her tonight. Shantai was wearing heels and a long, black tight-fitting dress with a long slit on the side. The dress was showing the outline of her hips and butt very well. Cynthia walked over to her and the closer she got to Shantai, the more she can see this girl was wearing the hell out of that dress. Damn, she is fine.

"Shantai hi, I didn't know you were even here. I didn't see you tonight."

She looked at Cynthia with mixed feelings. Part of her wants to cut her throat for how she blackmailed her into having sex. The other part wants her back in bed because she was fantastic. She is a total freak, just the way she likes her women and looking at her now in that very tight bodysuit was making her hot.

"I saw you when you came in and so did everybody else in this place. Girl, you are killing them with that bodysuit. Anyway, I came a little late and I sat in the back. We need to talk, now."

"Okay, no problem. What do you want to talk about? And don't step to me with no drama, because I'm not the one," she stepped closer to her staring at her eyes, "you wanted me just as much as I wanted you," she whispered in her ear, "you are such a sexual freak." She leaned away smiling.

Shantai could smack the taste out of her mouth, right now. Yet, having her physically this close again and feeling her warm breath on her ear caused her own desires to wake up and make

RONALD GRAY   (267)

her inner thighs hot. She has a plan for Cynthia and Stacy tonight.

"I would like for us to talk about Stacy. I have a plan and I need your help to pull it off."

"If it is what I think it is, then count me in. Let's go find someplace to talk."

They walked away and see Stacy talking to Keith.

Stacy turned toward Keith.

"Baby I will see you at home and be careful. I have a bad feeling about tonight. So, don't do anything stupid."

"Relax, everything is fine and after tonight we retire." He kissed her softly on the lips, loving how soft and warm her lips always are. Then he walked away.

Stacy got up and walked over to Sheila's table.

"Miss O'Neil, it was good to see you again and I enjoyed the show but now it's time for me to go home. Grandma Harris, Diana you have a nice evening." She walked away but looked at Diana with anger but she still sexually desired her.

All the drug dealers are standing by the runway talking to Keith and Ron.

Keith waved his hand to get their attention.

"Gentlemen, I hope everyone enjoyed the show. We have all your purchases and we will all meet at the warehouse and do some business."

Frank and his men walked over to Victor's table. Victor and his men stand up.

"Victor Augular, the show was very nice but I can see people perform and watch half-dressed woman back in Atlantic City. My patience is wearing thin, we need to talk and talk now."

"Mr. Cantina, I apologize for your inconvenience and appreciate your patience. There are some men over there that I need to briefly speak with, after that, we will do business. I promise you that. He and his men walk toward Keith and stood next to them. "Gentlemen, I hope all has gone well and everyone has enjoyed themselves. I know I did, many times and over."
One of the drug dealers stepped closer to Victor.

"Mr. Augular the show was fine. Now it's time to see some product."

"And so, you shall. I will see you all at the warehouse."
All the drug dealers walked away and out of the room.

Ron turned to look at Victor.

"Mr. Augular, we have all the purchases from everyone. A total of twenty-five thousand nine hundred kilos. Twenty-five thousand kilos of cocaine and nine hundred kilos of heroin."

"Perfect. I can handle it. I will see you two at the warehouse." He and his men walked over to Frank.

Keith and Ron walk toward Sheila.

"Mom, I have to go and take care of some business. I promise to call and come see you tomorrow."

"Ron please don't go, not now. I beg you please stay," she started crying, "is money more important than me or Jesus?"

Diana walked over to Ron and grabbed his hand.

"Ron if you truly do love me, please stay and stop breaking your mother's heart and mine," she started crying, hugged and kissed him.

"Ron," Keith yelled, "we have to go and we don't have time for all of this crying. Money is calling partner, damn. Let's get this money." He said frowning.

RONALD GRAY   (269)

Grandma Harris pointed her finger at Keith.

"Shut up devil. Hold thy peace, in Jesus name."

Sheila walked over to Keith.

"I have loved you like my own son, and now all you care about is your stinking drug money. The same thing that got my husband killed." She slapped him.

Ron pulled away from Diana.

"No matter what you think, I do miss you, Diana. You are my wife, and I love you deeply." He stepped closer to Sheila, hugged and kissed her. "Mom, I promise to call you tomorrow. He stepped toward Keith, "Keith, it's time to do this." He and Keith walked over to the far corner of the room where all twenty of the   are waiting.

Diana called out to Ron.

"Ron wait!" Tears were coming down her eyes.

Grandma Harris put her arm around Diana and Sheila.

"I know all seems like it is lost, but God is not finished with Ron. Just let go and let God, my Lord and master has all power."

The *Young Wolves* are aware of the big drug deal going down tonight and they have been waiting for Keith and Ron. One of them stepped toward them.

"Keith, Ron we are ready and loaded down in the trucks. We have four fifty-calibers rifles, three sixty-calibers machine guns, three Remington's M24s sniper rifles, three boxes of explosive hand grenades with thirty in each box, twenty Mac-10s machine guns, some pistol grip shot guns, some 44 Magnum hand guns, a few Striker street-sweeper shotguns, two flamethrowers, and two Rocket Launchers. We have enough ammunition for everything." Looking at Keith and Ron.

RONALD GRAY   (270)

Ron was looking at him, trying not to show his true thoughts, but he was wondering are these people for real. They have enough fire power and the skills to use everything, to start a war. This was ridiculous.

"Is that all you have. Do you think you need a little more?" Ron said smiling at the guy.

He stared at Ron with no emotion on his face.

"We can get more."

Keith nods his head at the men. They all got a little closer to him and Ron.

"Gentlemen, Ron and I appreciate all of you for being combat soldiers, ready at all times, but we need all of you to stand down on this one. Go to the office and just chill and wait for our call. We are done with the illegal stuff after tonight and we need all of you to keep your hands clean because we have some big plans after this and no one can have dirty hands. All of you can carry the weapons that you do because of your high-security clearance. We need to keep it that way."

Everyone nodded their heads and they walked away. Ron and Keith looked at each other.

"Damn Keith, where did you get these guys from? They are ready to take on the world." He was staring at him.

"I recruited them here and there. Preparation is the key, my brother, you know that partner. Let's go." They walked away and out of the building.

Mr. Augular was talking to Mr. Cantina.

"Mr. Cantina, again I appreciate your continued patience, now there is a more private room we can go to for our business.

If you will follow me," he turned to look at Greg, "Mr. Johnson you can go ahead and take care of that other business."

"Yes sir." Greg nods his head and walked away and out of the room.

Victor and his bodyguards, Frank and his men all walked together and out of the room. Grandma Harris, Sheila, and Diana are walking out of the building.

Mr. Bones was walking down the hallway of the Renaissance Hotel which is about a mile from the convention center. He stopped at room twenty-three fourteen, mumbled some words and tapped his cane against the door frame. The door opened and he walked in and the door closed by itself. He walked around the room mumbling and tapping his cane on all the furniture. He looked at the bed mumbled some words and spat on the bed then tapped his cane on it twice. He throws his bones in the air and they hover over the bed and turn into a thin mist that settled on the bed. He walked in the bathroom mumbling words and spat all over the bathroom.

"I curse this room and everyone who walk in here." He mumbled some words and disappeared in a cloud of smoke.

Stacy was not in the mood to go home. She caught a cab to the Renaissance Hotel, to walk around and maybe get something to eat. The hotel was very lavish. She also has been feeling very lonely and extremely horny. As she was walking through the lobby, she sees Shantai walking toward her. This was the last person she wanted or needed to see right now because of how she was feeling.

"Shantai hi. I didn't know you were here. Did you enjoy the show?"

"Yes, it was good and I saw some very nice outfits that I would like to buy, but I really need to see you. I don't want to go home right now. Can we have a girl's night and just have fun." Stacy knew what this could lead to.

"Shantai I don't want to turn my back on you but I just can't right now. I have some deep thoughts on my mind and I need to think."

Shantai walked closer to her and put her hand on her waist.

"I understand, but can you just hang out with me please, no pressure. I could really use your company and a friend. Look, I already have a room here and something to drink. It's Friday, so let's just listen to some music," she stepped closer and whispered in her ear, "I got some weed if that's your thing." She stepped back from her, "don't say no." She stared in her eyes. Stacy knew this was all a bad idea but she has been under a lot of stress lately, so why not.

"Okay I will come, but I can't stay long, and don't push up on me."

Shantai was thinking. *Yea right if Stacy only knew what was on her mind.*

"Great and thank you. We are going to have so much fun." She kissed Stacy on the cheek and they walked through the lobby toward the elevator with Shantai's arm around Stacy's waist. As they were walking, Shantai slowly slid her hand on Stacy's butt, very lightly caressing it, knowing she was already getting to her.

Stacy knew she should have moved Shantai's hand the moment she put it on her butt, but it did feel good, and it was relaxing for her. When they got on the elevator and the doors closed, Shantai grabbed Stacy by the waist, pulled her closer,

RONALD GRAY   (273)

kissing her passionately. She grabbed her butt, with both hands, nibbling on her ear. Stacy was done, weak to a point where she didn't care anymore.

The moment Shantai grabbed and kissed her, she felt a very powerful seducing spirit, flow into her body and wanted to slap her but she didn't. She wanted Shantai so bad. A lot more than the first time when they were together. She pushed Shantai away.

"Stop Shantai, I told you about that."

"You are right I could not resist you. Nobody told you to be so damn fine." Smiling at her.

They got off the elevator and walked down the hallway towards the room. Stacy was watching Shantai's butt, while she was walking and instantly some very erotic and nasty thoughts come to her mind.

Shantai knew Stacy was watching her walk, so she decided to make it more tempting for her. She pulled her dress up from the back, so Stacy could see her big, round shapely butt, and caressed it for Stacy to get turned on. She took her panties off earlier, just for this moment. She looked back at her while walking and smiled.

"Did you like what you saw?"

Stacy wished she had followed her first thoughts and not come up here. Because the moment Shantai flashed her butt, she wanted her. Her body was so sexy, so tight. Stacy could feel herself getting wet.

"That was not funny Shantai. You better stop playing with me or you are going to see a side of me that you can't handle." Shantai stopped walking and stood by room twenty-three fourteen and turned to Stacy.

RONALD GRAY   (274)

"Well, this is the room. Anyway, don't talk about it, do it, because I will."

That was it. Stacy felt like she was being compelled to do what she was about to do. She walked over to Shantai pulled her dress up and smacked her very hard on the butt.

"Ouch! Damn girl that hurt. Why did you do that? Don't make me…"

Stacy put her hand over Shantai's mouth before she could finish her sentence and then kissed her on the lips while grabbing her butt with both hands.

"Stop playing with me. Is this my ass?"
"Yes baby, it's yours, you know this. Tonight is our night."
Stacy was staring at her and was feeling guilty.

"No, I can't do this Shantai, I need to go." Stacy turned away to leave.
Shantai was not about to get this close and not have her way. She quickly grabbed Stacy by the waist and pulled her back.

"I miss you so much, please don't leave me." She kissed Stacy while whispering words Stacy couldn't understand and slid her tongue into her mouth, "I have a surprise for you."

She opened the door and Cynthia was sitting on one of the beds with no socks or shoes on. She was wearing a tank top with no bra and a pair of short, tight shorts showing her butt cheeks.

She stood up holding her arms out.

"Surprise Stacy."
Stacy and Shantai walked in and closed the door.

"Cynthia, what in the world are you doing here? This is a surprise." She walked over and hugged her.

When Stacy hugged her, Cynthia grabbed her butt under her dress and started caressing it with both hands, kissing Stacy on the lips. That's when Stacy knew, all of this was a setup. Before she could react, Shantai came up behind her kissing and sucking on her neck, while caressing her hips and butt as well. She was caught in the middle of them and getting hotter by the second.

"I can't believe you two would do me like this. Cynthia, you are supposed to be my friend. Why are you doing this," she leaned her head back, "ohhhh you two are driving me crazy. I got to get out of here." She stepped away from them.

Cynthia grabbed her pulling her back and started licking Stacy on her neck, while Shantai was taking Stacy's heels, dress, panties, and bra off.

"I'm your friend Stacy but I have wanted you for so long, so please baby don't get mad at us, just relax and allow us to have you. I promise you that it will stay with us." Cynthia took her shorts and tank top off and started licking and sucking on Stacy's breasts.

Shantai has her hands on Stacy's hips, licking her upper back working her way down to her butt.

"You know how much I miss you Stacy." She lowered her body and started licking and sucking on her butt while Cynthia has her head between her legs licking and sucking her wetness.

Stacy has never felt this good in all her life. Having two women pleasing her at the same time is beyond words.

"Oh yes, ohhhh you two are making me feel so damn good. Ohhhh just take me."

That was all they wanted to hear. They guided Stacy to the bed and began to turn her out. Shantai and Cynthia did it all to

Stacy. While one was eating her pussy, the other was licking and sucking her ass, at the same time. They each had a strap-on and took turns fucking her. They had Stacy spread out on the bed, with her legs spread, while one was licking her pussy and the other was sitting on her face. Stacy screamed so much, from having such intense orgasms, one after the other. They licked, kissed, and sucked her entire body, repeatedly. Then they all entwined their bodies together, and started fucking, sucking, each other into one big three- some. They smoked weed, poured wine on each other, and licked it off. Their sexual acts became so intense. You could see their facial expressions, turning almost demonic, with so many lustful spirits in the room. They were hissing, growling, spitting, biting on each other and licking every inch of each other's body until no part was untouched.

They could not get enough of each other. At one point, Stacy was begging them for more and they gave it to her repeatedly.

Stacy lost count of how many times she climaxed. Their juices were all over each other. All three eventually got up and took a shower but Stacy was the last one. Shantai and Cynthia decided to do one last thing to her. When they heard the shower water go off, they walked in on Stacy and both were wearing the strap-on. They sandwiched her by lifting one of her legs up while she was standing and one slid into her pussy while the other put it in her ass and started slowly fucking her.

Stacy thought she would fall out. It hurt a little at first, but they were so gentle and helped her body to relax by talking to her. Whispering words, she could not understand, while kissing and sucking all over her neck, until the pleasure was so intense she started shaking and screaming. She was screaming when

RONALD GRAY   (277)

climaxing so hard they had to put a hand over her mouth. Stacy started crying, it was so intense and it felt overwhelmingly good. She was begging them to keep fucking her, even after she climaxed, because, she could feel another orgasm coming, right behind that.

All three showered again and got dressed to leave. Promising never to speak of this moment to anyone, but Stacy knew her life would never be the same when she walked out of room twenty-three fourteen. She knew she was hooked on erotic, freaky, sex that not even Keith could satisfy unless he got on her level. As she was walking out, a wicked thought came to her mind. Diana, yeah, miss goody. I need to see just how committed she really is to the Lord. She was walking and smiling.

CHAPTER THIRTY EIGHT
Victor Frank and Mr. Bones

Victor, his bodyguards, Frank, and his men are in a small room. Victor was sitting down at a table with his bodyguards standing behind him. Frank was sitting at the same table, across from Victor, and his men are standing behind him.

"Mr. Frank Cantina, I feel the offer that I made you concerning your hotel and casino was a very generous one, considering its financial state."

"Yes, your offer was very interesting, and I have carefully considered it, which is why," he reached into his suit jacket pocket removed some papers and laid them on the table, "I have brought the necessary papers for my hotel to sign over to you."

Victor looked at his men and smiled.

"Perfect and your timing could not be better. Let's sign some papers and you can come with me and I will give you the money and the drugs and this will conclude our business."

"Not so fast Mr. Augular, it is not that simple. You may run things in Maryland and other parts of the world, but not in Atlantic City. Which means you will need a license for the casino, which the board doesn't like outsiders, and the fact is, I don't like you or the way that you do business. You can't muscle in on my territory or scare me."

Victor shook his head.

"It's a shame that you feel that way," he looked at his men, "gentlemen we have a situation."

His bodyguards quickly pull out their automatic weapons, with silencers on them and shoot Frank's men, and then aim their guns at Frank.

"Now look what you made me do." Victor yelled then quickly stood up pulling out his two three fifty-seven magnums. He put both guns to Frank's head, "now sign the hotel over to me, you, stupid idiot," he smacked him in the head with both guns one at a time, "now look at you. Sign the papers boy."

Blood was running down Frank's head. He rubs his head then looked at Victor with hate, but he signed the papers. He looked up staring at Victor with blood coming down his face.

"You made a very big mistake. You will never get away with this and my arm is just as long as yours."

Victor put his guns away and stepped back.

"I think not. Mr. Bones." He yelled."

A cloud of smoke appeared behind Frank and Mr. Bones appeared dressed in all black, holding his cane and black pouch. Mr. Case was standing next to him, dressed in his black ninja suit with his sword on his back.

"You called, Mr. Augular."

Frank stood up and turned around.

"What the hell is this? Where did you Halloween freaks come from? You can't scare me, I'm Mr. Frank Cantina, a made man."

Mr. Bones pointed his cane at him.

"Shut up boy. You, stupid sinners, are alike, thinking you can dance with me and not pay the price. Well it's pay time boy, time to go to hell."

Frank started laughing and pointed his finger at Mr. Bones.

"You stupid freaks don't scare me, I'm untouchable. Stupid freaks."

"Shut up fool, I'm Mr. Bones and I don't like people calling me names," he turned to Mr. Case, "Mr. Case, it's time to go."

Mr. Case moved with the speed of lightning, pulled out his sword and cut Frank's head off and grabbed his severed head even before Frank's body hits the floor. He grins slightly while putting his sword away and blood was splattered on the floor.

Mr. Bones tapped his cane on the floor twice and smoke appeared, covering the room. When it disappeared Mr. Bones, Mr. Case and Frank's entire body are gone, but his bodyguards are still lying on the floor.

Victor's bodyguards looked around to locate Frank and his bodyguards. They were bewildered at what just took place. One of Victor's bodyguards said.

"They're gone man, what the fuck! I don't know about this man. They all sat down. Victor does the same and shook his head.

"I keep saying this but never have I seen such power. That man must be the spirit of Satan himself in a body. Damn, he has powers, but Mr. Bone's time is very short. Now it's time for us to go get this money and hopefully send some people to hell," he and his bodyguards walked out of the room.

Mr. Bones cane appeared in the room, in a small cloud of smoke standing up right. It tapped itself on the floor twice and smoke appeared underneath Frank's bodyguards. The smoke covered their bodies then the cane tapped itself on the floor again once and more smoke appeared in the room, when it cleared, the bodies on the floor, the blood, and the cane are gone.

RONALD GRAY   (281)

CHAPTER THIRTY NINE

Stacy Cynthia and Diana

When Stacy left the hotel, she was feeling so bad for all that she did with Cynthia and Shantai. It was as if it was not really her doing and saying all those things. Her feelings of direct betrayal of what she and Keith share was overwhelming. She threatens him constantly about cheating, but look what she has been doing. Cheating! Being with females makes no difference, cheating is cheating.

When she got back to the condo all she wanted to do was take a long hot shower to try and feel clean. She spent an hour in the shower, scrubbing her body, over and over. She felt a little better after her shower. She wrapped a towel around herself and sat on the sofa to watch TV. She knew Keith would probably be out all night. She was very worried about him, more so than usual. She was also feeling very lonely, desperately wanting to talk to someone, so she called Cynthia, of all people, hoping she would tell her why she betrayed her because she thought they were good friends. She picked up her cell phone to call Cynthia when she heard a knock at her door. Stacy was surprised, because she didn't expect anyone this time of the night, except for Keith. She walked to the door and peeped through the hole and was shocked to see Cynthia standing there.

She was wondering, should she open the door and snatch this bitch in her house and beat her down or find out what she was doing here. Still wearing a towel, she was uncomfortable, knowing who was at the door, but she knew she could beat her down if she had to. She opened the door. Cynthia was wearing

RONALD GRAY　　　　(282)

tennis shoes, some very tight sweats and a short top displaying her tight waist.

"Cynthia what are you doing here," she said with serious attitude, "and how did you find out where I live."

"Can I come in so we can talk, please?"

"Yeah, come on in because we need to talk but you can't stay long." She stepped aside to let her in, trying not to notice how tight her sweats are, that are hugging her hips and butt very well.

They both sat on the sofa but Stacy felt very self-conscious sitting close to her and kept her legs crossed tightly. Anger suddenly overcame her. She slapped Cynthia so hard across her face, her neck turned then she quickly reached down between the cushions of the sofa and pulled out her razor, and put it to Cynthia's throat.

"What the hell is wrong with you, setting me up like that? I thought we were friends. I should cut your throat right now, you Judas."

Cynthia knew she would be upset, but didn't expect Stacy to react so violently. She felt the blade on her skin and was terrified, knowing Stacy was not to be played with. Tears quickly come to her eyes.

"Stacy wait, please don't cut me, I can explain. I'm so sorry for what I did to you, but the truth is, I'm bisexual and have been for years and I have always desired you. When I ran into Shantai she told me what happened between you two," she lowered her head then looked back at Stacy with tears in her eyes, "I felt so hurt and betrayed by you. We have known each other for years, ran the streets together, shared secrets and you go and be with someone that you just met. You could have come to me, I would have taken good care of you. Why turn to a stranger? Now, you tell me, who betrayed who?"

Stacy never thought about it like that because it was just an instant strong lust moment with Shantai. She never really knew Cynthia was bisexual, she heard rumors but didn't believe them. She was now staring at Cynthia feeling her sincerity and hurt. She removed the razor from Cynthia's throat, putting it back in the cushion of the sofa.

"I didn't know you felt about me like that and what happened with Shantai and I was just a moment that should not have happened. I feel bad for several reasons but I do not want to talk about it. I appreciate you coming over to explain all of this to me and it does make me feel better knowing the truth about you. I'm sorry for slapping you and putting the razor to your throat."

Cynthia exhaled, rubbed her throat, inwardly thanking God Stacy didn't cut her. She smiled at her.

"No problem, I still deserved it but you don't know how angry I was at you when I found out. I was determined to have you then," she stared at Stacy, "can I have a hug?"

"I don't think that's a good idea, you might jump me," she laughed but held her arms out to her, "okay, one hug."

Cynthia moved closer to her and they hugged. The moment they hugged Stacy could feel all her deep desires rise to the surface once again and allowed Cynthia to hug her too long. They stopped hugging and stared at each other, slowly moving closer, they kissed. Cynthia kissed her with so much passion because she really does love her. She stopped kissing Stacy and leaned back staring at her.

RONALD GRAY   (284)

"I know you are going to think I'm crazy, but I have never loved anyone like I love you," tears fall from her eyes, "I have to go," she stood up to leave.

Stacy is caught off guard by what Cynthia just said, she can feel the love that she has for her. Keith is the only person she ever did fully open her heart to. She understood real love. She gently grabbed Cynthia by her sweats.

"Cynthia wait," she stood up in front of her, "I didn't know you felt this way and I don't know what to say to you but I'm touched. I really am. If you want, we can be friends but I can't..."

Stacy never finished her sentence because Cynthia pulled her closer hugging her very tightly then looked in her eyes with her arms still around her.

"Thank you, I would miss you so much if we could not be friends," she stared at her then moved closer kissing Stacy very slowly, sliding her hands under her towel caressing her butt, "I love you Stacy, I really do," she kissed her again but with more passion and desire grabbing her butt harder, pressing her fingers into it.

Stacy knew she should have pushed Cynthia off but the truth is, she wanted her. She grabbed Cynthia's butt and it felt so good in her hands but she backed up from her.

"Cynthia, you know I want you but I can't, I love Keith."

She pointed her finger at Stacy and raised her voice.

"And I love you. Who is going to love me?" Cynthia throws her hands up in total frustration and hurt. "Who Stacy? Who is ever going to love me? She started crying.

Seeing Cynthia like this was breaking Stacy's heart and she had to hold back her own tears. She stepped closer to her.

RONALD GRAY   (285)

"Cynthia, do you really love me or just want sex from me?" She looked at her with tears flowing from her eyes.

"Don't do that, don't make fun of me, you know it's not just sex. I'm in love with you. Not just your body but you."

Stacy was looking at her with increased desires of her own because of Cynthia's emotions and words. That did it for her, she wanted Cynthia.

"Then come here and make love to me," she gently grabbed Cynthia's hand and leads her to the sofa. Stacy dropped her towel on the floor and Cynthia sat up on the sofa, removed all her clothes, except for her heels. Stacy climbed on top of Cynthia, pushing her head back, stroking her hair and her breasts, gently and takes her finger sliding it, slowly across her own lips. "Do you want me" taking her finger, sticking it into Cynthia's pussy.

"Ohhhhhh," Cynthia moans with excitement, "Stacy, you know how I like it," faster she yelled, "faster." They began to passionately finger each other, moaning in ecstasy until they both climaxed. Stacy suggests taking a shower together. They were touching, squeezing each other's breasts, and butt, laughing and biting each other. They washed and pampered each other's bodies, lightly kissing each other while doing so. When they got out they massaged and put lotion on one another. They walked back to the living room wearing towels and sat on the sofa.

"Stacy that was truly wonderful for me a dream come true. You are so good," she started laughing, "forgive me for laughing but I was just thinking about Keith's friend Ron. The plans I had for him girl, but he turned out to be such a disappointment. What's up with him and Diana? Are they still married?"

"Yes, they are but don't waste your time with him. Ron is fighting a spiritual battle of his own. His heart for some reason is with her. He thinks she is all that. Miss goody Diana. If he only knew. No one is ever that pure."

"Yeah, true that. I have seen her and noticed she really thinks she is super holy, but she is very attractive and has a nice body." Stacy playfully hit Cynthia on the arm.

"Oh, so you want her now?"

"Girl, stop playing. I want you," she kissed Stacy and licked her lips, "but I would like to teach her a lesson but we can't even get next to her. She is Jesus crazy."

"Maybe, maybe not. Is she really sold out to God? Well, let's find out how much she really loves the Lord. Be quiet, I'm going to call her and get her to come over here." She got her cell phone and called Diana. "Hi Diana, I know it's late, but I really need to talk to someone. I know you don't like me, but I really need some help. I feel like I'm losing my mind. Can you come over here and talk, and pray with me, please? Okay, I understand and thank you very much," she hung up the phone sitting it on the sofa.

Cynthia is looking at her.

"So, what did Miss stuck up say?"

Stacy was smiling.

"She said she was asleep, but will come over for a while, and it will take her about an hour to get here." She stared at Cynthia, "I got something for her goody, goody ass."

Cynthia was surprised and stared at Stacy, not knowing what she was going to do.

"What is your plan and can I help."

"My plan is to act like I'm very emotionally hurt, and then seduce her. I have a nice digital camera which I'm going to set it up and film the whole thing. Later, if she tries to deny it, or get smart with me, then I'm going to use it and rock her whole world. As much as I would like for you to be here, you can't because she would be too much on guard. You have to go, but you will be the first one I show the film too, okay."

Cynthia was looking at Stacy and becomes sad, and Stacy noticed.

"What is wrong? I thought you would be happy."

"I know and it is a great plan but the truth is," she stared at Stacy, "I don't want you to be with her like that, I don't want to share you."

Stacy understood how she felt but she must do this.

"I understand how you feel and I feel the same way about you but I need to do this and I hope you understand," she leaned forward kissing her, allowing their tongues to taste each other. Stacy slowly stops and pushed her back, "baby, we need to stop because you are making me wet and I want you," she kissed her again and they get up and Stacy walked Cynthia to the door. They hug and kiss passionately and Cynthia walked out the door.

Stacy quickly walked to the bathroom then stop and put her hand on her hips and began talking to herself.

"I know I'm good, but damn, my juicy must be the bomb, man or woman, I get them all sprung." She laughed and kept walking to her walk-in closet. She put on a simple dress that was not tight, with no bra or panties underneath. She set up the camera in the living room in a well-hidden place and turned the lights down, not too low because it will look too obvious and sat on the sofa waiting for Diana to show up.

Ten minutes later Stacy heard a knock at the door. She got up, exhaled and forced herself to start crying then answered the door. Diana was standing there wearing a long dress with her Bible in her hand.

"Hi Diana. Thank you very much for coming, please come on in."

"Hi Stacy, and I'm glad you called me."

She walked in.

Stacy was thinking. *Not half as glad as I'm that you came.* She smiled and pointed to the sofa.

"Please have a seat."

They sat down and the first thing Diana does is start praying, which Stacy can't stand, but she lowered her head to fake it. This gives her more time to push out some more tears. When Diana finished praying, Stacy started telling Diana how hurt she was and how she feels like throwing herself in front of a train at times. Anything to get Diana to feel sorry for her. She started crying hard and Diana leaned over to hug her.

"It is going to be alright Stacy, just trust in the Lord to be your strength and guide. He will protect you."

Stacy stared at her and stopped crying.

"I thank you so much for coming over and for the prayers Diana. Look I know you said you can't stay long but Keith is, well, God knows where and I don't want to be alone. Can you please stay, we can sit here and watch movies?"

Diana feels like she should leave and that inner voice was telling her to leave, but she feels bad for Stacy and wants to help her.

Stacy can feel Diana's hesitation, so she reached over and grabbed Diana's hand holding it, "please stay, I'm begging you," she quickly kissed her hand several times, "please stay, don't leave me."

This touched Diana's heart.

"Okay, I will stay."

Stacy quickly hugged her tight making sure to press her breasts into her. Smiling and thinking to herself, *I knew this would work and laughed on the inside.*

"Thank you so much," she walked to the entertainment center and put a movie in so they could watch it then walked toward her bedroom, "I will be right back, I have to use the bathroom and I will get us a blanket." She walked into her room.

"Okay," she yelled at Stacy, "do you have any popcorn?"

Stacy purposely put in a porn movie and took her time going back into the living room. When the movie came on it was two women in a room talking then one started telling the other all her problems and they started kissing and caressing each other. Diana has never seen a porn movie and was repulsed by it but she kept watching it. She knew this was all wrong but she felt so drawn to the movie. The women in the movie were fingering one another, making each other climax. That's when Diana started feeling very horny and knew she needed to leave, so she stood up. Stacy was watching her and walked into the living room carrying a blanket looking at the TV.

"Oh my God, I'm so sorry Diana. I put the wrong movie in, please forgive me," she quickly walked over and changed the movie to something else and walked back over to the sofa throwing the blanket on it and pulled Diana's arm so she could sit down with her, "again I'm sorry. Are you okay?"

"Yes Stacy, "I'm fine, but I think you put that movie in on purpose. Look Stacy, I know you are hurt and you think I betrayed our friendship but I had to make a choice for me. I chose God and never want to go backwards. It is God and my husband."

Stacy looked at Diana thinking. *Damn this girl is so stuck on that man.*

"Diana, I understand that and I know you love Ron a lot. And regardless of what you say, you are an undercover freak. Girl, you were riding that man's dick good." She started smiling and laughing.

Diana lowered her head in shame, truly regretting Stacy seeing them together.

"Stacy, you know I regret you seeing us like that and I don't. want to talk about it."

No problem. Come on, let's get under the blanket and watch this movie. I don't have any popcorn." She grabbed the blanket and covered them up and hit the switch on the remote to turn the lights out.

They both fell asleep while watching the movie. About three hours later, Stacy woke up, but Diana was still asleep. She was so horny and want Diana badly. She slid her hand under her dress and started masturbating, leaning all the way back, fingering herself.

RONALD GRAY   (291)

Diana woke up and sees Stacy playing with herself and it turned her on. She was trying to fight her inner sexual desires, but Diana slowly slides her hand under her dress and inside her panties rubbing her wetness. She leaned back because it's feeling so good.

Stacy sees Diana's hand moving under the covers, so she removed the covers and sees Diana's hand under her dress and she can smell her sex, which smells so good to her. Diana was shocked and quickly stopped.

Stacy moved closer to her and caressed her leg.

"Diana, it is okay. Don't be embarrassed. It is not wrong to please yourself. God gave all of us sexual desires. Let me help you," she started caressing her leg again and lifted Diana's dress putting her hand inside her panties feeling her wetness and was just about to slide her finger inside her.

Diana quickly jumped up and yelled.

"No, in the name of Jesus, I rebuke you devil, you will not have me," she quickly smacked Stacy and run out of her condo pleading the blood of Jesus while running.

Stacy hit the sofa out of frustration. She walked over to the door to lock it, then walked back over to the sofa and sat down.

"Damn, I almost had her again," suddenly, a spirit of shame and guilt hit her hard and she fell on the floor crying like a baby, "oh God, what am I doing to myself, oh Lord! Don't let me be destroyed," she screamed very loud, "Oh God help me, don't let me die in my sins, help me, oh God."

Diana practically run out the building and to her car. She got in and closed the door leaning her head on the steering wheel and started crying of shame.

RONALD GRAY   (292)

"Lord, forgive me for not listening to your spirit when you were warning me not to go and to leave. I didn't listen and my disobedience caused me to betray your word, "Oh Lord. Let no unholy spirit attach itself to me. Protect me from the arrows of darkness sent my way. Deliver Stacy Jesus, don't let her be destroyed by the powers of darkness. Clean me now oh Lord and make me whole again. Thank you, Lord, amen," she cried so hard but ten minutes later she can feel the spirit of the Lord comforting her, she looked up, "thank you God" she started the car and drove away.

Stacy fell asleep on the floor and woke up when she heard her cell phone ring. Not looking at the caller ID she answered it thinking it could be Keith but it wasn't, it was Cynthia wanting to know how it went with Diana. She explained all that happened and how badly she feels and tells Cynthia she was going to destroy the tape. Cynthia was angry at her and was thinking maybe Stacy was getting weak and not the same girl she knew from the streets. She was very erotic and sexy, but as hard as they come. She talked to Stacy on the phone for an hour and they ended up having phone sex, leaving Cynthia satisfied, but leaving Stacy with so many mixed thoughts and emotions.

CHAPTER FORTY
The Warehouse

The drug deal was taking place in a very large, two-level warehouse, in an industrial area in Jessup Maryland. Armed guards are walking in front, outside, and standing inside the warehouse against the wall, holding automatic weapons, top, and bottom floor. There was a helicopter sitting on the warehouse roof and a tractor trailer was parked inside the warehouse, with drugs and armed men in it. There are thirty vans inside the warehouse. They all belong to dealers, who are sitting behind a row of long tables. They all have a brief case full of money sitting on the table in front of them. Standing behind each drug dealer are three of their own bodyguards. Ron, Keith, Victor and his five bodyguards are standing about thirty feet in front of the tables. Victor's bodyguards have Mac-10 machine guns in their hands. Victor waved his hand in the air.

"Gentlemen, I thank all of you for being here today and we will do this as quickly as possible. For everyone's safety, all the security that you see is very necessary. There is one and a half billion dollars in cash in this room, so if anyone even blinks wrong, you will wake up in hell today. Please, for your own safety, no sudden or jerky moves. All of my men are paranoid and have been instructed to shoot with intent to kill."

One of the drug dealers at the table stood up.

"Mr. Augular, we all know just how ruthless and evil you can be, so you can skip the threats. We came here to buy drugs, not to hear you run your mouth."

RONALD GRAY   (294)

Victor turned and looked at his bodyguards

"Gentlemen, we have a situation."

Victor's bodyguards shoot the drug dealer who just spoke and his three bodyguards that were standing behind him. All the other security men, in the warehouse, clicked their weapons and aimed them at the drug dealers sitting at the table. Victor pointed to the men who were shot.

"He was a stupid idiot. No one disrespects me and lives. Is there anyone else?" He yelled and looked around the room. "Good, I love free money." He looked at Ron. "Mr. S&D, hand me my briefcase full of money, please."

"Absolutely." Ron walked to the table and got the briefcase, then walked back to Victor and put it on the floor next to him and walked back to where he was standing.

Victor looked at Ron. "Thank you, sir. Now let us do some, intelligent business, men."

CHAPTER FORTY ONE
The Police Station

Reed drives up in front of the police station and sees S.W.A.T trucks and a lot of police officers loading weapons, getting ready to ride out. He parked his car and walked toward the front door of the station. He sees Rick walking out of the door and waved at him.

"Rick, what's going on? What's up with all the police activity and all the guns?"

Rick walked toward James and they shake hands.

"Your timing is perfect. We received a solid tip about a huge drug deal going down now over at that big empty warehouse on the south side, and guess who owns it?"

"Mr. Victor Augular."

"Yes sir, Mr. Untouchable himself, who is at the center of it all. We are finally going to get him and I hope he resists. I don't see this night going well at all because there will be casualties in this one."

James was staring at him thinking about Ron and Keith.

"I know. Anywhere that Victor goes, violence will soon follow but from the tone of your voice, I sense something more."

"You are very observant counselor. Victor will have extra security in place for a drug deal like this, along with his regular killers. And we know Keith's new security company, *Young Wolves* Inc., is just a front to cover his dirty businesses."

"I have heard about them but they are a legal, high-profile security company. A good friend of mine ran their background checks for me. His team members are squeaky clean and they all have high-security clearances that allow them to carry some serious fire power. They also travel a lot, domestically and internationally, to protect high profile clients all over the world."

Rick shook his head and smiled at him.

"You have well-informed friend's counselor and all your information is accurate. If Victor and his team of killers are teaming up with Keith and his team of killers, that could only mean one thing. A mini war and a lot of dead bodies."

James frowns and shook his head.

"All of this sounds like a war in some foreign country, not in our city streets. No offense Rick but even local police and S.W.A.T. do not have the resources that these guys are going to have. You will be out-manned and out-gunned."

"True again, but what you see here is just a small amount of what we are putting together tonight. We will have assistance from other police departments from various counties. Also, the Feds, DEA and ATF will be there."

"Wow, that's a lot and all we can do is pray for the best."

"Amen counselor. Now, would you like to come along?"

"Yes sir, I wouldn't want to miss it."

"Good, you can ride with me, but don't go in the warehouse because I know before this night is over, a lot of people are going to die and you are one of the good guys. We need you to stay alive." He looked at the police getting in the S.W.A.T. trucks, then at James. "It's show time. Come on, my car is over here."

James got into Rick's car. Police cars begin leaving the station and S.W.A.T trucks drove away. Rick drives behind them.

RONALD GRAY   (297)

CHAPTER FORTY TWO

Showdown at the Warehouse

Back at the warehouse. The vans inside have been backed up to where each drug dealer and his men are now standing. All the vans have been loaded with drugs and all the briefcases are line up on the floor in front of Victor and his men.

"I thank you for everyone's contributions and intelligent behavior. There is one more thing. Mr. Bones!" He yelled.

A cloud of smoke appeared between the drug dealers and Victor and his men. Mr. Bones appeared dressed in all black, holding his cane and black pouch in his hand standing next to Mr. Case, wearing his ninja suit with his sword on his back. Mr. Bones is lightly tapping his cane on the floor.

"Mr. Augular, thank you for inviting me. Now, who can I take to hell with me today?" he asks while looking around the room. "I like this, a room full of fuel for hell. A room full of sinners, I love it, burn baby burn." He started laughing.

One of the drug dealers hit his hand on the table.

"What the hell is going on here and what is with this freak show?"

Victor smiled and waved his hand at the drug dealers.

"There has been a change of plans. I want all the money and my drugs back and all of you can go to hell."

The drug dealer hits his hand again on the table.

"You are a double-crossing bastard," he yelled. "Everybody, kill him."

RONALD GRAY   (298)

Gunfire immediately erupted outside the warehouse and two S.W.A.T. trucks crashed through the warehouse doors, and a shootout began. Ron and Keith quickly pulled their guns out, dropping down on one knee to shoot the drug dealers. Their armor piercing bullets rip through the men's flesh like paper. Victor and his men start shooting at the drug dealers and police. Rick jumped out of the truck and started shooting.

Victor dropped down on one knee shooting his .357 magnums. Then he turned to Mr. Case while pointing his finger at Mr. Bones.

"Mr. Case, do him." He yelled.

Mr. Case quickly pulled his sword out and cut Mr. Bones' head off. When his head hit the ground, it sounds like thunder and the entire ground shook. His body was still standing until Mr. Case kicked it and it felled to the floor with the cane still in Mr. Bones' hand, but his pouch fell out of his other hand with some of the bones falling out of the pouch.

Victor grabbed two of the briefcases and started running up the stairs, and then he set them down and pointed toward Mr. Case.

"Mr. Case," he pointed towards Ron and Keith, "kill those two clowns." He picked up the briefcases and runs up the stairs towards the roof.

Keith sees Mr. Case pull his sword out moving toward Ron. He waved at him.

"Ron, look out." He yelled.

Ron quickly moved out of the way and Rick shoots Mr. Case three times. He stopped moving but doesn't fall. He raised his sword over his head and charged toward Ron and Keith,

RONALD GRAY   (299)

growling. Rick shoots Mr. Case many times and he stopped, leaned over, still holding his sword which is holding him up as the tip of it rests on the floor. He slowly raised his head and growls again. Ron, Keith, and Rick look at each other, then aim their guns at Mr. Case and shoot him multiple times. He fell to the floor and they walk over to him. Keith pulled the mask off. Mr. Case quickly reached up and grabbed Keith's arm and Ron shoots him several times. He slowly lets Keith's arm go and laid down. Keith kicks Mr. Case in the side.

"Damn, this guy is unreal and now I know why. I always hated him. Mr. Case and Greg Johnson are one and the same. This man was truly a cold-blooded demon from hell."

One of Victor's bodyguards was lying down as if he was dead, but he quickly stood up and shoots Ron several times. He fell to the ground. He shoots Keith in the arm and leg and Keith fell. He then shoots Rick in the arm but Rick shoots him back several times and he fell, then Rick fell to his knees, holding his arm.

Bullets are flying in every direction as the police and security guards trade gunfire. Bodies are falling on both sides, but the police keep coming into the warehouse jumping out of trucks shooting. They are met with a barrage of Mac-10 bullets from Victor's guards, killing them, before they even hit the ground. For the next thirty minutes, the warehouse looked like a full-scale battle zone and death has no discrimination. Finally, the police overwhelm them with numbers and constant fire power. Dead bodies, body parts, and blood are everywhere.

Suddenly, the lights go out in the warehouse and it was almost pitch-black. Black smoke appeared and covered the entire warehouse. Mr. Bones cane tapped itself on the floor twice and his head speaks.

"Bones come to me." His bones on the floor begin to shake and they float over to his body and land in his hand and he clutches the bones. His head slowly slides across the floor and reattached itself, and his body stood straight up. The black smoke disappeared and all the lights come back on. He raised his arms.

"I'm back. I told you, no one can kill the bones." He tapped his cane and disappeared in a cloud of smoke.

The pilot was sitting in the helicopter. Victor was putting his two briefcases in the helicopter and was about to step in when a cloud of smoke erupts behind him. Mr. Bones was standing there with his cane in his hand. Victor turned around in total shock.

"What? How in the hell? I saw your head get cut off." He said with a look of horror on his face.

"Shut up fool. So, you like cutting my head off?" He pulled a sword out of his cane and cuts Victor's head off. His head hits the ground and rolled a few feet away, then his body fell. Mr. Bones pointed his cane at the body. "Now look at you Victor, you, stupid fool. You can't kill or trust me. I'm the devil, the father of lies and I come to kill everybody that I can and take them to hell with me."

The helicopter pilot pulled his gun out and shoots Mr. Bones. Mr. Bones stepped toward him and the pilot keeps shooting.

"Oh God help me Jesus." He yelled.

"Now you want to call on God. It's too late fool. You rejected him, now you are going to hell with me." He snatched the pilot out of the helicopter and cut his head off. Then he raised his arms, "I'm the bones, I will ascend into heaven, I will exalt

RONALD GRAY   (301)

my throne above the stars of God, I will be like the most high,
I'm the world's *Master Deceiver*." He tapped his cane on the
ground and smoke appeared and when it cleared, Mr. Bones was
gone.

When the shootout is over, police are walking around checking
everything and making sure no one is hiding, waiting to attack.

James walked inside the warehouse seeing bodies, body
parts, and blood everywhere. He got out his handkerchief and
covered his mouth, and then he sees Rick standing next to Ron
and Keith who are lying on the floor unconscious. James quickly
walked over to them. Rick looked up and sees James.

"James, be very careful where you step. There is blood, guts
and dead bodies everywhere. This place looks like a war zone,
much worse than what happened in Miami. This scene is a
nightmare and you know these two." He pointed to Ron and
Keith.

James stepped closer.

"Lord have mercy. It's Ron O'Neil and Keith Washington.
Please tell me they are not dead."

"No, they aren't, but this one," he pointed to Ron, "was shot
several times and it doesn't look like he is going to make it."

James was thinking. Lord, please let him make it.

"He has to. I couldn't face his mother and family." He looked
around. "I have never seen so much blood and this many dead
bodies in my life. It's making me sick."

Medics are scattered throughout the warehouse taking care of
the wounded. Some come over and take Ron and Keith away in
an ambulance. Rick waved his hand in the air.

RONALD GRAY   (302)

"Welcome to the world of Satan and his demons, the master deceiver and liar." He looked around. "Damn, look at this slaughter house. Television and movies always show the glamor of the drug lifestyle, fancy cars, big money and pretty women, but this is the true reality. Blood and death!"

"So very true! After Satan uses you, all that's left is broken homes, increased prison population and a lot of funerals to attend. All because people chose to serve the master butcher, the devil himself, instead of the master builder, King Jesus."

"Amen counselor."

Police are everywhere still searching for any of Victor's men and security guards that are not already dead.

Rick stepped closer to James.

"I saw Mr. Augular running up the stairs toward the roof," he pointed towards two police officers, "You two follow me to the roof." Rick, James, and the two police officers walk up the stairs.

They reach the roof, looked around and see Victor's body and head lying on the ground near the pilot's body and head. One of the officers immediately threw up and the other officer stepped away and threw up.

James covered his mouth with his handkerchief.

"God almighty, it's Victor, but who cut his head off? Lord have mercy."

Rick looked around and kicked Victor's body.

"God's mercy has run out for the untouchable Mr. Victor Augular, and I don't care who cut his head off. He got what he deserved. You live by the sword, you die by the sword. You reap what you sow."

RONALD GRAY   (303)

"Yeah, he has finally fallen and his voodoo has backfired on him. The Bible says, *Be not deceived, God is not mocked, for whatsoever a man soweth, that shall he also reap.* Look at the untouchable Victor Augular now."

"Amen to that counselor," he stared at Victor's body, "Look at you now. So much for being untouchable, devil worshiper. You are now reaping what you sowed. Burn in hell."

Rick and James stared at each other, shook hands and walked off the roof.

CHAPTER FORTY THREE
No One Dances for Free

It is a beautiful morning, but not for Ron. He is lying in a hospital bed in his room in a coma. Sheila, Christine, Diana, Grandma Harris and Pastor Williams are standing around his bed. Christine and Diana are crying.

Christine is feeling so uncomfortable right now around her family. It was as if they all know she is no longer a virgin and has been with, of all people, Mr. Reed. Her guilt and shame were beyond words and she has been praying so hard, asking God to forgive her for this and all her sins. She also knows Mr. Reed feels very badly as well. They talked over the phone for a while and he told Christine how extremely hurt and ashamed he was because of what he did with her and promised he would never disrespect her like that again. He begged for her forgiveness. She told him she forgives him and they both promised to never speak of it again. Christine knew it was more her fault than his and she also deeply regrets being with Tonya as well. Tonya and she talked on the phone and Christine made it very clear that what they did would never happen again. Tonya felt bad as well and agreed. Christine wants the closeness back with God and her family healed.

Diana was staring at Ron with great sadness in her heart and spirit. She can't help but think about visiting Stacy. Not praying ahead of time and not listening to the voice of God, before she went caused her all this pain. Yes, she had good intentions but no permission from God. The Lord has forgiven her, but she needs to forgive herself and listen to the voice of God more.

Sheila was looking at Ron trying not to allow her emotions to get the best of her, but her pain is tremendous.

"I begged him not to go, but he said he didn't need God anymore. Now, look at him. Lord have mercy, first, my husband was killed, then Sandra was paralyzed and goes into a coma, now my son is all shot up and is in a coma. I feel like Job. Lord help me, father." She started crying.

"I told Ron that God was about to bring him down, but I didn't know how. Disobedience to God brings much pain, but it ain't over. The devil is a liar," Grandma Harris said and lightly stomped her foot on the floor.

"Grandma, look at him. He is full of holes and in a coma. He said he would call Miss O'Neil tomorrow, but tomorrow is promised to no man. Lord God." Diana continues to cry."

"It is not over. The devil is a deceiver and he wants people to give up their faith. You must trust in God because his will shall be done. Ron tried to run from his calling, but you cannot run from God. He knows just how to bend your knees and break you," the pastor said.

Christine stared at the pastor frowning, thinking. Listen to him talking about my brother like that. Lord, I love the pastor, but sometimes some of the things he said seem so cold.

"Yes Pastor, but at what cost? My dad is dead, my sister is in a coma, and now Ron. It's all just too much." She lowered her head trying to control her pain.

Dr. Hardy walked in the room.

RONALD GRAY   (306)

"Hi everyone. I'm sorry for being late, but there was an emergency. Well, concerning Ron, it is out of our hands. We took the bullets out but they did serious damage to his body and it will take a miracle just for him to come out of his coma. If he does, he will never walk again. The bullets did severe damage to his spine."

"No Lord, not like this, not my husband," Diana yelled, then looked up and started crying even harder, "not like this, please God."

Sheila looked at the doctor with great determination on her face.

"I will not embrace this. I cannot. God cannot lie." She spoke with great conviction.

The Pastor stepped closer to the doctor and looked at him.

"Dr. Hardy, how is Keith Washington doing?"

"He was shot in his arm and leg and he lost a lot of blood. He may not have full use of his arm because of nerve damage, but time will tell and he may walk with a limp, but he will walk again." He looked over at Ron and lowered his head, then looked up. "Ron, well he is alive, by machine."

Diana shook her head back and forth.

"Nooo!" She yelled crying hysterically. Grandma Harris hugged her tightly.

The pastor looked up then yelled. "Hallelujah, Lord I thank you, Jesus. Dr. Hardy, you are wrong. God just spoke to me and said he will deliver Ron from his afflictions in three days from today, fully healed and very anointed by the Lord."

He stared at the Pastor like he was crazy.

RONALD GRAY   (307)

"Fully recovered in three days, medically and physically that's impossible."

"Jesus said, *If thou can believe, all things are possible to him that believeth.* Ron O'Neil will rise from this bed in three days fully recovered."

"I hear you pastor, you spoke it. From what I have seen with this family and your faith, anything is possible, but it will really take a miracle. I need to go and make my rounds. I will be praying for Ron." He walked over to Sheila and hugged her. "Sheila, keep the faith." He walked out.

"God also said for all of us to go on a three day fast and pray for Ron, Sandra, and Keith and he will do the rest." The pastor said looking at everyone.

They all nodded their heads and the pastor began to pray over Ron with everyone joining him.

CHAPTER FORTY FOUR

Mr. Bones' Continued Assault

In a supply closet in the hospital, Mr. Bones appeared in a cloud of smoke, dressed in black, holding his cane and his black pouch is tied around his neck.

"Stupid fools. Don't they know I hear everything? I really hate these born-again Christians, always praying and fasting and faith. I hate faith, I hate the world but it ain't over yet. I'm going to kill Ron O'Neil and his whole stinking praying family. I'm killing that old woman, Grandma Harris too. I hate that smart-mouth old woman. I don't care how much they pray and fast. I will be killing that chosen boy because he left the Lord and came over to my side, so he deserves to die and come to hell with me. God and his protection of back sliders, I hate love. All people have to do is serve me and I will give them what they want," he started laughing, "then I will trick the dumb souls and to hell, they go. I'm the bones."

A nurse walked to the closet where Mr. Bones was standing, she opened the door.

"Ahhhh," she jumped and screamed, "What are you doing in here?" She looked down the hall, "help, somebody help me, a thief."

"Shut up slut." He grabbed her throat, pulling her into the closet and tapped his cane on the floor and the door closed by itself. "I know you. You had your ass up in the air last night getting hit from the back, doggy-style. But that wasn't your husband. You were committing adultery, you nasty stinking slut.

RONALD GRAY   (309)

You were getting some, out of marriage dick, shame on you. And you deep-throated him too. Oh, you're a real nasty seed swallower." He took his hand off her throat and slapped her on the top of the head.

"Please don't hurt me. Lord help me, my children."

"Shut up you fool. You are just like all the rest. Calling on God when you get in trouble but you never want to serve him. You should have prayed over your children regularly and I wouldn't be able to get to them so easily, but you are selfish and determined to get what you want when you want it. Last night you wanted some new dick, shame on you. Now you are coming to hell with me. Later, I will be back for your children. I will send your son to prison and kill him and I'm going to put a strong lust spirit in your daughter and get her hooked on sucking penises, just like her slut mother."

"Nooo!" She screamed.

Mr. Bones put his hand over her mouth and mumbled some words, tapped his cane on top of her head twice and they both disappeared in a cloud of smoke.

RONALD GRAY   (310)

CHAPTER FORTY FIVE

Keith and the Hospital

Keith was lying in his hospital bed. He has a cast on his leg and a bandage on his arm. Three *Young Wolves* are in his room talking to him, and five are in the hallway close by. All are wearing Armani suits and dress hats and carrying Mac-10s under their jackets.

Stacy walked in the hospital and all eyes were immediately on her. She was wearing heels and a skin-tight jean bodysuit fitting her like a glove. The top of the suit is unbuttoned to the point she was showing a lot of cleavage and she was not wearing a bra. She was also wearing more makeup than usual. Men and women are staring at Stacy as she walked by shaking her hips and butt. She knows she got it going on and was not to be played with, on any level. One guy was staring at Stacy so hard, when he was coming out of the bathroom, he walked into the wall. Stacy laughed and kept it moving, but thought to herself. *Look at this real FULL SEVEN coming through.*

When she reached Keith's floor and saw the *Young Wolves* standing in the hallway, she smiled on the inside, because she liked the fact that Keith has such a loyal team, but it irritates her at the same time. She does not want to live like this, having to have security guards wherever she and Keith go. They all nod at her when she walked by and one of them opened the door for her. When she walked in and sees Keith hurt and laid up in bed like this, it breaks her heart, but she shows no sign of emotions.

RONALD GRAY   (311)

Keith and his men stare at her from the moment she stepped into the room. He has seen Stacy wear many sexy outfits but this was too much for him, especially since he can't be with her right now and hold her hand as she walked down the street.

The three guys in the room all nod at Stacy, then walk out. Stacy nods back at them as they leave. She walked over to Keith and kissed him softly on the lips and looked at him.

Keith was looking at her thinking, *Why, she is wearing this outfit that's too tight, showing the outline of her camel toe, hips and ass.* Arguing with her was the last thing he wants to do, especially in his present situation.

"Damn Stacy. You are a serious FULL SEVEN walking. Damn you are one fine lady. So how is Ron doing?"

"Ron was hurt very badly. He was shot several times and the bullets did a lot of damage to his body. Keith, he is in a coma and may never come out."

He lowered his head then looked at her.

"It's my fault. He was never cut out for this business. I should have talked him out of it. He was chosen by God but tried to run from his calling doing the devil's work."

"I know you are hurting emotionally and physically, and this may not be the best time to mention this, but I don't want this life style anymore. I have been thinking about the future and my life, I just need some time."

Keith can feel his temper rising and wants to reach over and slap Stacy. He is from the streets and knows how it goes in the game. You ball until you fall. Then when you do, others get missing. He was not stupid. The way Stacy was dressed and acting was letting him know she has met someone else or was leaving him.

"What? Don't tell me you are getting soft on me, not you. I don't believe this."

"It is not a question of getting soft Keith. Ron is in a coma and look at you. Think of your life and soul. You have made more money than most people even dream of, but all the money, the fine clothes, and cars, it's just not worth it. I'm finished with all of it."

"Oh, so you are going to just leave me? That figures. The good time is over. Ron is in a coma and I'm all shot up and on my way to prison. And you, well you can always find another sucker to care for you and put that meat to you," he pointed his finger at her. "Look how you are dressed now, wearing that skin-tight outfit showing your ass and your breasts. Damn, you found someone else that fast or you just want to look like you are on the market? Or are you so hot between the legs, you are just giving that ass up?"

Stacy stepped closer and slapped him, then stepped back and started crying.

"I can't believe you would talk to me like this after all the things we have been through. Have you ever thought for once you, stupid idiot that the only reason I'm with you is because I love you? Right now, I feel like stabbing you. How dare you talk to me like that?" Stacy stared at him gritting her teeth. "Damn, I'm so angry at you right now I feel like getting my razor out and cutting your throat for talking to me so disrespectfully. You better remember who I'm." She was staring at him.

RONALD GRAY   (313)

Keith looked at Stacy knowing he went too far in what he said and he knew he does not want to ever lose her.

"I didn't mean what I said. I don't want to lose you. Come over here but leave the razor." He smiled at her.

Stacy stared at Keith with mixed emotions. She knew she loves this man with all her heart and she really does feel guilty for all she has done recently with Shantai, Cynthia, and Diana but she has been walking around feeling so very horny. She wants sex so badly.

"I don't know what the future for us is but the way we lived is over. The drug business, everything is over. I'm not going to leave you but I have some thinking to do." She walked over to Keith and kissed him.

The moment their lips meet, his body responds with an immediate erection and he pulled her closer to the bed with his good arm and rubbed her butt discovering she was not wearing any underwear.

Stacy's body responds to Keith's touch quickly. She feels the wetness between her legs building. Stacy wants him, now.

"Keith, I want you so badly right now. Give me some of that good dick baby."

He has always liked the fact Stacy was hot, but this was extra even for her, but considering this may be his last time to get some pussy for many years, he is going for it. He pointed his finger at the door.

"Go tell one of my men not to let anyone in and lock the door baby."

She walked over to the door shaking her butt hard with each step, opened the door and looked at one of the *Young Wolves.*

"Don't let anyone in." He nods his head at her.

Stacy locked the door, kicked her shoes off and takes her bodysuit off standing there completely naked.

Keith stared at her with lust so strong he could bust right now, but he was thinking he hopes his injuries do not interfere with his dick.

"Damn baby, you are too damn fine. Get over here, but take it easy and watch out for my leg and arm."

She walked over to him thinking, *I love you baby but I'm getting mine.* She pulled his robe up and sees he was already erect. She started sucking him to make him harder and bigger, then climbed on top of the bed and lowered herself onto his hard dick and started riding him hard, fast, and deep.

Keith was trying hard to raise up matching Stacy riding him, his leg is aching and his head is throbbing, but he is determined to get the job done. Her passions seem a lot stronger than usual.

"That's it Stacy, damn you are riding the hell out of me."

Stacy was so close to a strong climax. She grabbed hold of the bed rails and started rocking back and forth on Keith feeling him getting even harder knowing he was close to release as well.

"Oh Keith, that's it, ohhhhh I'm cummming, fuck me, fuck me, fuck me, fuck me. I'm cumming baby, ohhhhhh Keith. It's so good, ohhhhhh I need, sex, sex, sex, ohhhhhh I got to have it, Keith get this hot, wet pussy baby. Fuck me damn it."

He was looking up at Stacy like she was crazy. He loves her great passions but damn, she's acting like she was possessed.

"Yes baby, oh yes, I'm about to bust, ohhhh Stacy take this nut baby, take it."

RONALD GRAY   (315)

They both reach their peak and released. Stacy leaned forward and kissed Keith.

"I love you so much Keith, so much baby." She started crying dropping tears on his face. "Get well soon baby. I need you."

She got off Keith and walked over to her clothes picking them up and walked in the bathroom. She comes out still naked but she cleaned herself while in the bathroom. She has a wet warm washcloth in her hand and cleaned Keith up, then walked back into the bathroom. She comes out still naked, walking over to Keith and stared at him. Her orgasm was strong and good but she was craving more and does not want to leave Keith until she was totally satisfied.

Keith knew something was wrong with her.

"Baby, what is it? Why are you staring at me like that and why are you still naked?"

Stacy stood there staring at him, then slides her fingers between her legs rubbing herself and rubs her fingers across his lips.

"I'm not finished with you, Keith." She climbed up on his bed and straddles his face looking down at him. "Eat this pussy Keith Washington." She started moving back and forth on his face while massaging and caressing her breasts.

Keith was surprised by her boldness, but who was he to argue with her, especially now. He used his good arm and grabbed her butt pushing her back and forth as she slides her body on his face, he was licking and sucking her like his life depends on it.

Stacy was moaning and hissing because Keith was making her feel so good and she was very close to climax. She grabbed

RONALD GRAY   (316)

Keith's head and pulled it toward her more as she rocked back and forth on his face, harder and faster.

"Ohhhhhh Keith, that's it baby, that's it, I'm cumming Keith, eat this pussy baby, and suck it good, ahhhhhhh Keith." Stacy was looking down at him while she has his head in her hands holding him in place while she smothers him with her pussy, drowning him with her juices. She calmed down, and raise up, turned around squatting over Keith again, but she put her butt on his face. She looked back at him, "lick it Keith, lick this big, sexy ass you like touching so much baby."

He loved Stacy deeply, but his body was hurting very badly from all her rocking and shaking of the bed and he was very tired.

"Baby, I'm hurting so bad right now and I..."

"Shut up Keith. Have I ever turned you down? No! I always take care of you and give you some good deep throat, pussy or ass. Do I complain when you want to fuck me like a mad man? No! Now lick this hot ass of mine and lick it good." She started sliding her butt back and forth on his face.

Keith used his good arm again and grabbed her waist and started licking her ass, long and slow.

Stacy reached down and gently grabbed her butt spreading her cheeks apart so Keith can satisfy her better, sliding her butt on his face until she feels his tongue slide in her ass which feels so good to her.

"Yes, baby now you are doing it slide that tongue in my ass, ohhhhhh Keith it feels so good baby, Ohhhhhh." She slides two fingers inside her pussy fingering herself fast and hard using her other hand to hold the bed railing, shaking the entire bed. "Oh

RONALD GRAY   (317)

yes, oh yes, Ohhhhhh Keith I'm cummming again baby, yes, yes, yes, oh Keith, my ass baby, lick this ass, ohhhhhhhh Keith, I'm your freak baby, I'm your freak, ahhhhhhh Keith." Stacy is ramming her fingers in her pussy faster and faster exploding her juices all over Keith's face. She finally relaxes and climbs down off the bed and walked to the bathroom. She is dressed when she walked back out carrying a warm wet washcloth again. She wipes Keith's face then kissed him so passionately. She walked back and put the washcloth in the bathroom and walked back over to Keith.

Keith grabbed her hand and stared at her wondering what is wrong with her. "I love you Stacy." She kissed him.

"Nice words Keith, but if you really do love me, you would marry me. Don't just put a ring on my finger, marry me. You can't have me and your criminal life anymore. Choose Keith. And don't give me that A.M.O.A, Always Money Over Ass, street garbage." She walked toward the door.

"Stacy wait! Where are you going?"

She turned around. "I'm going to church Keith, I need help. I feel like I'm going crazy. I need Jesus." She walked out.

CHAPTER FORTY SIX

Attorney Reed's Office

It is late at night and Rick drives up to James' law office. He gets out of his car with his arm in a sling, walked into the office building and knocked on his door.

James is sitting at Diana's desk when he hears the knock at the door. He gets up and opened the door.

"Rick, come on in sir. I'm glad to see you are among the living and how is that arm?"

"Attorney James Reed. I like saying that. It makes me feel like I'm part of an elite club. I have discovered that my body is not bulletproof, but my arm is doing well, all things considered, and I really appreciate you staying late so we can talk."

"No problem. Let's go to my office." James sat behind his desk and Rick sat in front. "Tell me the news."

"Well, that drug bust may end up being the biggest in the country with multiple arrests, twenty-five thousand, three hundred kilos of cocaine and heroin. A street value of five billion five hundred million dollars and we confiscated one and half billion dollars in cash. We also found crates of military-issue weapons. Every agency is trying to get a slice of that money and credit for the bust."

"I'm sure. A political nightmare. That's an awful lot of drugs and money. You probably have local police, FBI, IRS, CIA, ATF, DEA and the treasury department in on this."

"Again, you are right, but the worst part is, two dozen officers lost their lives and many seriously wounded in that raid, officers I have known for years. In one night, they get seriously hurt or wiped out, all because of one man." He lowered his head then looked at James. "Forget prison, I'm very glad Mr. Augular is dead. I know this is bad to say but I hope he rots in hell for all the evil he has done. The good news is we know your friend David O'Neil's killer was Mr. Greg Johnson who was also Mr. Case, Mr. Augular's personal assassin. The man was pure lethal. Special forces training, explosives, weapons, martial arts and communications, you name it and he was an expert."

"The military trains them and we receive the fallout, but how do you know he was David's killer?"

"We found a gun on him that matched the one used to kill David. We triple checked it and it was a perfect match. Now, the weird part. His body and Mr. Augular's body have disappeared from the morgue. All the drug dealers and their bodyguard's bodies have also disappeared. Isn't that weird?"

"Regarding this case, it's normal. What about the criminal charges against Ron and Keith? I have read the reports and their charges are very extensive. I'm good but I'm not that good to get them out of this. I don't think anyone is."

"I'm glad you asked and you are right. No lawyer could get those two out of all their state and federal charges, but no charges will be filed. If they keep their mouth shut, forever."

James stared at him.

"I don't get it. How is that even possible?"

"Oh, you are going to love this part. Those two have seen a great deal and they know a lot about some people you don't talk about. Their testimony could hurt a lot of people in high political positions, domestically and internationally. They are considered a political embarrassment. Those two get to walk away." He leaned forward in his seat and stared at James. "Mr. Keith Washington was smart. He pulled a J. Edgar Hoover move and kept files, pictures, and tapes on all the people he did business with. If he or Ron so much as fall down the steps, all this information will end up in the attorney general's office and on CNN. He made that very clear. For them, this case is closed but those two can't even run a red light, ever."

James leaned back in his seat and smiled.

"Wow. That was a dangerous move by Keith but very smart at the same time. Still, I would not want to be in their shoes. Thank God they will have their freedom."

"Freedom yes, but not that drug money. Keith and Ron did a very good job hiding their money in overseas accounts but the government has been doing this before either one of them was born. They found their accounts and took all of their money."

"You are baiting me so I will ask. How much did they have?"

"They had two hundred and fifty million dollars."

James whistles and shook his head.

"What! Those two young men made that much money? Unbelievable. Well, I would rather be broke and have my freedom than being rich and in prison."

"Amen to that my friend."

"I have two curiosity questions. Do you really think the government found all their money, and what about the many legal businesses they own?"

"Good questions. Those two have proven to be smart, so I would say, no. I'm sure they may have a few dollars hidden somewhere. Concerning their legal businesses, you should know this. The government said fruits from a poison tree, but they may end up being able to keep them or at least some of them because of the deal they made. It is too early to tell right now."

There was a knock on James' office door and Mr. Zechariah Brown was standing there dressed in a suit.

"Are you expecting anyone this late counselor?"

"No, I'm not." He reached into his desk drawer and pulled out a gun and stood up.

Rick stood up and pulled his gun out and they both walked to the front door. James answered the door with his arm behind his back hiding his gun.

"Yes sir, can I help you."

"Yes sir, I hope so. My name is Zechariah Brown and I'm looking for Diana Brown. I'm a friend of Ron O'Neil, who I know has been seriously hurt and is in the hospital in a coma."

"What is your relationship to Miss Brown?"

Zechariah stared at James.

"I'm her dad. I have been trying to locate her for many years and Ron made this possible. She was raised by her grandmother, Miss Esther May Harris whose daughter was Diana Brown. She was a very special friend of mine from many years ago."

"Lord have mercy, Mr. Brown please come in. We have a great deal to discuss." James put his gun in his belt behind his back and pointed to Rick. "This is Detective Matthew."

Rick put his guns in his pocket and they shook hands.

"Mr. Brown, please come to my office, we have a lot to discuss."

CHAPTER FORTY SEVEN
The Power of God

Three days later, Ron was lying in his hospital bed still in a coma. Sheila, Christine, Diana, Grandma Harris and Pastor Williams are in his room standing around his bed. Christine looked at Sheila.

"Mom, why is he still in a coma? This is the third day of the fast. Oh Ron, please wake up. You have so much to do. Lord deliver him."

Diana gently rubs Ron's head, then leaned over and kissed him on the lips staring at him until her emotions come to the surface and her tears fall on Ron's face.

"Ron wake up. I need my husband. Baby, please wake up." She stood up straight stepping back looking at him.

Pastor Williams touched Christine's shoulder.

"Lord, we know your will shall be done," he looked up, "Lord Jesus, God almighty, we have obeyed your word and we are on one accord. Now let us see your mighty hand at work and deliver Ron."

While they are praying for Ron, Mr. Bones was in a closet in the hospital. He was dressed in black with his cane in his hand and there is a picture of Ron on the floor with a circle of bones around it. He was tapping his cane on the floor.

"Die Ron O'Neil die, die, die, die. I come to steal, kill and destroy and by the powers of the bones I command you to die, boy."

RONALD GRAY   (323)

Back in Ron's hospital room, everyone was still praying. Grandma Harris was walking back and forth across the room.

"Yes Lord, I feel the powers of darkness trying to interfere with your will. Satan, we rebuke you in Jesus name, now flee."

Sheila waved her hand in the air.

"Oh hallelujah, hallelujah. No weapon formed against us shall prosper and every tongue that shall rise against us in judgment thou shall condemn. We are more than conquerors oh God."

Pastor claps his hands together several times.

"Oh, mighty God. Your word said, *Call upon me in the day of trouble, I will deliver thee and thou shall glorify me.* We speak deliverance for Ron and Sandra O'Neil, thank you Lord."

They all say.

"Thank you, Lord."

Back in the closet with Mr. Bones, he started jumping up and down.

"Nooo," he screamed, "not that name, I hate that name and these born-again Christians," he screamed again. "Ahhhhh the only power that can defeat me." He mumbled some words and tapped his cane and disappeared in a cloud of smoke.

Back in Ron's room, everyone was still around his bed praying and Pastor Williams was still clapping his hands.

"Lord we thank you for the victory, and now let thy will be done," he laid his hand on Ron, "in Jesus name."

Ron's body shook and he opened his eyes.

"Praise the Lord Pastor."

Everyone began shouting hallelujah and praising God. Sheila hugged and kissed him.

RONALD GRAY   (324)

"Thank you, Lord, thank you, oh praise the Lord, my son is back." She started crying.

Diana was jumping up and down and she put her hand over her mouth, crying and dropped to her knees patting the floor several times and looked up at Ron.

"Oh my God, Lord you did it. You brought my husband back."

Ron pushed the button on his bed to sit up.

"Diana, come over here." He looked at her smiling.

Diana practically runs over to him and hugged him so tightly, crying and kissing his lips and cheeks repeatedly.

"Oh Ron, thank you, oh Lord. You are back, my baby is back. You will never know how much I have missed you." Kissing him again and looking at him with a huge smile on her face.

Ron pulled Diana closer and whispered in her ear.

"I'm so glad to see you Diana and I'm very sorry for many things but when I get out of here, can I have some of your booty?" He laughed.

Diana playfully hits his arm and smiled.

Christine walked closer to the bed and touched Ron's hand.

"Praise the Lord, Ron." She stared at him and started crying, then hugged him.

"Praise the Lord Christine, mom, praise the Lord everybody, Grandma Harris, Pastor Williams."

Grandma Harris walked closer to him.

"Praise the Lord baby." She hugged him.

"Praise the Lord Brother Ron, hallelujah, Lord we thank you." Pastor shook Ron's hand.

RONALD GRAY   (325)

Dr. Hardy walked in the room, then stopped and stared at Ron sitting up in bed.

"God almighty, I don't believe it."

Sheila walked closer to Dr. Hardy and touched his arm.

"Believe it Dr. Hardy God has all power to heal and deliver."

He stared at Ron shaking his head.

"This is truly unbelievable. Well, let me check you out son." He checked Ron's temperature and blood pressure then looked at his wounds. "I don't believe it, even your bullet wounds have completely healed, not even a scar. I have never seen anything like this in my life. Another miracle with this family that only God could have performed. The so called impossible becomes instantly impossible."

Pastor raised his arms clapping them together then looked at Dr. Hardy.

"For with God, nothing shall be impossible. Luke 1:37."

Dr. Hardy walked over to Sheila and tapped her on the shoulder.

"Excuse me, Sheila but I need to go get some witnesses to this miracle and take some pictures." He almost runs out of the room.

Ron was looking around the room smiling at everyone.

"So when can I get out of this place and put some real clothes on."

James and Zechariah Brown walked into the room wearing suits. Ron looked at them and leaned forward in his bed grabbing his bed rails.

"Oh my God, will you look at this." He started hitting his bed rails and smiled hard. "You did it again. One more time you are still doing the so-called impossible. Another miracle just walked in this room."

James stopped walking and stared at Ron, totally bewildered by what he is now seeing.

"Lord have mercy, Ron you are awake, moving and talking. It's truly unbelievable. The last time I saw you son, you were lying down full of holes and bleeding. You were like a dead man. Now look at you."

Zechariah stepped to James and touched his shoulder and smiled.

"Nothing is too hard for God and Mr. Ron is truly a chosen child of God. Welcome back among the living Emmanuel."

Sheila was staring at Zechariah looking at his face and can feel the strong anointing on this man even from a distance. She also noticed he was very handsome and built. The spiritual and physical attraction she feels for him was instant, but she feels guilty for even having such feelings for anyone.

"Baby, who is this man that's talking about my Lord and is calling you Emmanuel and you are not even getting emotional?" Sheila asked.

"Man, it is great to see you. Well, don't just stand there, come over here and give me a pound, a hug or something."

Zechariah confidently walked over to Ron with swagger but humble. He was a man who would stand out in any crowd. He and Ron trade pounds and they hug.

"Praise the Lord Ronald Emmanuel O'Neil. You look great for someone who has been shot several times and who just came out of a coma."

RONALD GRAY   (327)

Sheila was watching them interact with each other and was smiling inside. She has never seen Ron connect with anyone like this. She was thinking. *Lord, it has been so long since I felt anything for any man, could he be the one. And he is so good-looking Lord, really good-looking. He could butter my biscuits any day. Oh, forgive me Lord. I'm sorry for thinking like this about this man. Forgive me.*

She looked over at Grandma Harris and it was as if she can read her inner thoughts.

Grandma Harris felt Zechariah's anointing as well and noticed how Sheila was staring at him. Sheila would not admit it but she knew that she was very attracted to him. Who would not be? The man was fine. She pointed at Ron.

"Boy, God has brought you out of a coma and healed you, so use that big mouth of yours and start talking." She pointed at Zechariah, "who is this man? He is big and fine." She looked over at Sheila and smiled and Sheila rolled her eyes at her.

"I love you too Grandma Harris. Everybody, this is the man I told you about, whom God used to show me and him his mighty hand. He was stabbed and died and God brought him back to life. A walking miracle." He pointed to James, "Mr. Reed the introduction is all yours."

James smiled.

"My pleasure. Everyone, this is Mr. Zechariah Brown. Mr. Brown, this is his mother Sheila, his sister Christine his pastor Elder Williams, and everyone's favorite Grandma, Mrs. Harris and this young lady over here," he and Zechariah stepped closer to Diana, "is Miss Diana Brown."

Zechariah stared at Diana.

"You will never know how badly I have wanted to meet you. How long I waited and continued to pray and believe in God that one day, one day I would see you." Tears fall from his eyes. "You look so much like your mother and you even sound like her. You are truly beautiful, just like her."

Diana was thinking. How does this man know so much about my mother?

"You knew my mother?" She looked at Ron. "Baby who is this man?"

Ron was staring at Zechariah and Diana having to keep his own emotions in check because of the love he has for them both, knowing what was about to happen.

"Go ahead Zechariah, tell her. It is long overdue."

Zechariah gently grabbed Diana's hands stared into her eyes.

"Your mother's name was also Diana and she took my last name. I'm your Dad."

Diana's mouth dropped open.

"Lord have mercy. You are my dad."

CHAPTER FORTY EIGHT
The Church

It was a beautiful morning. The sun was shining and there was a light breeze blowing. It was morning church service and people are still driving up to the church and walking in. The church was full, the choir was singing and Pastor Williams was sitting in the pulpit. Sheila, Ron, Christine, Diana, Grandma Harris, James Reed, Rick Matthew, John Hardy, Zechariah Brown, Stacy, and Keith, who has a cast on his leg and his arm was bandaged, are all sitting together. Keith has a crutch next to him. The choir stopped singing and Pastor Williams walked up to the pulpit wearing a red and black robe.

"I greet you all in the mighty name of Jesus Christ, who is worthy to be praised. I thank God for the choir and all of you being here on this very blessed beautiful morning. My message this morning is a very simple one and comes from the book of Mark, chapter nine, verse three. The passage reads, *If thou can believe, all things are possible to him that believes.* I tell you this morning that, with God all things are possible. Can I get an Amen?"

Everyone said Amen.

"God has all power and is a miracle worker no matter what the devil tries to do. When God speaks it shall come to pass, his word is true and holy. Everlasting to everlasting, and we have such a fulfilling of his mighty hand and spoken word, sitting with us here this morning." He waved his hand and pointed to Ron, "Brother Ron stand up and testify for the Lord."

Ron stood up.

"Praise the Lord everyone in the name of King Jesus. I thank God for just being here today. I have truly seen the mighty hand of God, but I walked away from him out of total frustration and deep emotional pain. No excuse, but I'm just keeping it real. I was shot several times and ended up in a coma. I stand before you completely healed and spiritually restored in Christ. I know I do not deserve it but thank God," he raised his arms, "*Is anything too hard for the Lord?*" he yells, "Hallelujah, I thank God for his grace and mercy upon my life. Lord, I truly thank you." Tears come down his face and he sat down.

Diana put her arm around Ron and kissed him on the cheek and whispered in his ear.

"I thank God for restoring you. I truly do love you my husband, and if you ever break my heart again, I will slap your eyes out." She kissed him again.

Pastor stared at Ron and tears escape his eyes.

"Brother Ron, you are a walking testimony of the power of God. Don't you ever turn your back on God again, or you will be destroyed. Somebody say praise the Lord."

Everyone said, "Praise the Lord."

"Praise the Lord, praise the Lord. Mr. Zechariah Brown, stand up and testify for the Lord."

Zechariah stood up.

"Pastor and everyone here, praise the Lord. I have also seen the Lord's power. He delivered me from prison on a life sentence when there was no way, but before I was released I was stabbed and died. God used Ron O'Neil to pray and bring me back to life and healed all my wounds. Thank God for this and his mercy and love for my life and soul. I must obey his holy word. *Is anything too hard for the Lord?* Thank you. Remember me in your prayers." He sat down.

"Thank you, brother Brown, and Brother O'Neil, for such powerful testimonies of the Lord's love, power, mercy, and grace. As God spoke to Abraham and I speak to you, *Is anything too hard for the Lord?*"

He walked down from the pulpit to the floor by the altar and stood there.

Ron walked up to the altar and faced the pastor.

"Thank you pastor," he turned and faced the church, "Diana, I asked the pastor if I could do this, just for the record. I know we have not been married that long and in that time, I have not been the husband to you that I should have been. For that, I have asked God to forgive me. Now, I ask you to forgive me for all my wrong doings and shortcomings. First, I will be the man that God wants me to be, which will allow me to be the husband to whom, you desire. I love you Diana O'Neil." He turned toward the choir and waved at them. They stood up and he turned back around facing the church, "Diana these are my words to you." He raised his hand.

The choir sings, just four words but sing it three times.

"You are my lady." Then they sat down.

"Diana, I know God brought us together and kept us despite me, and I truly want to spend the rest of my life with you. If you hold my hand, whatever we go through, we will go through it together." He held his hand out.

Stacy was sitting next to Keith and looked over at him and smiled.

RONALD GRAY   (332)

Diana's heart was so moved by Ron's words tears flowed from her eyes.

Grandma Harris tapped Diana on her leg.

"Don't just sit there, get up and go hold your husband's hand, all that praying you have been doing."

Diana walked up front and took Ron's hand.

"Ron, you are something else," she turned and faced the church. "Dad, what do you think? Should I forgive him?"

Zechariah stood up.

"Yes, and you couldn't find a better hand to hold. Stand by your husband as he stands by God."

She turned and faced Ron.

"Yes Ron, my wonderful husband I forgive you and I will hold your hand for life." She moved closer and kissed him on the lips.

Everyone in the church started clapping. Ron grabbed her hand, looking directly into her eyes and kissed her hand.

"I love you baby." He leaned over and whispered in Diana's ear. "I can't wait to get you and that fine body of yours in bed. I got something for you, wife."

Diana squeezed Ron's hand and whispered in his ear.

"Pray my brother, pray. I got something for you, husband." She smiled and kissed him on the cheek.

CHAPTER FORTY NINE

Sheila's House

After the morning church service, Sheila decided to have a celebration dinner at her house. Sheila, Christine, Ron, and Diana are sitting next to each other. Grandma Harris, Zechariah, Stacy, and Keith are sitting next to each other, on the other side of the dinner table. The food was everywhere and the music was playing. Sheila stood up.

"I thank God first and foremost for this day and for everyone being here. To my lovely daughter-in-law, Diana, and to Mr. Zechariah Brown for finding Diana, his daughter. And once again to the Lord for delivering my son physically and spiritually. For my daughter Christine, and I know the Lord will deliver Sandra from her coma. I pray that Keith and Stacy fully submit their life to Jesus and I thank Grandma Harris for too many things to even start mentioning, but all her prayers and sweet loving spirit is truly priceless." She sat down.

Everyone said Amen.

Zechariah tapped on his glass to get everyone's attention.

"Miss O'Neil, I thank you for inviting me to your home. Being here with all of you and looking at my daughter, well it's hard to put into words without becoming emotional. It is truly an answered prayer."

Keith tapped on his glass.

"I know I don't deserve it, but I thank God for sparing my life and soul." He looked at Ron.

RONALD GRAY   (334)

"None of us deserve God's grace or his love for us, but thank God for it." Ron said.

Grandma Harris tapped on her glass.

"Well, let me go ahead and get my thanks too the Lord. Speaking of God, his grace and love," she looked over at Keith. "Keith, when are you going to give your life to the Lord and marry that pretty lady sitting next to you? You can't keep getting free milk boy." She leaned forward staring at him.

Stacy started laughing and looked at Keith, hitting him on his arm.

"You heard what Grandma Harris said," she waved at herself, "all of this loving ain't free." She leaned closer to him gripped his arm tighter and kissed Keith softly on the lips.

Keith stared at Stacy and smiled.

"Grandma Harris, you are something else. I have been thinking a lot about my life and soul and I really do love Stacy. She has been a true friend to me despite my ways. So how can I lose with the Lord, my baby and I know, she got it going on." He kissed her on the cheek.

Grandma Harris lightly hit the table with her hand.

"Boy, this ain't no hotel so don't bring any lust spirits in here and don't get your lips busted at the table."

Keith nods and lowered his head.

"Yes ma'am."

Diana was looking at Stacy and is thinking. She must really love Keith to remain by his side no matter what. Maybe I underestimated her, but I still don't like how she tried to seduce me again, but never again, oh Lord.

"Stacy, you have been through a lot with Keith and you are still with him. That say's a lot. You must truly love this man."

Stacy has been trying not to even talk to Diana because she has been feeling so guilty about trying to seduce her again. She knows Diana was trying to be smart putting her on the spot like this but she better be glad I didn't turn her all the way out. Oh God forgive me. Help me, Lord Jesus.

"I do love Keith very much and I have remained by his side because my heart is true. I'm a real, *Montar a caballo o morir,* believe that.

Diana frowned a little thinking Stacy was trying to be slick and say something smart to her in Spanish.

"What did you just say? What does that mean?" Diana said.

Zechariah smiled, shook his head, knowing that Stacy was a true warrior.

"*Montar a caballo o morir* means ride or die," he waved his hand at Stacy, "respto mucho mi hermana, respto mucho."

Stacy smiled and is thinking, Finally a real warrior. Real recognize real.

"*Guerrero a Guerrero mi hermano. Reconocer Real real. Gracias,*" Stacy said.

Ron tapped the table with his hand.

"Zechariah, I didn't know you could speak Spanish and what did Stacy say?"

Keith was looking at Stacy very surprised wondering how long she has been speaking Spanish and what else he does not know about her.

"Yeah, what did she say?" Keith said frowning with irritation in his voice.

Zechariah laughed feeling the slight tension in the room.

"Well, I learned a lot spending so much time in prison. Stacy said warrior to warrior my brother and I said, much respect my sister. This has truly been a great day."

Stacy has been checking Zechariah out. She was attracted to him and knew he is all that, but she still would rather have Keith.

"Thanks, Zechariah and I'm glad God has done so much in your life," she said smiling at him then kissed Keith on the cheek.

He smiled and nods his head at her.

Everyone started eating, talking and laughing.

About twenty minutes later, when most of them are eating dessert, Stacy's heart was feeling very heavy and she has no desire to continue feeling this way. She looked at Keith then leaned closer to him.

"Keith, we have been through so much and you are my best friend. I do love you, baby, more than you know and I don't want to lose you, but my heart is so heavy and," she started crying, "I'm so tired of not having real happiness and peace and running from God. I really want Jesus in my life but it's so hard. I need help." Speaking to him very softly.

Keith reached over and held Stacy's hand.

"I understand Stacy. You need to do what will bring you peace, no matter what. I will always have your back." He kissed her hand.

Stacy squeezed his hand and smiled at Keith, and then turned towards Sheila.

"Miss O'Neil, will you help me, please. Pray with me."

Sheila's entire face lights up and she smiled.

RONALD GRAY   (337)

"Praise the Lord. Baby, God is calling you and we can pray right now." She stood up, "We can go in the living room. Grandma Harris, would you help me pray for her?"

Grandma Harris tapped the table with her hand.

"Yes Lord, my father is doing his thing," she waved at Stacy, "Come on baby."

Grandma Harris, Sheila, and Stacy walked into the living room. Diana was thinking. *I'm glad Miss O'Neil didn't call me. I don't feel comfortable praying with Stacy right now."*

Sheila touched Stacy's shoulder and looked in her eyes.

"Stacy, what do you want from the Lord?"

She lowered her head and looked at Sheila.

"I've had many things in life but I have never had ultimate peace and joy. I want Jesus in my life. I want God to take away all my heartache and deep-rooted pain and give me true peace and real joy. I want Jesus to come into my heart."

Grandma Harris stomped her foot on the floor.

"Hallelujah, yes Lord."

Diana looked up, then looked at Ron and clapped her hands with tears coming down her face.

"Thank you, Jesus, thank you Lord."

Sheila raised her hands.

"Praise the Lord. Let us pray. Dear Lord, we know you manifested yourself in the flesh for us and died on the cross for our sins and rose from the grave on the third day just like you said you would. Now Lord, deliver Stacy from darkness and into your marvelous light, right now Oh Lord. Your word says, *If thou shall confess with thy mouth the Lord Jesus, and believe in thy heart that God has raised him from the dead, thou shall be*

saved, for with the heart man believeth unto righteousness, and with the mouth confession is made unto salvation. Now Lord let thy will be done."

Stacy fell to her knees shaking and started yelling and screaming very loudly, and started throwing up.

Grandma Harris knew exactly what was going on with Stacy. She had seen this type of deliverance many times before.

"Yeah, that's it, let God have his way. Thank you, Jesus."

Stacy started coughing up spit and fluid and slowly calmed down and stood up feeling something that she had never felt in her life. True peace and joy.

"Forgive me for all my sins Jesus, come into my heart and deliver me from darkness," she started crying. "Thank you, Jesus, thank you, thank you, thank you." She was smiling like she had never smiled before in her life. She felt like a huge weight had been lifted from her.

Sheila and Grandma Harris hugged Stacy. Zechariah and Ron walked over to Stacy and shook her hand and hugged her. Christine walked over and hugged her. Stacy was wondering if Diana would come over and hug her. She felt so different, but she would understand if she didn't. Diana really does not want to hug Stacy but it would look bad on her part. So, she walked over and lightly hugged Stacy, but this time she felt no lust or seducing spirit from her. Diana hugged her again and just held her, very happy that God has delivered her.

Keith stood up staring at Stacy and she walked over to him.

"Keith, I still love you but my life will never be the same or what we had."

He looked at her and smiled.

RONALD GRAY   (339)

"I know, the bible says, *Be not unequally yoked with unbelievers, for what fellowship has righteousness with unrighteousness.* I'm very happy that you have answered the master's call. Keep praying for me, and I know you can't come home with me now."

"Thank you for being so understanding and I will pray for you daily." She kissed him on the cheek.

Ron was looking at Keith and Stacy smiling. No one in this room was as happy for Stacy as he was, and he knows Keith was next. He looked up.

"Lord have mercy, I feel God calling me to pray." He walked into his bedroom and closed the door. He got on his knees and began to pray. "Yes Lord, I hear you, but Lord, am I ready for this Mr. Bones? Yes Lord, I know, *greater is he that's in me than he that's in the world.* Yes, Lord you have all power in heaven and earth and you will be with me. I thank you." He stood up and walked back to the living room.

Sheila, Christine, Diana, Grandma Harris, and Zechariah are in the living room talking and Stacy was talking to Keith by the table. Keith was standing on his crutch.

Sheila turned her head and looked at Ron. She noticed he has a very determined look on his face. She walked over to him.

"Baby, are you, all right?"

"Yes, on fire for God, but I have to go somewhere and be used by the Lord to do battle right now."

"Go where and do battle with whom? You just got here." She was staring at him keeping her emotions in check.

Grandma Harris stepped to Sheila, touching her shoulder.

"Yes Lord, I know. Ron is being called by God to do battle with that devil, Mr. Bones."

Keith and Stacy walked in the living room.

"No Lord. Have mercy." Sheila said raising her voice.

Keith stepped to Sheila. "Mom, what's wrong?"

Christine walked closer to Keith and grabbed his arm holding on to him.

"Ron has to go do battle with Mr. Bones. That man or whatever he is, pure evil."

Stacy was looking at the way Christine was holding on to Keith's arm and was thinking. I know she better let my man's arm go. I know I just gave my life to the Lord but I'm still me and she better not get it twisted. She walked closer to Keith and put her hand on his back and stared at Christine and rolled her eyes at her.

Christine stepped away from Keith knowing this was Stacy's way of claiming her man.

Keith knew Stacy very well and looked at her and smiled, feeling good that she was still claiming him. He kissed her on the cheek.

"I have seen this Mr. Bones up close and personal. Ron and I ran into him in the park. We saw him transform from a dog to a man or whatever he is. Anyway, we shot him full of holes, he fell but he got right back up. We ran. He's not human. How can you kill something like that?"

Ron looked at Keith and hope he gives his life to the Lord soon so they can still be the best of buddies.

RONALD GRAY   (341)

"You can't beat the devil with bullets or weapons of this world. You can only beat the devil with the word and the spirit of God. Now I have to go."

Sheila stared at Ron and was proud of him for his courage in embracing what he must do.

"Let us all pray before you leave."

They all form a circle around him except for Keith, who is standing away from them.

"Diana, pray for your husband."

"Let us pray. Lord your word says; *the weapons of our warfare are not carnal but mighty through God to the pulling down of strongholds.* All things are possible through you. Now let thy will be done. Protect your chosen one, Ron, and we know that victory shall be yours. Thank you, Lord. Amen."

They all hug him.

Zechariah can feel Ron was about to enter the battle of his life, but he knows God was in control.

"Ron, I don't know exactly what you are up against, but I know that God is with you and he has never lost a fight. We are living proof."

Diana kissed Ron.

"Be careful Ron and hurry up and come back. You know I will be missing you and remember the devil is only a deceiver. Baby I love you."

Ron was staring at her thinking. *It has to be God in order for Diana to still be by his side and want and love him so much.* He hugged her tightly and looked into her eyes and kissed her softly on the lips. He stepped back and looked around.

Christine tapped Ron on the shoulder and hugged him and gripped his hand looked in his eyes.

"Ron, I have seen and felt his power so don't play with him. Let God use you to destroy him." She hugged him again.

Stacy was standing next to Keith, holding his hand. She looked at how he was staring at Ron realizing he was very concerned for his safety. She felt his spirit of great sadness because she knows Keith felt like he was about to lose his best friend. Keith would never show this because, for him, it would be a sign of weakness. She lightly kissed Keith on the lips to comfort him, in the only way she can now.

Keith loved Stacy dearly. Out of habit, he rubbed her butt. She moved his hand and whispered in his ear.

"Baby don't," she kissed him on the cheek, "marry me and I promise to rock your world for life."

Ron was looking at Keith and Stacy and sees the great love they have for each other and he noticed the sadness in Keith's face. He walked toward him.

"Don't look so worried. I will be back."

"I know, just be careful Emmanuel. Now go and show that Mr. Bones who really got the power." They pound up and hug.

Sheila walked over to Ron and hugged him.

"I will be praying for you baby."

Ron hugged everyone, then walked out and got in his Bentley and drove away, praying as he drove.

Zechariah has been looking at Sheila, trying not to be obvious. He finds her very attractive. Not just in a physical way, but her spirit was so strong in the Lord, and she has such a loving spirit. He wants to approach her but does not want to offend her

RONALD GRAY   (343)

or disrespect Ron in any way. He was staring at her but for some reason, he instantly felt the urge to look at Grandma Harris and she was looking at him. She nods at him, turning her head in Sheila's direction smiling and she nods her head at Zechariah toward Sheila. He knew this was a sign from God and he walked toward Sheila.

Sheila was standing off by herself in deep thought about her son. Suddenly, she heard the voice of God speaking to her spirit saying, "I have answered your prayer." She immediately turned her head and sees Zechariah walking towards her and becomes nervous like a school girl.

"Hi Sheila, I know this may seem like the worst time to hear what I want to say to you, but I would like to get to know you. Let me rephrase that. I would like for us, to get to know each other." He was thinking, *Lord, if she is truly the one for me; then allow, her not to speak, but just hug me.*

Sheila was staring at him and blown away by his words. For the very first time since David has been gone, in her heart she lets him go. Immediately her feet seem to move all on their own, closer to Zechariah and she hugged him.

Keith looked at Stacy and they both are looking at Zechariah and Sheila. Diana looked at them, then at Grandma Harris who was looking and smiling at them.

RONALD GRAY   (344)

CHAPTER FIFTY

Mr. Bones' House

Ron has been driving for hours not knowing exactly where he was going, but just being compelled to drive by the spirit of the Lord. He was driving down a road that was so dark if he didn't have his headlights on, he would be in total darkness. He was compelled to slow down then sees this dirt driveway. The spirit of the Lord told him to drive down this road until he sees a grave yard that was surrounded by woods. Next to the grave yard was an old raggedy, dilapidated looking house that has many dogs laying in the yard and on the porch.

Ron got out of his car and immediately all the dogs stood up barking and growling at him. He was praying while walking through the yard and onto the porch. He was about to push the front door open. when it opened by itself. Ron walked slowly through the house, constantly praying and looking around. He reached the den and sees Mr. Bones sitting on a couch in the corner of the den. He was dressed in black holding his cane and there was a pile of small bones sitting on the fire place mantle. There was old torn furniture throughout the den and the room was dimly lit and has a very bad smell to it.

Mr. Bones waved his hand.

"Welcome to my house boy and your place of death. I have been waiting for you a long time. First, you walk with God, and then you turn from him and live for me. Then you come back to God and now you think you can defeat me, stupid idiot. Don't you know who I really am? You are no match for me, I'm the

RONALD GRAY   (345)

bones and I come to steal, kill and destroy. Today you shall die, you fake Christian." He stood up.

"Shut up devil. Jesus said, I come to give life and to give it more abundantly."

"I hate that name and I hate you," he pointed to the bones on the mantle. "Bones come to me."

A few of the bones on the fireplace mantle started shaking and float over to Mr. Bones and land in his hand.

"Time for you to die, boy." He mumbled some words and tapped his cane on the floor twice.

Fire erupts on the floor and it forms a circle around Ron's feet. He looked down at the fire and at Mr. Bones, pointing his finger at him.

"*He that dwelleth in the secret place of the most high, shall abide under the shadow of the almighty.*" He pointed to the fire, "now be gone fire." The fire goes out. Mr. Bones stomped his feet.

"No, I'm tired of you boy."

Ron looked at the bones on the fireplace mantle and walked toward them.

Mr. Bones waved his hand at Ron.

"Stop boy," he tapped his cane once, "power of the bones, do my will." He mumbled some words.

Smoke comes from under Ron's feet surrounding him. When it disappeared, a large anaconda snake was wrapped around his body. Mr. Bones pointed at the snake.

"Kill him, my servant. Crush every bone in his ugly body. Choke the life out of that boy, so I can feed him to my dogs."

RONALD GRAY   (346)

The snake began to squeeze Ron tighter until he felt he was about to go unconscious, but he has enough strength left to pray.

"No weapon formed against me shall prosper. Lord, deliver me from the hands of darkness in, Jesus name."

The snake caught on fire and dropped to the floor, twisting and rolling around while burning, leaving nothing but ashes. Mr. Bones tapped his cane on the floor and a sofa quickly slid across the floor hitting Ron hard on his legs knocking him down. Mr. Bones mumbled some words, tapping his cane twice on the floor. What Ron sees was shocking. Mr. Bones slowly began to metamorphosis into a large wolf.

Ron shook his head.

"Good God almighty." He stood up pointing his finger at the wolf.

"For there is nothing covered that shall not be revealed, neither hide that shall not be known, Lord let thy will be done."

The wolf began to turn back into Mr. Bones.

Mr. Bones was standing there looking at Ron with so much hate, his body is twitching.

"Damn you boy. I hate you Christians and your mama. Play time is over hypocrite." He tapped his cane and disappeared in a cloud of smoke and reappeared behind him. He kicked Ron in the back of his neck and he fell to the floor hard and was very dizzy but he got on his knees.

Mr. Bones hit himself on the chest.

"Damn, that felt good to put my foot on you. I should have kicked you in your ass." He smiled while looking down at Ron. "That's right boy, bow down to Mr. Bones and serve me. I have the power."

RONALD GRAY   (347)

Ron looked up.

"Lord help me, *when I'm weak thou have made me strong*," he smiled, "thank you Jesus." He stood up and stared at Mr. Bones. "I'm dressed in the whole armor of God," he pointed at him, "at the name of Jesus every knee shall bow and every tongue shall confess that Jesus Christ is Lord, so bow down devil."

"No." He yelled and his entire body started shaking and he slowly began to bow down to his knees while holding his cane. It was as if the hand of God was upon him pushing him to his knees and he is trembling. Seconds later he tapped his cane on the floor, "bones help me."

The bones on the mantle begin to shake and float up in the air turning into large knives. They fly toward Ron's head. Mr. Bones stood up.

Ron turned to face the knives.

"Peace be still and I rebuke the powers of darkness."

The knives stopped within inches of Ron's face and fell to the floor and began to melt.

Mr. Bones reached into his pocket and pulled out his black pouch and extended both arms in the air with his cane and pouch in his hands.

"Backslider, you can't defeat me. I have the power. I'm God," he screamed, "Bones."

The house started vibrating and shaking and furniture in the room started sliding across the floor, windows started breaking, books are flying across the room, the floor started shaking and breaking up. The roof started shaking and boards start falling from the roof.

RONALD GRAY   (348)

Ron pointed at Mr. Bones.

"Blasphemer! God said, I'm the first and I'm the last, and beside me, there is no God. God said, I, even I'm the Lord, and beside me, there is no savior." He runs and kicked Mr. Bones in the chest.

Mr. Bones fell and his pouch and cane flew out of his hands.

"No," he yelled, "not my bones, not my bones." He mumbled some words and stood straight up. He looked at his black pouch on the floor and pointed to it, "Bones come to me now."

The pouch opened and the bones began to slide across the floor towards him.

Ron pointed toward the bones. "In Jesus name, peace be still devil bones. Greater is he that's in me than he that's in the world."

The bones stop moving.

"No, not my bones, I will not be defeated, boy." He extends his neck and opened his eyes very wide staring at Ron. "You will die tonight chosen boy." He started stomping his feet hard on the floor and the front door quickly swings open. Dogs began walking in the house barking, growling and slobbering at the mouth. The dogs keep coming and some are on the roof looking down at Ron through a hole from missing roof boards. Two dogs jump down from the roof landing close to Ron and start snapping their teeth at him. Ron stepped back until his back was against the wall.

Mr. Bones pointed his finger at him.

"Now what are you going to do boy, and where are you going except to hell with me? I smell the spirit of fear on you, soft cupcake. Tonight, I take your soul."

RONALD GRAY   (349)

Ron stared at Mr. Bones and the dogs as they move closer to him. For the first time since being here, he was afraid. His spirit compels him to start praising God for strength and courage. Seconds later, he was over shadowed with bravery and no longer afraid. He pointed toward the ceiling and looked at Mr. Bones.

"God didn't give me the spirit of fear but of his power, and I can do all things through Christ who gives me strength." He pointed toward the dogs. "The spirit that's in me is greater than you. I can defeat you, for with God nothing shall be impossible," he looked up and shouts, "Lord Jesus, fight my battle now Oh Lord."

The wind started blowing hard and it started thundering, lightning strikes inside the house landing close to some of the dogs. The dogs started howling and whimpering and they all quickly run out of the house.

Mr. Bones looked around the house shaking his head back and forth then looked at Ron.

"No! You can't defeat me and my spirit. I'm death walking, I send the spirit of death upon you, boy."

"Shut up devil," he yelled, "Death and life are in the power of the tongue and I call those things which be not as though they were. In Jesus name burn devil."

Fire erupts on Mr. Bones' feet and his entire body becomes engulfed in flames.

Mr. Bones is screaming, yelling and turning around twisting and shaking.

"Nooo, you can't kill me I'm the bones I will be back. I will be back."

RONALD GRAY   (350)

Mr. Bones' body burns and all that's left is a pile of ashes on the floor.

Ron raised his arms.

"Lord, I thank you. Victory in your mighty name." He dropped to his knees, "Yes Lord, I will *remember the former things of old, for I'm God, and there is none else, I'm God and there is none like me.* Yes Lord, I will remember who delivered me and I shall glorify your name forever oh God." He stood up and walked out the house.

Ron looked around the yard and the dogs are gone. He walked over to his car and got in, praising God as he drove down the dirt road.

The dogs were laying down at the edge of the woods so Ron could not see them. They all stood up barking and growling and started running around the house in a circle.

CHAPTER FIFTY ONE
Finishing What He Started

People are smiling and laughing as they are walking in church service this Sunday morning. The church was almost full and music is playing. Pastor Williams was sitting behind the pulpit wearing a white robe smiling and looking at the people as they come in. Sheila, Christine, Ron, and Diana are sitting together. Grandma Harris, Stacy, and Zechariah are sitting together. Walking into the church are Rick Matthew, James Reed, Cynthia, Shantai, Tonya, John Hardy, Judge C.P. Woodard, and Keith whose leg cast is gone but he is walking with a cane. He sat next to Stacy. The rest sit behind Ron. The music stopped and the choir stood and started singing.

When Mr. Woodard sat down he tapped Ron on his shoulder.

"Mr. Ronald Emmanuel O'Neil."

Ron and Diana turned around.

"Judge Woodard, how are you doing sir? I'm very surprised to see you."

He leaned closer to Ron.

"Son, when I heard you were released from prison I was shocked and I have to admit, very angry. So, I did some research concerning how you got out. The police made a big mistake concerning your Miranda rights. They were violated repeatedly. This information was not in any of the initial reports that I had. It was much later when the reports mysteriously became available. I read you mentioned several times to the investigating officers during your interrogation that you had contacted your attorney and he informed you not to make any statements but the police continued to interrogate you for hours. The appeals court overturned my court ruling which I had to admit made me very angry, but the law is the law. This was a miracle as far as I'm concerned and I don't believe in miracles. I found out this was the church you attend, so I had to come here to see you, and well, just be here."

Ron stared at the Judge.

"Sir, I know I do not deserve it but my heart and soul thanks God daily and I have truly changed."

"Hello Judge Woodard," Diana said smiling at him. "My name is Diana, Ron's wife. Ron has changed and I thank God for it. I'm glad you are here." She gave him another smile then turned back around.

"Amen to that sir. You are in the right place at the right time and I will be praying for you." Ron smiled, turned around and kissed Diana on the cheek and held her hand. The choir stopped singing and sat down. Pastor Williams walked toward the pulpit.

"Praise the Lord everybody. It is by no accident or chance all of you are here today. It was by the Lord's divine master plan for your life. You can try but you cannot run from God. He knows what it's going to take to break you so he can mold and shape you to be fit for the master's use. Tomorrow is promised to no one so don't allow the devil to deceive you another day. Bow down to his mighty hand today and let God deliver you. God is going to do something today that only he can do, deliver souls." He raised his arms high in the air. "Who will let go of the world today, right now and come to Jesus?" He walked from the pulpit and onto the floor in front of the altar. "Brother Ron O'Neil,

RONALD GRAY   (353)

come up front please and say something for the Lord. God is not finished with you."

Ron walked up front and stood by the pastor and they shook hands.

"Praise the Lord everyone. Once again, I'm a living witness that you cannot run from God and I truly thank him for his grace, love, and mercy because truly God chose me. All I did was answer the master's call, because after all, it was, *My Call*. Now, who else will answer the master's call?"

Pastor Williams raised his arms.

"Lord let thy will be done, come to him no matter what. The Lord can and will deliver you. Whatever your problem may be, it is not too big for God. Don't let another day go by that you don't hand everything over to him. God can and will deliver you from any spiritual bondage that you may be dealing with." He raised his arms again, "come to King Jesus, come to his glory. He will give you true peace like you have never known."

The choir started singing very softly the song, "Come to Jesus."

Stacy was sitting next to Keith and she turned her head to look at him with tears falling from her eyes, tears of happiness because she knows the true peace the pastor was referring to. For the first time in her life, she has true peace and joy. All the great sex, money, and material things could never do this. She kissed Keith on his cheek.

"Please Keith, stop running from God, it is the only way. Don't do it for me or anyone else, but do it for you."

He stared at Stacy, gently grabbing her hand.

"Will you walk with me up there?"

"I will always walk with you Keith. I'm still a ride or die baby but God is first. Just be real baby, be real."

Keith stared at her and tears fell from his eyes.

In all the years Stacy has known Keith, she has never seen him cry.

Keith gently squeezed her hand and they stood up and walked to the altar together.

Rick, James, John Hardy, Judge C.P. Woodard, Cynthia, Tonya, and Shantai all stood up and walked to the altar.

The Pastor sees all the people coming and must hold back his tears at the power of God.

"I thank God for all of you who have come forward and answered yes to the master's call but God is not finished," he turned toward Ron. "Brother Ron, continue to pray that the Lord's will shall be done." He makes a hand gesture to his other ministers to come forward and help him pray with the people because there are many and he can feel some very dangerous and strong spirits from some of these people, but God was in control. He began to talk and pray with some of the people.

James was on his knees crying like a baby because his heart was still very heavy concerning what he did to Christine. From his heart, with tears coming down his face, he was crying out to God for his divine forgiveness. He stood up feeling that weight has been lifted from his heart and he will be forever grateful.

Cynthia, Shantai, and Tonya are on their knees also crying out to God for his forgiveness and deliverance. All three are shaking and trembling because the devil was trying to keep them spiritually bound, but God delivered them like only he can. They stood up praising God and his mighty name for true joy.

RONALD GRAY   (355)

The doors at the back of the church swung open and Sandra O'Neil was pushed in the church by nurses. She was lying on a hospital bed and was still in a coma. She was pushed up front and Pastor Williams stood beside her.

"It is not over for the hand of the Lord." He turned toward Ron, "Brother Ron, let God use you. Pray for your sister. His word says, *being confident of this very thing, that he which have begun a good work in you, will perform it until the day of Jesus Christ.* Finish what God started son."

Ron was staring at Sandra thinking various thoughts. What if I pray for her and nothing happens, or she gets worse and dies. I can't do this. The pastor should do it, not me. No, I will not be defeated by the devil. The spirit of fear is not of God. The devil is a liar. Use me now oh Lord, use me. He stepped closer to Sandra and began to pray.

"Oh Lord, all power is in thy hand. Death and life are in the power of the tongue. Lord, I speak life to Sandra. Jesus let thy will be done." He put his hand on her head.

Sandra opened her eyes.

"Praise the Lord Ron."

The entire church stood up and started clapping their hands. Ron was beyond words and he can't hold back his tears.

"Praise the Lord Sandra. Praise the Lord." He stared at her with tears running down his face.

Sheila and Christine stood up crying and shout hallelujah and run up front to Sandra. Grandma Harris and Diana stand up crying and shout hallelujah and walk to Sandra.

Pastor Williams stepped closer to Sandra.

"Praise the Lord Sandra, this is truly a day that the Lord has made but "God is not finished with you." He turned towards Ron, "Brother Ron, finish the Lord's work."

Ron laid hands on Sandra again.

"Sandra O'Neil, be thy healed arise and walk in Jesus name."

Sandra slowly sat up and tried to stand up but couldn't, she started to cry.

"I can't Ron. I just can't, please help me Ron, help me Lord. I want to run."

Ron was thinking, I knew it. Now, look at her. Jesus, I have the faith but for any unbelief that I have, send me the right help.

Diana walked over to Ron and put her hand on his shoulder then leaned closer to him and whispered in his ear.

"*One can chase a thousand, two can put two thousand in flight*. I got you, just believe baby. Believe in the power of God." Ron looked at Diana and smiled then turn towards Sandra.

"Sandra, if you have faith the size of a mustard seed, then stand and walk in the name of the Lord." He was smiling at her.

The church was quiet and everyone was looking at Sandra.

Sandra looked at Ron and nods at him as she slowly stood up and walked towards Sheila.

"Praise the Lord, praise the Lord mom."

Sheila was overwhelmed with emotions and crying tears of great happiness seeing her daughter walk.

"Praise the Lord baby, oh God, oh God." She has her arms open and hugged Sandra tightly, "thank you Jesus, my baby, thank you."

Sandra heard the voice of God speak to her, *I thought you said you wanted to run,* she kissed Sheila on the cheek and started walking slowly away picking up her pace one step at a time until she was smiling so hard she couldn't help but take off running through the church thanking God along the way.

Everyone in the church stood up and started shouting and dancing seeing this miracle. Tears were falling from so many people's eyes and others were dancing in the spirit, and praising God. Christine caught up with Sandra as she was running and started running with her praising God as well for her own deliverance.

Keith was standing next to Stacy. She kissed him on the cheek.

"Baby, I know the government took all your money but I don't care. I have always loved you for you, not your money." She kissed him softly on the cheek.

Keith fell in love with Stacy even more and he had no intention of letting her go. He leaned closer to her and whispered in her ear.

"You are the best woman I could have Stacy. Don't react to this news but they didn't get it all baby. It is not much in comparison to what I had, but we can start over with three million dollars." He kissed her on the cheek.

Stacy squeezed Keith's hand and whispered in his ear.

"I knew you were smart and so am I Keith. I have been saving money for years even before meeting you. I have three million dollars spread out in banks across the country."

Keith smiled and leaned closer and kissed Stacy on the cheek.

"I miss you so much Stacy. Can I have some booty?" He laughed.

Stacy pinched him on his side.

"No, you can't have any more of my booty Keith unless you marry me, brother."

Keith smiled and kissed her on the cheek again.

"Soon baby, real soon."

He walked over to Ron and extends his hand to him. Ron shook his hand and they hugged. Keith put his hand on Ron's shoulder.

"Brother Ron, I never thought I could ever feel this good and have so much peace as I do now. So, now are we friends for life in the Lord?"

Ron stared at him and laughed.

"We are friends for life in the Lord my brother in Christ." They shook hands again and hugged.

Ron walked away and fell on his knees and started crying.

"Lord I thank you Jesus. I thank you, only by your mighty hand. No one can run from God, no one."

Stacy walked over to Shantai and Cynthia. They stared at each other and hugged and started crying, praising God.

Pastor Williams looked around the church and tears fell from his eyes seeing the marvelous works of God. He threw his arms high in the air.

"Lord, we thank you." He looked over at Ron on his knees praising God.

Ron looked up with tears falling from his eyes, tears of joy.

"Lord I thank you for, *MY CALL*." He yelled.

Everyone up front was praising God and hugging each other thanking him for their complete victory. Or was it?

RONALD GRAY   (359)

CHAPTER FIFTY TWO

Mr. Bones' House

Back at Mr. Bones' house, the dogs have returned and were running around the house in a circle barking.

Mr. Bones' cane was lying on the floor. A dog walked into the house toward the cane. It sniffed and licked it and walked over to where there was a small pile of bones laying on the floor. It picked up one in his mouth and brought it back over to where the cane was and dropped it on the cane. It walked over to where the pile of ashes was laying on the floor and started eating the pile of ashes until none was left. The dog walked back to where the cane and the one bone was and started vomiting up the ashes and they land on the bone and cane. It lifted his head up and started barking and all the dogs outside started barking. The cane began shaking and the dog backed away growling, looking at the cane then run out of the house.

The cane stood up tapping itself on the floor twice and the small pile of bones laying on the floor started shaking and the vomit turned into ashes. The ashes began swirling on the floor and floated up in the air hovering. The cane started tapping itself on the floor repeatedly and the bones continue shaking.

The sky grew instantly dark and lightning started streaking across the sky. A cloud of black smoke appeared in the yard and Doctor Eyes was standing there. He walked inside the house and sees the ashes hovering in the air, bones shaking on the floor, and the cane repeatedly tapping itself on the floor. He knew what he must do. He leaned over and held his hand out in front of his eyes, and hit himself hard on the back of his head. His eyeballs pop out landing in his hand. He placed them on the floor and stepped back. The eye balls started vibrating and floated up in the air alongside the ashes, and both started swirling around in the air. Doctor Eyes started stomping his feet.

"I call upon the spirit of the Prince of Darkness, come back, come back." He held his arms out to his side and leaned his head back opening his mouth very wide. The cane floated over to his hand and the ashes floated up and hover over his head and slowly go into his mouth. The bones slid across the floor into the black pouch which floated up and lands in Doctor Eyes hand. The eye balls floated over to his head and his eye sockets open and the eye balls go into them. Doctor Eye's entire body started shaking and trembling and he screamed so loudly the dogs started howling. He raised his hands in the air and started laughing.

"I'm back, the prince of darkness is back and I'm stronger than ever. You can kill the body but you can't kill the spirit," he started laughing and his face contorts into a look of pure hate and anger. "Look out chosen boy, I'm coming to get you and your family. The spirit of hell was unleashed upon the entire world." He walked out the house and across the yard, holding the cane and the black pouch. An earthquake hit the yard and a large hole opened and Doctor Eyes began going down into the hole.

"I'm coming back, boy. Hell will be unleashed." The hole closed.

RONALD GRAY   (361)

COMING SOON...

"MY CALL III"

THE SPIRIT OF HELL UNLEASHED

Ron and Diana are a very happily married couple. Keith and Stacy could not ask for more because they have each other. The O'Neil family is doing well and Sheila is talking to Zechariah. Grandma Harris is still around praying and praising God.

The spirit of the prince of darkness finds bodies to possess and a fury of pure anger and revenge is not only sent Ron's way but the entire O'Neil family comes under attack like they have never known.

This spirit has no remorse, no compassion, and no mercy, just hate with no discrimination! My Call III makes I and II seem like slight irritation from the devil, in comparison to what he is about to do.

The spirit of Mr. Bones is coming with the hand of death and he is using sex, money, and violence just to get your attention. The O'Neil family will suffer greatly but whom? How many? When the smoke clears who will be left alive? The spirit of hell has been unleashed!

RONALD GRAY   (362)